Praise for Neil Spring

'Explosive'
Daily Express

'A deft, spooky psychological drama based on a true story'
Daily Mail

'Surprising, serpentine and clever'
Sunday Times

'Spooky and tense with a truly horrifying denouement'
Sunday Express, S Magazine

'Close the curtains, pull up a chair, open a book –
and prepare to be pleasantly scared'
Metro

'A sinister tale'
Heat

'A triumph of creativity . . . the conclusion will shock
and amaze you'
Vada Magazine

'A real page-turner'
Tatler

Neil Spring is the author of several novels, many of which are inspired by real events. His debut novel, *The Ghost Hunters*, was adapted into a critically acclaimed television drama for ITV starring Rafe Spall. *The Haunted Shore* is his fifth novel. Originally from South Wales, Neil lives in London and can be contacted via his website, www.neilspring.com, or followed on Facebook at https://www.facebook.com/Neilspring.author, and on Twitter as @neilspring. Neil is represented by the literary agency, Curtis Brown.

Also by Neil Spring

The Ghost Hunters
The Watchers
The Lost Village
The Burning House

THE
HAUNTED
SHORE

NEIL SPRING

Quercus

First published in Great Britain in 2020 by

Quercus Editions Ltd
Carmelite House
50 Victoria Embankment
London EC4Y 0DZ

An Hachette UK company

A CIP catalogue record for this book is available
from the British Library

PB ISBN 978 1 78747 010 1
EB ISBN 978 1 78747 008 8

10 9 8 7 6 5 4 3 2 1

Typeset by CC Book Production
Printed and bound in Great Britain by Clays Ltd, Elcograf S.p.A.

Papers used by Quercus are from well-managed forests and other responsible sources.

In loving memory of Ellen Theresa Cooze,
my dear gentle Nana

I hear those voices that will not be drowned.

– Benjamin Britten, *Peter Grimes*

– 1 –

MY TERRIBLE MISTAKE

Have you ever visited somewhere and known, in your core, that there was something terribly wrong about it? Somewhere that felt not just uncomfortable, but which provoked a mental shiver and caused the hairs on the back of your neck to prick up? The sort of place you could quite easily imagine was the scene of an appalling, tragic incident?

The events I'm telling you about, the horrors that I feel compelled to share, happened somewhere very much like that, a loathsome place where the skies seem permanently veiled in gloom, where shells whispered secrets of buried sufferings and dark waves threatened your sanity.

I first saw this isolated stretch of shore when I was twelve years old, clinging fast to my mother's hand as we watched removal men lumber up the steps to the lonely Martello tower with our furniture. I suppose Shingle Street became my home then, but I never thought of it as that, and never wanted to.

The tower confronted the North Sea, an endless grey folded into brooding mist. It can't always have been that way, of course, but that's how it has stained itself on my memory. Dad always said this location was 'magical' and maybe he was right, but not in a good way. There was nothing here: no shops, no pub, just a row of battered Victorian coastguard cottages strung out along a shingle ridge. And about a hundred yards away, separated from the shore by a lagoon-like stretch of water, Orford Ness – the 'island of secrets' – a former military testing ground deemed uninhabitable after the war. Abandoned. Forbidden. Its looming structures rising darkly against the bruised sky.

A bleak, desolate place to make a home. My father was an architect and, judging from the many awards to his name, a successful one; but this project was different, on a whole new scale to his other work. Artistry was in his blood, that was true, and he had a grand vision for the tower. The problem was, it was a vision only he could see.

Why he had wanted to live here, miles from the nearest town, walled up in a gloomy tower, was a mystery to me and my brother, Colin. To our mother too, I think. I found some of her papers in the boathouse after she died, poems she was working on, notes. She wrote: 'It is impossible to set foot in Shingle Street without a shudder of trepidation. As the dark stones crunch and shift beneath your feet, you sense the blood-soaked secrets beneath.'

Anyone reading that might think it an exaggeration, but Mum was in tune with these things. 'I must be mad,' she said. 'I don't know why I let him talk me into coming here.'

The stark truth is this: those who lived near this lonesome shore, where the gulls scream and the fog rolls in thick, had at least a vague idea of its strangeness. A place where weirdness was multiplied.

Now, I know that better than anyone.

I blamed my brother for what happened. Carelessness. Neglect of duty. In truth, though, the whole sorry mess began with me.

Before coming back to Suffolk, to the tiny hamlet of Shingle Street, I lived in London. And I was *someone*: Elizabeth Valentine (Lizzy to my friends). Top-floor apartment in Vauxhall. Membership at Soho House. Salon highlights, designer clothes. This was fifteen years into my PR career and from the weight of my cuttings book, I suppose I must have been pretty good at it. Maybe that's what makes the truth even harder to acknowledge.

The life I squandered.

My boss always said I had the potential to go all the way. But you know what they say about the higher you climb? Well, when the wheel turned and my number came up black thirteen, I fell just about as far as I possibly could. And it didn't help that I was infatuated with the guy who sacked me. Or that we were embroiled in a deeply passionate affair.

Since our Oxford days, Mitch had been one of my closest friends. Loyal. You see, it was Mitch who gave me my second job after my first ended badly. He did that to help me, but that's not the whole truth. Sure, he knew he could rely on me, brought me in to manage a team of young, ambitious upstarts; but somewhere along the way – around when he had as many as fifty employees – the lines became blurred and we became close. In and out of the office. We were addicted to one another, despite the risks. Maybe even because of them.

Mum used to say that if something seems too good to be true it usually is. Cynical? Maybe, but that saying came back to me fairly regularly in those early years when Mitch was grow-ing his company. The sheer pace of its expansion. I had more than one question about his business dealings, how opaque they could be. His client list, for example. There were a few foreign governments on that list; I was just never completely clear about the sort of work the agency was doing for them.

But at the time, I closed my eyes to this and instead focused on our relationship.

Whenever Mitch talked about his wife – and I swear I'm not imagining this – his face would turn grey, so grey. He didn't love her; he didn't light up around her like he did with me. There were no kids involved (had there been, I'd never have gone near him), so a separation would be straightforward. At the time my world fell apart, Mitch had instigated divorce proceedings and I had spotted the engagement ring hidden in his desk drawer at work. I was hopeful. By then I was thirty-seven: the prospect of a wedding was looming and, after that, if I was lucky, a baby. All at once this perfection was within reach, and I yearned for it.

Perhaps I yearned for it too much.

Perhaps that's why I did what I did.

I read somewhere that everyone has a trigger that can throw our decisions off. Mine? Uncertainty. Spiralling and uncontrollable. That black fear of losing control, of being let down. I wanted a life with Mitch so badly. I wanted him to love me, be proud of me. And how did I feel on that late autumn afternoon when he strode into my office and told me one of our biggest clients was putting their account out to pitch?

Anxious – that's how I felt.

Raptor was worth sixty grand a month to the agency, and I'd been leading it for the best part of five years. Not the sexiest client – they manufactured railway navigation technology – but our press coverage was steady and impressive. If you've ever found yourself compromised in a work situation, you'll know that I felt insecure and eager to prove myself. Mitch didn't say it, but I had a sense that the problem with the account was something to do with me personally. I wasn't the issue, though. The only thing that had changed recently was Raptor's director of communications. Maxine Hall. Barely in her twenties. Never entered a room – no, she advanced into it. Always poured a coffee before being asked if she would like one. Her ice-chip eyes said, *I might be new here, but I'm in control and I intend to shake things up a little.*

'They think we've become complacent,' Mitch said, 'that our approach doesn't fit with their brand in the way it used to.' Subtext: *Maxine doesn't think your face fits.*

If Raptor were putting the account out to pitch, the vultures would be circling. It boiled down to this: if we didn't deliver the pitch of our lives, we could kiss a sweet goodbye to that sixty grand monthly retainer.

I gave Mitch my best PR smile. 'We'll pull it out the bag, right? We always do. Mitch?'

Finally, after an uncomfortable pause, the man I loved and wanted more than anything to spend my life with said, 'It's probably best you step away from their account. For now.'

Those words hit me like a kick to my stomach, along with the annoyance that flashed in his eyes. Of course he had every right to feel annoyed at the situation, but at me?

'You agree?' he said, and it wasn't a question.

'Fine,' I replied, not looking at him. 'You're the boss.'

I waited until he had gone back to his office to shut my door. I felt the sting of hot tears pricking at my eyes, but I would *not* cry. That was weakness. Instead, I checked old emails just to be sure I hadn't overlooked something on Raptor, something they could blame me for if it came to that. But no, everything was in proper order. Or seemed to be. Which heightened my frustration. Our biggest client was showing us the door, and I was getting the blame!

*

For once, I went home on time that night. Alone. Slumping on the sofa, it wasn't long before nervous exhaustion pulled me into the depths of sleep.

I dreamed I went to the shore. I was a child again, standing in the twilight on a ridge of dark shingle. Watching the waves roll in. Listening to the babble of curlews.

Something was wrong. In that dream, there was a distinct atmosphere of otherworldliness. My father was beside me; a much younger man, but there seemed to be an infinity of sadness in his eyes as he surveyed the shore, only to focus on the exposed shingle stretch of Orford Ness, the forbidden zone across the water. So desolate. So unknowable.

In my dream, Dad could not take his eyes off the mysterious observation towers and crumbling concrete laboratories. What else did those ruins symbolise, if not loss?

As the sky darkened, a sudden and disquieting thought went through my mind:

A darkness is rising.

I had no idea what that meant. In time I would, but not then, which was probably a good thing. And suddenly, I was awake. Agitated. In a cold, clammy sweat.

Was it a memory? It had seemed so vivid.

Just a dream, I thought, and for a moment hoped what had happened that day at the office was also just a dream.

Except you know that's not true, I realised. *If we lose this account it'll be on your head.*

I got up off the sofa and went into the kitchen. The clock on the wall said it was getting on for nine. I should have microwaved my favourite meal (lasagne), or watched something light on Netflix; that would have been the relaxing, sensible thing to do. What I did instead was go online, to the games that helped me escape whenever I felt things were spinning out of control.

For weeks until that moment I had been making a genuine effort to keep my habit at bay. A temptation that seemed to creep up on me from nowhere. That irrepressible urge which made me want to win, whatever the odds.

Sounds sad, doesn't it? But all the money I had in those days went straight towards feeding my gambling habit. So many websites, so many games, made all the more alluring and pernicious through technology. Holdem. Poker. Blackjack. The adrenaline they unleashed satiated me: a heroin addict might call it their fix; I called it 'a good day', when really it was my vulnerability, my corrosive vice. Especially my poison of choice: blackjack. When it comes to creating the irresistible illusion of control, the rush, there isn't a game to match it – and that night, I overdosed.

Big time.

An hour later, I got a call from my bank.

By then, of course, the damage was done. I was in a cold sweat of panic, fifteen grand down, overdrawn on my current account and out of control. The worst thing was, I had no comprehension of how bad the problem actually was until the bank called.

If you think that this spectacular crash and burn sprang from nowhere, you'd be wrong. I had played the online games for most of my career, without ever seriously asking myself why. In fact, I knew so little about 'problem gambling' that it was a permanent feature of my life long before I knew it was classified a 'behavioural disorder.'

I think this was because I didn't see myself as a 'gambler' in the typical sense (which looking back on it sort of fits the pattern). Watching sports on TV wasn't my thing. Neither were casinos or betting shops. Still, my behaviour was no less corrosive. For me, it was the thrill of escape.

In some ways, my whole life has been that way.

Ever since Mum died.

'We thought it proper to check you were making these withdrawals. Hello? Ms Valentine . . . hello?'

I froze, with the phone gripped in my hand, and stared wordlessly at the screen. When I say I was out of control, I mean I couldn't have stopped, even if I had wanted to. The addiction was telling me it was fine. *Carry on, chase your losses, Lizzy!* And why not? I was better than this. I'd never lost this badly. Hell, I was a winner!

Except I wasn't.

The truth is, most gamblers lack any skill at all. We tell ourselves a different story, but that doesn't make us right. What it makes us is fools.

I can't remember exactly how much I'd lost before that night when I made my terrible mistake. I'd been buying scratch cards, lottery tickets, and dabbling with the websites for most of my career. Small amounts mostly. But over fifteen years that was *a lot* of small amounts. It wasn't a problem for a good while because I earned enough to cover the losses. Sure, I was supposed to be paying into a savings account and a pension, and at first I was! But it wasn't too long before those payments lapsed. Being broke crept up on me from nowhere with slow, insidious steps.

The bank wanted to know if the transactions were genuine and I told them they were. What they weren't were recoverable or refundable.

'You're well over your overdraft limit.'

'Can you extend it, for a few days?'

'I'm afraid not. Either transfer the necessary funds imme-diately, or we'll close the account and refer the outstanding amount to a debt collection agency.'

I hung up. Hurled the phone at the wall so hard it exploded into fragments of plastic and glass.

Anyone else, anyone sensible, would have cut their losses. Me? I was wide-eyed and paranoid and pacing the floor. And at the back of my head, the temptation was calling to me. Goading.

'Enough,' I told myself, 'just stop,' but the addiction only whispered back at me.

One more time. Get back online. It's your right, Lizzy.

Was it? Probably not, but still: I had been lucky before, so why not again? The injustice of feeling cheated out of my dues was burning in me.

Which explains, but does not excuse, what I did next: reached for my credit card. My corporate credit card.

Borrowing, that's all it is. You can repay the money later, once you've won it back.

Sly temptations, looping in my head.

Mitch probably won't even notice. Even if he does, you'll have put the money back by then.

I thought I had this under control, mostly. I didn't know that I was about to commit an illegal act. Or maybe I *did* know, but it was impossible for me to listen to the whispers in my head: *Liar. Thief. Cheat.* The truth was, I needed to gamble like I needed to breathe.

After depositing fresh funds from the credit card, I trans-ferred a new balance to my gambling account and sat down to a hand of blackjack, staking the maximum allowable amount on one hand of three grand. Hit after hit followed. Relief flooded me: I was a winner again, with enough winnings recouped to repay my overdraft twice over. The adrenaline was pumping and, like an alcoholic reaching for the next bottle of gin, my hand returned to the mouse, gripped by that hope of just one more shot. After putting ten grand on, I hit blackjack and just clicked and clicked.

And clicked.

I don't need to tell you what happened next. Or maybe, I don't *want* to tell you because it hurts, even now, to go there. The despair, the self-loathing.

In twenty minutes, with eight consecutive hands, I lost the best part of eighty grand.

And ruined my life.

More than once I wondered: was it the fear of disappointing Mitch that led me to play that night? Or was it because he removed me from the business pitch? A way of elevating myself from the feeling of inadequacy and reasserting control? A way of escaping? Maybe it was all of those things. Either way, it took a while for me to realise the enormity of what had happened, what I'd done. I sat stiffly before the screen, my hands trembling. The room seemed to be spinning around me. I wanted to believe it was a dream, a nightmare. The figures on the screen negated that lie.

Eighty grand – squandered. Eighty grand that did not belong to me. It belonged to Mitch, his company. And one way or another, Mitch would know. Eventually, whether I liked it or not, he was going to know.

Oh God . . .

I stared at the string of black zeros on the screen. Incontrovertible. Undeniable. I would lose my job, everything

I had worked for. Worse, though, much worse, I would lose the man I loved.

My stomach gave an awful lurch and I threw up, all over the kitchen floor. Slid off the chair and hunched there, sobbing and retching. When there was nothing more to vomit, words spilled out of me:

'You were drunk, you were under stress, worried about the pitch, and you made a terrible mistake. That explains it, work pressure, you lost control. If you explain, Mitch will understand. There's a chance he'll understand . . .'

But Mitch did *not* understand. Two days later, after our weekly management meeting, I was summoned to his office. He sat across the desk from me in his sharpest suit, looking at me with quiet, black fury.

Sitting on Mitch's left was a man I didn't recognise, a slim sixty-something with cold eyes and a chiselled jaw neatly defined by a salt-and-pepper beard.

'Elizabeth, this is Connor Metcalf. Our new FD,' said Mitch, as the man snapped open a briefcase and drew out a slim file of papers. 'Since you told me what you did, Connor's been checking over the accounts. Checking everything's in the proper order.'

I was suddenly acutely aware of the sounds of traffic drifting up from seven floors down.

'Of course,' I murmured. 'You need to take the proper precautions.'

Mitch leaned towards me over the desk, pinning me with his gaze. 'I trusted you, Lizzy, your professionalism, your judgement,' he said coldly. 'Most of all, I trusted your friendship. And now you've let me down, and in the worst and probably most hurtful of ways.'

It was true, I knew – I'd hurt him, and it was killing me. Wasn't love about forgiveness, though? This was the man who loved me, who wanted to marry me. The future father of my children. He had to see beyond this mistake!

I didn't like the way he was looking at me. Not at all. 'Do I need my solicitor?' I asked, hearing the strain in my voice and at the same time disgusted at myself.

Metcalf clicked his pen. His demeanour was that of an auditor – any wonder I felt intimidated? 'We're not going to prosecute, this time. Can't afford that sort of publicity right now, not with the Raptor pitch looming. However, we can't turn a blind eye to fraud. Understand?'

I opened my mouth; closed it. Once, when Mitch was applying for a loan to help grow the business, he had told me he had lied about his income and outgoings to get the bank onside. He had asked me to collude in that deception and I had, willingly. No, I never signed anything, but I went along with it, never tried to stop him. Not proud of that, but I wanted to help, to see him succeed. And here we were.

In fifteen years of working together I had never felt so let down. I had a problem and I had owned up to it: what I had done was wrong, utterly wrong, and I was sorry. But the man I loved didn't even want to understand.

'Mitch. It was reckless of me; I'm truly sorry.'

He glared at me and for a moment I saw something quite unsettling in his frown. Something menacing. It caught me off guard because I hadn't seen that look in many years; not since he'd applied for that loan from the bank. Which, I remembered now, was rejected.

So, where, exactly, had he found the money to grow the business so quickly? How was it that he could employ so many staff so soon when our monthly income only just covered their expenses?

It suddenly occurred to me – with the clear, cold clarity that only hindsight can douse you with – that perhaps there was a side to Mitch I didn't know so well. Mostly, I think, he showed me his full self, and that was good; but at the same time, here was a man who had been happily lying to his wife for a long stretch of time. You can call me paranoid, but men like that, I suspect, tend to have more than one secret.

And how did Metcalf fit into all this? How long had they known one another, and why hadn't I heard about his appointment before now? As these questions flashed through my mind, my insecurity, my sense of vulnerability, had never felt more acute.

'I'll pay the money back, I promise. Every penny.'

Mitch exchanged a quick glance with Metcalf, who said, 'The two of us will make sure of that, Ms Valentine. It's not beyond us to have you placed under surveillance. The fraud investigators I use can be most tenacious and I should warn you that my debt collectors like to make home visits. Their methods can be very heavy-handed if necessary.'

'I don't understand,' I said, shaking my head. 'Mitch, what sort of operation are you running here?'

It was Metcalf who answered, with a threatening undercurrent to his tone: 'We will do whatever it takes to recover the funds. From this moment you're suspended from your duties.'

'Mitch?'

'You'll be hearing from Connor.' His voice was hard and his body was still. Tense.

But his feelings for me? I wanted to believe some remnant of affection remained.

'Mitch, please?'

Jaw set, frowning, he angled his head away, and from across the table I scrutinised the face I knew so well. Had I seen that expression before? I worried I had. I worried he looked the way he did when he spoke about his wife.

I said, 'Can we please speak in private?'

'No.'

'I didn't do it out of malice. Mitch, I'm going to get help, I promise. I have a serious problem.'

'You're right about that,' said a new voice, and I turned in my chair to see piggish Jane Nixon from HR standing in the open doorway. I'd been so distracted I hadn't even heard her come in, which was kind of surprising for a woman of her size.

Jane was brandishing a big cardboard box, the sort of empty box that says, *This is all you are now, and guess what? It's all you deserve.*

It seemed to be my cue to leave.

Even so, as I stood, on shaking legs, I couldn't help but make one more desperate attempt.

'Please,' I managed, looking directly at Mitch – ignoring Jane with her tight-lipped smile, and Metcalf with his clicking pen. 'We can make this good. If you just give me a second cha—'

Mitch raised his hand. 'Get out, Lizzy. Just get the hell out.'

And that was the last thing he ever said to me.

With no job and little in savings, what the hell was I going to do? No clear answer. And it didn't help that there were unopened bottles of wine at home.

My memory of that night is of sitting cross-legged on my living-room floor, hopelessly flipping through the scrapbook of cuttings that had been my life's work, and slowly getting drunk. I sat up most of the night, resisting the temptation to call Mitch and tell him he had got it all wrong, that I was innocent, because I knew it would be pointless. I'd moved past denial, the first stage of grieving for a life I knew I would never get back, and fast-tracked to depression.

What a spectacular fall from grace. I had hit rock bottom, and the shame was enough to make me hide from the world in my apartment, the curtains drawn. I stayed in there, in the darkness, for days. All hope drained out of me. Time lost meaning. A stranger confronted me in the bathroom mirror, a woman I had come to loathe.

Then, one evening, my new phone rang (the old one was still in plastic tatters on the floor). I stared at it, watching it light up and buzz. It was a call from Sarah Keaton, an old work colleague and friend. It pains me to admit this now, but I was furious that she should be calling me, and afraid of all the inevitable questions: *Is it true, Lizzy, did you really take all that money? How long has this been going on?*

When the phone finally stopped ringing and my apartment was filled with the thick, obdurate silence that was sapping my sanity, my fury turned inward.

Gambling had cost me my friends, my job, and the man I loved. Now, it seemed only right that it should cost me my life.

It was what I deserved.

I got up off the floor and went to put on my coat, to take a final walk.

Here's the memory that keeps me awake at night: a woman on Lambeth Bridge peering down through the inky darkness, the oblivion offered by the cold waters below a grim but welcome escape.

As shivers racked my body, I thought of Connor Metcalf, the

new FD, who would hound me for every penny I owed. No way could I find that sort of cash; and so long as I couldn't, I would never be free.

How easy it would be to climb onto the bridge wall, to step nearer to the edge and just . . . drop. No more debt, no more shame. I could disappear.

What had happened to me? The shiny, self-confident girl fresh out of university? How had it come to this?

The wind was seething as I removed my jacket, dropped it on the pavement. Within seconds I was up there on the side of the bridge. From where I stood, I could see the majesty of London's glittering skyline, perhaps now for the last time.

Do it!

There was no one about to talk me down, no friendly policeman. This was my choice, so I had no right to feel abandoned, but that is how I felt. Alone. And about to learn the true meaning of solitude? I didn't know. Decisiveness was called for, and soon. A black cab was bound to drive past at any moment. I just had to jump.

If I hadn't waited a second longer, I would never have felt the phone in my back pocket, buzzing.

I hesitated. What was the point in answering? The decision should have been simple. But curiosity got the better of me. The desperate hope that it was Mitch calling to say all was forgiven.

'Hello, Lizzy?'

My brother.

'Colin . . .' The water below drew my gaze again. 'This, uh, isn't a good time.'

'We need to talk.' He sounded restless, agitated. 'It's Dad.'

I waited. For one helpless second, I thought he was going to tell me our father had passed away, and what I felt was an immediate pang of sorrow. I hadn't had the chance to say good-bye, or that I was sorry for missing so many family Christmases. That I was proud of him for making a life on his own after Mum was gone.

'He's depressed. Withdrawn, fearful. Honestly I'm struggling to cope on my own.'

I let out the breath I'd been holding. Dad wasn't dead then . . . but in trouble?

Colin lived with our father. Unusual at his age, but a convenient arrangement: he was a painter-decorator (a good one and often much in demand) and could help keep the tower up to scratch. When I say the arrangement was convenient, I don't mean that it was perfect. Like everyone, Dad and Colin had their annoyances, but mostly they rubbed along pretty well, and that was good. Meant they looked out for one another.

This wasn't the first time Colin had warned me that our father had reached an age where we may need to rethink his domestic situation. The conversation a few weeks earlier had been brief and curt, every word clipped with sibling rivalry, but the meaning clear: *He can't go on living in the tower. The stairs are too challenging.*

'Sometimes he's volatile, unpredictable . . .' Colin trailed off and left a pause so long I thought, worried, he was about to add 'violent' to that list. He didn't, but he might just as well have. 'It's a lot for me to deal with, Lizzy. Sorry. I need you to come home.'

It was sincere, pleading, hard to ignore. Like me and Dad, we weren't close, but for a moment I remembered us playing as kids on the Suffolk shore next to the tide-breakers. That helped bring me out of my fog of desperation.

Helped me step back from the edge.

'I didn't realise things were so bad for you,' I said, glancing around to see if anyone was coming, any cars.

'We need to discuss Dad's long-term situation.'

A prolonged silence. Below me, the city lights gleamed in the dark water.

'He's not like he was, Lizzy. A different man. I can't do it any more. Not on my own. I'm afraid it wouldn't take much to push him over the edge.'

And there it was. A reason to pause, to reflect.

A reason to go on?

Like I said, Dad and I weren't close; he had never allowed that. In many ways we were strangers to each other. Always a handshake, never a hug. That was Dad. But I knew he loved me. Losing a child at his age? How would that affect him? Could he possibly understand, would he ever?

No. A grim image surfaced in my mind: my elderly father hunched forward at my funeral, tears streaming down his flushed cheeks. It was enough to coax me down from the ledge.

'He was asking about you the other day. He misses you,' Colin said, although it's possible he made that up to tempt me into going home. He told me it would be good to have me back to help for a bit, if I had the time.

I had to shake my head at the irony: my brother was talking me down from suicide and he didn't even know it. Time was *all* I had.

'You there, Lizzy?'

'Yeah.' I was back on the pavement by then, putting my jacket on, letting out a long breath with my head tilted back and my eyes on the stars. To say I was suddenly thankful for Colin's phone call was an understatement.

'Will you come?'

'Yes.'

'When?'

'Soon.'

'Are you sure—'

I will beat this.

'Yes, soon, I promise.'

I left the bridge then and walked back to my apartment and packed my case. Going to Dad's wouldn't cure my addiction, but my family needed me, and for the moment that was as good a reason as any not to end things.

I thought about Colin as I got into bed, hardly believing how selfish I had been. How close I had come. My brother unwittingly saved my life that night and I've never thanked him for that, but I was grateful then, and despite everything that has happened since – the whole horrible business – I still am grateful. Sometimes all it takes is to remember that other people need you.

As I laid my head on the soft pillow I kept telling myself: *I will beat this*, without knowing if I would or could. Only knowing I had to try. It was another roll of the dice and the odds were against me; but the addiction's *One more time* was not a thought I was willing to entertain again.

Tomorrow I would drive out to the Suffolk coast and check on Dad. And then maybe I could rebuild. I wasn't free yet, but I genuinely wanted to move past my terrible mistake.

As I drifted into a restless sleep I was almost optimistic.

But that was before what happened at the tower.

Before I was accused of murdering my father.

– 2 –

A TOWER BY THE SEA

I left London the next afternoon, not with a great deal of hope, but enough to remain focused on my destination.

Swinging my legs out of bed, already I was visualising the Martello tower, a sentinel presence beside the foaming sea, surrounded by vast banks of dark shingle. A wilderness.

The weathered grey tower had stood empty for decades before we moved in, which wasn't so surprising. All about it there hung an air of desolation and abandonment. Blank windows. A sturdy iron door. Walls thirty feet high and fifteen feet thick at the base. I was never sure where he found the money, but Dad was the first to buy up and renovate one of these old Napoleonic fortifications in the remotest parts of Suffolk – the sort of project you expect to see on one of those television shows where middle-class developers with more money than sense risk everything to create their stunning dream home.

His passion, if not his outright obsession.

For me, the wind-wrapped Martello tower was a building out of time. I'd never felt comfortable there. Never completely safe. Too many nights kept awake by the groan of the sea.

Too many nights feeling watched. Trapped. Vulnerable.

I'll grant you this: I was young back then, and yes, of course I was highly impressionable – show me a child who isn't. And yet, it was only when Dad moved us into that damned tower that my bad dreams began. My nightmares.

I called ahead to let Colin know I'd be there by the evening. I remember that clearly, because I made the call from my home-office just after opening the mountain of bank statements I'd been avoiding for the past year. There was no reply, but that was hardly surprising. My big brother was never great with picking up messages, except when it suited him.

Fifteen years my elder, Colin was unfailingly gentle. Quiet. But his greatest failing – we all have them – was that he just never listened, at least not to me. If he had, the horrible things I want to tell you about might never have happened.

Louise Weston, my neighbour, caught me on the way out of my apartment and I saw immediately from her inquisitive look that she knew something was up. 'Going anywhere nice?' she asked, when I told her I'd be out of town for a few weeks. 'You take care, okay?'

The smile was warmer than usual. She even offered to help me with the case I was lugging down the stairs – and that told me something that made me uneasy: I was failing to suppress my inner turmoil. I was ashamed, deeply ashamed, and the mask was slipping. If I couldn't fool my neighbour that everything was all right, I was going to have a hard time with Colin and Dad.

'Just say if you want me to go in and turn the lights on at night. I still have those spare keys.'

'Thanks so much, Louise,' I said, but I didn't care about the lights, or the flat, and not just because it wasn't mine. I could no longer afford it.

'See you soon, Lou!' I beamed.

This smile, I think you can see through it, right?

Which is why I didn't look her in the eye as I went out on to the street to find my car.

My one comfort that morning – strange as this might sound – was my car. A classic Mini Cooper. Small. Sporty. And great fun.

For some reason, I'd always needed to own a car, and Jules (yes, I had a name for her) was a vehicle I cherished. She was red; the brightest red, and quite beautiful. Sure, sometimes the steering was a bit off and sometimes, if you slammed the passenger-side door hard enough, the window fell out (it happened to me twice). But for all her faults, I was proud of her. She belonged to me, and that meant a lot, because for a time, growing up, we didn't have a car. We took the bus or walked or got friends to drive us.

I don't know why we didn't have a car. Only that Mum was very quiet around that time. Permanently worried, it had seemed to me.

I tried not to think about that as I buckled my seat belt and set off. Getting out of town was the easy part. The hard part was what came next. Considering the mess I'd fled from in London, escaping to the edge of nowhere should have felt like a tonic. Instead, by the time I arrived in Suffolk, my mouth was dry. Just watching the skeletal trees and wilderness of mudflats zipping by I thought I could feel my heart urgently beating out a warning to turn the car around. But my conscience was telling me that a U-turn wasn't an option now, and my conscience was undoubtedly right.

'You'll think of something, and pay the money back,' I told myself, sounding far more confident than I felt. I was beginning to realise I should have conquered my gambling habit a long, long time ago, and something else – that every debt catches up with you. In the end.

Looking back on that car journey, what I remember most is the mental image of Mitch, so disappointed. Saying nothing. Just staring at me in terrible, furious silence as I explained, through my sobs, about my financially ruinous compulsive behaviour. How I couldn't physically stop myself. How every time I lost a bet, I had to take another in the hope of winning back what I'd lost. Worse, I also saw the imagined faces of our children, who would never be born, whom I would never know or love.

Regret was prowling around me.

In the rear-view mirror, my eyes were grim, resigned. But not completely defeated. Because here was my chance to renew, to recover. If I was sensible.

If I was extremely lucky.

A bumpy narrow track leads to the remotest part of Suffolk. It snakes through a wilderness of mudflats and forests and farmlands, estuaries and heathland, and as I turned on to that track, the guilt was gnawing at me. In my heart I knew I should have come home long before now, and that didn't make me feel good about myself. How long had it been? Two years, longer?

Easily.

So, why had I stayed away?

That question brought to mind Colin's first phone call about Dad.

'Look, how can I put this? He's just not . . . himself any more. I looked it up, Lizzy – I'm worried. What if it's dementia?'

I remember scowling, as if he had used a dirty word, because a part of me didn't want to believe that – who does? But something in Colin's tone warned me I would soon *have* to believe it, that facing up to my duties as a daughter would fast become a reality.

'Sure you're not overreacting?' I asked, trying to sound rational and in control, and, in the background, I thought I heard the faint sound of a woman clearing her throat. 'Colin, you're not thinking of moving him out, are you? He loves the tower, it's his home, so it's right that he remains there.'

At once my brother's exasperation was unleashed. 'Have you heard yourself, Lizzy? How do you know what's best for him when you're never here?'

I gripped the telephone so tightly that I'm sure my knuckles were turning white. How dare he? It was churlish of him not to acknowledge that I had our father's best interests at heart. I sent money home frequently; not because I felt he needed it, but because I wanted to make a contribution to the tower's running costs.

What bothered me was his attitude. Colin resented my ambition, I was sure. Did he feel inferior? Maybe. If he worked just one of my days he'd have realised there was no need to.

Still. My annoyance was of the brutal sort that only the guilty can feel. I wanted to tell my brother where to stick his outrage, but right then I could only reply with cold silence, because the truth was, he was right; and I knew it. Aside from my hidden addiction, Mitch and the company and the career were everything to me.

'Swanning around in London, leaving me to get on with

it. You've no idea what it's like, none. The burden falls to me every time, and I have a life, too. You get that, right?'

'I can't have this conversation now,' was what I said next, gaze fixed on my computer screen and that evening's losses. 'It's not a good time.'

'When is it ever?' He spoke with trembling resentment and I sensed that he was building to something else. Probably another problem I couldn't resolve, when enough of my own were already threatening to pull me under. 'Look,' I said. 'Sorry, but I've got to go.'

'Wait, there's something I need to—'

I hung up.

Now, on the homeward straight, I didn't feel good about that. Colin deserved more than such a cursory dismissal. I would apologise. And, once I had worked out precisely how to pay Mitch back, I'd explain to him about my wastefulness and profligacy. That was only right.

But Dad? He could never know. For a moment I saw his face crumpling with humiliation. *No. Never.* Was that calculated dishonesty? I guess so; but not every lie is based on self-interest. Show me a daughter who doesn't want to make her father proud.

By the time I reached Shingle Street, the sky was a sickly dark yellow, with grey mists drifting in from the marshlands.

A wild sequestered spot. Creepy.

If you're going to change your mind, now's the time.

It was the same mental voice I'd heard in recent weeks urging me not to gamble, except this time it was louder.

Be sure, Lizzy, be very sure.

Then the right turn appeared, along with the battered road sign: MARTELLO TOWER. With a pang of nostalgia, I remembered helping Dad paint that sign one Saturday morning, one of our rare father–daughter moments. Now, to my dismay, the black lettering was flaking, barely legible.

And that struck a nerve, brought the childhood memories flashing back: my best friend Nick Strickland and me, picking our way home from school, passing the old anchors, spooking ourselves with some of the legends:

'There were bodies on the shore, so the story goes; bodies on the shore; from where, no one knows.'

The sort of myth appropriate for a location such as this; because what made Shingle Street unusual – apart from its name – was that it had once been evacuated and used by the military for training.

And top secret experiments – if you believed the stories.

As I made the turn, the single narrow track dipped and turned into a rattling bridge that crossed a mud-slicked stream. Only when I had reached the enclosed gravel car park did I stop and take in the view. What most astonished me, perhaps, was its air of desolation. But it was as it had ever been: the wide shingle ridge lined with cottages, the old anchors and the stretching groynes, long low walls made from wood running down the beach and out into the grey churning sea.

It was with a mixture of hope and trepidation that I got out of the car and faced into the gusting wind and salty sea spray. Because of the density of the fog, I couldn't yet see the Martello tower; it waited some distance along the beach. What I could see, directly ahead, was another sign, this one noticeably better maintained than the last:

Shingle Street
Site of Special Scientific Interest
The land and track beyond this sign are privately owned.
Shingle Street is special.
Only you can help keep it that way.
DO NOT DRIVE BEYOND THIS POINT

I didn't have much luggage; the case and the three bags I had brought could wait on the back seat of the car. Clothes and some old books.

What mattered now was finding Dad. Coming here was a chance to close the distance between us. And I needed his help, his guidance. That's what I told myself as I locked the car and started walking.

I headed quickly along the shore, by the banks of black shingle, looking out at the fishing shack – abandoned to ruins, for who would want to fish in this extreme and dismal environment? Further down the beach, shallow lagoons glimmered darkly, and beyond, the sea pounded in.

There was no one else about. Still, by the time I passed the great Victorian coastguard cottages – which had always looked to me more like imposing London townhouses – I did not feel that I was alone. It was almost as if I was being observed.

But there was no one.

I passed Dumb Boy Cottage, the end house and the only one that did not look vacant. The cottage was a holiday rental owned by a well-to-do family in Woodbridge, and in all the years Dad had lived out here I'd never known a guest stay for longer than a few days. It was hard to imagine living under that cracked slate roof or behind those moth-eaten curtains.

But right now, something did make me pause and think about it, something I'd never seen before: a long line of bright white shells running from the door of the cottage some hundred yards onto the shingle ridge.

Despite the fading light, that line of white shells was clear and visible against the banks of dark stones. Powerful, almost. It trailed right down to the water, where it ended in an intricate circular pattern. It didn't look like a natural formation. Clearly, these shells had been laid with a great deal of care and attention.

I started walking again, wondering what it meant, who had made it, why? And soon enough, the Martello tower greeted me, looming out of the murky autumn dusk.

Once, this tower had defended this shore. I took a moment to study it, already visualising the circular chambers within; the dank bedrooms; the daunting spiral stairway leading up to the roof, which had once served as the battlements but which now, thanks to Dad, was a chic, open-plan living space with kitchen-diner.

A home now maybe, but as I stood there on the shingle ridge, staring, all I could see was the way it had been: three feet deep in water and mud, the rough grass sprouting from its battlements.

Next to it, just yards from the beach, was the boathouse. When we first came here, I'd asked Dad why we needed the property when none of us had an interest in boats and I've always been afraid of water, and he'd said he intended to fix that up as well. Add a few bedrooms, convert it into a home-office. The job took him just a couple of months; then we had somewhere to stay while the renovations on the tower were completed.

Now, with the wind at my back, I went towards the rickety fence that enclosed the boathouse and peered through the mist into the small garden. Abandoned. A tangle of weeds. The coiled hosepipe on the distant wall was almost falling apart. Which was odd. Normally, Dad took pride in the garden.

What came to mind then were Colin's comments about Dad seeming fearful and distracted, maybe depressed, and all at once my guilt returned to overwhelm me. Suddenly nothing else mattered. I had to see Dad – now.

I turned towards the tower and walked faster. Urgently. As I headed up the steel staircase – the entrance to the tower was halfway up the wall – I noticed the iron handrail was rusted and loose, that the building's cement skin was chipped and cracked, like the macabre surface of an abandoned tomb. These signs of neglect made me uneasy as I knocked loudly and waited, hugging myself against the cold.

Almost a minute passed and still no answer.

Next, I tried the door handle. It turned, I pushed, and the sturdy iron door swung open.

Weird. Would Colin leave it unlocked? Possibly, but Dad never would, even when he was at home; and the cavernous chamber into which I stepped was ill-lit and cold. Why wasn't the heating on?

'Dad?' I called out, but again to no response.

As the wind moaned around the tower, I gave an involuntary shiver, looking up, past the brick arches, to the spiral staircase.

Not to worry, I told myself, *he's probably on the top floor, can't hear you.*

He loved it up there, and was it any wonder? Over the years that room must have appeared in dozens of home design magazines.

The looping stone staircase led me up.

'Dad, hello?'

The room was empty – and it smelled. In the kitchen area the sink was loaded with dirty plates, the bin was overflowing, and the floor looked like it hadn't seen a mop in months. On the table were stacks and stacks of unopened letters. I picked one up, noted the postal date.

What the hell?

I could have been standing in the house of a dead man. Some of these letters were almost a year old!

Outside, the sky was darkening. And far below, the mudflats, grey and vast, glistened coldly.

Glancing around me, confused, I was trying not to think the worst, before I thought – with some anger – of Colin. How could he have let the place deteriorate like this? And anyway, just where the hell was he?

My next thought was logical but comforting: perhaps he had taken Dad somewhere, a trip in the car maybe, shopping in Woodbridge?

That seemed possible. They would be back soon. I would clean up the kitchen. It would be a surprise when Dad got home. Then, over a cup of tea – definitely no wine – I would talk to them both about getting a cleaner in.

That was a sensible plan, or would have been, if it wasn't for what happened next: from beneath the floorboards, far below, the hard clang of the iron door slamming shut. Which was wrong.

Hadn't I taken care to shut it behind me? I was sure!

Except then the clang came again, harder. So loud that my whole body reacted involuntarily with a jolt.

The front door must be open, I thought, without fully

understanding: *it's open and catching on the wind.* I would go down and close it.

But as I descended the spiral staircase and entered the lobby area I saw I was wrong. For a moment, my eyes refused to believe it: the front door was closed and locked. Totally secure.

Something wrong here, was the thought that broke in, *something definitely not right.* It was all too still, too unnervingly quiet. If this tower had been a ship, then I'd suddenly boarded the *Mary Celeste*.

But I had overlooked something. My gaze shifted to the stairwell leading down to the bedrooms. What if Dad had just come in and headed downstairs? It had to be worth checking.

I headed down, holding on to the bannister as though I was holding on to life. The stairs were uncomfortably steep, looping around the circular walls, which were cold and grey and rough. As I descended, it occurred to me that here it was, my addiction, playing out. The need to maintain some semblance of control. I suppose it was ironic that the bannister wasn't fastened to the wall properly, was shaking.

Something's wrong, I thought again.

And I was right, because what I saw next tightened a cold, vice-like fist of fear around my heart.

For a moment my brain refused to process what I was seeing. Then my vision sharpened. Horribly.

He lay there at the bottom of the stairs, a thin man with a tangled grey beard.

'Oh my God, Dad!'

His glasses were crushed under his face and a dark puddle of blood had poured from his nose and pooled around his head.

In panic, I flew to his side and gripped his marbled hand,

which was as cold as the stone-flagged floor. As I ran my hand over his wispy hair he didn't move. Didn't even flinch.

'Dad, please!' I shook him gently. 'DAD?'

Grey-looking. Purple lips. Cheeks caved in.

With a slow, numbing dread, I began to process the thought that he was dead.

Please no, please not like this!

I was leaning over him, putting my ear to his mouth, when a shadow dropped over me. I raised my gaze.

And there, halfway down the stairs, was the formidable figure of a woman. Gripping a claw hammer and raising it, as if to strike.

HAZEL

'How did you get in?' the woman demanded. Hard. Accusatory.

She stopped at the bottom of the staircase, right at the point where it began to bend around into a spiral, with the hammer raised high, ready to swing. She looked somewhere in her mid fifties. A buxom, rather porcine woman of medium height with short, frizzy dark hair, thick glasses and a tight mouth. Over a white blouse, she wore a dark red, cable-knit cardigan. Flat, sensible, lace-up shoes and a plaid, pleated skirt completed the overall impression of a stern matron.

Still brandishing the claw hammer, she took what I interpreted as a deliberately threatening step towards me.

'What the hell have you done to him?' I asked.

She recoiled. 'I am here to *help! Who are you?*'

The next few seconds seemed to pass very slowly, but I quickly understood that this situation could escalate into the worst sort of misunderstanding. Whoever she was – a friend, a neighbour – my fear was this: she would assume I was an intruder, that I'd broken in perhaps to prey on a vulnerable man, that I'd pushed him down the stairs.

And suddenly, in my mind, a sequence of events unspooled like one of the horror movies Colin used to make me watch when I was a kid. Me leaping to my feet to protect myself. This accusing woman looming over me, hammer raised high; then, out of fear or panic, or both, bringing it down hard. Smashing it into my skull over and over, until the metal was thick with lumps of flesh and tufts of blood-soaked hair.

'*Woah*, *woah*, *woah*!' I instinctively threw up a protective hand. 'Stop, okay? Please, I'm Lizzy, his daughter!'

She froze at the bottom of the stairs. The hammer remained raised. It was almost as long as her forearm, and heavy, I knew. I remembered Dad buying it twenty years ago at a car-boot sale in Woodbridge.

'His *daughter*!' I stressed, and her eyes narrowed, flicking to Dad at my side and back to me.

'He never mentioned a daughter,' she said in a gravelly voice.

Disbelief welled up inside me. My hands twisted in frustration. I was frightened to death and only too aware of my father crumpled up next to me. I said, 'Look, I've no idea who you are, but you must trust me! Help, please, call an ambulance!'

'I already did,' she said, holding my gaze. 'Wi-Fi was down; I went outside to get a signal.'

The slammed door. Was that her?

Maybe.

'What happened here?' I asked. 'He fell down the stairs?'

'Actually, he collapsed right there.'

'And what did you do?' There was an allegation in my tone.

'We were having a conversation when it happened. I went for help.'

'You said he collapsed. Why didn't you catch him?'

She was about to reply; but as I was clutching his hand, I felt suddenly the spark of life. A feeble pressure from his fingers.

And a lesson from school jumped into my head. It seemed so obvious.

'We need to put him into the recovery position!'

For a moment, she seemed locked in thought, eyes fixed on me. Then, finally, she dropped the hammer. It clanged heavily to the ground as she hurried to my side and crouched to assist.

'Like this,' she said, rolling my father onto his side, tilting his head back. She seemed to know precisely what she was doing, which was good; but the obvious question remained, and it was one that I found distinctly troubling.

She said she was with him; so why didn't she do this sooner?

'Support his head,' she instructed, and I did, with both hands, all the time listening to the voice of doubt. *Recovery position, Lizzy! It occurred to you. So why not to her?*

The woman was now close enough that I could smell her sweat. Stale. I didn't want her this close, so I lost no time in getting to my feet and moving to crouch down next to Dad on the opposite side. And as I did that, I noticed another distinctive smell. An earthy smell that reminded me of Mum, when we would cook together on Sunday afternoons. Rosemary.

'Who are you?' I said, but she spoke over me.

'I want proof you're who you say you are.'

I clung to my father. 'You're not serious?'

She said nothing, just fixed me with a penetrating stare that lacked compassion. Lacked any warmth at all.

Infuriated, I took my purse from my coat pocket, whipped out my bank card and thrust it out. She took it and looked down with a needle-like stare, inspecting it closely, as a headmistress might an examination paper, until eventually handing it back to me. By the time she did that I had realised I had no right to own the thing. Sure, my name was on that card, along with my account number and sort code. What it lacked was a stamp of personal responsibility.

She fixed me in silence from behind her glasses. As we waited for the ambulance I gently took Dad's wrist and checked his pulse. It seemed weak to me. The thread of anxiety entwined around my heart tightened – not helped by this stranger regarding me appraisingly.

'So, who are *you*?' I challenged.

'I'm Hazel,' she said, as if that were all the answer I needed. 'Hazel Sanders.' Then she turned her attention to my father and a smile softened her face. 'Lizzy and I have had a small misunderstanding,' she said, pressing a hand to his forehead as if to soothe him. 'But that's all right, pet, isn't it? I mean, misunderstandings happen all the time, don't they?'

I scowled. Who was she to call my father *pet*?

'But why the hell are you here?' I said sharply.

The smile vanished. With her head cocked on one side, she gazed at me with a look of intense interest, or defensiveness. 'I *live* here,' she said in a tone of abject finality.

I froze. My whole body went cold. 'You what?'

'Oh, didn't anybody mention that?' she said, assessing me with concern. 'Sorry, pet. Gosh, how awkward!'

I stared at her. This was unbelievable. Outrageous. Or something I deserved for staying away for so long? Finally I said, 'I'm out of the loop.'

I watched as she checked Dad's breathing and his pulse. She seemed so confident in the role, capable.

Finally she said, 'Your brother employed me.'

'I don't understand,' I said feebly, and reached out to stroke Dad's hair. But she stuck out a hand, blocking me.

'*I'm* his care-giver,' she said, her eyes blazing. 'Your father is *my* responsibility. Do you understand that?'

Thus my nightmare began.

'Who is she, Colin?'

As if there could have been another question while we were waiting outside Dad's hospital room.

It was seven hours later. Two o'clock in the morning, and the hospital ward was as silent as a tomb. Or would have been, if it weren't for the incessant squeaking of my brother's trainers as he paced back and forth, back and forth, his eyes on NHS posters, the vending machine – everywhere it seemed, but on me.

'Colin?'

'She's a professional.'

'I'm not talking about her job! Who the hell *is* she?'

'Why so cynical? She takes care of Dad.'

'Really?' I exclaimed. Maybe working in PR had made me cynical, but that didn't mean I was wrong. I saw again the stairwell looping down into the gloomy bedroom area, Dad helplessly splayed on the cold flagstone floor.

'Tell me: if she's so perfect, why did she leave him when he collapsed?'

My memory called up images of the dirty dishes in the kitchen sink, the stacks of unopened mail.

'And why is the tower so filthy? What is she paid to do? I mean, Christ, Colin, when were you going to tell me?'

He stopped pacing and I looked up at him. My brother was grey and despondent; a weak man with watery eyes who had always needed strong women about him, ever since he had flunked out of university and allowed drink to take over his life. After that he got sober and made the best of himself. Not a bad man; in his own way, he was kind, well-meaning; just not particularly strong. He just about managed to meet my gaze.

'Well?'

He shook his head, swallowed, shook his head again.

'This woman—'

'Hazel. She's been living at the tower almost a year now.'

'With *both* of you?' I asked.

There was a pause as he cleared his throat. 'With Dad.'

I processed that.

'Just the two of them?'

The guilty look on Colin's face said it all.

'Where did you find her?' I asked. 'You went through an agency, got the proper references?'

He shrugged, but it was half a squirm. 'Mary at the post office said she knew Hazel, that she was reliable—'

'What were you thinking?' I snapped, exasperated. 'Colin, really, she could be anyone!'

He held up his hands in a gesture that said, *Please just hear me out, okay?*

'Agencies are expensive. And different carers working different shifts?' He shook his head. 'That wouldn't work for us. Dad gets confused, repeats himself, and until Hazel came along he insisted he didn't need help. What he needs now most of all is consistency. A friendly face. Every day. Someone reliable.'

That was supposed to be you, I thought. *That was the deal.* Before another, quieter voice said: *Well it was never going to be you, was it, Lizzy?*

But I had to shut that voice out.

'Don't you think you should have told me?' I asked.

'I said there had to be changes at home, didn't I?'

'How often do you visit? Where are you living now?'

'The Melford estate. I've met someone. Sandra. She's important to me.'

'Fine, but . . .' I swallowed. Then it burst out of me: 'You moved out without telling me! Brought a complete stranger in to look after our father! I had a right to know! You see that? I had a *right*!'

My brother shook his head, looking at me with complete exasperation. 'Lizzy, please, don't overreact. Whatever you've assumed, Hazel *is* hard-working, okay? And she's dedicated, and—'

'And our father is in *hospital*. On *her* watch!'

His lips compressed. And I felt my face flushing.

'Dad doesn't look well fed to me, and he doesn't look well groomed. Colin, he looks malnourished!'

'You've heard too many horror stories,' he said. 'Hazel isn't that person, okay? She's just not. She knows what she's doing. She used to work at Rose Cross House and—'

'She threatened me with a hammer!' I all but shouted. 'Are you just going to pretend that didn't happen, or would you like me to go back and tell you again how she forced me to show her my ID? Christ! She didn't even know I existed!'

Colin shook his head. 'Of course I mentioned you.'

'Really? Where were my graduation photos?'

'I told you, Dad's been moving things around. Hiding them. Convinced we're going to have a break-in.'

'Why would he think that?'

'He's paranoid! And if it's any consolation, the pictures of me are gone, too, okay? He's hiding things away in the boathouse. God, Lizzy, there's a lot you don't know.'

'And whose fault is that?'

He looked at me with a dubious expression. 'If I'd thought

you cared,' he said bluntly, 'I might have kept you in the loop, okay?'

That hurt; I winced as if he had struck me, and he must have seen it because he immediately held his hands up in a gesture of apology.

'You didn't want to keep me in the loop,' I said, 'but it was okay to keep taking my money, right?'

He squirmed where he stood.

'So,' I asked, 'how much are you paying her?'

'It's worth it,' he replied, at once defensive.

'How much, Colin?'

'Way above market rate,' he rushed to answer, 'but the cleaning, his meals, his medication. Honestly? I couldn't manage it any more. Not on my own.'

My shoulders tensed. We both knew he had meant to say: *You left me to get on with it.*

Clearly, I had underestimated the toll on him, which, I saw now, had become a burden, and that was sad. How could I not feel guilty? A parent should never be a burden.

Don't get me wrong, I loved Colin for taking care of Dad in the only way he knew how, and I was grateful. On the other hand, I couldn't help resenting his lying to me, pretending he was at the tower when he wasn't, and all the time keeping silent about the stranger he had brought into our father's home.

'He's hard to manage, Lizzy. Cut off from all his old friends. Isolated in that damned tower. Completely paranoid. The way he is now . . . no, I just couldn't cope.'

I made a bewildered gesture with my hand, and he finally stopped standing over me and sat beside me on the row of hard plastic chairs.

'Look, I know your job is stressful,' he said, 'so I didn't want to worry you. But about fifteen months ago, Dad became con-fused, disorientated. He collapsed, Lizzy.'

'Why?' I asked. 'How?' These were the words that fell from my lips, but there were others that didn't: *Why didn't I hear of this earlier, when it happened?*

'He has diabetes. It's pretty serious. He has this ulcer on his foot, it's always infected. They've already amputated his big toe.'

I stared, couldn't believe what I was hearing.

'He's often disorientated, very forgetful, confused. Sometimes it's as if he fades out of this life and tunes into another. And then there's the depression . . .'

I didn't know if he was exaggerating or if there was a deeper truth here. Neither option seemed appealing. When it came to telling the truth, maybe we both had a problem and that might have been the thing we had most in common. Still, I needed to know; what else had he kept from me?

'How bad, Colin? How bad is the depression?'

He looked at the floor and took a breath before saying, 'We think he made an attempt on his own life.'

'What?'

'Or he was going to.'

'When? Where? How?'

His eyes, when they met mine, were glistening with sad-ness. 'We were outside, walking. Dad wasn't alone for long, I swear. But when we came inside . . .' His face tightened . . . 'We found the leather belt. Fastened to the bannister at the top of the stairs.'

For one horrible moment I saw my brother, with Hazel at his side, in the entrance chamber of the tower, looking up at my father's lifeless body hanging over them.

'Thank God he didn't go through with it. You know where we found him? In the kitchen, muttering something about testing the strength of the bannister.' Colin shook his head, like a man trying to shake off a nightmare. 'I'm not even sure he remembered doing it; but if we'd left him just a moment longer . . . I think about it all the time, it haunts me.'

I fell silent, aching for Dad, my memory of that night on the bridge, so cold and so alone, still uncomfortably close.

'So, you see,' Colin said, covering my chilly hand with his, 'it's not sensible for Dad to be alone, is it? And we can afford Hazel.'

I stared at him. 'You need to understand something, okay? My situation has changed, Colin. Drastically.' Never had a truer word been spoken, but I struggled to get those words out. 'I'm out of a job.'

'What happened?'

'Redundancy,' I lied.

Colin was looking closely at me. My mind jumped back to the office, all shiny glass boxes and chrome; the cardboard box packed with my belongings, the inquisitive looks downstairs in the lobby, the security guard guiding me past the lavish fountain towards the exit.

Your laptop and corporate phone have already been removed from your desk and confiscated. Do not attempt to re-enter the building.

'Sure there's nothing you want to tell me?' he asked.

From behind me suddenly, the shuffle of feet. I turned and recognised at once those lace-up shoes, the plaid skirt, the cable-knit cardigan.

'Well,' Hazel announced, 'they've only just completed the MRI, so they should be bringing Dad up soon.' She sounded satisfied with herself, annoyingly so.

'I made them do it immediately. They suggested it wait until tomorrow, but I said no, no, no, and that's how to manage the NHS, you've got to be on their backs. You know, I feel sorry for those poor sods with no family to look out for them, don't you? Only the best for Dad!'

The first 'Dad' had me gaping at her. The second had me on my feet.

'*What* did you call him?' I said, incredulous.

'Elizabeth, please,' said Colin, tugging on my arm. 'Hazel's just trying to help—'

'No!' I shrugged him off. 'He's *our* father.'

There was a moment of uncomfortable silence.

'Look, pet, we agreed that—'

'Don't!' I held up a hand. In her right fist she was gripping a cluster of plastic bags stuffed with Dad's bloodied clothes; but that wasn't what made me feel queasy. What did that was her sour, sweaty smell. In my mind, I could still see her regarding me coldly with the hammer raised high.

'You crossed a line,' I said. 'Just then, *and* at the tower.'

'A misunderstanding,' she said, 'but we're all under a lot of stress, aren't we? We had no idea you were coming, so I naturally assumed the worst . . .'

She trailed off, dropping her gaze apologetically.

'Well, now,' she said, 'I feel thoroughly awful. I hope I haven't come between the two of you? Siblings look out for one another, or should do,' she added heavily. 'Can we please put this whole unpleasant business behind us?'

When I said nothing, she moved a little closer to me. 'A trying time is coming,' she said, 'and it's essential now for your dad's sake that we all get along. Isn't that what he would want?'

I said nothing, just stepped back into my own space. We were immediately next to an open ward and it was quiet except for the haunting high-pitched *beep, beep* coming from the machine next to the adjacent bed, in which lay an elderly black man. His head was lolling to one side, facing us, his eyes heavily lidded. Looking at him, I felt my tear ducts burn.

'I should go,' Hazel said with reluctance.

Yes, you should.

'Hazel, no, please. Dad needs you here.'

I glared at my brother. Why was he defending her?

'Well, now then, these are going to need a good wash,' she said, her manner common-sense. Brusque. She was looking down at the plastic bags again. 'I'll bring some fresh shirts back tomorrow. Some slippers and a robe, too, so he's nice and comfortable. Sound good?'

'Perfect, thank you Hazel.'

'It's no trouble at all,' she replied, giving my brother a warm smile.

'If you can wait, I'll give you a lift,' Colin offered.

'No, no, don't you worry about me,' Hazel said, 'I'll order a taxi. Call me if you hear anything, okay?'

'Yes, of course,' Colin said, 'as soon as we hear.'

Away she went, the squeak of her shoes following her the length of the shiny corridor. When she was gone I said heatedly: 'I can't believe you're defending this woman.'

Colin looked nonplussed. 'She's punctual, consistent. Helpful.'

'The wrong sort of help,' I said, 'a stranger!'

'*She's* always around.'

'Listen. We must talk about this. It's essential that we—'

Suddenly, the corridor doors burst open and two

exhausted-looking nurses appeared, wheeling towards us a bed with railed sides.

'Not now,' Colin said, 'please, for God's sake, not now.'

My father's name was Clifford Alastair Valentine. His friends called him Cliff. When I was little I'd say, 'Like the singer?' Among the pictures I kept of my him and myself from my childhood was an old Polaroid of him standing prominently in front of the Martello tower, before its renovation. In the photograph Dad is wearing jeans, a flannel shirt with the sleeves rolled up, and a baseball cap. He looks strong, but with a sad, distant look. Standing off to the left, Mum and I are looking pensively at him. That picture came with me to London and I studied it from time to time, trying to understand more about Dad, but never with much success. Over time that picture kept fading. I told myself that one day I would have it restored, but I never did. Eventually, Dad's face faded to nothing more than a blur.

With a pang of nostalgia and regret, I thought about that as we stood aside and let the nurses do their work. Eventually, one of them – a friendly young man called Patrick – said we could sit beside Dad's bed. Feeling apprehensive, I did just that, entering a small white room where the only noise was the beeping heart monitor and the hiss of oxygen from a tube under Dad's nose. My breath caught at the instant I saw him. His nose was broken, swollen, set in a splint, his face horribly gaunt. Worst of all, his usually intelligent, bright eyes were closed and cruelly sunken.

'Oh, Dad,' I said, stroking his fine hair. It felt as though it hadn't been washed for several weeks.

My apprehension turned to guilt. I should never have left it so long. My thoughts returned to Hazel, perhaps inevitably. I see now that I was probably looking for someone to blame.

Where did she come from? How can I trust her?

The questions looped in my brain, as they had done since the moment the ambulance arrived at the shore.

'She said she called the ambulance immediately,' I said, and Colin looked uncomfortably at me. 'She said they were having a conversation when he collapsed. A conversation about what?'

My brother opened his mouth to reply, closed it, and we sat in silence for a long, ponderous moment.

Eventually he said, 'She likes to get him talking about the past, distract him from the present, from the things making him unhappy.'

'Oh?' This I had to hear. 'Tell me.'

He drew a reluctant breath. 'She thinks Dad feels neglected by his family.'

His family?

The words impacted with a mental thud.

'Lizzy, you all right?'

For a moment I just gaped, unable to meet his eyes.

He means me. My fault, it's my fault Dad's depressed.

The monitors beeped hauntingly as I put my head in my hands, then turned and studied my father, all the time wondering if any of this had been avoidable, if there was more Hazel could have done, and why she didn't even know about me.

'Why didn't you warn her to expect me?' I asked. 'You knew I was coming. Why didn't you tell me about her?'

Silence.

'I called you yesterday, remember?'

He stared blankly at me.

'Colin – I left you a voicemail, asked if you needed anything picking up on my way – remember?'

He looked at me like a concerned mother might regard her seven-year-old who thinks her imaginary friends are real.

'No Lizzy, you didn't call, there was no voicemail.'

A stunned look must have hit my face. Was I misremembering? Had I blanked out again, the way I sometimes did when I was in the throes of addiction? No. It would be easy to check the call records; and I was about to do just that when Colin said something that threw me completely off guard.

'Decisions need to be made. When – if – Dad wakes up, we'll need a power of attorney to handle all his affairs, and I think it's best you take control, Lizzy. You're reliable, you're good with money.'

I swallowed.

'And in time we'll need to think about changing his living arrangements. The tower just isn't a safe environment for him, not any more, but a care home would be—'

'No,' I said, hardening. 'No, Colin. No way.'

'Even if he needs specialised care?'

I tried imagining it: Dad in slippers and a stained flannel robe, slumped in a vinyl-covered armchair at the back of a television room stinking of urine and faeces.

Locked up and on a slow slide into invisibility with people he had never met? Entrusted to the care of strangers, to await the creeping decline towards senility?

Never. He would rather be dead than endure that. I shook my head and told my brother so.

'Fine, but if you insist on keeping Dad at home you'll have to find a way to cope with that, for his sake, and for mine.'

Sensing his seething resentment, I decided to take some heat out of this argument. Dad would have wanted us to pull together.

'Look. We'll get someone in,' I said confidently, 'someone else, someone we can interview together, and—'

He cut me off. 'No. We can't just send Hazel away.'

'Why not?'

'She signed a contract of employment,' he said, folding his arms. 'Even if she did leave, she's entitled to three months' notice.'

I was chilled.

'Three months! You're not serious?' I said.

But his steady gaze told me that he was, utterly serious.

For the moment, Hazel was going nowhere.

Colin was holding Dad's frail hand as I slipped out of the hospital room. He was red-eyed with exhaustion. I could see that he was running the emotional gauntlet while doing battle with his conscience, and I could see it clearly, because the same turmoil was distressing me. More and more under the spell of guilt, I thought about the past.

What would Mum have said?

'Stay strong; please Lizzy. Do that for me.'

Her favourite words, as her end drew near. After she was gone, I hadn't been able to cry, but the sense of loss was unbearable. She died in October, when the leaves in the vast and gloomy Rendlesham Forest were falling. The year of my graduation. I was twenty-one; I needed my mother. I still do. I've never stopped missing her. And I've never stopped hearing her final words – that we must 'do our best', 'stay strong'. But strong was the last thing I was feeling.

Pessimistic. Sad. Worried.

These were closer to the truth, because though it pained me to admit this, what I felt at that moment was the ache of grief still to come. I hoped to God that Dad would pull through, but I didn't think he'd be walking out of this hospital any time soon, perhaps not at all. And then what?

Worse. What if his body recovers, but his mind doesn't? Have you thought about that? What if he's confined to his favourite chair in the corner, without even knowing where he is? Worse still. What if he can't bathe himself; what if he can't see me properly; what if he wakes in the night, screaming, and begins to—

Thinking about that wasn't an option. So I shut my eyes, told myself it was all going to be okay. It crossed my mind to go back and give Colin a great big hug. I didn't. Colin wasn't a hugging sort of person; he never had been – a bit like Dad, I guess. If I had known of the trouble awaiting us on the shore, I would certainly have gone back with that hug. I might even have opened up about my own troubles, attempted to unite us. But I didn't know. Life's cruel like that; keeps us guessing.

The hospital corridor, windowless and creepy, smelled strongly of disinfectant. As I walked to the lift, something Colin had said needled at me: *'Lizzy, you didn't call, there was no voicemail.'*

The more I thought about it, the more it worried me. I *had* called, I knew I had. Yesterday. After opening all those old bank statements that confirmed so bleakly the problem I'd denied for too long.

So why doesn't he remember, Lizzy?

It seemed a good idea to check, so I paused next to a poster that read CLEAN HANDS SAVE LIVES, pulled my phone out and scanned the list of recent calls. Plenty of numbers listed. None were Colin's.

My head was spinning. What had he said?

'You're reliable, you're good with money . . .'

But my judgement obviously wasn't as good as he thought.

I closed my eyes and the image that flashed up on the dark screen of my eyelids was of Mitch sitting at his desk, ordering me to get out, just get the hell out.

My eyes snapped open. Light-headed, I had to steady myself against the corridor wall. Feeding my addiction had already cost me so much – what else would it cost me? My family?

My sanity?

By the time I reached the lift, I needed caffeine. Maybe some fresh air, too. I pressed the call button and waited. With a ping, the elevator doors swished open.

'Lizzy?'

I spun around. My oldest friend was standing there, along the corridor, in a white doctor's coat, staring at me with a smile I remembered well, one of the few smiles that has ever made me feel safe.

'Nick!'

I rushed to him and threw my arms around him, realising even as I did that it had been more than two years since I had last seen him.

Obviously, he already knew Dad had been brought in, and obviously he cared. The warmth of his embrace told me that. At least I thought it did. As we separated, his eyes searched mine and a sudden desire to cry washed over me.

'Lizzy, I just came on shift, heard about Clifford . . . What's his condition?'

'Stable now.' My voice was trembling. 'They've just run an MRI, but—'

'Okay. I'll find out what I can.'

'Would you?'

He gave me a warm smile, which was the only answer I

needed, and our eyes locked long enough for me to speculate briefly how different my life would be if I hadn't moved to London.

If I hadn't turned him down.

Close personal relationships have never been my forte. Before her illness, Mum would warn me about men – how you could always rely on them to let themselves down, and let you down. When she died, it was Dad who encouraged me to spend more time with Nick. 'He's from a good family,' he said, speaking in the reasonable, encouraging tones parents use when they're trying to say in a not-too intrusive way that they know what's good for you. 'If you're lucky you might find that one day he's keen to take care of you. Your mother and I met when we were around your age.'

That might have been his guilt talking, I suppose. This conversation happened after Mum found the letters in the boathouse. And besides, I didn't need taking care of. I wanted to do that myself. Plenty of guys at college showed an interest in me, and I'm sure many of them felt dismissed or shut out. Why? I don't know for sure, but what I think is, after Mum's death, my way of coping with negative emotions was simply not to experience them; denying closeness with others to avoid being anxious or vulnerable. Being a successful overachiever was easier, probably, but it had its price all right. Emotionally unavailable. Distant. To some of the guys at college, these must have been my middle names.

But I never felt good about that. Nor about myself; not until I found something I *was* good at. Public relations? Selling journalists tomorrow's headlines? Now *that* excited me. Maybe it was the illusion that I could exert some control that way, keep things together.

One thing I know, and it's with sadness: Nick was the only man I've ever regretted letting go. I suppose he was a bit like my dad. Distant, silent, but always with a warmth about him. So, yes, maybe I pushed him away, because I was afraid of dating someone *too* much like Dad – and who could have blamed me for that?

What made it harder was knowing Nick was so reliable, so steady. Now, in that soulless hospital, I saw that steady and reliable were two qualities I really needed. I thought, *If I'd said yes, we might have made it work. We might even be together now. And he'd be able to help me think clearly. And he would never have abandoned me as Mitch has.*

After he had gone, I went in search of coffee. The hospital cafeteria was in darkness, the doors locked, so I had to make do with steaming black water that spluttered noisily out of a machine into a disposable polystyrene cup. After just one sip, I tossed it away.

I found somewhere quiet to sit for a moment; a hard plastic chair at the end of another corridor. Here was another poster: DO YOU WANT TO STAY WELL THIS WINTER?

As I sat there, vacantly staring, thinking about Dad, my attention was drawn, as if at a summons, to a fluorescent ceiling light at the far end of the corridor. The light was flickering harshly, blinking on and off.

As if it's flashing a warning, I thought, oddly.

And after a few seconds, to my confusion, that harsh light briefly threw into relief something shifting in the shadows. Twenty or thirty paces away was a figure.

Someone watching me?

With an inward shudder I told myself I was being silly, to

get a grip. But another part of me was adamant that I was *not* being silly, because the more I focused on the shadows, the more I was sure I could pick out a dark shape reminiscent of a human form. More than that, I could sense it; a definite presence intruding on my consciousness.

I was about to call out to whomever it was when a hand dropped on my shoulder.

'Lizzy?'

My body jolted. Then, feeling a little absurd, I looked up.

Nick was standing over me. He smiled.

'Sorry,' I said, 'my nerves are shot.'

'You ought to get some rest.'

I glanced back towards the end of the corridor and saw, in the next flash of the light, that it was empty. Only the blinking light remained, flickering and buzzing.

Nick sat next to me, cleared his throat.

'Now, I've spoken to your father's consultant, and it seems he suffered a minor stroke; what we call a transient ischemic attack.'

'But he will recover?' I asked, hearing these words more as a statement than a question, and it took a few seconds of what I sensed was professional diplomacy in action for Nick to compose his response.

'Look,' another pause, 'Clifford's in good shape for a man of eighty, but a stroke like this can have a formidable impact. It has predominately affected the right side of his brain, so he's going to find it hard to focus, and his short-term memory will almost certainly be compromised. Then there's his mobility – walking, lifting, bathing; he'll be even weaker, shakier. You want my honest opinion?'

'Of course.'

'The safest place for your father is probably a care home.'

I felt resistance rise up inside me. The very mention of the words 'care home' turned me cold, made me think of the television exposés, with hidden cameras catching nurses slapping or dragging defenceless elders who weren't only powerless to prevent their abuse but were also very likely to forget it had even occurred.

'That's just not happening.'

'You should think carefully about this,' he said, 'otherwise you're likely to be making life hard for yourself.' Was there the slightest hint of self-reproach in his tone, or was I just being overly sensitive? 'If he continues to decline, and I sincerely hope he doesn't, you may find that you have no option.'

He slipped his hand into mine and his voice returned to the compassionate tone of earlier. 'But in that eventuality, could your dad afford the care fees, could you?'

'Sure,' I said, not quite meeting his eye.

Nick smiled. 'God, I am so proud of you, Lizzy; I always knew you'd make a success of your life. That unshakable self-confidence, you've always had it.'

I forced a smile; looked away. 'Thanks. And I mean it; Dad's staying in his own home.'

Colin and I had promised him years ago he would never go into a care home, and it was a promise I intended to honour. If necessary, I would take care of him myself – with or without anyone's help.

I reasoned that the familiarity of his own home might hasten his recovery. 'We've got some help,' I explained. 'Colin employed a private carer.'

Nick looked at me, frowning a little. 'Why do I sense there's a "but" coming?'

I had to smile. He had always known how to read me.

'Because she and I haven't exactly hit it off,' I explained, remembering the fear of being bludgeoned to death. But then remembering how bad Hazel seemed to feel about the misunderstanding, her attempt to build bridges with me.

'It must be uncomfortable for you,' said Nick, 'having this stranger in your house. But if your father goes into a home, it'll eventually be strangers looking after him, anyway.'

I supposed there was some logic in that. 'Have you heard of her, Hazel Sanders?'

A look of vague familiarity crossed his face. 'Name rings a bell. Look, leave it with me and I'll see what I can find out; but in the meantime maybe give her a chance? It might help having someone to share the load.'

Suddenly I remembered Colin saying we would soon need to acquire a lasting power of attorney. He was probably right, though I still didn't feel anywhere near comfortable with the idea of managing someone else's finances. Not after my own spectacular mess. Maybe it was too soon, but I asked Nick if he knew anything about setting it all up.

He looked thoughtful.

'You can download the forms online from the Office of the Public Guardian and I can certify them, if you like. But in order to sign them, your father will need mental capacity. We won't know if that's possible until he regains consciousness.'

'I understand,' I said, and that was the truth. For me and Dad and Colin, there was a long, difficult road ahead.

'But I'll do all I can to help. Promise.'

'Thank you, Nick, you're a good friend.'

He stood, looking me over again, and said with affection, 'You know you can talk to me any time, right?'

With the tiniest smile, I nodded. Felt very small. He was looking directly at me, almost as if he was searching for his best friend from high school, the girl he had known before she was replaced by the sharp suits and flawless make-up. A part of me hoped he would embrace me in a hug again, but he didn't, and probably that was right. When there's history, when there's a past, sometimes even a hug is too awkward.

Then, as he moved away, something caught his eye over my right shoulder, at the end of the corridor.

'I'd better get someone to put that right,' he said casually, and I realised he was referring to the flickering light. But the look on his face wasn't casual.

'Hey, you okay?' I asked. 'Nick?'

For a moment, he was motionless, still staring off, strangely distant. I turned, but saw no one – just that harsh light, throwing ambiguous shadows. Buzzing irritatingly.

'Nick?'

'Uh, yeah. Sorry,' he shook his head, 'I'm fine.'

'Sure?'

I had to ask because, honestly, he didn't look fine. He was pale, staring with wide distended eyes, like someone wrenched out of a nightmare.

'Yeah, yeah,' he said briskly, 'and you'll be fine, too. Promise. I'll help you through this.'

I returned the bravest smile I could summon, but the moment he stepped into the nearest lift and the doors closed behind him, that smile flattened to a thin line.

Silence, all around me. Abruptly from behind, another buzz of the light. A glaring white flicker.

I stood there in that hospital corridor, completely alone, rubbing my arms as I thought again of what I had seen down there, at the furthest reach of the corridor. A dark figure in the shadows. A presence.

Observing us?

By the time the taxi dropped me back at Shingle Street, the dark stones were glowing under the bright half-moon. The tide was high, and as the waves folded onto the beach, they seemed to whisper secrets.

As I got walking – carrying the luggage I had rescued from my car – I saw for the second time the line of white shells trailing some hundred yards down towards the water. The dusky moonlight touched them with an ethereal beauty.

Again, I thought: *Who arranged those shells like that? Why?*

As I was thinking this, I turned my head and detected a greyish figure. A man, observing me, it seemed, from the entrance to Dumb Boy Cottage, where the shell line began. The cottage's exterior lamp cast him in a harsh orange light. He was well-built, bearded. Maybe a fisherman or, in another time, hundreds of years ago, he might have been one of the smugglers who worked these shores. He wore a thick, black wool jumper and a pair of dark green boots and was clutching a plastic bag.

As I trudged on by, he straightened his cap and raised one hand in a gesture of greeting. I was about to wave back, out of politeness, but with the slip of a shadow, he had gone; retreating into the house.

I remember many things about Bill Durrant, but that brief wave stands chiefly among them. He may have been a stranger to me back then, but there was something reassuring in that simple wave, something friendly.

And yes, something enigmatic.

*

The slam of the tower's iron door. A cold echo. And when it dispersed, just the chilliest silence.

Should have left the heating on.

Feeling crushed from exhaustion, I wanted nothing more than to go to bed, but I couldn't rest. I was uneasy at the prospect of seeing Hazel again. *Is she here? Did I wake her?*

With that echo, how could I not have?

Yet, as I stood there, motionless, in the gloomy entrance chamber, listening intently, I heard no footsteps from below. Just silence, which suggested maybe she had gone out, or not come back.

Cautiously, I descended the stairs that circled the interior of the tower wall.

'Hello, Hazel?'

Nothing. I took a few more steps down, then paused.

At the bottom of the staircase was a white chair, fastened to a rail. The mere sight of that stairlift made my stomach squeeze with sadness. And, as I stared at it, I felt something else: a lingering and unpleasant suspicion.

It was unplugged at the wall; the seat looked dusty, as if it hadn't been used.

Hazel said she was with him when he collapsed. Was that even true? Would a decent care-giver *really* leave a frail and stubborn man alone next to a steep flight of stairs? That thought spurred me on.

I passed Colin's room, then Dad's, until I came to the door of the room I suspected Hazel had selected for herself. My old room. And now I could smell something – the fragrant aroma of rosemary. Not an offensive smell, but certainly . . . curious.

I approached the bedroom door, reasoning that Hazel wasn't a member of our family, Hazel was an employee, and I was entitled to know more about her. But when I tried the handle, the door was locked.

I stepped back, confused. Since when did my bedroom door have a lock? I scanned the lower hallway. All the doors, I saw, were fitted with locks.

My eyes settled on Dad's room. And my mind quickly summoned a reason to try that door next.

It was looping in my head, Nick's question from earlier: *'Could your dad afford the care fees, could you?'* Even if work managed to write off the eighty grand I had embezzled, which wasn't likely, I was still without a job, and in the absence of any references I wasn't likely to find one soon. Sure, there would be freelance opportunities, if I searched hard enough, but none likely to cover these sorts of costs. And freelancing wasn't exactly a reliable way to make a living.

So, you should check Dad's financial situation. He had a cash savings account, remember? Cash.

Everything I needed – bank accounts, passwords, identification numbers – would be where they had always been, in the drawer next to his bed. Once I had those, it was simply a matter of logging in on my laptop and joining the Wi-Fi.

Go into Dad's room.

Wasn't it the prudent thing to do? The sensible thing?

If the door had been locked, perhaps I would have forgotten about the idea altogether, but it clicked open and a musky, heavy smell wafted out.

No. This felt strange. Wrong. And that wasn't completely surprising. Dad's room had always been off limits.

But you're doing this for him.

That's what I told myself as I crossed to the bedside cabinet. I gripped the drawer handle, pulled, and there was the leather-bound file, thickly padded with paperwork: bank letters, home insurance forms, pension statements. I grabbed it, took the stairs to the top floor, and unpacked my laptop on the kitchen counter.

My fingers hovered over the keyboard for the best part of a minute before finally, I landed on the bank's website and clicked 'log in'.

You're doing this for Dad. This is the responsible thing to do.

So why was my mouth dry, my palms itching? Yes, logically it made sense to check Dad's finances, to plan for the future; but was that the *only* reason I was contemplating accessing his bank account?

It was useless lying to myself. To my shame, the addiction was pulling at me:

Just one bet, Lizzy. One won't harm. One big win could solve a lot of problems.

I was in a cold sweat, knowing this was wrong, but also knowing that I might have a realistic chance now of repaying the money that I had stolen. Flirting with the cruellest temptation and a pathetic lack of self-control.

A series of numbers punched into the laptop, a few clicks, then Dad's bank accounts blinked up on the screen. And I held my breath. Not in anticipation and not in relief, but in cold, white shock.

Dad's current account showed a balance in the low hundreds. And his savings account wasn't just running low; it was empty.

Completely empty.

– 4 –

UNUSUAL SUSPECTS

Where's the money gone?

There had *been* money. I remembered a few years ago how Dad had called me for advice on the best savings accounts, how I'd asked him for specific figures and held my breath in surprise and a little shock that he was keeping so many savings in cash.

So . . . where's the money gone?

I sat there in the glow of the laptop's screen staring unbelievingly at the pitiful sum, the only sounds the suck of the waves far below; the tide lifting and grating the shingle. Then I thought I must have made a mistake; what other explanation was there? So I quickly searched for other accounts in Dad's name.

Nothing. Only two accounts – one empty, one showing a balance in the low hundreds.

I flipped the laptop shut, and for a moment I felt blessed relief. I couldn't be tempted by available funds if there weren't any, and that was good. But Dad's money, all of it, gone. Where? How?

With a sigh, I turned away from the laptop and sat there on the high stool, staring across the room. It was already clear to me that sooner or later I might have to see what government grants were available to help elderly people in need.

But there should have been no reason for financial difficulties, not after his successful career in architecture and certainly not after the money from the sale of his parents' house. So, either he had deposited the money elsewhere, or . . .

Or someone has taken it.

I worried about that as I went back downstairs, into Colin's old room, and lay down on the creaking bed. And as I stared at the cracked ceiling and listened to the sea kicking the shore I wondered, inevitably, about Hazel.

Was she dishonest? Was she – God forbid – the sort of caregiver who accompanied elderly men on their weekly shopping trips, but also to the bank?

To the cash machine?

The idea was as chilling as the wind off the sea. But it wouldn't be sensible to rush to unfounded conclusions. Telling myself this, I listened to the slide and the drag of the shingle and went down into the depths of sleep, hoping – praying – that I had judged Hazel too harshly.

I dreamed I was at sea, *in* the sea.

All around me was darkness. Freezing. I was flailing against the current, my legs kicking madly for the seabed, when a great wave broke over me.

In seconds, I was being sucked under, helpless with panic. When I surfaced, my lungs were screaming as I heaved a breath, and as I struggled for dear life, I felt it: an intense heat against my face. Fire.

All around me were bobbing bodies and the orange glow of flames.

The sea was *burning*.

*

With a gasp I was awake suddenly, my whole body clammy and cold. The neon digits on the bedside clock blinked 5 a.m. I sat up in bed and stared into the thick darkness. After the long wait at the hospital and the mystery of Dad's missing funds, what I needed was rest. But I couldn't settle. There was a chill in the room; my curtains were flapping in a gust of wind. If I hadn't forgotten to close the window, I might not have heard the noise outside. I was exhausted and probably a little irrational, so of course I questioned myself; but it really did sound to me as if someone was out there.

At this hour?

I listened hard. The sound of shoes grinding on the shingle was unmistakable. My heart was beating anxiously. Who would be roaming around on the beach so late?

With a flare of relief, I remembered the bearded man who had waved to me from Dumb Boy Cottage. That was the nearest house; so perhaps it was him? I clung to that idea until it calmed me, then I lay down. Eventually, the murmuring sea carried me towards sleep once more.

But any hope that I would sleep peacefully at last was dashed when I heard a new and more alarming sound. Breaking glass. A shattering that was caught on the wind. I knew that it had come from outside, and wouldn't have been so alarmed if it weren't for the footsteps, which I heard again now, scrambling and clashing away over the shingle.

I sprang out of bed and flew out of my room, heading for the stairs. It was then that I cannoned into a figure looming from the shadows.

'Yes, I heard it, too,' Hazel said, gripping my wrist, 'but you shouldn't go out there alone! We don't know—'

But I was already pulling away, taking the stairs, then bolting across the circular, vault-like hallway, grabbing a torch from the table, shoving my feet into shoes, before withdrawing the bolt and plunging out into the night in my pyjamas.

'Elizabeth, please, come back!'

The beam from my torch slashed the darkness, revealing nothing.

'Who's out here?' I cried.

In reply, only the seething wind. The murmur of the sea. All else was still.

'Answer me! What do you want?'

At that moment, the sensible thing to do would have been to go back inside and call the police; and I almost did do that. What stopped me was the strange odour: pungent, acrid. Wafting in my direction, that smell was a direct challenge for me to determine its source. I stepped forward, jaw set.

'Wait!' Hazel again, behind me, an overcoat thrown over her nightdress. She held up a hand, sniffed the air. 'You smell fire?'

I could. Very soon it was overpowering. A strong smell of burning. And now, in the beam of my torch, the drifting smoke could clearly be seen.

'Quickly,' I yelled, beckoning Hazel to follow me out, and to her credit, she did. Together, we hurried around to the back of the tower, stumbling on the shifting stones, until we were standing just yards from the weatherboard boathouse. And now a new sound arrested me.

Crackling.

To my horror I was confronted with a sight that I knew would break my father's heart: smoke streaming from the boathouse roof, pluming from one shattered window. And behind that window was a flickering orange glow, fierce flames licking at the curtains of the room within.

The dining room!

Where Dad kept the family albums, I knew. Old pictures of Mum.

'We have to put it out!' I yelled and, without thinking, I stepped forward to reach for a coiled hosepipe hanging on the nearest wall.

'Get back!' Hazel cried, just before she threw her arm around my waist and yanked. We fell together, tumbling backwards, just as the window nearest to us exploded.

Whoosh! Against my face, a flare of immense heat; shards of glass scattering; tongues of flame leaping from the windows.

After a few terrifying moments, Hazel drew herself up, her face bathed in the glow of the blaze.

'Fire brigade,' she uttered, 'we have to call the . . .' but she tailed off, and her voice lacked conviction. Which wasn't surprising because by then it was clear to both of us that the boathouse didn't stand a chance; the air was thick with enough sparks and embers to tell us that.

'Come on, Elizabeth. We have to get inside,' she said, and taking my hands in hers, she hauled me to my feet.

Coughing against the drifting smoke, I let her guide me back into the tower, and as Hazel slammed the door and got on the phone to the emergency services, I slumped down on the steps and wept uncontrollably.

By the time Colin arrived, the sun was coming up and scattering streams of silvery light across the shore. Silence between us as we stood on the beach and regarded what little remained. A yellow cordon surrounded nothing more than a shell. The dark ground smoked, the boathouse crackled. Blackened and seething.

Naively, I clung to the hope that we would yet recover the family albums, even though the fire crew had told me it was impossible. Only one room, an old guest bedroom, remained intact.

Forlornly, my brother dropped his head. 'If only I'd been here, I could have done something.'

'I doubt that, Colin.'

Quickly, I told him of the events preceding the fire: the footsteps I had heard on the shingle, the shatter of glass. The fire crew had found a brick wrapped in cloth inside. And something else: an empty petrol can.

'Arson?' he said. 'But who would do that?' His tone was sincere. Perplexed. But it was then that I noticed something off about him. His eyes were watery and unfocused, and his breath smelled strongly of booze. That was odd. Worrying. Because to my knowledge, my brother hadn't taken a drink since his late teens – for good reason.

He asked again: 'Who would do this? Why?'

Good questions. The police seemed to think it was a random crime, but Shingle Street was so remote I struggled to believe that. Whoever had started the fire had come prepared. I wished now I had given chase down the beach. Maybe I'd have glimpsed the culprit, or at least their vehicle.

'I've no idea, Colin.'

'This is gonna cost a fortune to put right,' he said wearily, 'the insurance had better be paid up.'

He was slurring, ever so slightly, but I pretended not to notice and instead said: 'I wouldn't bet on the insurance being in order.'

'What do you mean?'

I looked at him closely for a moment. 'Don't you realise how dire Dad's financial situation is?'

His blank expression told me he didn't.

I explained how I had checked Dad's bank accounts and found them empty.

'There's no money left, okay?'

Colin stared at me. On his face, a mixture of shock and guilt. 'Well, he must have put the money somewhere else,' he speculated. 'Investments?'

'I'd love to know what they are,' I said doubtfully. 'The only thing he's ever cared about is this property; you know that as well as me. He poured everything into the tower.' I hesitated. Then I asked: 'Does Hazel handle Dad's money?'

He flicked his gaze at me. 'Writes a few cheques, I think.'

'A few cheques? For God's sake, Colin!'

His eyes flared. 'You're not blaming me for this, sis.'

'I'm not blaming you, I'm asking about Hazel!'

'Keep your voice down,' he said, casting a furtive glance towards the tower. 'She might overhear.'

So what if she does overhear? She works for us! Or at least, she's supposed to work for us.

'You're being paranoid, Lizzy.'

I remembered Hazel's words: *'Your father is my responsibility.'*

'I am NOT being paranoid. Colin, listen to me. Significant sums of money are missing.'

'And you were quick to look, weren't you,' he said caustically.

I folded my arms across my chest. 'What's that supposed to mean? You told me to look into his finances, remember? At the hospital?'

He nodded reluctantly, as if he wished now he hadn't said that, and curiosity gleamed in his eyes, an uncomfortable scrutiny. It reminded me of the way Mum used to quiz Dad on where he had been each weeknight while she had been at home with us, cooking dinner.

'Colin, you're the one who suggested I acquire power of attorney.'

'Which requires Dad's expressed *consent*,' he said, his tone suspicious suddenly. 'Which obviously, you don't have yet because Dad isn't in a fit state to sign anything. So, what did you do? Dig out his bank statements? Open his mail?'

'Colin—'

My brother turned away from me, but not before I noticed again how haggard he looked. Puffy-eyed.

He suspects me, I thought, *I don't believe this*. And I felt a vulnerable disquiet settle over me. *Remember he's been drinking*, I told myself, *so he's probably just hungover, paranoid. He doesn't mean it*.

'We should talk about this another time,' he said, 'but I want to know exactly what you've checked.'

He isn't serious? I thought. *He really can't be. Can he?*

Just how worried was I after that conversation? The answer is very. Even setting aside Colin's hurtful questioning and his paranoia, which flowed, I suspected, from his drinking too much, I had reason to be worried. Because his suspicions of me weren't entirely baseless, were they? My decision to come home had been motivated by a need to run and hide from a financial secret I was still keeping. I was his sister, but I felt more and more like an imposter.

An hour or so after Colin had left, when I was confident Hazel was down below, I went up to the top of the tower and sat at the floor-to-ceiling window, cradling a coffee and silently crying. My career was in tatters, I felt completely adrift, and the gambling was only part of it. The life I'd built for myself was unravelling and, while coming home was supposed to be a comfort, after Hazel, after the missing money and Dad's stroke, after the fire, life had never felt so uncertain or so overwhelming.

Tendrils of black smoke traced my grief against a wintry blue sky.

A childhood of memories. Obliterated.

I looked down, watching the sea surge over the shingle. The natural beauty of the shore was striking, as it always had been, but increasingly I felt uneasy. That I shouldn't be here, and there would be consequences to staying, none of them good.

When I had dried my eyes, I took out my phone and called Nick, told him what had happened.

'Jesus, Lizzy. What can I do? Are you all right?'

'Still processing it,' I told him numbly.

'Well, I have some good news,' he said, and the reassurance in his voice made my breath catch. 'Your father's awake . . . Lizzy?'

'Still here,' I said. 'Oh, Nick, thank God! Is he making any sense?'

'More than I would have expected. We need to run some tests and it's early days, but yes, he's not too bad. It's his mobility that's most compromised. I'd expect us to begin endovascular therapy as soon as possible.'

'Okay . . .' I had no idea what endovascular therapy was.

'Improves blood flow in the brain. We'll assess his mental capacity in due course, and I'm going to ensure he gets the best possible treatment.'

I stared through the window at the trailing black smoke and felt my heart squeeze a little. Nick went on giving me medical details, but it was hard to take it all in; because the more I listened to his calm, steady voice, his reassurance, the more I was thinking about the past. The memories of my time with Nick floated around me now as I stood up, crossed to the opposite side of the room, and looked towards the vast forest that spread out for miles behind Shingle Street.

I had never expected to call my childhood friend my lover, but that was almost what happened the autumn we graduated, when Nick suggested we celebrate by popping some champagne in Rendlesham Forest. A mist that smelled heavily of salt was drifting in when we had ventured into the trees as the sun went down; and, led by the bobbing beams of our torches, we had found our way back out again not long before it came up.

It was our journey into the forest that I remembered most clearly now as I stood at the window and gazed down upon it; the soft, scuttling sounds of animals in the underbrush on all sides; the gnarled and twisting tunnel of trees that unwound before us, as if leading us into the deepest recesses of a grim fairy tale. We had heard the legends about this forest, everyone had; about the screams of invading Nazis shot down in the woods as they fled from British defenders. But that night, neither of us was afraid. Nor did we believe the old tales. There wasn't a scrap of evidence that the Nazis had landed on this shore.

After contending with a mile of jutting branches and underbrush that snagged at our ankles, eventually we emerged into a small clearing. We lit a fire and sat together, clinking plastic glasses brimming with champagne, toasting the future, the flames reddening our cheeks and our breath pluming in the cold night air.

That night, with the rest of our lives before us, there was a spark of magnificent possibility in the air. I hadn't seen it coming, but when he kissed me, I didn't flinch. I enjoyed it, even though my head was hazy, my vision swimming from the champagne.

Then he asked me a question.

That night I learned something that never quite left me: sometimes, even the people you know the best can surprise you. Sometimes, we sabotage what we love the most.

And sometimes, things get weird in the woods . . .

'Lizzy, you there?'

I blinked; came back to the present. 'Yes. Sorry.'

'I was talking about your father's capacity. Once we're satisfied that he's capable of making his own decisions, you should be able to progress with registering the power of attorney. That will grant you the legal power to make decisions on his behalf, if it should ever come to that.'

A wave of anxiety swept over me. That was a big responsibility. Massive. But all that mattered was helping Dad, protecting Dad.

'Nick,' I said, 'please, whatever you do, don't mention the fire to my father – at least not yet. I really think it would break his heart.'

'No, of course not.'

'Can I come and see him?'

'Give it a day or two. We've still some tests to run, and he needs rest.'

We promised to meet soon for lunch at his favourite pub in Woodbridge, and when the conversation was over, I clicked off my phone and stared at it for a long time.

The last thing Nick had said to me before the end of our conversation was: *You know, Lizzy, I think your father might surprise us all.*

'I hope so.' That was how I replied, and I meant it. Now, looking back, I wish I hadn't.

The relief of Nick's good news must have helped me fall asleep, which would have been good, if I hadn't dreamed once again that I was standing at twilight on the shore. Once again I felt the distinct atmosphere of otherworldliness, and saw my father crouching down beside me, his gaze locked on the forbidden zone across the water – on Orford Ness. And once again I had that sudden and inexplicable thought:

A darkness is rising.

Just a dream, I thought, when I woke.

But it was a warning, of course – I see that now.

The buzz of my phone brought me out of it. I sat up on the sofa, trying to focus on the flashing screen. It showed an unknown number.

Thinking, hoping, it might be Nick again calling from a hospital line, I answered it.

'Hey, Elizabeth.' The voice was male, cool and overly familiar. 'You there?'

'Nick?'

'It's Connor Metcalf.'

The penny dropped as I visualised a pair of pale blue eyes; an electric blue suit; immaculately manicured nails.

'So, Elizabeth . . .' A sharp edge in his voice.

I held my breath, hoping my voice would remain steady. I pictured him now in his shiny glass office behind a chrome desk, the new king of the castle. My employment had been terminated, but that didn't mean their investigation was over.

'I'm assuming you're not calling to ask how my job search is going?' I said, finally.

'Funny.' He didn't laugh. There was a pause. 'Mitch wants the money back.'

'Of course, I said I would—'

'*All* of it.'

'Mr Metcalf,' I lowered my voice, looking furtively around me to be sure Hazel wasn't anywhere near, 'I told you everything.'

Now he did laugh, but it didn't sound remotely good-humoured. What it sounded was malicious. 'Oh, come now, Elizabeth; it wasn't so long ago that you worked in perception management.'

He probably had me on speakerphone with Jane from HR. She would be sitting off to his side on a white leather sofa, attentively scribbling notes.

'You didn't tell Mitch *everything*, Lizzy. Did you?'

Somehow, I managed to keep my mouth closed, which was good. Because the shot of anxiety in my blood right then probably meant whatever I said would be wrong.

'My brother used to gamble, you know. Don't feel proud sharing that, but I know the pattern . . . Which is why, after your dismissal, I immediately took the liberty of digging a little deeper into your time with us. Checked every expense claim you ever made. And there were quite a few.'

My stomach plummeted.

'Hey, Lizzy, you still there?'

'Yeah,' I said eventually, 'I'm here.'

'Turns out, some years back, your expense claims were submitted when you were off sick. Funny that, hey?'

He must have gone back years.

I felt a great wave of shame, but I was *not* that person any more. I just wasn't. And the idea that I could once have done such a thing, and worse, forgotten about it, left me trembling with a mixture of shame and fear.

'Let me be clear,' he went on, 'Mitch was prepared to let you pay the eighty grand back, with interest, over two years. He was quite prepared to be reasonable. Lenient.'

'And now?' I asked hesitantly.

'Now? Let's just say those expense claims of yours were like a kick in the teeth. I guess something in him just snapped. Can't say I blame him, either, can you?'

A slideshow of images flashed through my mind. Mitch and me strolling through Hyde Park, hand in hand. Mitch taking me to dinner and ordering me two desserts, because I couldn't choose. Mitch beneath my sheets, his delicate touch, his lips locking with mine. Now every memory was tainted with the dark cloud of my betrayal and weakness. Now these memories were all I would ever have of him.

Tears rolled down my face. It was hard to choke out the words:

'You'll get the money back. Every penny.'

'Expecting to win the lottery?' Connor said.

'You'll get your money.'

'When?'

'Give me a year.'

'Three months. With a year's interest.'

I nearly dropped the phone. 'How do you expect me to do that?'

'Ways and means. Your father was a successful architect, wasn't he?'

'Leave him out of it.'

'There will be savings. So, if you can't pay up, maybe your father will,' he said intimidatingly.

He was serious, I knew that – like most financial directors, this was a man who wasn't afraid to be demanding.

'Otherwise, we will apply pressure to recover the funds. Legal proceedings? That will mean professional and financial ruin for you. And . . . if that doesn't work . . . well, there are other methods of persuasion.' He paused, and this time it wasn't just oppressive; it was ominous. 'You wouldn't want another fire . . .'

A chill swept through me.

'I trust that no one was hurt?'

In my head, suddenly, was something he had said the day I'd been sacked: *'It's not beyond us to have you placed under surveillance. The fraud investigators I use can be most tenacious . . .'*

'It was you!'

'I'm sorry, what?' Feigned innocence, not even halfway convincing.

'I should warn you that my debt collectors like to make home visits.'

'You bastard. Do you have any idea what the belongings stored in that boathouse meant to our family? I'll go to the police.'

'No you won't.'

'Why won't I?'

'Because no one can trust the word of a compulsive gambler.'

This comment plunged me into silence. And I had every sense he was enjoying listening to that silence.

'You're going to find the money, hear me? Because if you don't, there will be consequences. I've ended bigger thieves than you. Clear?'

It was crystal clear. 'Yes,' I said.

'Good.' I heard the smile in his voice. 'So, no more chasing your losses please; not until we have our money. Three months. Better hurry now.'

I was about to hang up, and would have done. But he did it first.

Bastard!

Mitch wanted that eighty grand, one way or another, and that was fair enough. But how far, beyond a reckless and sense-less arson attack, was his new finance director prepared to go? How dirty would he get his hands?

He won't use his hands, I thought. *They're too well manicured, remember? He'll send someone else. Like he did with the fire. And God only knows what else they'll be capable of.*

I ought to have called the police, right then, but it would be my word against his, and he had a point – who would believe the accusations of a thieving gambling addict?

Just three months . . .

If I didn't come up with the cash by then, what next? A personal visit, probably. Some ex-enforcer from the Russian ganglands. That felt about right to me; a brutal thug in a black balaclava with a crowbar. Metcalf's man already knew where I was staying. He could come at any time. Abusive phone calls? Arson? That was just the beginning. What about breaking my fingers? A battering? A stabbing?

Stop thinking like this, stop it now! He works for a PR firm, not a gang of organised criminals. But I wondered if I was entitled to draw that conclusion, considering how little I knew about the com-pany's finances. That was a pretty unsettling thought, actually, and one that only made me think harder on the past.

Remember, Lizzy, how surprised you were that the company was able to grow so quickly? Remember the bank loan Mitch was refused? So, where did he find the money?

And then there were the private clients. The businessmen whose identities were confidential, and the foreign regimes. Saudi Arabia. The oil-rich Kazakhstan government. Clients Mitch never spoke about. He had kept professional secrets from me, that much was clear, and so it was natural now to wonder how many of the 'communications' activities he sold were illegal or unethical.

I suddenly felt very cold. Heart racing, I paced to the window, looked out at the dark shoreline and felt a premonition of fear. With mounting unease, I pictured an intruder prowling out there, just as he had last night. I wanted to jump, and if the window could have been opened fully I might have done, but suddenly a voice from behind made me start.

'Who were you talking to?'

It was Hazel, standing at the top of the spiral staircase.

God, did she overhear any of that?

I sure as hell hoped not; the last thing I needed was her rushing to judgement. I could show her every control I had in place to help restrict my online gambling activities, and she'd still label me a gambler beyond hope, with a problem for life, never to be trusted. She'd want to know all about the mistake that had landed me here, how deeply I'd delved into Dad's finances, and once she learned about my profession – PR? – she'd surely question whatever answer I gave. Wasn't it my job to have an answer for everything? And wasn't it more than a little coincidental that I had returned to the family's valuable home just as my dad's health was failing?

'Just an old work colleague,' I explained, hoping the lie didn't show.

Hazel looked at me with a question in her eyes. After an

uncomfortable moment, she moved across the room to my dad's old chair beside the great fireplace.

'Mind if I sit a while, Elizabeth? Been cleaning all afternoon and I'm just about beat now.'

You should have cleaned already, is what I was thinking. Besides, in my heart I didn't want her to clean or to sit; I wanted her *out*, and it was on the tip of my tongue to say so, but I remembered my conversation with Colin:

'You've got your doubts about her,' he had said, *'and I get that, but she's not doing the job for the money, she's well off. She does the job because she cares.'*

A financially secure woman in middle age puts her life on hold just to care for a stranger? Yeah, right.

'I know what you're thinking,' Colin had said, *'but she's lonely, and she has a good heart, one of the best. So please, just sit down and have a good chat with her, okay? Promise me.'*

As if reading my mind, Hazel said: 'We could do with getting to know one another, don't you think, Elizabeth? Or should I call you Lizzy?'

'Doesn't matter,' I said, lowering myself into the other armchair that was usually reserved for guests. Then I realised how childish that had sounded and added, 'Lizzy. I prefer Lizzy.'

Hazel sat and smoothed down her thick wool skirt. Her eyes found me, and with self-conscious appraisal, I found myself wishing I'd worn better clothes, that I'd had my roots touched up as I'd promised myself on promotion. Never mind that the promotion had never happened. Never mind that I couldn't even now *afford* highlights!

'The boathouse,' she said with a sigh, 'it's deeply disturbing to me; such a shock. And you must be devastated – part of your home, your family history, in ashes. The question now is who would do such a thing?'

Christ, maybe she did overhear!

I rushed to change the subject. 'He's awake,' I told her, 'Dad's awake now.'

She brightened. 'Well, that *is* a relief. Was it a stroke?'

I nodded.

'Thought as much,' she said, nodding. 'We'll know more about the long-term effects when we get a good look at those scans. Told you – the MRI is vital. My own father waited two weeks for one of those. *Two whole weeks*, can you imagine? Outrageous, really. And by then it was too late.' A pause. She eyed my laptop. 'Oh, I'm sorry. Am I interrupting your work?'

'Not really. Just catching up on a few things.'

Naturally it was on my lips to ask her about Dad's bank accounts, whether she had access to his funds, but something was telling me that wouldn't be wise, at least not yet, anyway. The way things were between us, brittle, doubting, a question like that would only sound accusatory. No. I would talk with Colin again, and speak to Dad. There may be an explanation for the missing savings.

'Now listen, Lizzy, I deeply regret our misunderstanding. We got off to such an unfortunate start, and that's all my fault – I totally overreacted. It's this place' – her eyes roamed to the window and the spit of shingle below – 'so desolate, sometimes it sets your nerves on edge. Makes you feel out of yourself, some-how. Damned lonely. And that works on your mental health after a while. But that's no excuse. We ought to get along. We both have your dad's best interests at heart.'

I studied her, thinking that she sounded utterly sincere. Should I believe her? Would that be reckless of me?

'It's entirely understandable that you'd have your doubts about me,' Hazel said smoothly, as if she could hear my thoughts. 'I felt the same way when I had help for my parents.'

I said nothing. This was the first time she had mentioned anyone in her life.

From the pocket of her cardigan she drew out a plain white envelope.

'My references,' she said. 'They're not perfect, I'll grant you that, but whose are, right?'

I flinched inwardly, but she didn't seem to mean anything by it; she just held out the references.

'Hopefully you'll find everything in order,' she said. 'Reassuring.'

I nodded, taking the envelope but not opening it, not yet. In my head a question had surfaced and I wanted it answered. 'Why do you do it, the job, I mean? Have you always been a carer?'

'I should explain,' she said, and her tone grew pensive. 'I'm fifty-five now. Getting on. This job is not as easy as it used to be, but I know what you're going through, how hard this must be, because . . . I've been there myself. Some years ago, my own father collapsed struggling to get out of bed, in a care facility over two hundred miles away from his home. Heart failure. I'd cared for him myself, at home, until the strain became too much. And it does, you know. Colin will attest to that. What made it worse for me were the injuries he suffered . . .'

'Injuries?' I asked, shaking my head, frowning.

She tailed off and squeezed her eyes shut. Her face, I noticed, had turned as white as salt. The room around us was suddenly very quiet, so quiet I could hear my own breathing.

'Hazel?'

Eventually, she opened her eyes again; they were glistening with painful reminiscence. 'I blame myself.'

'You mustn't.'

She nodded absently, as if agreeing to something she hadn't even heard. 'But don't you see? I put him there, and that was *my* fault.' Her hand went to cover her chest, just above her heart. 'Bless his soul, my father died under the care of strangers – because of *my* decision to put him in a home. And his ordeal was horrific, Lizzy. Utterly horrific.'

I started to feel deeply uncomfortable, and something else. I felt sorry for her.

Hazel was staring mournfully at the window that formed the wall of this room. After a few seconds she said: 'They couldn't find the DNR order, so the emergency services were called. More strangers. They did what they were supposed to do – compressed his chest over and over, until finally' – her voice broke into a sob – 'until finally . . . his ribs . . . *snapped*.'

My hand jumped to my mouth.

'You may know, Lizzy, that it's not uncommon for ribs to be unintentionally broken during CPR; a horrible but sometimes necessary evil. And they managed to bring him back, to resuscitate him, but then . . . I like to believe that the Alzheimer's had robbed him of most of his awareness, but the pain' – she shook her head – 'the pain must have been unimaginable.'

At that, she screwed her eyes shut. I was staring in horror. No words seemed adequate. To say I felt guilty now would be an understatement.

'Hazel, you mustn't torture yours—'

'I picture him, sometimes,' she said, shaking her head, 'his eyes screwed up, his hands clenched into fists, crying out in agony—'

'*Stop*,' I said, 'please stop.'

I was beginning to feel nauseous. As much as we had got off to a bad start, I had no wish to see her – or anyone – relive this suffering.

'He died shortly afterwards, and for every second of every day since, I've carried the guilt, the terrible loneliness.' Her voice wavered. 'Let me explain, Lizzy – you give to a charity, volunteer in an old people's home, start doing home visits, you think it will help ease the pain, your conscience, you never think that will become your life, your vocation.'

'You carry his memory with you still?' I said, and Hazel nodded sadly. Then she leaned nearer, fixing my gaze, and I saw the liquid sheen in her eyes.

'There's a huge void when the person you're caring for passes away. It's different for some families. Yeah, sure, they show up at the funeral and say all the right things, they fork out for the nicest casket if it appeases their conscience. But those families don't feel the void *we* feel. How can they? Because for them it's family *business*, and always was. For them, the suffering of a parent was something they could *afford* to lock away, just so they could go on attending their cocktail parties, or their tennis matches, or turning up at their jobs, or doing whatever it is that brings comfort and security to their neat little lives.'

She rolled her eyes. 'Sometimes, families turn a blind eye, Lizzy. Trust me on that. And us – care-givers? We're left behind, forgotten. No one prepares you for that. For us, it's a double loss. You lose them *and* you lose your identity, because you're the only force keeping them alive; the first person they see when they wake; the last person they might ever see when they go to sleep. After the funeral, though, what's left is a big black hole of isolation. And I dropped into that hole – boy did I ever.'

She lapsed into contemplative silence. All of it was desperately sad; but I felt a bristling annoyance sweep through me all the same. Did she think it was 'family business' for me? Did she think that I had 'turned a blind eye'? I had stayed away too long, and I was sorry for that, but in the end I had committed to being here for Dad. Short of him dying in hospital, there was no way I would see him live anywhere else, other than here, in the home he had built.

I took a sidelong glance at Hazel and saw that her body was quite still now. It had grown dark outside and the room was in gloom, so I reached across to the nearest lamp and snapped it on. As the light bloomed, illuminating her face, I thought perhaps I was being too sensitive. The self-reproach in her eyes, and the regret, was obvious, and I felt sympathy: she had suffered with this burden for a long time and clearly it had influenced her choices.

'Try to imagine,' she explained, 'knowing that if the worst should happen, if the person you're caring for should pass away on your watch, the last thing they see is *you*. Your face. Just knowing *that* is a colossal responsibility, and as a carer, it makes you do the right thing. Every time. It keeps you honest, Lizzy.'

Conscious of her gaze on me, I averted mine. Since my terrible mistake, the word 'honest' had an unfailing and unwelcome ability to touch a nerve.

'It hurts me to see other people suffer, but too many people turn a blind eye. Isn't that what our government, our entire society does? You can't deny it; we look away. Even when the doctors write reports of neglect, of elderly people distressed, with dementia sometimes, and totally dependent, lying in their own faeces, their legs swollen, their skin chafed and covered in sores, their limbs covered with infections, lying in their wet beds, crying themselves to sleep and calling for their own mothers. *We look away*, perhaps not because we want to, but because maybe looking away is *easier* – especially when there are inheritances involved. Vested interests. Secrets?' She nodded. 'Always plenty of those when it's family business.'

The tone wasn't accusatory, not quite, but it was bitter. Her talk of family secrets had got me thinking about Dad, again, about his missing money. And of course about Colin, who was drinking, and who had spent so much time alone with Dad, out here, in the middle of nowhere.

Before he met his new girlfriend. What was her name?

Sandra. Lives on the Melford estate, near Woodbridge.

'Like I said, all too often you find that the families are complicit, Lizzy. Of course,' Hazel added hastily, 'I don't mean you and Colin. Of course not. But many are, even if they can't admit it to themselves. And that makes me *furious*. Makes me want to step in and do the right thing. Other times, like when your brother asked me for help, I step in because I see they can't cope. But know this: I sure as hell don't do this job for the money.' She held my gaze. 'I don't do it because it's expected of me. I do it because I hate to see anyone suffer. Simple as that. I do it because it's kind! Because from bitter experience I know it's not just care that our elders deserve from us, but dignity. Compassion. Because I remember once, visiting my own father, only to walk in and find him on the bed, on his bedpan, and he was falling off it and calling out for help, in agony. The nurses had left him like that for the best part of an hour! Bullies, that's what they were. I hate a bully. The worst sort of person. Was it any wonder my poor father was terrified? He pleaded with me not to let him die in that home. And in the end, I let him down. I don't intend to make that mistake again. I'll do my job, always with kindness, always with compassion.'

Her eyes, so accusing when she had first confronted me, now looked earnestly considerate. Seldom did I see warmth in those eyes, but I thought I saw it then, which was good. Despite my earlier cynicism, I now had little doubt that Hazel lived for her job. And that made me angry, too; I was mad at myself for rushing to judge her.

With a shrug she said: 'So, I help people in need. People like you and Colin. People like dear old Clifford. It brings me meaning. Purpose. Maybe a chance to set things right.'

'I understand. I intend to stay as long as possible and do what I can to help.'

She flinched a little, her gaze narrowing slightly, then smiled warmly. 'Well. That's good to hear. So, what do you say? I'd dearly like to stay, and I believe that would be good for you, too. Maintaining this place? It's a mammoth undertaking, and you're no superhero.'

'It does take a lot of upkeep.'

Hazel nodded. 'Better to share the load; that's not failure. Sometimes asking for help is what's right, Lizzy. There are two things you need to know about care-giving. It's relentless. And it takes its toll. God, does it take its toll! But honestly? I can't imagine doing anything else. Like I said, caring for people is in my blood.' She paused. 'Let me talk to you about Dad – sorry, *your* dad, and his needs, yes?'

I nodded. She was looking at me now with unnerving curiosity. At last she said, in a cautious voice: 'Lizzy . . . I must ask, is there something about this tower, or maybe this stretch of shore, which unsettles your dad?'

'How do you mean, exactly?'

Her face darkened. She cast a glance at the floor-to-ceiling window as an especially strong gust of wind smacked it with rain.

'I suppose what I'm asking is – did he ever *fear* the shore?'

'Fear it?'

'Was there anything here that caused him distress?'

Odd question.

The truth was, I could never understand what had caused Dad to barricade himself in this fortress. Nor could Mum; and over the years I'd wondered about that. Whether the tower, or this shore, had anything to do with their blazing arguments.

'Lizzy?'

Her eyes remained intently questioning.

Perhaps there had been something. A long time ago. In the dark days before Mum left us. But I didn't want to think about that now; I couldn't.

'I very much doubt Dad would ever have bought the tower, renovated it or stayed for so long if he felt that way. Why do you ask?'

Behind her thick glasses, Hazel's eyes were a flurry of blinks. 'You mean to say that Colin never mentioned Clifford's restlessness? His . . . episodes?'

'He told me he suspected a suicide attempt, with a belt. And that didn't sound wholly convincing to me. My brother is rather paranoid, he tends to exaggerate things and—'

'No,' she said, 'Colin is *not* paranoid, and he *was*

exaggerating.' Her gaze locked with mine. 'I'm sorry, Lizzy, really I am, but there have been . . . incidents. Too many. Beyond the suicide attempts, there's much you need to know. And I'm afraid it's not good.' She leaned forward where she sat. 'Are you ready to hear this?'

A heavy dread flooded my stomach.

− 5 −

NIGHT TERRORS

'How many times has this happened exactly?'

This was some twenty minutes later, and Hazel was still sitting across from me on the other side of the coffee table. Outside, wind-driven rain lashed incessantly at the window.

'Five, maybe six times in as many weeks.' Her eyes pinned me again as she raised the coffee mug to her lips. 'I think that's worrying, don't you?'

For a moment I didn't know what to say.

'He hears the strangest sounds from outside. Or thinks he does. Sounds that originate as if from nowhere.'

'What sort of sounds?'

'Sometimes it's whistling, whining noises from the sky. Other times, it's voices. The cries of men suffering extreme agony. Other times, it's the "*malicious whisperings*" − well, you can pull that face, Lizzy, but that's exactly what he calls them!'

'Hallucinating?' I asked, worried now. And I think Hazel saw that worry.

'Hearing voices is a surprisingly common phenomenon; for some people it happens perfectly normally as they fall asleep. But this is so much worse. Sometimes, in the middle of the night, Clifford wakes bawling, inconsolable, drags himself out of bed, drenched with sweat, heart thundering. Then he's up here at the window, staring, pointing.'

'At what?' I asked.

Slowly, Hazel lifted her bulk from the chair and went to the window. 'He seems to believe there's someone down there, watching the tower. He's described it to me many times – a figure that observes from the shadows, or lumbers along the beach. Approaching.'

As Hazel told me this, the surf was pounding the shingle beach below. It wasn't long before my legs carried me to the window. She moved over, and I stared through the glass, stared hard. I saw . . . nothing. Only Hazel's ghostly reflection, gazing back at me. And the more I studied her reflection, the more I wondered.

'Was it you?' I asked.

'I'm sorry?'

I turned to her. She looked confused.

'At the hospital? At the end of the corridor.'

Her face was blank. 'I'm not sure I follow.'

'I *saw* someone. Or thought I did.'

'Who?'

Even though I could still picture the figure beneath the flickering light, I shook my head in a gesture that said *never mind*. Going into detail would only make me sound paranoid. Weird. So I swiftly brought the conversation back to Dad.

'Look, if he thought he saw someone approaching the tower, that's possible. Maybe it was the same person who was responsible for the fire? Or sometimes there are dog walkers who come from miles away and—'

'In such foul weather? On nights as filthy as tonight? Without a torch?' Hazel looked at me cynically. 'Besides, the beach is mostly deserted. But I agree with you about the fire; the police said it was random, but I suspect otherwise. We both heard someone pacing around out there. They knew how and where to strike; the only questions are why, and who.'

She stared at me, but I couldn't meet her gaze for long. 'There's someone living at Dumb Boy Cottage,' I said hastily, 'is it possible he was involved?'

'I don't believe so.'

'Why not?'

'He paces the beach every weekend laying those shells, no idea why. An artist, I'd say. Never comes down this far. Spoke to him once; seemed harmless to me. Just a regular holiday guest.'

From outside suddenly came a crack of thunder. I stood there motionless, and listened to the rain pelting the window, and a realisation hit me: if Dad was afraid of a trespassing stranger, and if Hazel knew about that fear, then wasn't it perfectly understandable that she should have been so suspicious of me, the night I arrived?

Hazel had reacted precisely *because* she was doing her job.

That thought made me feel very small, and something else I didn't much like. Responsible.

I returned to where I had been sitting, not so much sinking into the armchair, but perching.

'This figure, Dad's "intruder" – did you call the police?'

'What, and drag them eight miles from Woodbridge for something I wasn't even sure existed?' She shook her head. 'That hardly seemed justified. No crime was committed.'

She came to sit in the chair beside me. Then, as if summoning some inner resolve, she turned to face me with a look that said, *I'm sorry you have to hear this.*

'I'm deeply concerned that Clifford is trapped in his own personal war zone. You should know that he can become terribly angry. Aggressive. Sometimes violent.'

I looked at her, aghast. 'That does not sound like my father.'

'I've seen this before: the distress, the agitation, the hallucinations. Delusions. I'm afraid, Lizzy, that all of these are symptoms consistent with the early stages of dementia.'

I heard that word and didn't. In the darkest recesses of my imagination I saw myself, for a wretched moment, gently kissing Dad's cheek, combing his hair as he sat, frail as a broken bird, glassy-eyed, just staring; but somehow none of this was real to me, failed to impact. Like cancer or Parkinson's, dementia happened to other people, didn't it?

'Did you hear what I said, Lizzy?'

I did, but it was hard for me to meet her gaze. It's true to say that I have always had a fear of ending up that way myself. A disease that can so indiscriminately take control, and at any time? Who doesn't fear something like that?

'I'm sorry, really I am, but if it *is* dementia, that isn't a battle your father will win. The stroke may only hasten his decline. And that won't be easy for you. Dementia is the most insidious illness of them all. The cruellest. It could come to you or to me, and we would never know; not until our world begins to slip away and someone told us.'

After a moment I said, 'You sound convinced he has this?'

'Oh, my dear.' Gently, she took my hand in hers. 'I'm merely trying to prepare you for the worst. They fade away, and when their world unravels, we become part of their chaos. Sometimes, in the fog of their confusion, they show you something of what they used to be. To glimpse them as they were, restored, that's a rare gift and one to cherish. But inevitably there will come a day when he asks who you are, or even *where* you are, while staring directly into your eyes.'

I had never heard something so distressing. I didn't *want* to hear it.

'He may act as if he is possessed by the soul of another. And if that day comes, if your dad should become confused or frightened or violent, then trust me; you'll need all the support you can get.'

As Hazel released my hand, I closed my eyes. Wrong. She just had to be wrong. Aren't we supposed to take care of our parents? But dementia would render me utterly incapable of doing anything to help my father. So Hazel had to be wrong.

But what if she isn't?

And of course, there was something else to consider: dementia or no dementia, it was clear that Dad was tormented by *something.*

'*A figure . . . lumbers along the beach. Approaching.*'

'His paranoia,' I asked, 'how bad does it get?'

'The screams,' she said in a low voice. 'I pray you never have to hear his most godawful screams.'

I suddenly felt both sick and scared. 'Tell me.'

She shook her head as if in rebellion at the memory. 'Your father suffers with night terrors.'

'You mean nightmares?'

'Night terrors are *not* dreams. Yes, they occur when people are sleeping, but when they are in the grip of that terror, crying out for help and flailing . . . poor souls, they give every appearance of being wide awake.'

She was looking directly at me now, her eyes unwavering. 'The body becomes paralysed, completely, from the feet up. Your father says it's like an invisible snake, coiling around his legs.'

I fell silent. Outside, the wind was getting up to a howl and the rain was pelting against the window. A rough night. I remembered again the strange figure at the hospital. It wasn't pleasant, but I was dimly wondering if seeing things like that perhaps ran in the family.

'The first time, I found him in his bedroom, thrashing around in a wild panic, on the floor, like he was suffering some mental horror movie.' Hazel's voice was quiet, her face paling at the memory. 'That awful look on his face, I'll never forget it; such profound terror. He was convinced, *adamant*, that someone was coming for him. I almost believed him.'

'Why didn't you?'

'Because he couldn't elaborate in any detail.'

'Maybe he forgot?'

'That's possible.' She rubbed her arms. 'Of course I remained at his side, holding him, until the episode passed, but during that time, his perception of his entire environment was warped. Distorted. He couldn't see me; at least I don't *think* he could, but the awful way he was staring past me, tears streaming down his face . . . Honestly, Lizzy, it was as if someone, or something else, was in the room with us.'

As I sat there, stunned, listening to the storm rolling ashore, I was trying to understand what could possibly invoke such an ordeal. Then something else occurred to me. Something I'd meant to raise earlier and which now made a little more sense. 'Downstairs,' I said, 'the bedroom doors? The locks – that was you?'

She straightened and nodded. 'Don't think having those fitted brought me any pleasure, but I had to keep him safe from the hazards of the tower. The stairs, the terrace. That ghastly drop . . . Couldn't risk him injuring himself, or getting out.'

I thought – but didn't say – *you could have put a gate at the bottom of the stairs.*

Instead I said: 'Any idea what causes the night terrors?'

Her eyes did a circuit of the room, taking in the old family photographs. 'Something on his mind?' she suggested softly. 'A trauma?'

Could I remember much about Mum's illness? I could, if I wanted to; but that wasn't often, because that wasn't a memory that felt good. But right then, as I sat looking across at Hazel and feeling more insecure than I could remember feeling in a long time, I did remember. I thought of the dark days, when Mum got sick.

Her last words to me: 'Don't cry, we've all got to leave the party some time.'

I thought of the funeral and the long nights listening to Dad across the hallway, quietly weeping. I remembered longing for some certainty to return. Wishing I could escape.

'Lizzy?'

I shook my head. Traumatic it certainly had been, but this wasn't the time to go into Mum's death. The agony I felt when she left us remained deep within me, a mental pressure cooker waiting to explode. On reflection, that's probably what led to my problems, that insatiable need for control that manifested itself in my efforts to overachieve and yes, convince myself I could win at any game – whatever the odds.

Back then, during the dark time, somehow we had got through it all. Moved on. But there was a reason why Dad had moved the family albums from those years into the boathouse. A very good reason.

'Whatever the root cause,' Hazel said, 'if the night terrors recur, we'll be here for him, won't we? Together.'

I nodded, not completely convinced Hazel and I were a 'we' (remember I still had her references to check), but glad we had talked, reassured by her honesty.

'And I'll try not to be in your way.' She smiled. 'It's my job to blend in, to be invisible.' Then she looked at me speculatively. 'I'm curious, though; have you ever suffered from night terrors, Lizzy?'

I didn't believe so. My own night terrors were of a very different kind – out of control on the usual websites, chasing big wins – but nothing like this.

'Why do you ask?'

'Only because the condition often runs in the family.'

'You mean—'

'That's right.' She stood up and put a hand briefly on my shoulder. 'Night terrors tend to be hereditary . . .'

With Metcalf's threatening demands ringing in my ears, I took care to lock my bedroom door that night. Not that it did much good, because soon the nightmare visions of the debt collector were in the room with me. For too long, I lay awake in bed listening to the sea churning in rhythm with my stomach as paranoid speculations slid into my mind. How many more fires would we suffer before the final confrontation?

With trembling fingers, I pawed for the bedside lamp, snapped it on, and in the blooming light, caught sight of my laptop. The first thing I did was get back online to check Dad's accounts, just to be sure I hadn't dreamed it.

I hadn't. His bank accounts were vastly depleted, and there was no arguing with the final-demand bank letters I had photographed and saved to my phone.

With a sigh of confusion, I flipped my laptop shut, and gazed towards the window.

'*Your father seems to believe there's someone down there. A figure that observes from the shadows, or lumbers along the beach. Approaching.*'

I didn't know much about night terrors. But I was horribly conscious of the stress of financial liability. Debt.

Was it money – or lack of it – distressing Dad? Was that why he woke at night, screaming? Why he thought someone was after him?

The more I thought about it, the more persuasive the idea was: Hazel said night terrors ran in the family. So, what about addictive behaviours? Did *those* run in the family?

What if Dad and I weren't so different, after all?

I got back into bed, wondering about that. Listening to the waves crashing over the shingle and feeling horribly cold under those sheets. They were musty and smelled of damp; the way they had when Mum was no longer around and when Dad was absent, mentally, I mean.

'*Was there anything here that caused him distress?*'

I recalled how, late one afternoon, I had come home from school to find him standing entirely motionless at the window on the top floor, gazing blankly over the black and rolling sea, as if drowning in his melancholy. Staring off, towards the abandoned military facility on Orford Ness.

Back then, so soon after the funeral, the explanation seemed clear. *Of course* he was sad. That was normal, to be expected. He was grieving for Mum.

At least, that was my assumption.

*

The dream came again that night, as I suspected it would. The shore at twilight. My father, standing silent beside me, gazing sadly off towards Orford Ness and its desolate watchtowers. And once again, beneath the surface of that dream, was an unsettling thought:

A darkness is rising.

Precisely what this meant or why I should dream of the Ness and its history, I could not say; but I had a growing idea that the abandoned test facility over there, and its secrets, had always been a source of intense fascination to my father.

I cannot say why, but at some time during the early hours, I awoke feeling agitated, shivering, and as my eyes scoured the darkness, my senses suddenly on alert, I had the distinct feeling that someone was in the room with me.

With a jolt I sat up and flicked on the bedside lamp, half expecting to see a figure standing there, looming over me.

Of course, there was no one in my room; how could there be? I'd locked the door. Still, I wasn't yet ready to lie back down; the adrenaline was pumping.

I got out of bed, padded to the window, and looked out with tired eyes into the darkness. The wind was gusting harder now and the sound of it, along with the roar of the ocean, made me shiver. All at once, I was keen to get back into bed.

Then I saw something strange, a bright, angry red glow quivering on the water, far out to sea. Flames licking the watery darkness. But that made no sense, not unless . . .

An accident, I thought, *a boat's got into trouble.*

I would have to go and see; there would be a number for the coastguard upstairs.

Quickly, I headed out of my room and up the looping stairwell, but then I paused.

Take another look before calling and reporting anything. That was the sensible thing to do.

Taking my coat from the nearest hook, I shrugged it on, flung the door open, and stepped out into the bitter cold.

I want to say it was an unnatural darkness out there, and I believe that it *was* unnatural, because whatever the source of the fiery illumination I had just observed, I could see absolutely no sign of it now.

When the morning dawned, windy, wet and steel grey, I headed out. I didn't want to waste another moment. Dad was awake, so it was vital I saw him.

The sounds of the hospital. Machines beeping. They had moved him to an open ward. To my surprise, he was sitting upright in the high-backed chair next to his bed. Clean. Dressed in elasticated tracksuit bottoms and a chequered green shirt.

It was good to see him out of bed, but it took a second longer than I would have liked for him to recognise me. When he did, a smile broke on his lined face.

'Oh Lizzy, you came.' The slur was noticeable, as if he'd had too much to drink, and his mouth was slightly crooked on one side.

I pressed a gentle kiss to his forehead. Then pulled up a chair next to him.

'How's your memory?' I asked softly, as if talking to a child. I reached across and poured him a glass of water from the pitcher next to the bed. 'You remember what day it is?'

He nodded cautiously. 'Monday?'

'The name of the Prime Minister?'

He got that right, too.

'Good.' I handed him the glass. 'And what's *your* name?'

He jerked his head up, and stared directly at me.

'Patrick!'

The name burst out of him as if from nowhere, which was alarming.

'Patrick,' he said again, and for a moment his eyes drifted and all the colour seemed to drain from his face.

'No, no, not quite,' I said, and tried to keep the distress out of my voice. 'Patrick is one of your nurses, remember? Try again.'

He hesitated, shaking his head, frustrated with himself. 'Stupid, stupid, old man, what's wrong with me? Can't remember my own name? And so unsteady on my feet, Lizzy. I could barely walk to the loo earlier without help. I don't want to live like that.'

Maybe I just hadn't prepared myself mentally, but at that moment, a wave of emotion broke over me and tears sprang to my eyes. It happened so quickly that I had to make an excuse and leave the ward and, for the next five minutes, leaning on a hand-gel dispenser, I couldn't breathe for tears.

The bleeding on the brain had robbed him of something, that was undeniable. Upsetting. But I wasn't crying just for Dad. I was crying for all the times I'd never had with him. Crying for Mum. Being back in this hospital with all its familiar, unpleasant smells brought memories of her illness, the dark times, flooding back. Horrendous memories of the cancer that had spread from her bowel to her spine and finally to her brain.

Mum left us when we needed her most, when we were struggling, in so many ways, financially and emotionally, in a new home none of us had wanted. None of us except Dad, anyway. The sense of loss was overwhelming, but I didn't cry back then, even after the funeral. I wanted to, of course I did, but my body didn't seem to know how.

After a few minutes I pulled myself together. When I returned to the ward, Dad seemed more alert and was smiling. 'Clifford,' he said, more confident now. 'My name is Clifford . . . *Cliff*. Like the singer, right?'

'Exactly,' I said, with a sigh of relief. 'Like the singer.'

And I hugged him, closer and longer than ever before.

About half an hour later, I pulled up outside the council house on the Melford estate, where Colin had told me he was now living. The road was badly maintained, the pavements uneven and cracked. Three teenagers with shaved heads and tracksuit bottoms ambled by. One of them was carrying a mud-encrusted football. He looked back at me with a grin, whistled, as the others laughed. They walked on past low walls sprayed with graffiti, and litter bins overflowing. I drummed my fingers on the steering wheel, wondering why on earth my brother would choose to live here.

Sandra must be very special.

There was no doorbell, so I knocked; a young woman in a baggy grey tracksuit answered the door, took one look at me and curled her lip.

'You here to sell me something I don't want?' she asked.

Her hair was platinum blonde. A tattoo on the back of her hand; her fingernails colourful plastic talons.

'Actually, I'm looking for my brother. Is he here?'

Her mouth tightened and she nodded primly. That expression said, *Great, now I'm going to have to invite you in, aren't I? And I'd really rather not.*

I was smiling, hoping the gesture covered my surprise; I was a little taken aback that Colin had gone for a woman less than half his age.

'You'd better come in,' she said, begrudgingly, and I followed her through a narrow hallway into a kitchen that looked right out of the nineteen seventies. Brown and orange wallpaper. A few cupboard doors were hanging off their hinges, and there was a sour whiff of cat's piss.

'This is about your father, I suppose?' Her tone was curious but distinctly lacking in any genuine concern.

I was about to explain that, thank God, Dad was awake and talking, when I looked past her into the dining room and saw two half-packed suitcases lying on the floor.

'Going somewhere?' I asked, and at that, Colin appeared in the doorway, unshaven; face flushed; eyes watery and unfocused.

'So, uh, you've met Sandra?' He was slurring again. Not as much as before, but it was noticeable. 'Did you find out what happened to the missing money, Lizzy?'

'I haven't come here to discuss finances,' I said. 'Dad's awake; I thought you might want to go see him, but . . .'

I trailed off, eyeing the half-packed suitcases, and allowed the silence to spin out.

'Look, there's this job come up, in Scotland,' he said finally. 'Loch Ness. Some massive renovation project with this old manor they've rebuilt. You remember my old mate, Tony McAllister? Well, he put me forward to help with the decorations, and the charitable trust involved want me to help, Lizzy. It'll be a few months, easily – maybe longer – but they need me on site, understand?'

I didn't, not with our father so unwell. Not with everything else that had happened. I needed my brother's support.

'I can't afford to turn this down,' he added. 'And it's not like you're alone, Lizzy – now you have Hazel—'

A realisation hit. 'Wait. Is this why you asked me to come home? Because you knew you'd be gone, because you knew Hazel would need some extra help?'

'No, no of course not.'

Did I believe him? Not really. Jobs like this weren't confirmed overnight, and the idea that he was lying to me only spiked my anger, but I tried not to show it.

Then: 'Look sis, the way I spoke to you before, at the tower, it was a bit much. But I'm not well, you can see that, right? I think I need help, to get away for a while . . . This job . . . it could be good for me.'

What I felt next was an uneasy blend of relief and concern, and fear.

Siblings look out for one another, isn't that what Hazel said? And in an ideal world, maybe that was true, but it was clear that Colin wasn't well enough to look out for himself, let alone for me.

'Just one thing,' Sandra said, and I turned to look at her. 'Next time you're dealing with Clifford's finances, it would be good if you consulted with us both.'

'I beg your pardon?' A flush of anger heated my cheeks.

'Only, I'm a part of this family now, and I have a right to be consulted, I think; in case anything should happen to Clifford – if you see what I mean.'

I did. And I found this outward display of greed both distasteful and outrageous, which is why I glanced sharply at Colin, hoping he would see the inappropriateness of this remark and support me. Instead, his eyes only drifted. I couldn't decide if that was the alcohol or weakness or ill-concealed unease, but it was one of the most depressing expressions I had ever seen.

'I assume your father *has* written a will?' Sandra asked.

'That's enough,' I said. She had gone too far, and now my mind was beginning to wander somewhere I really didn't want it to go. How involved, exactly, had Sandra been with Dad's affairs? 'You have a most unhealthy interest in matters that have nothing to do with you,' I said flatly, then shook my head with a gesture I hoped conveyed disgust. 'I should leave.'

'That's maybe a good idea.' She folded her arms.

'Colin?'

'I'll be on my phone, Lizzy,' he said, as if that made this all okay, but he was running away from the family problem, we both knew that. Leaving it to me, and maybe that's what I deserved, but I was worried for him. Worried by how alike we were. Because by the time I was walking out into the hall, I heard the snap and fizz of another beer can.

'Talk soon?' he called after me.

But I already had a pretty good idea that mobile phone reception in the Highlands wasn't as reliable as it could be, and I doubted we would be speaking often.

Or any time soon.

My chat with Hazel last night had put most of my doubts about her integrity to rest, and there were no red flags in her references. But it would have been remiss of me not to follow up. Just to be sure.

The journey took just under an hour. Rose Cross House was on the outskirts of Woodbridge, set within acres of open fields. An isolated Gothic mansion of black stone. Depressing. As I parked outside, I had to wonder why anyone would have thought this building desirable as an old people's home.

Debbie Charter was a gangling woman for whom retirement can't have been far away, with wintry grey eyes and straight black hair (dyed, with a tell-tale purple hue). Although she wore a lace-trimmed blouse and pink cashmere cardigan, her confident, crisp demeanour left no doubt she was every bit the businesswoman, and that was fine, but something about her smile was forced, I thought, impersonal. Which was probably why I didn't warm to her immediately. In her office, surrounded by numerous Care Home Awards, we exchanged pleasantries for a minute before I came to the point.

'Hazel Sanders?' She clenched her hands together and stared across her pristine desk. 'Yes, she worked here. Three years, or thereabouts. How is she?'

I explained.

'After-stroke and dementia care. Is that the sort of work she did here?'

She nodded and her face assumed a look of open sincerity but, like her smile, it lacked warmth.

'Hazel put a great deal of effort into her work. A lot of overtime. She didn't need the money. People like that must truly care, don't you think?'

You tell me, I thought.

She went to a filing cabinet at the back of the office and thumbed through the files. 'Here we are. Hazel Sanders. Yes, I was correct: with us three years and two months, to be exact.'

She brought the file across to the desk. I couldn't help noticing it was rather well padded.

'Our problem, as an industry, is immigration.'

I forced a smile, nodded.

'Way too many care assistants coming from abroad these days. Way too many cultural differences, too. Creates barriers with our residents. Even our English staff can lack empathy sometimes. But Hazel? Well, she was a true star. Always built

the best rapport with our residents, which is what they deserve.
She had the human touch. A rare skill, Ms Valentine, but one
we value greatly here at Rose Cross House.'

I nodded.

'Did she enjoy the job?'

'You'll have to ask Hazel, but I feel sure she must have done.
Before she came to us, she worked for a private client, which
you know about, of course.'

'Actually, no.'

'You mean her references didn't mention—'

'Only two references,' I told her. 'One from yourself, the
other from Woodbridge Hospital.' I lifted an eyebrow. 'Who
was the private client?'

'Sorry. That information is confidential.' Mrs Charter closed
the file in front of her. 'As far as I'm concerned, Hazel is a com-
petent and trustworthy care worker, which is why we were
happy to employ her.'

'And yet, here in your reference you say that Hazel could sometimes do better to improve her communication skills. Why?'

'It was a long time ago,' she said carefully.

'Did she say why she was moving on?'

'Not really. But I think she wanted a change of scene.
Understandable.' Her eyes concealed something as she hooked
a button on her cardigan. 'You may know that Hazel Sanders is
a wealthy woman. At her age, I couldn't blame her for wanting
some time to herself.'

'Can I cut to the chase, Mrs Charter?'

'By all means.' Her tone said: *'I wish you would.'*

'Was there any trouble during Hazel's time here?'

'Trouble?' She reflected for a moment. 'This is a care home,
there's always some sort of trouble.'

'But is there a complaints procedure?'

She frowned and sat back. 'Well, of course there is. Why?'

'In case anyone should have concerns about standards.'

She stared at me as if I had used an outrageous profanity. 'Ms Valentine, when it comes to the care and treatment of the elderly, Rose Cross House is one of the finest establishments in the country. As you can see,' she added, gesturing to a framed certificate on the nearest wall, 'we're rated outstanding by the Care Quality Commission. Our residents and their families truly value our work.'

Now that she was riled up, I figured I may as well press further and ask the question that had been on my mind since I'd discovered my father's money was missing. 'When Hazel was employed here, were there ever any instances of residents "losing" valuable possessions?'

'Good heavens!' said Mrs Charter. 'Certainly not! If I had *any* suspicion of theft in this home then I would have personally, and thoroughly, investigated all allegations or evidence. I run a tight ship, you know. There's an inventory of every resident's belongings, and photographs are taken of every piece of jewellery that is brought in.'

She sighed impatiently. 'I think I know what this is *really* about; it's that trouble we had in the newspapers. Am I right? The unpleasantness?'

Now we're getting somewhere.

I knew nothing about any 'unpleasantness', but it seemed logical to pretend I did; so I nodded, holding her gaze. 'Exactly,' I said, 'the trouble in the newspapers. It's bound to make one wonder . . .'

'Oh, I thought as much,' she said sourly, shaking her head. 'A hullaballoo over nothing is what *that* was, and a long time ago. Tell the truth, I could have sued the *Gazette* for damages. Those stories—'

'You mean *allegations*,' I said. The comment was a complete stab in the dark but not necessarily a wild one.

'Damn careless hacks, throwing around aspersions. And for what? To besmirch someone's good name for the sake of a shocking headline. Makes me sick. A free press? Don't make me laugh. It's the ones who point the finger who keep their freedom. The ones they name have to live with the fallout. You coming here today only proves the point. For heaven's sake, it was four years ago!'

I knew I had to pursue this, by pretending I knew what she was getting at. Poker face.

'And there was no substance to the allegations? Obviously, you understand why I'm asking.'

She spread her veined hands wide. 'Look. There were some unexplained incidents. There always *are* when you're working with confused patients. Like I said, always *some* sort of trouble. Over time, the residents can become very different people, you realise that? There are behavioural problems. Aggression. Sometimes violence. And that is troublesome, believe me, for everyone.'

Again, she hooked a button of her cardigan. 'But the business with the newspapers was a whole other matter and blown completely out of perspective.'

I studied her. That impression I had that she was distanced, impersonal, was reaffirmed in her compressed lips. The smile was gone. Here was the real Debbie Charter, a hard-nosed businesswoman who cared more about preserving her own standing than the well-being of the residents who relied upon her.

'Tell me, please.'

Indecision on her face, her lips tightening again. 'Hazel would use certain techniques with some of the guests to improve their memory. Admirable. Some of her work was experimental, some might say unconventional. But her work was showing considerable promise, no doubt about that. Some of the residents were improving, and that was to Hazel's credit.'

'Then why wasn't her work continued?' I asked.

She sat back. 'Now, there you go. Just like the pack of reporters who came to my door. Making assumptions without knowing the facts.' She eyed the file of papers on her desk. The 'facts' were in that file, I knew it.

'Now,' Mrs Charter said, rising from her chair, 'you'll have to excuse me. I'm already well behind with my day.'

I folded the reference that bore Debbie Charter's signature and slipped it into my bag. As I stood, I asked, 'I suppose there's no chance you left anything else out of this reference, is there, Mrs Charter?'

She sighed heavily. 'Ms Valentine, if there was anything else I thought you ought to know, I'd say. Hazel's a good woman. Bossy, yes, a little righteous maybe. But she means well.'

I thanked her for her time, and turned to go.

'You know,' she said, sweetening her voice, 'if you change your mind about live-in care, there could be a place here for your father.'

'That's very kind,' I said.

And left.

As I drove back through Woodbridge towards Shingle Street, I couldn't think of anything except that folder in Debbie Charter's office. What sort of 'memory work' with the residents of Rose Cross House had attracted such stinging attention from the press? And why, I wondered, hadn't Hazel mentioned any of this when we chatted about her background?

I thought of calling Nick at the hospital, hoping he would now remember why Hazel's name had 'rung a bell'. The reason I didn't do that was simple: I'd left my mobile at the tower. Probably it was charging next to my bed.

Then I saw, along the road, a familiar squat, grey stone building. The public library – I could look up the newspaper reports. I found a parking spot and strode towards the pillared entrance.

Even though the library was equipped with just six computers, getting online was easy. No queues. What was distracting was the dishevelled bearded guy sitting two screens away opening so many colourful windows and minimising them just as quickly. When the librarian finally accused him (rightly) of looking at porn and instructed him to leave, I brought up Google news and entered 'Rose Cross House', hesitating before I typed 'Hazel Sanders'.

And once I hit enter, I saw I was right to have come here.

The first result was an article published four years ago in the *East Anglian Gazette*, and Rose Cross House was the lead story: 'WOODBRIDGE CARE HOME CRITICISED FOR PUTTING RESIDENTS AT RISK.'

Sensational as the headlines were, the articles confirmed Debbie Charter's protestations. Hazel Sanders had been dragged over hot coals for doing little more than administering a mixture of herbal remedies to elderly residents who were suffering from the advanced stages of dementia.

All right, I could see why people had been concerned. '*The inspectors discovered that certain unregulated herbal remedies were administered to patients without consideration of reduced effects of other prescribed medications.*'

There was a risk that some of these remedies could have had adverse side effects. But no one was harmed. No charges were brought. So, there was no case to answer. Carelessness? Certainly, but not criminal. Nor, to my relief, were there any allegations of stolen valuables or missing money.

What the newspaper articles did not explain was *why* Hazel had done it. Why exactly had she decided to improve patients' memories? Was it kindness? Delusions of grandeur?

Her words came back to me: *'Sometimes, in the fog of their confusion, they show you something of what they used to be. To glimpse them as they were, restored, that's a rare gift and one to cherish . . .'*

The penny dropped, and I knew why. *She was trying to help*, I thought as I went back out to my car. *She was only trying to help.*

THE SHELL LINE

Visiting hours.

I sat on the bench in the hospital garden waiting for Dad to say something. With a warm blanket across his lap, he looked comfortable enough in the wheelchair. He had insisted on fresh air, but it was too chilly to stay out here for long.

'Do you remember how your stroke came on?' I asked again gently. 'What you were doing?'

'Hard to remember,' he said, peering at me with rheumy eyes. 'I was downstairs, I think. Speaking with Hazel?'

'Do you remember what you were speaking about?'

Beneath his dressing gown, his bony shoulders shrugged. 'Something about the past, most probably,' he said. 'It's always about the past with her. Hazel does like her questions. Always asking about my life, my younger days, when I moved to the shore and why.'

I could see how unkempt his beard was, the grime under his fingernails. It was hard not to wonder if Hazel spent more time asking questions than she did tending to his needs.

'Sometimes I get terribly confused, Lizzy. Not all the time, but when I'm stressed or anxious, that's when it's worse, and I have trouble remembering things from long ago. Hazel is able to help me recover some memories; the problem is they're not always good memories. And when the darker things surface, so does the pain. She does like to probe, though.' He hesitated. 'It's probably better you don't get into long conversations with her about our family history, Lizzy. Keep the work and the personal side of things separate if you can.'

'But do you *like* her?' I asked. 'You trust her?'

'Sometimes she can be short with me, loses her patience, but she's good enough mostly.' He gave a long sigh. 'I get so tired these days. Hazel sorts out the supper, gets me settled. Helps calm me down.'

'What's been worrying you?'

He rubbed a shaky hand across his face, almost as if he was trying to wipe it clean.

'Does Hazel ever deal with your finances?'

'Yes, yes, now and then.' A note of impatience. He fixed me with a blunt stare. 'I've never been especially good with money, Lizzy.'

You and me both.

'But it's all right, I'm going to go back to work,' he added. 'Soon as I can.'

My heart sank. Dad hadn't worked in ten years. No sense correcting him, it would only cause distress. 'That's the spirit. Good to be positive.'

He nodded, but already his bottom lip was trembling. 'Everything okay at home?' he asked, sounding worried.

'Everything's absolutely fine,' I said, trying to keep the uncertainty out of my voice. It wasn't just the uncertainty; it was the deceit. I hated lying to him, but now wasn't the time to tell him about the cherished family memories that had gone up in smoke. 'I'm keeping a close eye on things.'

A smile of relief broke on his gaunt face, which was good to see, but the tears soon followed, rolling into his beard. 'Look at me, Lizzy. I got old. I feel so useless. Maybe I should just walk into the sea and end things. Simpler for everyone.'

'Don't speak that way,' I said, with tenderness and pity. 'You'll get better, soon; you're lucky it wasn't worse.'

'I don't feel lucky. I deserve this.'

What the hell did that mean? He was confused, I realised. I told him things would get better. He would get better.

'Nick said you could find yourself coming home sooner than you—'

His gasp cut me off. He wasn't listening; his eyes, wide and frightened, were fixed on something across the hospital garden.

'Dad, are you—'

Before I could finish the question, he squeezed his eyes tightly shut, throwing up one hand. 'No!' he cried. 'Get away, get away! Please, just LET ME BE!'

I looked at him in desperate confusion as he writhed in his wheelchair, flailing his arms, as if to beat away some invisible horror. I had never seen him like this. Never.

'Dad,' I took hold of his arms, 'Dad, please, it's okay, stop it now, STOP IT!'

His eyes flew open. Finally, he stilled.

'Dad?' Taking his hand, I crouched down beside his wheelchair. Being so close to him made me think of my dream, the one in which we are standing next to one another at twilight on the shore. Him gazing sadly towards the abandoned Orford Ness.

. . . *A darkness is rising* . . .

The more I thought about that dream, the more intrigued I was about the out-of-bounds military zone, its secret history. As a kid he had warned me to stay away. I decided to ask him about it now, but instead of answering he let out a long exhale. There was something painful in that sigh, something anguished. His eyes drifted for a moment, then focused on me. 'You were smarter than me, Lizzy. Smarter than I ever was.'

'What do you mean?'

'The best thing you ever did was getting out of Shingle Street. Getting away.'

We held each other's gaze for a breath.

I thought of the shore in darkness, of my other dream of the burning sea. I thought of Hazel staring hard into my eyes. *Did he ever* fear *the shore?* she had asked.

Yes, I thought with a shiver. *Yes he did.*

The rains came, as they tend to do in Suffolk at that time of the year, and the next few days passed in a monochrome of grey uncertainty.

The loneliness of the tower was desperately depressing.

You could have gone back to London, I told myself. *You could have used your membership at Soho House. You chose to stay.*

But what option did I have now, with Colin away on his job in Scotland?

It was at the top of my mind to ask Hazel directly about her trouble at Rose Cross House, but the morning after our chat, she vanished. She had said nothing about leaving, and I was puzzled. A quick call to Colin didn't help. He gave me her number, but it rang out.

You may have thought it was a relief to have the place to myself, but the truth is I hated being alone in the tower, listening to its strange acoustics, and when it grew dark, I became nervous thinking of what might happen should our friendly arsonist make a return.

How did this affect me?

The slightest noise outside pricked my anxiety: shuffling, scraping sounds in the slipping shells. Did I really hear them?

Did it even matter?

Not all who wander are lost, that's what Bill Durrant says, but on those gloomy mornings when I rose warily, listening and watching for any sign of an intruder, I *did* feel lost. And desperately alone. Very much like a wanderer, oppressed by the dread of an unpaid debt; and that vulnerability put nettles in my stomach and racked me with worry.

The idea of calling Nick and telling him everything frequently recurred as I roamed the tower. *I came here to run away, because I hit rock bottom, and because I need help.* It was easy to picture us strolling, like we used to, along the water's edge. Confessing to him that I had embezzled tens of thousands in a gambling hand I couldn't control. But shame prevented me from doing any of that.

Sometimes – usually late at night while listening to waves kick the shore – the urge to escape returned, locking me in its grip, vice-like. And led me back to the old websites. At the sight of them, I felt like vomiting, like I had done that night back in London. But still, the compulsion to place a bet or two was overwhelming.

I needed to distract myself. When I wasn't visiting the hospital, the grey days lapsed into a rhythm familiar to me only from the distant school holidays. I walked the length of the shore and back again, collecting strange-looking shells. I stood on the shingle and watched the frothing waves recede, leaving brackish lagoons that glimmered.

From here, I could just about make out Orford Ness on the horizon; dark shapes of hangars, lookout towers and weapon storage areas languishing on a spit of land. Since the military had abandoned the place in the early fifties the locals referred to it as the 'graveyard', this necropolis of rusting structures. It was the strangeness of the place that drew the eye; the brooding, quiet, overshadowing sense of danger. Sometimes I would stare at it for minutes at a time, remembering my dream in which Dad stared at it, too.

It was on such a day, as I stood among the ridges and ditches of shingle, listening to the cries of the gulls and feeling the teeth of the wind at my back, that I had my first conversation with Bill Durrant. A lone observer, a mystery.

And a man I would come to rely upon as a friend.

'Hey there, miss! You all right?'

A gravelly voice. Distinct. With the bitter wind tearing at my hair, I turned and saw, at the edge of the water, next to the line of bright white shells, the bearded man. He wore faded grey jeans, a thick, black wool jumper, a pair of dark green boots, and a black cap pulled down low.

'He paces the beach every weekend laying those shells. Never comes down this far . . . seemed harmless to me.'

Now, as before, I had an idea he might be a fisherman, but then I doubted it. For one thing, the National Trust didn't allow fishing here, and for another, he wasn't equipped with any rods. What he was holding was a white plastic bag, and I wondered, eyeing the shell line once more, if he was in the process of laying down some more.

He called to me again.

'Hi there, yes, fine, thank you,' I called back, and instantly worried my tone was too abrupt.

I had no desire to appear rude, so I began walking to him,

and as he watched me approach, the stranger straightened his cap and extended a weather-beaten hand.

'Bill Durrant,' he said, and again I registered the gravelly voice.

'Elizabeth Valentine – Lizzy,' I said, shaking his hand without hesitating – not just out of politeness; he seemed genuinely concerned and his eyes were kind.

He was handsome, for an older man; late fifties, I thought. His face was heavily lined and tanned biscuit-brown, a clue to the amount of time he must have spent outdoors, but his cheek-bones were prominent and his jaw was strong. There could be no doubt that the years were treating him kindly.

'Wind's got a bite today,' he said, 'You warm enough in that coat?'

I wasn't, and I probably should have buttoned it up. I did that now, drawing it around me as I eyed his plastic bag.

'You laid these shells?'

'Aye, I did; guess it's my labour of love.' He laughed, but not in a happy way; there was something sad about that laugh. 'Guessing you're staying over there?'

He was looking towards the Martello tower, which was half obscured by the drifting fog. It felt good to have the tower partially out of sight. I nodded and he shook his head.

'Sorry about the fire; I didn't want to intrude afterwards, but the police said no one was hurt.'

I thanked him. 'It could have been a lot worse.'

'You renting the tower itself are you? Isn't it magnificent? If I had the money, I'm sure I wouldn't mind renting it myself one year.'

'No, no, I grew up there.'

A raised eyebrow. 'Well . . . I *am* sorry; must have come as an awful shock.' Then, with a look of open curiosity, he nodded at the Martello tower. 'Truth be told, I've always been curious to see inside. One hell of a restoration job, if the old photographs are anything to go by.'

He was right about that. 'A masterpiece' was the judgement of anyone who had ever ventured inside; 'an architectural triumph!' Dad had leaped at the project with the alacrity of a middle-aged man rediscovering his youth.

'My father won some impressive awards back in his day,' I told Bill, and his eyebrow remained raised. 'Best architect in the district, some say.'

'Must have been one talented man.'

'He *is* a talented man,' I corrected him.

'Wait . . . he's . . . *alive*?'

'Yeah,' I clarified, 'the tower is his home. Why?'

Now Bill looked even more confused. 'How old is your father?'

'Nearly eighty.'

Bill just stared at me.

'He's in hospital now,' I explained, 'but—'

'Oh, forgive me, I just assumed . . .' He tailed off. 'Guess your father must really like being indoors, huh?'

'Why do you say that?'

'Never seen him, for one thing. And I've been renting this cottage off and on, weekends mostly, for a couple of years now, from the Grayling family, over in Woodbridge. Now, maybe you think this sounds odd, but I've an eye for detail; reckon I recognise most faces I see on this stretch of beach, and I'm pretty sure I've never seen a man your father's age coming out of that tower, or anywhere near it, for that matter.'

Was I surprised? I shouldn't have been; Colin had mentioned

Dad's reclusive tendencies. Was I almost overwhelmed by sadness and embarrassment to think that Dad had become a living ghost out here, unseen and unheard? You bet I was. Sure, records would show that Dad still drew his state pension; and the chemist in Woodbridge would have copies of his prescriptions for blood pressure and diabetes. And yet here, on the very shore he called home, Dad had become completely invisible to even his closest neighbour. And dependent on the care of a stranger.

'Have you seen Hazel,' I asked, 'my dad's care-giver?'

'Glasses? Heavy-set? Middle-aged?'

'That's her.'

'Yeah, she comes and goes. Doesn't strike me as the sort of person who smiles a lot. Looks as if her mouth is filled with tacks.'

Hard to disagree; but when I remembered the awful fate that had met Hazel's father, the manner of his agonising death, that was understandable.

'Had a brief chat with her, but only the once,' Bill said. 'The two of you rubbing along okay?'

I shrugged. 'We've had our challenges.'

'Playing happy families, eh?' He nodded. 'That can get awkward. Boundaries. I used to have a cleaner who was *extremely* assertive. Just remember, Lizzy, please; it's your home. So you make the rules, okay?'

I nodded, and he smiled.

'Good. Now then. How long are you staying?'

'Until Dad's home and fighting fit, I guess.'

'You guess?' The smile vanished from Bill's face. 'Okay, but that could be a while, and I'll be honest Lizzy, because I always am – I don't much envy you cooped up in there with that woman. As you'll know only too well, winters here are exceptionally cruel – these old hands will attest to that.'

He spread them for me and I saw how cracked and reddened they were from the cold.

'Be sure about staying so long; especially with a stranger.'

'Why do you come back here so often?' I asked, curious, and keen to get off the subject of Hazel. 'Favourite holiday spot?'

'Not quite.'

'Visiting family?'

'Something like that.' There was an edge to his tone – regret, I thought. Then he gave a smile.

'Luckily, though, the Graylings only charge me a peppercorn rent for Dumb Boy Cottage' – he pointed to the Victorian dwelling further down the beach – 'I'm there most weekends now.'

'It's a weird name for a house,' I told him, wondering if he would be curious to hear some of the not-so-pleasant stories I'd heard about it.

'Weird name; weird shoreline,' he said. 'I'll explain what I mean by that some time, if you like?' His eyes had an enigmatic gleam. 'Sometimes I wonder if I've come to know this place rather too well.'

'Do you come here alone?'

He nodded. 'Solitude focuses the mind, don't you think?'

Maybe he was right about that. In my case, solitude *did* focus the mind, just not always for the better.

The wind was getting up now and it shook the plastic bag in Bill's hand. The clanking of shells was unmistakable. I looked again at the white line on the beach, tracing it from the front of Dumb Boy Cottage down to the waterline.

He saw me looking and said: 'You like it?'

'Yes, I do, very much. It's . . . quite beautiful.'

'Glad you think so,' he said, gazing at his work. 'Twenty thousand shells now. Or thereabouts. But who's keeping count, eh?'

'Does it have any meaning?'

'Oh, this and that. Frail and transitory it may be, but this line has endured for so many years now, and I hope it always will.'

'But what *does* it mean, Bill?' I asked again, assuming, as Hazel had, that it was a work of art.

'Survival, I suppose.' He nodded to himself. 'Yes, that's right; it means survival – and hope.'

He had left something unsaid, something that saddened him, I thought. I couldn't help but feel curious.

'Are you raising money for charity?' I ventured. 'If so, the shell line would make a great feature for the local newspaper.'

'You speak like someone who knows what newspaper people want?'

'Well, I work in PR. I mean, I used to . . .'

The cloud of introspection that had darkened his face lifted suddenly. 'Your other life, you mean?'

I nodded, and worried he might ask me more about that life. And was glad when he didn't.

'So, what about your *new* life; how's that treating you?'

'Guess I'm still working on that,' I said, thinking of Metcalf's demands for payment within three months, feeling the grip of fear: how was I ever going to meet that deadline?

'Finding yourself, huh?'

'Something like that.'

His eyes twinkled. 'Well, you wouldn't be the first to do that out here. As you grew up here, you probably know this already, but a hundred years ago, this beach was just a long row of small wooden houses and huts – fishermen mainly. Called themselves the "streeters".'

Actually, I hadn't known that; which wasn't necessarily so surprising. Since my father moved us into the tower, he had told us precious little about its history, and equally little about the area or its enigmatic past. Why not? Perhaps he was just being over-protective, I told myself, as if he was afraid we would learn something upsetting about the shore's history. Something disturbing, possibly?

Possibly. But I was sort of okay with him not sharing, because if my dreams were anything to go by, somewhere, lodged deep in my mind, was an early childhood memory about this shore that I did not want to revisit. Whatever it was remained deep in my subconscious, and there, for the moment, I was happy for it to stay.

Bill said, 'I think of the "streeters" sometimes, a frontier community living out here on the edge. I wonder if they felt it, too. When you cross the bridge to Shingle Street, when you hear that unmistakable rattle of the wooden boards, it's like you're leaving the rest of the world behind.' He flicked his eyes at me. 'Know what I mean?'

I did.

'This shore, something about it' – he hesitated – 'takes you out of yourself.'

I remembered Hazel saying: *'It's this place . . . sets your nerves on edge. Makes you feel out of yourself.'* The similarity wasn't just uncanny, it was striking.

'How do you mean?' I asked.

'Let me tell you, Lizzy, there's a stranger world than the one we walk through every day. Growing up here you may well have felt that.'

In a funny way he was right. Mum's old poem returned to me: *'As the dark stones crunch and shift beneath your feet, you sense the blood-soaked secrets beneath.'*

A small shiver ran through me, 'Why *do* you visit so often?' I asked.

'This is hard to talk about,' Bill said, 'but I guess the bottom line is, I'm looking for something.'

From overhead, suddenly, came the cry of a marsh harrier. My eyes were searching skyward for it when Bill announced that he ought to be getting back inside.

An hour or so later, in Woodbridge, I found the pub halfway down Market Street. All beamed ceilings, red carpets and creaking timber. The air was warm from the fire that crackled in the great stone fireplace. It was cosy – a complete contrast to the tower and the shore.

'There she is!'

On the opposite side of the bar, Nick was waving me over with one of his best smiles. A reunion of sorts. We had come here often just before our university days. He hugged me tightly, and I hugged him back, feeling so grateful for his warm acceptance after all these years.

His eyes searched mine as we drew away. 'Hey, you look peaky,' he said, 'you eating properly?'

I smiled at his concern. 'Don't fuss; you have enough patients without worrying about me.'

We found a cosy alcove and talked about Dad and his agitations and his recovery. We talked about Colin, his job in Scotland, and my concerns about his drinking. We talked about Dad's missing funds. Then we talked about Hazel.

'I overreacted,' I admitted, 'she's no super criminal. But she is something of an enigma. She's been gone these last few days – no idea where.'

'Hopefully she'll be back soon,' Nick said, 'but despite your father's outburst, physically he's making good progress. You never know, by the time he's out, you may find yourself glad to have Hazel around.'

'Maybe.'

Once we had ordered, he looked at me steadily and said, 'Listen, I have some papers for you. Thought I'd save you the hassle, with everything you're dealing with. And when it comes to tracking down your father's money, these should help.'

He handed me an A4 board-backed brown envelope. 'These forms grant you a power of attorney over your father's financial and health matters. I've certified them already, which means they only need your signature and his, when the time's right. My own view is that he currently does have mental capacity to make the decision, but that might not always be the case; dementia can worsen faster than the time it takes to secure the lasting power of attorney, so you need to get it done.'

Two glasses of wine arrived. Two lasagnes that looked too hot to eat. The cheese was bubbling.

'Thank you,' I said softly when the waitress had gone. 'But why have you certified the forms now? Why not wait until we can all sign them together?'

Nick's mouth compressed. He put his hand on mine.

'I have to go away for a time,' he said.

'With work?'

'No,' he replied, after a pause. 'Me and Jenny, we've decided to give it another go. A reset. She's hired a place in West Wales for us. Two months. I've asked for an extended period of leave . . .'

No! cried a voice inside. *You can't leave me!*

My reaction shocked me. This was Nick; he wasn't mine to keep in the first place. I had turned him down. Made a life in London. Fallen in love . . .

Mitch. He was the one who had abandoned me. And the pain of his rejection was engulfing and raw. But that wasn't Nick's problem; I couldn't put that on him. This was on me.

'The relationship has lasted eight years,' he was saying. 'I owe it to us both to see whether it's salvageable.'

'Of course you do,' I said, and forced a smile.

'Lizzy, look at me.'

I did. From across the table his gaze was reassuring.

'It doesn't mean I won't still be here for you.'

It does mean exactly that, I thought. *And with Colin gone, I'm on my own in this.*

'I didn't want to leave you in the lurch,' he said, lightly patting the brown envelope next to my plate. 'Now, be sure to take good care of these, they're important documents. Ask your father to sign them as soon as possible, but only when he's comfortable and clear-minded. Assuming, of course, that is what he wants.'

Would Dad want this?

That question trailed me as I drove back to Shingle Street, nervously biting my lip as I parked in the gravel car park. Would someone as private and controlling as Dad really want me knowing about, and managing, his financial affairs?

Quite possibly not. If he had been struggling with his own hidden addictions and shame, then *probably* not. And what about me? Could I trust myself?

That was the question in my head as I began walking over the muddy black shingle. It was late afternoon now, the sky was fading from purple to pink, and the shore, as ever, was eerily deserted; a world away from the bustle of Woodbridge, or the grind and rumble of my old tube journey to the office.

The roar of the surf was in my ears. Noticing my breath pluming out in little icy clouds, I tightened my scarf, and as I passed Dumb Boy Cottage, I thought of Bill. His words came back to me: *'Let me tell you, Lizzy, there's a stranger world than the one we walk through every day. Growing up here you may well have felt that.'*

Too superstitious by half? Absolutely. Almost amusingly so. And yet, despite myself, because of my recurring dreams, I was becoming ever more curious to know more about the disused facility on Orford Ness.

I turned to look that way now, across the river, to the silhouettes of ruined hangars and lookout towers rearing out of the mist. I thought of the military guards who had been based out there, the scientists and soldiers, and the watchtowers they had deserted behind the fences of barbed wire, standing derelict and decaying, creaking and rattling in the hard coastal winds. I remember thinking it was impossible to look at those structures and not to imagine that something sinister had happened there, but what?

It had always been a hidden place. Secretive. And in some ways, it still was.

'Snags the attention, doesn't it?' a voice said from behind me. It was Bill Durrant's voice, and it was uncanny the way it intruded at that moment, as though he had heard my thoughts. Uncanny that I hadn't heard his approach.

He came and stood beside me. From here, we could discern the oblong shape of a military watchtower. For some reason, it snagged my gaze, made me feel sad and lonely but also inexplicably curious.

'Orford Ness?' Bill said. 'Just a graveyard now, a military junkyard – but from the beginning of the last century, it was a government research site. Top secret. Surely, you must know all this, you grew up here?'

But Dad had never allowed me to know. The memory of him kneeling before me, glaring into my eyes with a warning never to venture to the Ness, never to ask about it, was vivid. Most kids would have responded to that with only greater curiosity, so why hadn't I? Part of me was wondering if I had always suspected – at a subconscious level – that asking questions about the Ness was not a good idea. As if the invisible weave of its perilous history might only entangle me in distress or fear.

'What sort of work went on out there?'

'So much of the detail is unknown, and most of what was there is left to the birds: guard huts, machine shops, the photo-processing facilities, the hangars. It's the National Trust running it now; building a museum I hear – damn fools. Come summer, there'll be a boat running.'

I shivered, and my gaze drifted over the vague shapes of abandoned military buildings – the watchtowers, the barracks. And those structures rising darkly against the sky, colossal and strange. Under the low late-autumn sun, they almost seemed to glow, and to me, they didn't look like military structures at all. More like Buddhist temples.

'Long after the Chinese labour camps, after the first ever purpose-built radar masts, those structures you see, the pagodas – that's where they tested vibrations.'

I frowned. 'Vibrations from what, exactly?'

'Ah now . . .' There was a half-smile on his lips as he tapped his nose with one finger. 'There's a story. Like I said, the files are missing, but if they weren't they'd still be classified. From everyone I've spoken to in these parts, what seems clear is that something happened out there, and on this shore. During the war. Something the government worked very hard to bury.'

Immediately, but for no apparent reason, I remembered that weird dream – flailing against the currents, the sensation of utter fear as my legs kicked madly for the seabed.

The heat of fire. All around me, the sea burning.

'Bill, tell me, what the hell happened?'

'That's an easy rabbit hole to disappear down,' he said with a grim smile. 'How far back do you want to go?'

'As far as you like.'

He nodded. 'There are some wild stories about this place. I don't believe all of them, but sometimes I think out here, the normal rules of reality don't apply.'

It was an enigmatic remark for someone who seemed so gruff and down to earth, and I had to think for a moment because honestly, he had me stumped. What could have happened to give rise to such speculation?

'Look,' I said, 'desolate, lonely places have always attracted these sorts of tales. I'm not saying they're made up, but . . .'

'The military are long gone, but the stories of what they did here remain. And legends like that?' He frowned. 'They stain the landscape, that's what I think; they seep into the very stones beneath our feet, and fester.'

'You're talking about folklore?'

'Call it that,' Bill said, 'if you like.'

I was intrigued, and that didn't surprise me, not really. How many times had Dad warned me to stay away from Orford Ness? How many times had he *insisted* it was to be avoided at all costs? And how many times had he resolutely refused to tell me why? It made no sense to me then, and still didn't: sure, he had an architectural vision, but why bring his family to live so close to somewhere that he believed to be so terribly dangerous?

'Before the military sequestered the land,' Bill said, 'the only people you'd find out there were the marshmen tending their livestock. Local folk who made the trip to gather eggs or oysters or hunt. Mostly though, if they knew what was good for them, people stayed away from the Ness. As you should, Lizzy.'

Bill pressed his lips together. I took it as a sign that this avenue of conversation was closed.

The wind keened. 'Well,' Bill said, 'best be heading back on inside now. Call in and see me some time, yeah?'

I said I would, and we shook on it. Then, briskly, he headed back to his cottage, leaving me gazing out towards the Ness. Before I started walking, I thought about what he had said. Something happened in that moment of reflection. I found I wanted to shut my eyes, and when I did, I saw Orford Ness as I imagined it had once been: a wilderness of lonely marshland, the low curves of military bunkers bulking against the sky. I heard the explosions of petrol tanks, the drone of aircraft as they lumbered overhead, their deadly cargo whistling to impact. I saw the young men and women in uniform crossing the river, their heads lowered. Soldiers. Pilots. Scientists. And the signs, hastily erected:

PLEASE KEEP OUT
WARNING: THIS IS A PROHIBITED PLACE WITHIN
THE MEANING OF THE OFFICIAL SECRETS ACT

All of these were images that came from somewhere else. Or seemed to. I had never been easily spooked. But it was hard to deny that I felt uneasy at that moment. Troubled by the significance of this place, and tantalised by its mysteries.

I opened my eyes and a new mental image imposed itself: I saw myself, alone, climbing the stairs of a rusted guard tower.

What the hell is happening to me? I thought. *Get a grip, Lizzy. Just get a grip.*

I think I glanced back towards Bill's cottage then because it was the one thing that seemed safe and stable on this shore. But my gaze snagged on something else – there, just beyond one of the black wooden wave-breakers running down to the water, a silhouette was outlined against the purple sky. A figure half-hidden in the drifting sea mists, and it seemed to be turned towards me.

'Bill?' I called out. 'That you?'

It remained still, gave no answer.

More drifting mist obscured my view; was there really someone there? Yes, I felt certain there was.

An icy finger caressed the back of my neck.

'Who *are* you?' I called, remembering Dad's fears of an intruder. Then, more loudly I shouted, 'Did Metcalf send you? Is that what this is about?'

I held my breath; no answer.

For a moment, I wondered if I was imagining this. As anyone would have done, I told myself it was the stress, my sacking, my debts. But then the figure moved. Towards me. Covering a distance of what seemed to be five or ten yards in a matter of seconds.

I jumped back. 'Leave me alone!' I yelled, and I turned and ran, so quickly I almost stumbled.

Then came a new sound, a voice on the wind.

'HELP ME, PLEASE!'

In a flash, I turned and looked back, only for a second, but that was long enough to see there was no sign of anyone on the beach.

The figure – whoever it was – had vanished.

The first thing I did was lock the front door. Then I went nervously around every room and flicked on the lights.

I would feel better after a large mug of hot chocolate, at least that's what I told myself. But I *had* seen someone; I would have put money on that – in my other life.

Who was it?

I shivered, mentally and physically.

Some sort of distraction was needed, however mundane.

Up on the top floor, I clicked on the TV, hopped a few channels, only to pause. Staring at the screen, my heartbeat speeding up, I felt like I needed a glass of wine, and although I no longer had the money for these live phone-in quizzes and competitions, that didn't stop my gaze drifting to my phone on the coffee table in front of me.

I reached for it, then stopped myself.

Switch the channel, I ordered myself. *Switch the damn channel.*

The impulse to dial the number on the screen was almost irresistible. It was the anxiety, triggering me.

Switch it now!

I did, to a music channel, and Gaga's 'Poker Face' blared out. Before I knew it, I had reached for the remote again and was turning her up loud, until I could feel the pulsation of the beats in the floor, in the walls, in every limb.

Somehow, that pulse soothed me, chased away the shadows, and I lay down on the couch. By the time Gaga was on the edge of glory, I was drifting away.

– 7 –

DEVIL TO PAY

'Lizzy, LIZZY!'

The voice pulled me out of sleep with a jolt. Hazel was looming over me, one hand clasped on my forearm, shaking me. The TV was off but every light in the room was on, blinding me.

'What's wrong?' I asked, sitting up in alarm. She was going to tell me we had another intruder outside. Or someone had broken in and was coming for us.

'It's your father . . . oh, Lizzy.'

My stomach gave a horrible lurch.

'The hospital called?' I asked.

'Yes, exactly. Oh Lizzy, I'm so sorry!'

My breath stilled as I braced myself. So this was it: we had come to the end. All thoughts of Dad suddenly diminished to the expectation of a funeral; a polite gathering of distant family members I had never met telling me how sorry they were as their speculating eyes crawled over his property wondering how much it was worth and if any of them would ever see a penny of it.

'When?' I asked, feeling numb. 'When did it happen?'

'Well, I brought him home just now.'

'You what?' I shook my head. What had she said? 'You brought him *home*?'

Horrified understanding bloomed in her eyes. 'Oh, my goodness, no! You've got it wrong. Your dad's alive, you hear me? He's downstairs in his bed. *Right now!*' she emphasised, her voice shaking with emotion. 'I brought him in the wheelchair from the car but he's not doing so well. He's running a fever.'

'Then why the hell isn't he still in hospital?'

'He had a turn when I got him home. They called when you were out and said they were discharging him. Well, naturally, I assumed you'd want me to go immediately and collect him.'

I was lost for words, in the grip of the realisation that she had brought him home and tucked him up in bed without telling me *anything*. Because, why? I'd been out for lunch? Just as I was beginning to trust this woman, to accept that we needed her help, she overstepped. It should have been *me* who collected Dad and brought him home; he was my father. The hospital should have called me first. Hazel hadn't even had the goddamned decency to call my mobile.

'Go see him, Lizzy,' said Hazel, patting my hand. 'He's been asking for you.'

Shaking her off, I started for the staircase. When I reached the top, I turned, glaring daggers at her.

'I wanted to be there for him,' I said in a low voice.

'Lizzy, really, I tried to contact y—'

'No, Hazel. You didn't. And that's not right.'

With a surge of resentment I turned my back on her, and headed down to see my father.

'Dad?' I whispered, but the word sounded wrong. Because the frail-looking man in the bed still bore little resemblance to my dad. They had shaved him, exposing the hollows of his cheeks. He looked painfully gaunt.

Swallowing, I looked around his bedroom. It was lit by a bed-side lamp that cast a sickening yellow glow. Swarming shadows. Worse, far worse, was the cloying odour of sweat.

As I approached the bed, his rasping breaths brought goose-flesh to my arms. Although he was lying down, he didn't look particularly settled, and it was hard to read his emotion, because his expression was one of vague detachment.

'Hi Dad,' I said gently, 'it's me.'

I studied his glazed eyes for a response. For a few seconds, nothing. Then finally, a slow and – I hoped, deliberate – blink. And that almost made me smile. The reason I didn't was a grim realisation:

Look at him. Unable to move.

What had I been thinking? What had Nick been thinking? He said Dad was making good progress, why? To lift my spirits? If so, they had just been dashed most cruelly.

You've turned his home into a prison. It would drive him mental knowing he wouldn't be able to get around the tower the way he used to. Cruel not to have him cared for in a proper facility.

Hazel was right about the fever; there were beads of sweat on his forehead. It had made him confused. Did he even know who I was?

For my own sanity I told myself yes, of course he knew. Hadn't there been the glimmer of recognition in his eyes just then?

Or was I only hoping I'd seen that?

Outside, the wind got up, battering the tower. Dad stared at me. *Why did this happen to me?* his expression seemed to say. *How long will I be like this?*

Quietly, I began to cry.

I was drawing a tissue from the box next to his bed and

drying my eyes when, from behind me, I registered the click of an opening door.

'Leave me alone,' I said, without turning around. I didn't want Hazel to see me vulnerable.

'Sorry to disturb,' she replied coolly, drawing the door closed a fraction. 'I already gave him a small sedation and paracetamol for the fever, but now he needs his medication.'

I closed my eyes, out of frustration mostly. If she'd known his medication was due, why hadn't she mentioned it before?

'Fine,' I said with a sweep of my hand, but I still couldn't bring myself to look at her.

She disappeared for a minute, then came back into the room carrying a glass of water with a plastic straw in one hand and, in the other, a little bottle of pills.

'What are those?' I asked, holding out my open palm.

Hazel handed me the white bottle and waited as I examined it under the bedside lamp. A name I didn't recognise and couldn't have pronounced was printed in capital letters on the label, next to an instruction to: SWALLOW TWO TABLETS TWICE A DAY.

'What are they for?' I asked.

'Blood pressure.'

She turned to my father and said, matron-like, 'Now, then, let's sit you up.'

His dry lips found the end of the straw and he coughed, choking on the water. I had to look away, my head filling with images that might have been lifted straight from the family photo album that no longer existed: Dad, strong and fit and agile, picking shells on the shore; holding me on my first bike. Dad as he would never be again: strong and independent. Good times. Diminished to this.

Frail. Weak. Confused.

I turned to look back at the bed. Hazel popped two capsules into his mouth. More coughing followed. Eventually he got them down.

'Well then, that should do for now,' Hazel said, dabbing his chin with a tissue she had drawn from the box next to his bed. 'I'll let you sit with him a while now, Lizzy. Maybe press a wet towel to his forehead. But remember, please, your father needs his rest.'

I waited with gritted teeth as she collected the tray and walked to the door. She paused before leaving.

'Lizzy,' she said. 'I did try to get in touch with you. I called, but there was no answer.'

She should have tried harder, I thought. We could have gone to the hospital together. And I was certain my phone hadn't pinged with any missed calls. But I was done arguing with her – Dad was what mattered now. I would get his temperature down.

'Goodnight, Hazel,' I said.

She nodded, and left the room.

When the door had clicked shut and I was sure she wasn't coming back, I went into his en suite bathroom, doused a hand towel with cold water, and pressed it gently to his forehead.

'Home now,' I said softly. 'Going to take good care of you. Hear me, Dad?'

No response.

And then, as if answering a prayer, his mouth widened into a smile, his expression clearing, gradually, like a bruised sky lit by a glowing sunrise.

'Elizabeth,' was all he said, but my name on his lips was beautiful.

'I'm here, Dad,' I said, squeezing his hand. 'I won't leave you.'

I dared to feel a little hopeful then. Maybe I had been wrong to doubt myself. At least here in the tower he had me near to watch over him. And his recovery would be quicker in familiar surroundings, with family.

'God, I am so sorry,' I said, leaning close to him, 'I'd have come to collect you if I'd known. But Hazel—' I broke off.

Enough. This wasn't the time for apportioning blame.

'We will make this right,' I said, gazing deep into Dad's eyes. 'Somehow, I will make this right.'

When Hazel finally went to bed, I went up to the tower's top floor and sat before my laptop with guilty temptation. My mind wouldn't stop racing because I knew what this feeling was; I needed to escape. The only way I knew how. Like Hazel, the addiction was sneaky, crafty; it did not want to go away.

Giving in to the old urges, I brought up a website I'd never used before: an online casino. 'DEPOSIT 10. PLAY WITH 40. AND GET 200 FREE SPINS.'

As my heart began to race, I pulled out one of the few credit cards I had that wasn't at its limit. Placing a bet would be as easy as the touch of a button.

Suddenly, Mum's voice was in my head: *Is this the way it's always going to be, Lizzy?* She didn't sound frustrated or angry; just desperately sad. *You can change direction any time you want. You know that, right?*

I did; but the pink flashing ads on the screen held my gaze, baiting me and, for what must have been a minute or longer, my finger hovered over the trackpad. One click away from the 'JOIN NOW' button.

My heart wasn't just racing now, it was pounding, so hard that I felt the rush and pulse of blood behind my eyeballs. All because of gambling. Life was as pointless as one of those bets. The Martello tower wasn't my escape, the Martello tower was my miserable prison. Where I deserved to be.

You're wrong, Lizzy, Mum's voice again. *Remember, it may feel like an escape, but you'll only trap yourself in a cycle of winning and losing.*

My finger was trembling, my chest tight. Could I change course? Surf the urge until it was gone?

I started to cry, and in that moment, I saw two future lives: one was beleaguered by multiple credit cards, failed deposits and cancelled withdrawals. Visions of gambling myself to prison, or standing on London bridges, looking down into an abyss.

And the other life? No more looking over my shoulder. Debt free. Bet free.

What's the old saying? Deal with the past and the present will take care of itself?

The debt was too overwhelming. Erasing the past was no longer an option, but I saw then that maybe I could learn from it. What if I locked my accounts? Put controls in place to restrict myself from every online gambling site?

A good idea, Lizzy. Maybe the best idea.

It was. New activities would replace the gambling. Feeding the addiction only gave it power, so I had to starve it. I would fill my days with long walks. Become obsessed with physical activity if that's what I had to do.

With a deep breath, I clicked the website shut and whispered to the empty room, 'Thanks Mum.'

Maybe, somewhere, she was listening, I hoped so.

And that was the last thought that went through my mind before I ran a search for the self-exclusion gambling helpline and removed myself from the games. Every game.

For good.

I think you know that night wasn't an easy one. For an hour, maybe longer, I lay in bed, reflecting on what I'd done, feeling proud but also worried. This was a new personal challenge and it sure as hell wasn't going to be easy; but for Dad's sake and for mine, it was necessary.

As I lay there, listening to the lonesome wind buffeting the tower, I realised that Hazel was up. I listened to her muffled footsteps trudging back and forth, resenting every one. Whispers through closed doors kept me from sleep. She must have gone in to check on Dad six or maybe seven times.

Why? What's she saying to him?

Lying there in the dark, listening to the heaving waves, made me think how exposed I was out here against the elements. I thought, perhaps inevitably, of London; how badly I missed its buzz, the company of friends. Mitch.

I thought for a moment I heard a phone ringing, but that sound soon blurred with others, mostly nightmarish screams – my own screams, as a burly stranger armed with a crowbar burst into my room and bound me with cord.

I came awake feeling cold and clammy. I was shivering slightly beneath the covers. Which was odd, because when I got out of bed and checked it, the radiator beneath the window was on full – was almost too hot to touch – and the window was tightly latched.

Uneasiness washed over me. My mouth became cork dry,

my shoulders and neck tense. I had an impression that was irrational. An impending sense of danger.

I told myself I was imagining it. I was tired. Overwrought. When it came to guilt, my subconscious was giving me a lashing. What I needed was caffeine.

I was almost convinced of that, but then I became aware of a peculiar noise outside, above. It was unusual enough for me to put on my dressing gown, and head on up to the top floor and out onto the balcony.

In trepidation, I listened to the darkness, feeling distinctly the spray of the sea against my face. I cocked my head, listening hard, and now the low drone of an aircraft was unmistakable. It sounded as if it was directly overhead. Weird. Never before had I heard an aircraft out here. And when I scanned above, there was nothing to be seen – just a coal-black, starless sky.

Then: silence, but for the gusting sea wind and the crashing waves below.

In an agony of suspense, I stood there, confirming to myself that I *had* heard it. I was so on edge that the palms of my hands were clammy. I almost expected someone to leap out, like in a bad horror movie.

No one did – but the anticipation was real, and I felt it in every limb.

Forget Dad's paranoia. Phantom aircraft? Perhaps it's your mental health you need to worry about.

But it was easier to entertain that thought than it was accepting it, which is why I allowed my feet to lead me downstairs and out, onto the beach for a clearer view of the sky. The shore was in thick gloom, the bitter wind whipping at my hair. I stood there for a long moment, all the time feeling a vague dread swelling in the pit of my stomach.

Until suddenly the sky was thick with engines, the hum and thrum of propellers.

There must be an explanation, I told myself, turning my gaze skyward. The planes were above the cloud cover, had to be; that's why I couldn't see them. That's why their drones sounded muffled.

Except when had I ever heard aircraft sounds like this?

A darkness is rising, I thought. *Rising, rising, rising*.

A wave of light-headedness crashed through my mind and in an instant I was adamant that some undefinable danger was close at hand. An intruding peril. But if there was someone, or something, out here with me, then only an owl could have seen it, for I was marooned in an impenetrable darkness.

Suddenly the ground was vibrating as I covered my ears against the screaming of the propellers and the roaring of powerful engines. A thunderous, unbearable crescendo of noise.

With a flash of unease that warned me to brace myself, I hunched down, clasping my hands over my ears.

What the hell?

Seconds later, a high-pitched whine. A deafening explosion that reverberated through my every limb. Off kilter suddenly, grabbing for support that wasn't there, I staggered back on the shingle.

My nightclothes were wet. My elbows throbbed painfully. Hemmed in on all sides by the gloom, I crouched there, shaking with fear at the roar of engines above, the rattle of impossible gunfire.

Then, abruptly, just silence.

And that was almost worse. Eerie. For a few uncertain moments I contemplated the terror of what had happened;

contemplated heading back inside. What stopped me was the smell of burning: a thick, acrid smell that made me think of valves and pistons and dirty oil.

I was struggling for breath now. Thick smoke was clouding around me, and foul black soot was in my mouth, my nostrils, my lungs.

'Please, help me!'

That's what I was thinking, but it wasn't my voice.

With my heart fluttering, I forced myself to my knees: *What the hell?*

'HELP ME!'

An anguished voice. And then there was a chorus of similar pleas, crying out to me on the shrieking wind.

'Help me! Dear God, please, HELP ME!'

The screams were muffled, as if they were at once close and yet infinitely distant. They were unmistakably the voices of young men, terrified and in agonising pain. Coming from the direction of the water.

There must have been an accident, my mind reasoned. *A boat collision, perhaps?*

What troubled me so dreadfully was the thought that there were people suffering so close to me, and that there was nothing I could do about it.

Cautiously, I struggled to my feet, straining to listen to the cacophony of cries that even now was dying on the wind. Eerie. As if a reality I could only hear and not see was melting away, and suddenly a fear unlike any I have known before swept over me. My skin crept with the certainty that I had to get away, for how could *any* of this possibly be?

At that instant there came more intolerable explosions, the rattle of gunfire. And with it, a horrible sense of some tragic presence, something that had once lived and now was most certainly dead.

That was when I ran, without looking back. I made it up the steel stairs to the tower, crossed the threshold, slammed the door and threw the bolt home.

After that, slumping on the floor, I took in deep gulps of air until my heartbeat slowed. Only then did I finally dare to unlock the door and look out onto the darkened shore.

Why would I do that, you ask? Why would anyone do that?

Fair question, and it's one that's come back to me in the time since. What I wanted, as ghastly as this sounds, was to hear the men's voices – God forgive me, to hear their screams – once more, if only for just a second. Why? To prove to myself that I hadn't imagined their inexpressibly terrible cries for help, which, I believed, had come from somewhere close by and at the same time far, far away.

Maybe decades ago.

Making sense of that belief, though, was another matter altogether, and not one I felt qualified to handle. For now, as I opened the door and gazed out into the night, the blank fact was that the phenomenon had ceased.

No engines. No fire. No voices.

The only sound was entirely natural. It was the sound of waves folding over the shingle – the shore whispering to itself in secret communion.

I awoke at first unable to understand why the clothes on my bedroom floor were dirty and wet, or why my hair was damp. Then, with a rising swell of anxiety, I could not helping thinking of the night's disturbing occurrences.

A dream? Surely not; even the most troubling dreams fade

shortly after waking, don't they? And yet, I remembered everything most vividly, from the deafening roar of aircraft engines to the ear-throbbing explosion that had brought me to my knees.

And those voices.

Those terrified voices crying out for help.

The memory provoked a shudder.

I remembered my immediate bewildered feeling, the need to know and to understand what triggered these sounds. Unless some elaborate hallucination had infected my senses, there had to be an explanation, but I was at a loss to know what it could be. I resolved to try to get to the bottom of the matter.

After checking on Dad, who was sleeping peacefully and whose temperature was – thank heavens – back to normal, I shrugged on my coat and went out onto the beach.

What struck me was the serenity of the moment, a stark contrast to the night before. I thought of those unnatural sounds in the thick of the night, that smoke-filled nightmare. The explosions and bursts of gunfire that had come as if from out of nowhere. After all that, the beach should have resembled a war zone. But a cautious search revealed nothing.

Standing there in the penetrating coastal wind and looking up into the clear blue sky, I felt strange. Untethered. I wrapped my arms around myself, remembering the horrible sensation of the supernatural that had gripped me outside in the gusting darkness.

You know you could have hallucinated all of that, right?

I did. Hadn't I read somewhere that anxiety was quite capable of inducing the most vividly convincing fantasies? I had been alone and scared and in the dark, with little visual information. The perfect conditions, some might say, to stoke my imagination and scramble my senses; for the brain to impose its own creations onto reality.

Doubt crept in, tangling my stomach with nerves. But it didn't seem possible that I had imagined it all; the memory of my terror had not faded – indeed, as I stood there on a bank of rough shingle, it was vivid.

I closed my eyes and heard once again the men's pleading cries for help. I could almost picture their faces.

One thing I knew: at that moment, the idea that there was something unnatural – perhaps even something ghostly – in those cries seemed not only possible, but plausible. Not *believable*, because I had no way of understanding how such things could even happen, but I *could* imagine the suffering of human beings on this shore. I could imagine military men, who had served their country during the war, when Shingle Street was evacuated and used for training exercises. Young men, called up to do their duty, training for the most brutal forms of warfare ever known, under conditions that weren't just horrific, but deadly.

Was it possible that soldiers were once killed here after an accident – some horrendous disaster, maybe an accidental mine explosion during a training exercise? Might it be possible that some trace of that occurrence remained? The ghostly remnants of some long-ago tragedy?

Was that what I had heard?

I decided I would speak with Hazel about the mystery. Why not? She had been in the tower when it had happened; there was no way she could have missed such a racket.

Reassured, I went inside and up to the top floor. Hazel was sitting at the breakfast bar, tucking in to a generous portion of bacon and eggs. Her meal looked divine: the baked beans in their own little china bowl, the eggs perfectly poached, the bacon neatly layered next to buttered sourdough toast.

'Morning, Hazel,' I said, somewhat tentatively given our falling out last night. I'd been hard on her, I realised. Put all my anger over failing Dad onto her.

She said nothing, just kept eating.

'Er, I was wondering . . .' How to broach the subject without sounding crazy? 'Did you hear anything unusual last night? Only I thought I heard a disturbance. Outside.'

She didn't look up, but she did reply. 'What sort of disturbance?'

'A very loud noise,' I said, thinking that in this case, the less said the better. It was perfectly incredible that she could not have heard it. 'A rumbling sound?'

She swallowed the piece of bacon she was chewing and looked at me.

'Haven't you seen the news?'

I shook my head, confused.

At that, Hazel plucked up the remote next to her plate, aimed it at the TV, and clicked up the volume. There followed footage, shakily shot, of cracked roads and fallen trees. The news presenter saying, '. . . *yesterday. A four-point-three earthquake on the Richter Scale, bringing scattered destruction throughout Suffolk . . .*'

Now, as I viewed the reporter standing among fallen branches and split trees, I wondered: was *this* the source of the rumbling sound I'd heard? Had everything else – the explosions, the harrowing pleas for help – all been in my mind? Natural sounds, rendered mysterious, to me, by the darkness and my own disturbed imagination.

But earthquakes didn't happen in Suffolk, did they?

Hazel seemed to read my mind: 'They can happen anywhere,

Lizzy, and this isn't the first time there's been a coastal earthquake in these parts.'

Was that true?

I had no idea.

Apparently, the tower had been unaffected – thank God. Hazel had carried out a top-to-bottom inspection earlier that morning, she said. The worst of the damage was a few scattered cookery books that had tumbled from the kitchen shelf.

Yet the news reporter was explaining that the earthquake had cracked windows and toppled chimneys. *'It woke me up because the whole house was shaking,'* said one interviewee. *'It was enough to wake the whole neighbourhood.'*

According to the news, the epicentre of the ground tremors was the forest immediately behind our own broad expanse of shore. Rendlesham Forest.

'Lizzy, you look very pale.'

She was right about that. I could see my reflection in the mirror above the coffee table. My face was drawn and the colour of milk. Mostly, it was because I was afraid I was losing my grip on reality. If I had imagined those events last night it didn't say much for my mental health. But it was also partly the mention of that place, the green gloom where no birds sang. Rendlesham Forest.

Hazel was staring at me. 'Whatever you heard was the earthquake!'

But I remained unconvinced and my confusion grew deeper than ever as I was sure that the sounds I had heard were real. Sure, an earthquake might explain the explosions or some of the louder rumbling sounds, but it did not explain the disembodied voices. It did not explain the harrowing and lamentable cries for help that hinted at some unspeakable catastrophe.

I wasn't sure how to believe in ghostly activity, but when I remembered the old tales – Shingle Street evacuated, the beach mined, an attempted wartime invasion – ghostly was the word that came to mind.

'Everything all right, Lizzy? With *you*, I mean.'

'Fine. Listen, about yesterday, I really think—'

'Only I'm worried,' she said, cutting me off. 'There were some odd phone calls. During the night. And to be honest . . . well, they didn't leave me with a good feeling – not at all. Are you in some sort of trouble?'

'Wait.' With a bad feeling, I fixed on her. 'You answered my phone?'

'Well, it kept ringing and ringing, such a racket, what was I to do? Could have been the hospital calling about your father – something we needed to know urgently for his care.' Her dark eyes were probing. 'Anyway. Why don't you and I have a cup of tea and a chat, huh?'

I didn't want a chat, mainly because something about her tone unsettled me, made me think she was needling for information. How much *did* she know? Maybe nothing. But I had no way of knowing who had called, not without checking my phone – and where was it anyway?

Hazel laid down her knife and fork and sat back on her stool. 'Look. I don't want any trouble here, Lizzy.'

'Who called? Where's my phone? I need it back. Now, please.'

'You're on edge, I see that. But you must trust me now.'

'Trust you?' It was on the tip of my tongue to tell her what I knew about her trouble at Rose Cross House, but her next words left me speechless.

'When were you going to mention you aren't employed any more? Was it redundancy, Lizzy? Or a sacking?'

A bolt of horror ripped through my chest. I think maybe she saw it, too, because the confidence in her tone grew stronger.

'Something's going on with you, Lizzy. We need a conversation, don't we? All this time, me feeling like the guilty party, when in fact it's you who owes me answers.'

But how could I tell her that I was guilty of embezzlement, had no money to my name and was being threatened?

'I'm just distracted, job hunting.'

She came towards me. 'You're trembling.'

I hadn't realised it, but she was right. I was trembling, and short of breath, and my stomach felt badly knotted up.

Firmly taking my arm, she said, 'How about I fix us a nice cup of tea?'

It wasn't really a question. And, as I thought about my five credit cards, the various loans, and the secret life, how enslaved I had been to an insatiable addiction, no wages, no savings, I realised that if I didn't tell someone soon, I might go crazy – if I wasn't already. The secret was killing me. And it suddenly seemed extraordinary to me that no one, not even Mitch, had ever noticed my problem, or suspected a thing.

So I told her. I told Hazel the truth.

We sat in awkward silence as the kettle boiled, shame heating my cheeks. By the time she asked the pivotal question, that damned kettle was screaming.

'So, how much do you owe?'

Stunned, I watched as her lips curled in a half-smile.

'Oh now, don't be embarrassed, pet. We've all had money troubles. Back in the day, I racked up a considerable debt. So, how much is it? A few grand?'

I saw the number in my head. The string of black zeroes.

Winced. Saw myself, getting home from work, slumping on the couch and taking out my phone, crying and shaking because I knew I was a slave to whatever game came next. While to everyone else, especially to everyone at work, especially to Mitch, I was always, entirely, in control.

'Over eighty grand,' I whispered.

I expected surprise to raise her brows, a widening of the eyes, but there was nothing. For a long moment, her face was just a mask of composure. Inscrutable.

Finally, without judgement, she nodded and said, 'Why did you do it? To escape? To reduce the stress of the job?'

'There's no excuse for what I did.'

'Oh, now, we all do things we'd rather not; don't be so hard on yourself.'

I wanted to say that the gambling had soothed a pain within me. Numbed it. The problem was knowing *which* pain. Since Mum died there had been so many. I *think* it started with a scratch card on Christmas morning. I can still see it, courtesy of the National Lottery: red and blue and decorated in fat white snowmen. Tucked away at the bottom of my stocking, which lay under the tree. Dad must have slipped it in there because it was the first Christmas Mum wasn't with us and presents were always her area of responsibility. It's what she loved to do. Make us happy. It's sad to think of it now, but I have an idea that that scratch card, that whole unbearable year, was the beginning of my problem.

'It was fun at first. Just the odd flutter. Then things got complicated at work. I fell in love and it was messy. He had a wife. Said he'd leave her. Didn't.' I shrugged. 'Soon I was gambling daily, always increasing the sums.'

'You felt neglected?'

That was true.

'The gambling replaced what was missing. Distracted you?'

'Maybe.' I nodded, feeling so ashamed. Weren't women like me, successful, ambitious, meant to hold things together?

'You must have felt very lonely? Living such a separate and secret life.'

That was also correct. I thought of the night I'd walked out onto the bridge in a daze, feeling that life was crumbling around me. How learning that things were wrong at home, wrong with Dad, had finally snapped me out of it.

'I haven't gambled since,' I said, and that was good and true. 'I've excluded myself from all the online games I used to play. And I understand that every day is going to be a struggle now, but I know this – I'm ashamed of the lies I told. I never want to be that person again.'

'Well. Why don't we see if we can work something out?'

'What do you mean?'

She went to the work surface and poured the tea with a steady hand. 'It's absolutely none of my business, but we don't want anyone making trouble for us out here, do we? Not with your dad the way he is.' As she placed a steaming mug before me, she added: 'It so happens that I'm in a fortunate position to help.'

Help?

'No.' I pushed the mug away. 'Thank you, but no. I'll pay it back. Somehow. I'll find a way to—'

'You fabricated expenses,' she said suddenly.

I flinched at the sudden change in her tone.

Now she was looking at me accusingly. 'You took advantage of an organisation that trusted you.'

'Hazel, I—'

'You defrauded your employer,' she said abruptly, and that lanced me with guilt. For the briefest of moments, I was in Mitch's office, flinching from his disappointed scowl. 'You also ran up many thousands in debt on a company credit card, which you confessed to spending on an online gambling site.'

'Hazel. Listen! I take full responsibility, okay? I'm beyond devastated by what happened. And I couldn't gamble again, even if I wanted to. I've installed software to prevent me from accessing any websites that—'

'Still. You have a problem. It must be dealt with.'

She put a hand on my shoulder and looked at me self-righteously. This stranger who had come into my family home from nowhere, who had displayed such concern for my father's well-being. Who'd threatened me with a hammer.

Now she was offering me money?

'Don't you at least want to know the terms?' she asked, and I shook my head; and yet she must have caught a glimmer of curiosity on my face, because suddenly she was reassuring me that she had the money, all of it, in the bank. And as if to convince me, she produced her mobile phone. Keyed in the numbers, angled the screen my way.

'Here. See for yourself.'

Awkwardly, I took the phone from her, looking down at the screen. 'This . . . this can't be right,' I heard myself say, staring unbelievingly at the string of numbers.

Hazel was indeed wealthy.

She took the phone back and buried it again in her cardigan pocket. As she did that, the obvious questions were looping in my mind: what was in this for her? Was she trying to manipulate me? Or did she genuinely want to help? All of these were good questions, but a better one – perhaps the only one that mattered – was what would happen if I declined? It gnawed at me, the fear. And Hazel seemed to scent it, because, with a tight smile, she asked: 'How *will* you pay the money back? Because you won't get a loan, pet, not now you're unemployed. And I'd wager that your credit score has seen healthier days.'

Her hand covered her heart. 'I only want the best for Clifford. For *all* of us. Problem is, Lizzy, I sense that your old firm could be mixed up in business they shouldn't be. And if that's right, the sort of men you're dealing with won't stop until they get what they want. Why, you saw what they did to the boathouse.' She eyed me knowingly. 'That *was* them, wasn't it?'

I looked at her blankly and nodded. There seemed to be no point in holding it back any longer.

'Whatever possessed you to get involved with a company that behaves in such a way? What's next? You don't think they'll stop with a harmless domestic fire, do you?'

The question reminded me of my nightmare. The thug with the crowbar. No, they wouldn't stop with a burned-out boathouse.

'For as long as your debt goes unpaid can you honestly say that your dad is safe out here, in the middle of nowhere? And what about us? You and me. Are *we* safe? Because honestly, if the answer to that question is no, then you know what I'm going to say. Your first duty is to clear your debt, quickly. No fuss.'

Her impassioned speech had at least whetted my curiosity about her terms, because in a way she was right, wasn't she? I did have a duty of care.

And I had promised Dad I would put things right.

I took a sip of tea. 'How soon would you need the money repaid?'

She shrugged. 'Whenever works for you. I'll draw up a simple promissory note, if it makes you feel better, and you can pay me back in manageable instalments.'

I said nothing, just stared into my mug, wishing I could agree, desperately wanting to clean away this awful mess.

'There are limits on how much I can transfer at once, so I'll need to make two separate payments. You could have the first instalment soon,' Hazel said, 'by tomorrow? I get the impression you'd need it soon. The man who called didn't sound like the sort who likes to be kept waiting.'

She had that right.

'How much interest would you charge?'

My head snapped up at her answer.

'None.'

A silence between us then; so profound that the frothing waves below sounded colossal.

I had to understand. 'You're offering to lend me the entire sum, immediately, with no interest?'

She nodded.

'*Free*?'

'Well . . . I didn't say free.'

'Then what *do* you want?'

She levelled her gaze, business-like. 'To not feel resented for doing my job. For this arrangement to work, we have to act as a unit. Like a family, Lizzy.'

I stared at Hazel, shocked. She thought she could buy her way into my family? That by doing me this favour, she'd be one of us? I knew she was lonely, but that was a step too far. Intrusive.

'Look,' said Hazel, 'I know you don't quite trust me. I know you paid Rose Cross House a visit.'

I felt myself flinch. She seemed calm, though. Either she had expected me to do a little digging or she saw nothing wrong with the fact that I had done so.

'I made a mistake,' she said, 'it's true, but my herbal treatments *did* yield the most encouraging health benefits. Oh, now, I don't mean they reversed the illness, of course not. That would be miraculous. The effects were inconsistent and unreliable, I accept that. But some of my patients, Lizzy, I *swear* their memories improved tenfold because of my remedies. Helping those people, in just a small way, was a tonic. Was that so wrong of me? Misguided, maybe, but not wrong.'

She put down her mug and reached out, taking both of my hands in hers. 'Accept my loan,' she urged, 'it'll make all your problems go away.'

She sounded sincere, but still my inner voice was screaming caution. So again, I declined.

Her face tightened. 'What about your dad? If he knew that people you'd upset had been here making trouble. If he knew what happened with the boathouse.' She leaned closer. 'And that it was all because of *you* . . .'

'You wouldn't tell him?' I said, appalled.

'No, no, no,' she replied, and she sounded sincere, but somehow I wasn't convinced.

Anxiety made my heartbeat pick up. And shame. Dad couldn't find out what I'd done.

Hazel's eyes were fixed on me, and something in her gaze unsettled me – reminded me of when she found me at the bottom of the stairway with Dad and raised the hammer.

'Colin mentioned you've already delved into Clifford's affairs,' she said softly. Insidiously.

'Yes,' I said, 'at Colin's express request!'

She hesitated. 'But Clifford hasn't consented yet, has he? I mean, not officially . . .'

It hit me then with sickening force: *she's blackmailing me. She's actually forcing me to take her loan.*

'Your father is proud of you, Lizzy, so proud. Imagine his disappointment if he knew. More worrying still, I'd hate to see him come to any harm because of what you did. Already we've had a fire – what's next?'

I opened my mouth to reply, but could find no words. Whichever way you looked at it, this was blackmail, and it turned my stomach.

'You've already gambled with other people's money,' Hazel said. 'Are you going to gamble with their lives, too?'

I was silent, wrestling with my emotions: fear, guilt, obligation.

'Take the money, Lizzy. You should. It's the *right* thing to do.'

At some point in their lives, everyone is coerced into making a decision they would rather not, and so it was with me at this moment; I genuinely couldn't see another way. So I nodded.

'You're doing the right thing,' she said, satisfied, and I told myself that this would all be okay. Somehow. It would have to be okay.

The lies we tell ourselves.

The truth was I was unable to speak; my mouth was dry with shock and a little revulsion, with her and with myself.

'Let me have your bank details now. I'll transfer the first instalment of funds by tomorrow; that's a promise.'

And it's a promise she will certainly keep, I thought, as I listened to her footsteps receding, down, into the depths of the tower.

You might think I was relieved then to know my debt to

Mitch would be settled. I was, to a degree. But there was no cause for celebration. All I had done was delay payment, shift it. And one grim lesson was haunting me; it had been haunting me since the moment I arrived at Shingle Street. It was the same lesson taught to Antonio by old Shylock, who had demanded 'the due and forfeit of his bond' and who bargained most callously for his pound of flesh. You can leave the past behind you, but it always has a way of coming back.

– 8 –

INSIDIOUS

True to her word, Hazel deposited half of the money in my current account the next morning, and by the morning after that, I had transferred the entire sum to Mitch's company.

I'll admit there was a moment in between those events, a very dark and tempting moment, when my old urges drew me to my laptop to get online. But the need to do my best for Dad intervened long before I could enter the web address for one of my favourite sites.

You're not that person any more.

I felt like a prisoner on death row who had just been granted a brief stay of execution; with luck, my payment to Metcalf would placate him – for now – and that was good.

When Hazel assured me that the second payment would follow soon, that sounded good, too.

And for a while, I believed her.

The loan was not mentioned again for a week or so. More than once during that time, while I was walking outside I caught Hazel looking out from her eyrie, observing me from the top of the tower.

The awful thing was, I should have felt at home up there on

the expansive top floor – relaxed. Some of my most memorable childhood Christmases had been enjoyed there. But with Hazel constantly busying herself – flower arranging, doing crosswords, eating plates piled high with food – I found myself retreating, like a scolded child, down below. Taking sanctuary there.

Something had changed between us the moment I accepted her money. She was sterner, sharper, and I felt like she was looking down on me. She seemed content, for the moment, to keep the three of us trapped in that tower. Why? That was one question. Another was: where did she get that sort of money in the first place?

One morning, I went upstairs to find a small envelope on the floor beneath the letterbox and the note inside was addressed to me:

Lizzy, good to meet you the other day. I'm going to spend the next six weeks or so with my sister in London, near Kew. She's not well at the moment, there could be an operation soon, and she could do with an extra pair of hands. But please, when I get back, come see me for a cup of tea or something stronger, if you'd like?

You seemed distracted on our walk, and I'm not surprised given what you've been going through recently.

Feel free to tell me this is none of my business, but if I was in your situation, I'd lay down some clearer house rules with your helper. She needs to understand you're the boss, that it's your family home.

At the same time, I wouldn't spend so long together cooped up inside. If you're anything like me, it'll do you some good to go walking now and then. But incidentally, I'd steer clear of Orford Ness. The old test sites and weapons store areas. Like I said when we spoke, it's not safe, and though you probably think I'm being paranoid, I mean it. When the military left, back in the fifties, not all the debris was cleared. They would explode bombs there, underground. There are pits out there deeper than hell, and I've heard tell of more than one unfortunate walker falling into one.

Seriously, Lizzy, the Ness is one of the few places I've ever set foot on that truly feels alien. There's nothing normal about it. And in my opinion, places like that are generally best left alone. Do me a favour and keep that in mind, will you?

We can talk more when I return, if you like, but I wanted you to know that you're not alone out here, even if sometimes you feel that way. For as long as I'm renting here at weekends, I'm your neighbour, and your friend.

Anyway, take care, and as soon as I'm back, I'll put the kettle on.

Bill

'Who's that from?'

The voice broke in just as I was folding the note. I started violently to find Hazel at my elbow.

'Oh, just a friend,' I said, hastily slipping the note into my back pocket. 'Please don't creep up on me like that.' Her swift glance of suspicion was not reassuring. 'How's Dad this morning?' I asked. 'I was about to go down and—'

'He's fine,' she said, cutting me dead, and her smile vanished just as abruptly. 'But we really ought to discuss how we divide our time with him.'

In a way, I was glad she'd raised the subject, because just a day earlier I'd gone in to speak with him, only to be chastised by Hazel for interrupting what she called her 'routine'. Reminiscence therapy. As far as I could tell, this consisted of her burning rosemary-scented candles in Dad's room, playing music to him from his younger days, and incessantly asking him questions about the past. His old friends. His passions. And why he had chosen this shore for the biggest architectural project of his life.

Why this tower? Why *this* shore?

I had wanted, needed, to talk to him about the question of his missing finances. Not that me asking would necessarily have been much help: we were out of sync because I would say things he either didn't understand or couldn't remember. Sometimes he didn't even know who I was, and that was the hardest part of all. But then he'd smile and say 'Lizzy', and re-energise my hopes that he was recovering, remembering.

The problem was Hazel – lingering, like the scent of her rosemary candles. Busying herself in Dad's room when I sat with him.

'It's important I'm with him,' she said flatly now. 'And most important we're not disturbed. Clifford's often disorientated and he panics; what he needs then is a familiar face.'

'Well, I'm his *daughter*, so . . .'

I saw the resentment in her eyes. *What right*, I thought, *do you have to push me out?*

She registered my annoyance, I think, from the way her face softened.

'Look, it's no trouble,' she said, 'we can manage between us, whatever you want. We can be flexible. Support each other.'

A not-so-subtle reminder that she had supported me, with her money, and I owed her. I nodded; even though my inner voice was screaming at me to rise up and declare: '*NO, you WILL NOT tell me how much time I'm allowed to spend with my own father!*'

'You look terribly tense. What's the matter?'

'Nothing,' I muttered.

'Not worried about the second payment, are you?'

'No.'

'I'm as good as my word, Lizzy. It'll be in your account soon enough.'

A moment of silence; I felt every second of it like a judgement.

'You trust me, don't you?' she asked finally.

I had heard that tone before, when she was cajoling me into accepting her loan, and I wondered if anyone had ever really argued with her. This was how control freaks went too far. It was how gamblers ruined their lives. They became accustomed to doing their own thing without anyone ever challenging them.

She has an inferiority complex, I thought, *or she's jealous of my life, or Dad's home. Why else would she need to exert such dominance?*

I kept seeing the bank balance on her phone, the money she had wired to me against my inner wishes. These memories were uncomfortable, and they were an incentive to draw meaning from Bill's note, which was secreted away in my pocket. Suddenly, I was inspired to challenge her. Loan or no loan, I was determined: she would not dominate me.

'Thank you for your care and diligence,' I said, 'but I'll see my father whenever I want to. Clear?'

Hazel bristled, primly straightening her cardigan, and that was satisfying to see. Spurred me on.

I saw the dishes piled up in the kitchen sink — envisioned her mopping the kitchen floor, polishing furniture.

'Remember you work for us,' I went on, 'so when you're not tending to Dad's personal needs, I suggest you help out a little more with the housework. How does that sound?'

Her face hardened just as much as I had expected it would, and that was pleasing – knowing I could rile her.

'Well?' I said.

For a moment, I scented victory, thought she was going to compromise. But then her lips parted in a sour smile.

'You think I envy you, Lizzy – is that it? Your fancy London job? That expensive suit you arrived in? Your swanky apartment?'

The smile vanished; what took its place was a look of sullen contempt.

'No, I don't envy any of that. Oh, sure, you may have *earned* more than me, you may be more successful on paper, but I work damn hard to help other people. Living out here, cleaning up after Dad, taking him to the shops, keeping him company, helping him cope with your trail of unresolved family issues.' With savage pleasure, she concluded, 'I suppose with all that I must have something you'll never have, right?'

I knew what she meant, and I hated her for it. The moral advantage. She had that much over me, she thought. And the worst thing? The worst thing was knowing she was probably right.

There was no Indian summer that autumn in Suffolk. The drawing-in of the days seemed quicker than usual, making Shingle Street feel ever more isolated.

There was little to distinguish the passing of the days except the turn of the season. In the forest behind the shore, leaves turned rusty orange and fell to the damp earth, decayed and crumpled, only to be lifted again and scattered by the wild west wind, driven like ghosts to the dark shore.

Halloween passed with the usual paraphernalia, though not a single door on Shingle Street received a visit from miniature ghouls seeking treats or threatening tricks. That was good because on Halloween night the spray from the frothing sea would have sent them running. The roaring November bonfires did appear, as they always did, along the Suffolk coast, and then were extinguished.

More than once I tried calling Colin to ask how the project in Scotland was progressing and more importantly how he was feeling; and more than once I got no reply.

I also thought about Bill's kindly note and found myself wondering how his sister was doing, hoping he would return soon. I had already made up my mind that as soon as he was back I would certainly call in and see him. His company would be a most welcome relief; that and an opportunity to discuss some of the stranger things that had happened to me out here. Bill was open-minded; he would have a view on these things, maybe an informative one, and if so, that was a view I was eager to hear sooner rather than later.

Dad's memory seemed to be improving. So was his mobility. As he slowly convalesced, Hazel and I waited, in a kind of co-dependent purgatory. It was a lonely time for us both, that early winter. We shared the Martello tower like two wandering ghosts, inhabiting it, most of the time, either at separate moments or in separate places, and each day felt longer than the last.

'Is he sleeping?'

A freezing November morning. Entering the bedroom, I took one look at the bed, at the lumpen shape beneath the covers, and immediately wanted to sit with him; but once again there was an impediment. She was there, standing over him.

'Hazel, I—'

She looked up sharply. 'Not now. We're in the middle of something.'

'But—'

'Leave us, please!'

Her use of 'please' was entirely perfunctory. With my heart-beat thumping in my ears, I looked defiantly at her. 'I will not leave.'

Hazel stared; murder in her eyes.

It was my father's voice that broke the silence. 'Please, Lizzy, it's all right. Just discussing a few . . . matters. We won't be long.'

Resentful, with quiet compliance, I did leave, hating myself as I did so, feeling Hazel's gaze needling into my back all the way to the door.

Exactly how long I stood in the chill of the hallway outside the room, recovering my temper, I cannot say. What were they discussing? I had heard Dad's screams in the night and his mut-tered cries, and I had seen his tears. But whatever was causing his distress, Dad had not confided in me. Had he told *her*?

Minutes later, I heard Hazel's shuffling footsteps approach-ing the door, and I instinctively backed away from it, not wanting her to find me eavesdropping. She slipped out of his room, pulling the door quietly closed behind her, and saw me standing near my room.

'Don't ever do that again, Lizzy. He was reminiscing. And you interrupted.'

'What did he say?'

She looked steadily at me.

'Hazel?'

'Your father's memories would give you nightmares.'

'What did he say?' I repeated. 'I'd like to know.'

'Trust me,' she replied, 'you really wouldn't.'

After that, things only got worse. One evening, I cried silently as I listened at the door and heard my father call her Lizzy.

'I'd take it back!' he was saying, over and over again. 'I'd take it back, if only I could. We were just exploring! You see that, right, Lizzy? Please tell me you see that, please tell me that you understand?'

The incoherent ramblings of a man gradually losing his grip on the world.

'He has his good days,' Hazel reminded me afterwards, 'more and more now. The trick is talking him into them. Reminiscence therapy. A bad day, though? They're not pleasant, and I'm afraid they're becoming all too common. Just remember,' she added with undisguised self-importance, 'the bad days are when you need me around.'

By the time Christmas songs were airing on the radio, I was spending as much time as I could with Dad when Hazel wasn't around; but he did not spend time with me – not in the same way. On too many days his eyes were clouded by confusion. But for the most part he seemed comforted to know I was there, even if he didn't always know who I was, and that was a small mercy. Sometimes I was his daughter, but mostly, I think, I was just a person who brought him his porridge or his tea or asked him about the past; and he was very good at talking about that! He would describe his long days at boarding school, and his time in London as a young man studying architecture. Over and over, the same stories. I soon learned to predict every hesitation, every smile. I could tell when he was struggling with names, dates. Other times, he made no sense at all, and that could be unnerving.

Something else bothered me. An intermittent sound that came from behind his door, usually in the dead of night. A scratching, gnawing sound. Like mice. Except I hadn't seen any mice, or rats. Odder still, Dad said he knew nothing about those sounds.

I wasn't sure I believed him.

One evening I was reading to him as he dozed off when he suddenly sat upright in bed, his mouth gaping. There was spittle around his lips and his grey eyes were startled, which wasn't so unusual these days, but they were also alert. Lucid.

'Dad, what's going on with Hazel? Are you sure you still want her around?'

His mouth tightened, and even as I asked the question I realised that sending her away wasn't an option, not while she had a financial hold over me. But she had chosen us, I believed now, for *something*. A secret purpose. 'What does she want from us?'

My father hesitated, his gaze nervously roaming to the door behind me – as if he was afraid he was about to see someone standing there.

'What's wrong?' I put my hand on his and noticed that some of his fingernails were torn, and he shook his head for a moment, as if all speech had deserted him. 'Dad?'

'We'll suffer for what we did,' he said gutturally. 'We'll all pay, in the end.'

'Dad, what are you talking about?'

He ran a shaky hand through his cloud of white hair, then looked at me.

'Oh, my darling, whatever will you think of me?'

'Rest now,' I said soothingly.

'Bodies,' he mumbled, 'so many bodies. We had to go, we had to see for ourselves; who wouldn't? Can you ever forgive me, Lizzy?'

Eventually, he calmed a little and I sat with him until he drifted off to sleep. That word, *bodies*, seemed to echo in the room long after he was silent, and speak to a distant part of me.

*

The next time he came back to himself was a few days later, on a Sunday afternoon. I went in to see him and found him rifling through a file of papers.

'Perhaps it would be easier if I moved into the boathouse,' he said anxiously, 'it's all one level, so easier to get around, perhaps?'

I pictured the boathouse burning, flames licking at the precious family albums. Why did he store them out there and not in the tower? That was a question for later. The question for now was: should I explain to him what had happened?

Soon he would be strong enough to walk outside. No good keeping it from him any longer. Finally, I told him, my heart heavy as his hollow face paled with shock.

'Was anyone hurt?' he asked in a small voice.

'No, thank God,' I replied, taking his brittle hand in mine. 'Nothing was salvageable though, Dad. I'm sorry, I'm so sorry.'

He put his hands to his head and let out a horrible wail, so full of pain. I remember thinking that wasn't a sound I would forget any time soon, perhaps not ever. Then the tears came, trickling down his face.

'An accident?' he asked weakly.

I nodded. It would have been cruel to distress or worry him further. In any event, that threat was behind us now, or would be when I made the final payment to Mitch.

Dad became quiet then. He sat still for maybe half a minute, looking introspective. Finally, he turned his gaze on me. Lucid.

'I've been thinking, Lizzy,' he said. 'The tower . . . it's beyond me now. Or will be, soon. And when that happens, I'll need someone to take care of my affairs. You.'

I couldn't shake from my mind the question of his missing

money. 'Do you have any investments you'd like me to check? Pensions?'

'A couple of private pensions. I've not yet drawn down on any of them.' He gave me the names of the funds, and it was a relief to know they existed. 'Let me check,' I said and a part of me assumed – hoped – this was where he had invested the cash he had kept in the bank.

A glimmer of hope at last.

'Will they allow you access?' he asked me. 'Won't they need my permission?'

I thought of Nick's envelope. 'Well. We prepared some forms, if that helps?'

He stared off, as if into some unhappy place. The past maybe, or the uncertainty of the future? These moments of clarity, I realised, were as much a curse for a failing mind as they were a blessing. I thought he might be about to nod off, or tune out, but instead he sighed and looked directly at me.

'Can it be done quickly?'

'Soon as you wish.'

'That would give me so much peace of mind. You handle it, please. Colin's not good at this sort of thing, not when he's on the booze.'

As he was speaking, I was aware of the fragrant smell surrounding my father. That scent of rosemary.

'How is Colin?' he asked, somewhat warily. The truth was, I had no idea. For days I'd been trying to reach him on the phone. Every email had gone unanswered. Perhaps the renovation project in Scotland was going well, that was what I hoped. But if he was in the midst of some fitful drinking binge, it wouldn't be good for Dad to know anything about it.

'You mustn't worry, Dad. Arranging your affairs . . .' I paused.

This had to be handled delicately. 'I'll make sure everything's in order.'

'I'm not so sure that's a good idea, Lizzy,' a third voice cut in. I turned sharply to see Hazel entering. I hadn't heard her open the door.

'We should talk about this,' she said, looking troubled. 'I'm not disagreeing with you, just wondering if you're the right person to take this on.'

'Lizzy?' said Dad, confused.

I turned to him. Smiled. 'It's okay, Dad. I just need a word with Hazel for a moment. I'll be right back.' I patted his hand and then stood. 'Outside,' I hissed at her.

She stepped back into the hallway, and I followed, closing Dad's door behind me.

'How is this any of your business?' I snapped. 'What gives you the right to—'

'I have a duty of care,' Hazel said.

Sly Hazel, always claiming moral superiority. From the sheer force of her will she had made our family home her dominion. As she stood there looking at me contemplatively, my anger erupted. Anger at her intrusiveness, anger at her over-familiarity, anger that she had probably been eavesdropping and thought she could just barge in – tell Dad what he could and couldn't do – and then have the audacity to censure me.

'Do *not* come in and interrupt when I am speaking privately with my father. If you have something to say then kindly wait to—'

'No.'

'I'm sorry, what?'

'I said no, Lizzy. What would *you* say if someone who had

proved incapable of managing their own affairs volunteered to take care of your affairs?'

'I—'

'You cannot assume that responsibility. Because as a gambler you—'

'Don't call me that, don't you dare!'

'As a *compulsive* gambler,' she continued, loudly and scornfully, 'who *defrauded her employer*, you *cannot* assume responsibility for your father's financial affairs. Not now, not ever. You must see that?'

'Just leave me alone, Hazel,' I said furiously. 'Go.'

She didn't move.

'You'll show me some respect!' I demanded.

Her eyes narrowed. 'You're in no position to make demands,' she said. 'I won't help you go down, Lizzy; and I can't allow you to take me or your father down with you.'

I had an urge to strike her, and, feeling alarmed by that, I turned my back. Retreated. When I heard a door open, I stole a glance over my shoulder.

And she stood there, outlined against the light spilling from my father's bedroom – like a sentinel, arms folded, watching me go.

For the next couple of days, Hazel was never away from my father's room long enough for me to discuss with him the power of attorney. Was she afraid I would have him sign the forms when she wasn't looking?

Then, on the Wednesday morning, Dad was lucid again, and in good humour. Hazel made him poached eggs on toast and was bringing it to his room just as I was coming down the stairs with the forms. It had to be now, while he was thinking clearly. It wouldn't be right to delay any longer.

She closed the door just before I could enter.

'Stop interfering!' I insisted. 'Just stop!'

Her eyes flared. 'What this comes down to, Lizzy' – again, that condescending tone – 'is a fundamental issue of trust. Or, to be more specific: my trust in *you*.'

I opened my mouth to protest, but she silenced me with a raised hand. 'You thought you could just waltz into your father's life, take control of matters, after *what you did*?'

'Who else is going to handle his affairs?'

Then, with a heavy sinking in my stomach, I understood.

'End of the road, Lizzy. We can make Clifford secure if you entrust the power of attorney to me. Or' – her voice hardened – 'our financial arrangement is terminated.'

She really is crazy, I thought, shooting her a horrified look. And regretted it immediately, because she seemed to savour that look; the satisfaction of knowing she had beaten me.

'No second loan,' she declared. 'If you deny me, then your debt is your problem. And in that instance, it would be my duty to inform your brother. You see that, Lizzy? Your family will have to know. Everyone. Including Doctor Strickland.'

When I didn't reply, knowing she had me backed into a corner, she snatched the brown envelope from my hand.

'It's the only thing to do,' she said, 'the right thing.'

Helplessly, I stared at her. If only there was another option. Any option. Even Colin would have been preferable to her; but now, when I needed him most, my brother was absent, physically and emotionally, and for all I knew was barely capable of taking care of himself.

'Now,' Hazel said, looking at me with a leer of triumph, 'fetch me a pen, please.'

She had said that yes, without question, she would handle Dad's affairs properly. Absolutely, she would consult with the family on any decision that was made in Dad's name.

But when the forms arrived authorising withdrawals from his state pension, that was the first I knew of it.

A day later, I was locked out of Dad's bank account.

Soon, more forms arrived. From his private pension providers.

'Lizzy, I think those are for me.'

Hazel came slowly across the hall and took the forms from my hand.

'What are you doing?' I asked. 'Is Dad aware?'

She gave me a flat stare. 'Yes, he knows. On his clear days. Not that there have been many of those in the last few days. God, if he asks me the same question just one more time . . .'

She can't be serious? I thought. And yet she looked it. Where had her compassion gone? Her empathy?

'He rabbits on – over and over. It's infuriating.'

'He's trying to find some sort of order,' I said. 'Don't you get that? He repeats because he must. It helps him feel in control again.'

'Pathetic, really, when you think about it – a man his age, muttering away. And weeping in the night like a little girl. Depressing.'

Pathetic? Depressing? The effort of holding back my outrage heated my face.

'You'll treat my father with respect. Understand?'

She shrugged. 'If you say so. But you know, he's losing his

mental capacity and that makes him unpredictable. Wicked man, your dad, when he has the devil in him.'

I wasn't sure what she meant; wasn't sure I wanted to know. But what I knew for sure was that if Dad was deemed to lack mental capacity, then under the power of attorney, Hazel would have full control.

'What are you doing with his pensions?' I demanded.

She smiled as if I'd said something funny, plucked a pink pen from her cardigan breast pocket, and began clicking it, up and down, up and down, in a rhythm that seemed designed to taunt me. I could almost count the weeks I had been here in those clicks; the sound of them wasn't just in my ears, it was in my head. Maddening.

'Your dad wishes to review his named beneficiaries,' she said, finally. 'Pensions aren't considered part of his estate; I don't know if you knew that, Lizzy? I didn't! But anyway,' she smiled, 'clarifying the named beneficiaries removes any element of doubt.'

I didn't like the sound of that, not at all. 'You need to keep me informed of what you're do—'

But already, Hazel had turned her back on me, and once she had snatched up the rest of the mail, she scuttled off like a rat.

'Hazel!'

'I'm sure he'll tell you all about it, in due course,' she called. And the next sound, from down below, was of the door clicking shut, as she went into Dad's bedroom.

The following day, she was sitting next to his bed again, turning through one of the few family albums that he'd kept in the tower, and Dad was smiling until, without warning, Hazel pointed to one image.

'Such a beautiful wife you had, Clifford. Was it a happy rela-tionship? I had the impression from Lizzy that there had been some family trouble. Were you faithful to your wife, Clifford? Or were you a dirty dog?'

She might as well have spat in his face, from the way it paled. Dad looked up disbelievingly. Saw me standing in the doorway. And began to cry.

For a moment I found myself unable to speak. This went beyond sly or controlling behaviour. This was outright cruelty. Shock turned to rage. 'What the hell do you think you're doing?' I demanded. 'Apologise and get out. Now!'

She remained where she sat, my father looking sorrowfully into his lap.

'Did you not hear me?' I said. 'Our family history is none of your business. Got it?'

'I'll decide what's my business,' she said finally. 'We have an arrangement, you and me, don't we Lizzy? Now then, what do you think? Should we tell Cliff all about it, or . . .'

She tailed off, raised her finger to her lips, and looked me in the eye.

'*You* employed her,' I said, fighting against the fury that was making my voice tremble.

On the other end of the line, Colin sighed. I was amazed he had even picked up.

'So you find out what the hell she's playing at, understand me?'

'Yes.'

'I *mean* it, Colin.'

'I'll have a word.' He was slurring. 'When I'm back, when this job is done.'

'Today.'

'Soon.'

'Don't start on me, Lizzy.'

'Why are you protecting her?' I demanded.

Silence.

'I won't tolerate her intimidating me or treating Dad with such disdain.'

'Are you sure she's as crazy as you think? That she hasn't just got inside your head?'

'Isn't that what crazy people do? Get inside your head?''

More silence.

'I don't trust her, Colin. She must understand that she works for us.'

'Sure.'

The next day, Hazel went out. Had errands to run, she said, important matters to attend to.

Well, that made two of us.

I had doubted my abilities but, in the end, picking a lock was easier than I imagined – thank goodness for YouTube.

With a click, the door to her bedroom swung open.

I looked in on her inner sanctum; it smelled of rosemary, which wasn't surprising. There were a few pots of the herb lined up under the window, and that was okay. I'd anticipated those. What I hadn't expected were the stains, dried to maroon, dotting the carpet by the window. Blood spots.

Had she injured herself? How? Did it even matter? Those blood spots could quite easily have been caused by stepping on something hard, a rogue piece of shingle, perhaps.

Putting these questions out of my mind, I went over to the bed. More specifically, to the storage drawer beneath the bed.

It felt like an intrusion to pull out that drawer, but there was no sense in stopping now.

What had I expected? Bundles of Dad's money? Stolen trinkets? Something damning, for sure. But all the drawer contained was old books and yellowed newspaper cuttings.

My gaze was pulled to a loud black headline: '*BRITAIN'S SECRET MILITARY HINTERLAND TO OPEN TO PUBLIC.*'

I scanned down to the rest of the article:

> *A windswept peninsula on the Suffolk coast has been acquired by the National Trust. Once home to a testing ground for secret British military technology, Orford Ness – known locally as 'the graveyard' – is to undergo extensive renovations in the hope of one day opening to the public.*
>
> *Senior Ranger Will Summerskill said: 'Orford Ness was always a good place to keep a secret. It's completely out of the way, and being cut off from the mainland by a river made it very handy to keep away from prying eyes. But now, if we can, we'd like to show the public what was so special about this site, taking care to preserve as much of it as we can.'*

I lowered the newspaper and sifted through some of the books. The range of titles was bewildering: *Unsolved Mysteries of World War Two*; *The Plot to Kill Hitler*; *Blood and Sand*; *The Burning Sea*; *The A-Z of Curious Suffolk*. A faded photograph was tucked into one of the books. A desolate beach, and there could be no mistaking our Martello tower, vast, magnificent, looming over everything else. As I stared at that image, the muscles in the back of my neck tensed. It was evident that Hazel had examined this picture many times; her smudged prints were all over it.

Where had she found it? Dad's private collection?

I didn't think so; this looked like it had been copied from a newspaper.

Why is she fixated with our home?

With mounting intrigue, I picked up the book in which the picture had been buried, turned to the page it had been marking, and here was a faded photograph of armed, uniformed men kneeling near breaking waves and barbed wire. Young men with strong jaws and questing eyes. The caption beneath the picture read: '*SECRET WAR AT SHINGLE STREET. GOVERNMENT DENIES ALL KNOWLEDGE.*'

Looking at this clipping, these books, brought a curious realisation into focus – Hazel had a surreptitious interest in the shore's history, perhaps in Orford Ness especially, yet the reasons were unclear. Now I was bound to wonder *why* she was interested, and that got me thinking, once again, about the Ness's secret military history, and about the bizarre and terrifying noises that had accosted me that night on the beach.

What was it about Orford Ness specifically that had captured her attention?

As I studied the photograph of the uniformed men, their brave young faces, it was natural to wonder if one of them had been related to Hazel. Why else would she be so interested in the shore's military history?

At the bottom of the drawer was a collection of old photographs, bound with a fragile ribbon. Pictures from her childhood maybe?

I untied the ribbon, began rifling through them. These pictures depicted Shingle Street decades ago. The Martello tower before its restoration, an eyesore in the landscape.

Finally, I came to a faded picture of a teenager with tousled hair. Sitting in front of a birthday cake decorated with candles, he wore a tight T-shirt and denim jeans. Overweight for a boy his age, not fat exactly, but well-padded enough for me to imagine he might have been no stranger to playground taunts from bullies twice as insecure as him. The sort of boy who would always forget his PE kit and be forced to litter-pick at the edge of the school field; or live in fear of being asked to do gym glass in his underwear. A boy who might look at himself in the mirror when he fully hit puberty and think, *Get up early, exercise, run, run, run.*

A group of other boys, a similar age, stood huddled around him. They were on the beach, not far from Dumb Boy Cottage, smiling, all of them, but something about the birthday boy's smile wasn't right. Looked forced to me.

At that moment, a sound from the floor above made me start. Footfalls? Unlikely. If Hazel had come home early, surely I would have heard the iron door slam shut? Nevertheless, with the wind gusting so hard, it was difficult to be sure.

Slip out now, just in case.

With trembling hands, I bound the photos with the ribbon, dropped them into the bed drawer, and shoved it shut.

I was on my feet in a flash, heading for the door, when a niggling voice at the back of my mind whispered: *Something about that photo was familiar. Not the kid . . . but something . . .*

And a part of me knew what that something was. Which was why, while almost pleading with myself *not* to look again, I returned to the under-bed drawer and pulled it open. But as my hand reached for those old pictures, I froze; and felt it before I heard it. One hell of a jolt.

What the hell?

Suddenly a low rumbling. It rolled through the floor, reverberating through my bones, through the walls.

Shelves shook, books tumbled. Panicked, I grabbed the bed frame, holding on for dear life. All the time, the light above me swung wildly.

Then . . . nothing. Just a long, eerie silence.

Shaken, I scrambled to my feet, casting my gaze around. My stomach flipped and I wanted suddenly to be standing next to a toilet instead of a bed.

Only when I was absolutely sure the earth tremors (for I told myself that's what they *must* be) had ceased did I slip out. Taking the picture of the birthday boy with me.

– 9 –

THE DEAD PLACE

The following morning brought murky grey skies, the sort of skies that threaten trouble. I could have lain in bed for another hour, listening to the waves lashing against the shore. But that isn't what happened. Someone was knocking on the front door.

No, not knocking. Pounding.

It was chilly as I shrugged on my dressing gown and went upstairs, only to find the door was already open.

Standing on the threshold was my brother, holding the set of keys he'd used to let himself in.

'Sorry,' he said, not sounding sorry at all, 'did I wake you? Forgot I had these on me.'

'You're back? Why didn't you tell me?'

'I'm telling you now.'

'What happened in Scotland? Is the project completed?'

'I'd rather not talk about it.'

There were blood spots, I noticed, on his shirt collar. Thin scabbed tendrils on his left cheek that looked as though he had been clawed by the sort of pink plastic talons supplied by a cheap beauty salon. 'You really don't look so good, Colin.'

'Could say the same about you, sis.' He stepped forward, his eyes watching me closely. There was a strange awareness in them, as if he was on the verge of revealing something. The overall effect was more than mildly uncomfortable, it was downright disturbing.

'We need to talk,' he said, glancing past me. 'Hazel out?' It sounded more like a statement than a question, and that was curious in itself. 'Dad sleeping I suppose?'

Again that knowing tone.

'I think so; look, what's this about?'

'Upstairs,' he said, closing the door behind him.

'Colin?'

But he was already stepping around me, heading for the stairs, striding up. I wasn't being paranoid; something was wrong here.

'Put the kettle on,' I called hastily, 'I'll make us some coffee,' as if that familiar ritual could distance me from this moment of deep uncertainty. And I followed him up.

When I entered the top-floor room, Colin had not put the kettle on. Instead, he was at the floor-to-ceiling window, staring out at the view of the stretching shore and limitless sky. I left him to his thoughts and made us both coffees. I'd drunk most of mine by the time he turned to me, his face grave.

'Everything all right with you, Lizzy?' he said. 'Only Hazel said she was worried about your . . . behaviour. Mentioned you thought you'd been hearing things? Maybe even *seeing* things? Hazel is a very—'

'Just to be clear,' I interrupted, 'you're talking about that awful woman *you* brought into our lives?'

'Are you still playing that record?' His face took on an expression that actually hurt me; it was one of ill-concealed contempt. 'You're unreal, sis, you know that? You should hear yourself sometimes.'

'Hazel is sly and devious,' I told him. 'She's interfering with Dad's finances, and you're okay with that?'

'According to you, they couldn't be much worse.'

He remained silent for a long moment, staring straight at me. Watching him, I realised how much he had changed. He was jowly, unshaven, and his eyes were flat and cynical.

'What's happened to you, Colin?' I said. 'Where's my big brother gone?'

He snorted with derision. 'I could say the same to you, Lizzy.' He set down his coffee, untouched. 'I didn't want to raise this, but I can't get past the doubt. I can't let it fester any longer.'

Doubt? What's he talking about?

I thought I recognised the look on his face, and I didn't like it. Accusation mixed with suspicion. Like Mitch's face – just before he sacked me.

'This was on your laptop.' He took out his phone and brandished the screen at me, like an officer might brandish his ID just before arresting someone. 'Can you explain?'

There, on the cracked screen, was a photo of my open laptop. Displaying a website that read: NEED CASH RIGHT AWAY? APPLY NOW!

'Money troubles, huh?' said Colin.

'I've never seen this website before,' I said, and that was true. Even when my addiction had been at its worst, I'd never turned to moneylending websites.

His eyes sharpened. 'You don't remember sending me this picture?'

'I didn't send it to you!' That was God's own truth.

'Except you *did*,' he replied, showing me the screen again, and I held my breath in shock.

Sure enough, where it said 'sender', my name and number were clearly visible.

I felt my heart quicken and my face flush. Of course he wanted to know: why the hell was his sister – successful, established, professional Elizabeth – looking at the websites of predatory moneylenders? The only problem was, I couldn't remember ever having done that!

The room began to spin then. This couldn't be right. How could I have forgotten? *How?* Was I losing my mind?

'You were so quick to ask me what happened to Dad's money, weren't you? So keen.'

'Colin, you can't seriously think I had anything to do—'

'You think you're telling me the truth now,' he cut in. 'Just like you thought you left me that voicemail that never arrived.'

How calm he seemed. There was no righteous indignation in his tone, and somehow that was worse, because it meant he had thought about how to do this, how to confront me. He was prepared for me to be defensive, prepared for any excuses. He'd thought about what to say if I denied it.

'Can I see your bank account?' he asked now.

'You're not going to bully me,' I snapped, wishing I could show him my bank account, but knowing I couldn't. 'Did Sandra put you up to this?' I could just imagine that common blonde drip-feeding him doubts as she painted her plastic nails.

'If she has access to his account, she has access to his funds. How much is left, how is she spending it? Where've the savings gone? If she hasn't pissed them all away yet, she will soon. You've got to confront her, Colin. Be a man for once in your life and stand up to her!'

'You're better than this,' I said, watching him go to the fridge and help himself to a beer. Drinking so early? Not reassuring! 'You can trust me.'

'You say that, Lizzy, and yet the money *is* gone.' A fizz as he snapped open his beer. 'Can't pretend I'm not worried about you, sis. And so is Hazel.'

Then it hit me. I wasn't crazy. This was *her*. The wicked, malicious bitch. How simple it would have been for her to get online, visit that site and snap a few pictures on my phone, then send them to Colin. This was Hazel administering her special concoction of slow poison. In this glasshouse relationship of ours, she was seizing control.

'Colin, listen to me,' I said urgently. 'This wasn't me – it was Hazel. She's trying to drive us apart.'

Suddenly, a voice behind me: 'Oh, not at all, pet.'

I almost jumped out of my skin. Hazel was climbing to the top of the stairs. For how long she'd been eavesdropping, I wasn't sure.

'I only mentioned to Colin that I was concerned for your well-being. What with all your paranoia recently, and those weird sounds you heard – or *think* you heard . . .'

'Stay away from me,' I said.

She adopted a sweetly condescending tone. 'You're imagining things. It's like I said, Lizzy, anyone involved with a sufferer of dementia becomes part of their confusion, in the end.'

'Shut up,' I said, 'just shut up.'

'When their world is so skewed, how can we not get caught up in it? Inevitably when you're caring for someone with dementia, your worlds become hopelessly blurred. It's awfully sad, I know, but can't you see that's what's happening to you?'

At her side now, Colin was nodding. 'Just listen to Hazel, Lizzy, will you?'

Infuriated, frustrated, I started shaking my head and backing away from them both. My heart was hammering to a frightening rhythm; all I wanted to do was flee.

'We've been so worried about you,' she went on, 'I was half tempted to call Doctor Strickland for his advice. Think I should do that, Lizzy? You've been under *such* strain.'

'SCREW YOUR STRAIN!' I yelled, and in rage threw my mug at the floor, where it shattered into jagged cuts of blue and white porcelain.

That momentary loss of temper that she had provoked in me was all Hazel needed to give Colin a look that chilled me to the core. Knowing and reproachful. A look that said: *'You see, I told you she was losing it . . .'*

I flung the front door wide open. Needed fresh air. Freedom. To be anywhere Hazel wasn't.

What does she want? Why is she torturing me?

On the beach, the wind pushed against me, as if urging me back, but I pressed on across the shingle, passing tide-breakers and the line of white shells trailing away from Dumb Boy Cottage. I walked on and on, until I came to a halt at the edge of the dark water, gazing across at the thin line of the horizon broken by the shape of early Cold War relics rising from the ground and bulking against the sky. Those rusting structures. From here, I could almost hear them rattling in the wind.

The crash of the waves made me focus. At my feet was a smooth memorial stone inscribed with the words:

FROM THIS QUAY MEN & WOMEN
CROSSED THE RIVER ORE
TO SERVE THEIR COUNTRY.

Bill's warning to me in his letter: *'Places like that are generally best left alone.'* He might have been right, but why?

It was natural to wonder. Plenty of birdwatchers and botanists crossed to the Ness, didn't they? It couldn't be all that unsafe, surely. Not if you kept to the concrete paths laid down by the army. And hadn't most of the unexploded debris been cleared away? Probably.

So what's the danger over there?

As the isolation of that desolate spot wrapped itself around me, time seemed to thicken, slow down. It was as if the ages were reaching for me. I closed my eyes for a moment and saw those abandoned structures looming large in my mind, temples to science, with the pits Bill said were deeper than hell, tempting me, drawing me.

Then something sliced through my mental vision. A cold shadow dropped over me. I had heard the phrase, 'it was like someone stepped on my grave', but I had never truly understood it. Until now.

Help me. Find me.

For a moment, I could almost hear the voices of the young men who had once served their country over there, calling to me across the water. Across the decades.

Stop. That's all in your mind, and you know it.

I told myself so. But that wasn't enough to stop the air feeling unnaturally still and colder than ever. A nagging sense of curiosity, of adventure, intruded on me. And then, as if arranged for me by fate, my attention was drawn to an empty, neglected-looking boat that was bobbing nearby. Tiny. From the looks of it, a little ferry boat for no more than six or eight passengers.

Abandoned, I thought, eyeing its warped, peeling boards.

But I was wrong about that. Because then, I noticed there was a woman in waders in the water, submerged up to her waist. Until now she had been out of sight, behind the boat. Now she was at the rear of the craft, giving it a good scrubbing down.

She was in her sixties, I guessed, and she looked strong, her face tinged red from the cold. She looked like she had grown up beneath these vast Suffolk skies and would probably live out her days here.

At the sound of my footsteps, she turned and smiled at me pleasantly, as if she was pleased at the opportunity to talk with someone, and in turn I introduced myself.

'Susan Winter,' she said pleasantly, wading out of the water. She stuck out a frozen but friendly hand.

I remembered something Bill had told me and now joined the dots. *They're building a museum I hear. Come summer, there'll be a boat running.*

It was a conversation starter. Yes, she confirmed, her work concerned the new military museum on the Ness, which should be up and running some time next year. Her job, she said, rather cryptically, was to keep an eye on its development. She was heading over there now.

I had a flash of my dream then. The shore at twilight as my father gazed sadly towards Orford Ness. That thought led to another, one that had me remembering the books and newspaper cuttings that Hazel had concealed in the drawer under her bed.

If the Ness was a source of fascination to her, then I needed to know why. I suppose we're all fascinated to some extent by abandoned places. Towns. Hospitals. Tunnels. Perhaps this was the extent of her interest. Except I wasn't convinced of that. Not even nearly. Call it a hunch, if you like; because that's what it was. A strong hunch.

'Don't suppose I could come along?' I asked.

'Members of the public really aren't permitted until—'

'Promise I'll be no trouble,' I assured her, and a useful lie occurred to me. 'I know the Ness pretty well, actually, my father used to take me out there as a child. He's not been well.'

Perhaps she was tired of making the trip alone, or maybe it was compassion for the sadness in my voice. Whatever her reason, I was grateful when she agreed, on one condition: I was to do as she said and not wander off.

'Fine by me.'

Next to the boat's steering wheel was a small waterproof container. Susan clipped it open. Inside was a key for the engine. I was mildly surprised it wasn't better protected; but then again, such was its shabbiness, this wasn't the sort of boat I imagined many people would be inclined to steal.

As we launched into the water, I raised my face to the wind and salty sea spray. Liberated. That's how I felt. Unshackled, for the first time since coming home to this bleak, wind-blasted spot.

It took maybe ten minutes to make the crossing. I observed her steering the boat with confidence, her right hand on the throttle. And struck up a conversation. 'What exactly is your role with the museum?'

Susan looked as if she wasn't entirely comfortable with this topic. 'There's a lot out there still to be cleaned up,' she said, 'the detritus of decades of military tests.'

'You mean unexploded ordnance?'

'That's part of it. Everything from machine guns to bomb ballistics was tested there.' She pursed her lips. They were tinged blue from the cold, I noticed, which meant mine probably were, too. I decided to try levelling with her.

'A friend of mine believes that the Ness is haunted,' I said lightly.

She flicked me a glance. 'Is that right?'

'Funny what some people believe, huh?'

Susan was quiet for a moment. Then she said, 'It's such a unique and extraordinary place that in all honesty, I wouldn't be completely surprised if there is something strange at the Ness. Several of the workmen say they've heard inexplicable sounds.' She gave a speculative shrug. 'I can only explain what I've experienced.'

'Oh?'

'Well, I spend a lot of time on the Ness. And you know what's funny? Don't see many birds there any more; and if you do, you never hear them sing.'

I felt a chill at that; waited for her to go on.

'There's a sadness there; no doubt about it. Some tragedies gnaw at the present, that's what I think. There are some places like the Ness, where the darkness and the sadness of the past never quite lets go. So much pain in one location is bound to leave a mark.' She shrugged. 'If that's what "haunted" means, then your friend may well be right.'

'Has it always felt that way to you? Sad?'

She shook her head. 'I wouldn't say so. Mysterious? It's always felt that; secret old places, particularly if they're abandoned, usually have an enigmatic air about them, right? But the sadness is new to me. The Ness has been sleeping with its memories for so long now, and sometimes I wonder if the new renovations might just have woken it up a little.' She smiled; shook her head. 'But that's just silly talk, right?'

'Maybe.' Given that she'd opened up a little, I decided to push it and ask again, 'What's the exact nature of your work?'

She looked away towards the approaching shoreline. I've wondered since about what she said next. And why she said it. Certainly, she could have chosen not to answer my question or just as easily palmed me off with a lie. Perhaps she was just lonely, or a skilled raconteur who hadn't known an interested audience for too long. Whatever her motivation for telling me, her answer aroused a deep response in me. The sharpest curiosity.

'When the military departed, they left various records behind. Documents. The kind our government would probably prefer had never existed.'

'Shouldn't they have been sent to the Public Record Office for eventual disclosure?'

'Oh my dear.' Susan gave me a look that made me feel not just idealistic but a little naive. 'What never existed never needs to be disclosed now, does it? Guess that's open government for you. When the old buildings on the Ness were made secure, some of the files, like everything else out there, were left to rot. The military have a phrase for this – "controlled ruination".'

'Isn't that a bit risky?'

'Not really. It was all sealed off until a few years back; a warren of tunnels and underground chambers. Now, with the museum on its way, proper precautions need to be taken.'

'Which is where you come in presumably?' I asked.

Susan didn't say yes. She didn't say no, either.

I thought of Bill, with his haunting shadowy suggestions of mysteries and perils. Bill saying something happened out here. Something the government worked very hard to bury; and that called up another memory: the roar of unseen aircraft, the eerie screams calling out to me from the darkness.

My imagination sketched a succession of unwelcome

pictures. Bloodied bodies. Young servicemen cut down in the prime of their lives. Reduced to burning corpses.

The cries of the dying, was that what I had heard that night on the shore?

'What's in these files?' I asked, but Susan only gave an evasive shrug.

'They pay me to retrieve them; not to read them.'

'Not even a peek?' I asked doubtfully.

'Nope.' She held my gaze. 'I do as any dutiful citizen would do.'

'And what's that?'

The tiniest smile touched the corners of her lips.

'I avert my eyes.'

The waves were slapping against the jetty as I clambered out of the boat, and I was grateful to Susan as she held out a hand of support. But the moment we set foot on that grey terrain, I gave an involuntary shudder, for it felt to me that we had arrived in a different country. On every side were derelict military relics surrounded by tank tracks and circles of bomb craters. I saw rusting rails and tangled metal, pad-locked doors, a watchtower, crumbling red-bricked barracks and, in the distance, flat-topped bunkers. Here, beneath the gunmetal sky, we were at the edge of the world. Bill was spot-on; this was a dead place – yet it possessed a beauty that was both haunting and strange.

'So,' I said to Susan, 'where are you headed?'

She pointed across the marshy terrain towards one of the low bunkers. 'I need to see how the latest works on the museum are developing. Come with me?'

We walked for some ten minutes or more, taking care to stay

on the old concrete military road. There could still be unexploded munitions out here, Susan said, among the reeds and tall grass.

Sure enough, our path soon veered to run adjacent to a chain-link fence and here a sign nailed to a tree read:

> PLEASE KEEP OUT. THIS SITE IS NOT OPEN TO THE PUBLIC. ALL THE STRUCTURES ARE VERY UNSAFE: THERE MAY BE A RISK FROM CONTAMINATION AND UNEXPLODED ORDNANCE.

Beyond the fence were the aircraft hangars. Bunkers and barbed wire spread out around the ghost of a runway. Rusting structures left to rot were now lonely homes for nesting gulls.

'Would you like to see the new museum?' she asked, and I almost said yes. What stopped me was the urge to explore. It was the same nagging curiosity that had first drawn me to the boat, except I felt it more keenly now.

'I'd like some time alone,' I said, 'if you don't mind.'

'Reflecting on childhood adventures, huh?'

I nodded. 'Something like that.'

'All right,' Susan said, 'I'll be ten minutes or so. Wait for me here?'

I nodded, and then, with a mixture of nervousness and curiosity, I watched her go and thought of the many oddities that had accompanied my return to Shingle Street: the vivid dreams of a burning sea; the unaccountable noises at night; the intrusion of felt but unseen presences.

I supposed that the lingering scent of rosemary also counted as an oddity, but not in the same way as the thunderous deafening roar of an unseen plane, or disembodied voices.

Were these, I wondered, the residues of things past – the shadows of things that had been?

And what of my persistent dreams, in which my father appeared to me as a young man – distracted, and so fixated with this forbidden territory? Even Hazel seemed fascinated.

I needed to know why.

Looking back, I wonder what Susan thought of me as she walked away; if she wondered about my real motivation for wanting to explore the Ness, and if she purposefully indulged my curiosity. After all, my reference to alleged hauntings had hardly been subtle and, in her own way, she too had said more, perhaps, than she ought. About the history of secret goings-on. I suspect that she knew just as much about those as she did the rumours of paranormal occurrences, and maybe she was trying to tell me something, or at least facilitate me finding something out.

Only when she was out of sight did I start walking again, leaving the concrete path and heading quickly out over the brackish wetlands, knowing time was short. I knew this was wrong, that I was breaking a promise, but I was on autopilot now. As if someone were – what? Guiding me?

Soon, I came to a high security gate, badly rusted, almost hanging off its hinges. It was flanked by a guard shack whose roof had fallen in and whose shattered windows were like blinded eyes.

I was standing in the shadow thrown by the square watchtower that rose up at the corner of this compound. Covered in red rust and broken in parts, it did not look remotely safe. The stairs attached to the side of the tower seemed perilously unsteady and the whole structure creaked and rattled in the wind.

And yet the idea that I should climb it was irresistible.

I started forward. I would climb right to the top, to the guard cabin, because . . . why? I could not say, and that fact bothered me immensely – until it didn't. Because what came over me then was a sense of unreality. My feet were leading me as if they had a mind of their own, and I felt detached. Outside of myself.

I put my foot on the first step and heard it creak. Felt it shake. *Definitely not safe*, I thought. And yet, still, I felt that the right thing to do, the only thing to do, was climb up.

Oddly, I can't remember what must have been a slippery and freezing climb; I only know that I *did* climb, because my next memory is of standing at the top, on the watchtower's outer platform. I gripped the rusted railing as I surveyed the stretch of bleak marshland and shingle, the rows of armament barracks, the double fences coiled with razor wire, all languishing beneath the heavy skies of East Anglia.

I have never known such utter loneliness. And then the certainty came over me that I was *supposed* to be standing here, now, at this moment, three storeys up at the top of the watchtower.

What gave me that feeling was something I hadn't expected. So many emotions sweeping over me, and none of them welcome. Not fear, but some inexplicable sadness that seemed to permeate the frigid air. More than sadness. A crushing impression of suffering and bereavement. These feelings held me, confused and puzzled, unable to move, not knowing why I should be feeling such wretched, extreme misery.

A voice in my head suddenly, no more than a whisper:
Find me. Help me.

Gooseflesh rippled over me as I felt, with conviction, that I was no longer alone. I looked around, but saw no one.

It can't be. It's just you and Susan out here. Just you and her.

'There's no need to be afraid,' I said to myself.

But then, over the whine of the wind, I heard the whisper of a voice. Not in my head, but behind me.

Turning sharply, I stared at the rusted door that led into the watchtower cabin. It was ajar.

'Hello?' I called. 'Is someone there?'

Nothing.

I stepped nearer, again feeling as though the action wasn't entirely my own. Looked at the decrepit cabin and its shattered windows, and hesitated.

Then I pushed on the door.

It creaked open. That sound felt like an invitation to enter. I stepped through into the musty space beyond and was confronted by the nauseating stench of stale air. Flaking walls stripped entirely bare except for a solitary old-style black telephone that hung from one corner, festooned in dust and spiderwebs.

Like the rest of the base, this guard tower had been left to decay among the lagoons, brambles and foliage. I had to wonder: how many men had kept a lonely vigil up here? How many had been thanked for their duty?

Were any of them still alive?

I turned. There wasn't much else to see – floorboards thick with dust and broken glass, a single chair toppled on to one side.

I should leave. Susan would be waiting.

Then my gaze snagged on the opposite wall and the mark

there. A handprint dragged through dust, no more than the faintest outline, only dimly discernible. But still, unmistakably, a handprint.

Help me. Find me.

That voice, no more than a sigh on the wind.

I ought to have got out then. I ought to have gone down the slippery metal steps and found Susan. Instead I remained, drawn nearer to the wall.

As I studied that handprint, the sadness I had felt outside returned, except now it was heavier, oppressive. There was some meaning here, I felt, some long-ago tragedy to be known and understood. And that chilled me to the core.

I whispered into the musty air, 'Hello?'

An extraordinary hush settled around me; not even the cry of the wind or the distant waves intruded. It was as if I had stepped into another time or place. And in that silence there was a vibration: the ghostly impression of something intangible and unseen.

But present.

Find me. Help me.

I had an irrepressible urge to lay my own hand over that print on the wall.

There was a sudden metallic sound behind me, the unmistakable clang of metal hitting the concrete surface below. And it came just as my hand moved towards the handprint. I whirled, my eyes widening in fright.

As I stood there, listening intensely and hearing only my quickening pulse, something came over me, a cold that spread through my body, stiffening my limbs, tightening my throat. It brought with it a feeling of utter helplessness – the way I had felt moments ago on the ground when I felt compelled to climb this structure. My feet had seemed to lead me to the top of this guard tower.

And now it was happening again. I felt as if I was being forced by someone, or something, to walk out to the edge of the guard tower platform. To get as close as possible to the edge, to that gap where the rusted railing was broken and had long ago fallen away.

The pull felt both deliberate and cruel and I felt oddly much, much younger. As if I was a teenager again?

Yes, that was it. What came to mind as I started walking were dim and distant memories of public humiliation. Playground visions from my childhood: the verbal attacks; taunts from kids forcing me to try a cigarette, making me inhale until I coughed and coughed and finally was sick like a dog; a particularly spiteful girl throwing a rock at my back as I ran away, knocking me to my knees on the concrete, where I hunched over and sobbed as they laughed.

These were torments I hadn't thought about since I was a kid, since before Mum died. Now they were all too horribly lucid – and why? What was it about this tower that could bring such horrors to the surface?

Outside, there was a panoramic view of the spit and the estuary and my father's home on the distant shore, but I had eyes only for the broken railing. I was so close to the edge now. How easy it would be to take one more step . . .

A voice called out from below. 'Lizzy? Lizzy! It's me, Susan! What the hell are you doing up there?'

Startled, I leaped back from the edge. It must have been the sheer alarm in her voice that wrenched me out of that state, and all at once the present returned, the bellow of the wind loud in my ears again.

But I could not deny what I had felt at the top of the watch-tower. *Something terrible happened here*, I thought, moving towards the stairs.

Whatever it was, someone, or something, wants you to know.

– 10 –

THE HAUNTING
OF BILL DURRANT

'It's kind of you to see me,' I called to Bill. I had spent the day resting, feeling inexplicably drained by my uncanny experience on the Ness. It was early evening now, around half past seven, and I was indescribably relieved to be warm and feel welcome, beside a crackling fire, in the rustic front room of Dumb Boy Cottage.

'No trouble,' Bill called back from the adjoining kitchen. 'Milk with your coffee?'

'No thanks!'

I'd always thought that milk (as well as cheese) made me dream more, and in my agitated state, I had no wish to do that; I was still feeling confused and shaken from earlier.

I was relieved that Bill had finally returned from London; relieved also that his sister was better now after recovering from what he said had been a 'minor operation'. Although from the concern in his voice I'm not sure I really believed it was so minor.

While I waited for him, I surveyed my surroundings. Unlike our Martello tower, this cottage had never been modernised to maximise light, so the atmosphere was rather gloomy. Cosy, though, despite the fraying brown carpet and exposed red-brick walls. I was sitting in a low, overstuffed brown chair next to a wooden chest that served as a makeshift coffee table. Directly in front of me was a smeared single-paned window that looked onto the beach. It was rattling and shuddering in its frame. You could smell the salt air as clearly as you could hear the slow collapse of the waves outside.

The shore, murmuring its secrets.

'You know,' I called, 'there's an intriguing tale about how this house got its name.'

'Oh?'

I nodded, remembering one of the stories the kids loved telling me at school just to freak me out.

'Well, if you believe the tales,' I said, 'one filthy night some hundred years back, a kid living here saw some smugglers out on the beach. When the old rogues caught up with him, they didn't want him talking, so they . . .'

'Cut out his tongue?'

'Exactly.'

I heard Bill in the kitchen chuckling to himself. Understandably. That yarn sounded very much like folklore to me. 'Stories like that grow with the telling,' I said.

'Oh, most likely,' he answered, treading back into the room and carrying a tray with a coffee pot and two steaming mugs. 'But who knows, eh? Remote. Sparsely populated. This stretch of coast was a natural haunt for smugglers. Still is. Within these few square miles you'll find places drenched with folklore – devilish black dogs; witchcraft; mysterious lights over Rendlesham Forest.'

He handed me a mug, his eyes glimmering darkly as they caught the glow from the crackling flames. 'Growing up here,

I dare say you've heard your fair share of those tales, but I can guarantee you won't have heard them all.'

He was right; I had heard many tales; but knowing about them wasn't the same as giving them credence, and I thought about telling him I didn't believe in the supernatural, despite all that I'd experienced. But what would have been the point in doing that? I had come here for his honest opinion, so I had to be prepared to hear it, however unlikely it sounded and however uncomfortable it made me feel.

'Go on, Bill.'

Having made himself comfortable in the armchair opposite me, he explained: 'I take the world as I find it, with an open mind. I look at the evidence, not what I want to believe.'

'What *do* you believe?'

He looked at me darkly, and I was again reminded of my initial impression: a fisherman, or a sailor. With his rough beard and thick grey woollen sweater, he seemed to inhabit the part, especially in this house. Nonetheless, I was glad he was neither of those things, because it was his enigmatic stories that had drawn me here; my impression, if you like, of his expertise.

'You said before that the normal rules of reality don't apply out here. What did you mean?'

'Time works differently here,' he said in a low voice. 'Moves more slowly. Matters less. Some people can feel it, some can't. But you know when you do. It's unmistakable; a sensation that slips coldly into your mind. A sort of nameless dread.'

His words made my skin prickle. 'Look, the thing is, Bill, I need your advice on something that happened to me earlier. Actually, more than one thing,' I added, remembering the phantom explosions, the cries for help on the wind. 'I've tried, but

I can't explain it. Something . . . I've never experienced before. Something really, really weird . . .'

'You went to the Ness, didn't you?' he asked knowingly.

I nodded, picturing the rusting rails and tangled metal, the padlocked doors, the derelict watchtower. I gave an involuntary shudder.

'And?'

What I wanted to say was: *Something called me there*. But that was fantastical, wasn't it?

After a moment, Bill said, 'Listen, Lizzy, you can tell me anything, okay?'

And in that cosy room before the fire, with his kind eyes on mine, I felt like I could share this, that it would be a relief to confide in him. So, as if some mental floodgate had opened, the details of what had happened out on the Ness came spilling out of me. I told him how I had felt drawn there, how I had been compelled to climb the guard tower and afterwards not remembered doing so. I told him how I had been sure I was not alone up there, and I described the whisper on the wind, the sound of breaking metal and the single handprint on the grime-encrusted wall. The only part I left out, because I was embarrassed that I had almost harmed myself, was the terrifying compulsion that had forced me to stand so close to the edge of the watchtower platform, by the broken railing.

I sipped my coffee, savouring its jarring bitterness, and listened to the fire crackle and spit as Bill said nothing for a few long moments.

'Quite a tale,' he said finally, pouring another mug of coffee, and I couldn't help wondering if it would taste a little better laced with a warming slug of brandy. 'So, what would you like me to say?' he asked. 'You want me to explain it? Debunk it?'

'I just need to *make sense* of it,' I said. 'According to Hazel, my father has been experiencing unusual happenings. Or thinks he has.'

'Tell me about your father, was he good with people?'

I hesitated. You think you know someone. You hope, of all people, you'd know your dad, right? But how many of us really know our parents? I mean, who was he before I was born? Where was he when I was born? Why were there so few pictures of him in his early twenties? In fact, I'm not sure I'd seen any.

'I wish I could tell you he was an easy man. But he chose to live in a disused Martello tower. That tells you how sociable he was. Hazel asked me if he was afraid of something here, said he'd been hearing voices, inexplicable sounds, but she's adamant it's all in his head. So, what if I'm also imagining things? Because this has happened before, Bill, in my old life, in London. Sometimes I did things I later regretted, and I forgot about them. Perhaps now I'm doing the same—'

'You shouldn't doubt yourself,' Bill cut in, and put down his mug. 'What I'm about to say might sound fantastic, and if you want to call me crazy, go right ahead; I won't be offended, all right? But I won't lie to you, either. I think you know it, anyway.'

I met his gaze. 'Tell me. Please.'

'Okay. I can't claim to know everything that happened on the Ness. But I do know there were accidents. Tragic ones. Innocent men perished in the name of a greater cause. The lethality was brutal. And not all the experiments on the Ness were documented. As you probably know, during the war, Shingle Street was evacuated and marked out for bombing target practice. Dangerous as hell. What you may not know is that dozens of young airmen were fatally injured in the most appalling ways imaginable. Not sure I believe some of the wilder tales, but this coastline has its secrets, and the powers that be have worked hard to keep it that way.'

'You mean the government?'

He nodded. 'Bombs were dropped. A great many lives were lost. So many that no one spoke of it for a long time. No one could.'

I shivered. Through the window, I could hear the suck of the waves over the shingle, the wind playing a haunting note.

'Exactly how many deaths are we talking, Bill?'

He frowned deeply. 'A year after the outbreak of war, something happened here. Something no one from around here ever forgot. Probably the locals don't talk about "the graveyard" because it's easier to pretend it's not there. Like a community living with a shameful secret. Talking about it only gives it importance. But pretending it's not there diminishes it; takes away its power. And Orford Ness has much of that, believe me. Even though it's uninhabited now.

'Whatever you experienced at the top of that guard tower is a mystery, to be sure, and not one I can explain. But I've had experiences like it. I've heard things out here, as I'm sure you have. Echoes from long ago. The secret sounds of Orford Ness.'

He took a breath. 'I believe that this shore is a domain for the living, and for the dead.'

'You're saying Shingle Street is *haunted*?'

His answer was coldly sobering. 'I'm saying it would be strange if it wasn't.'

Bill leaned forward in his chair, and his next words made my flesh creep. 'There are secrets buried here, Lizzy. Truths. Injustices. Unsettled scores.'

I thought of the memorial stone at the edge of the small river that separated Shingle Street from Orford Ness, remembered those eerie muffled detonations.

'Is it true that the beach was mined? There was a legend, something about a Nazi invasion?'

'The chances of invasion were high, especially on this shore. No German soldier could ever set foot on British soil.'

'So what did they do?'

'A scenario was devised. Ingenious, but horrific. The burning of oil on a grand scale. A sea of fire.' He gazed out of the window, towards the shore. 'Summer 1940, there was an invasion. German landing craft were attacked by flame barrages. Hundreds of bodies. Burned. German soldiers drifting into shore. Dead men, young men; their faces burned off.' Now he fixed his eyes on me. 'The sea raged with flames,' he said grimly. 'According to some, the waters were boiling.'

His gravelly voice and low, chocolatey tones would have guaranteed him a very generous audio-book deal. And I'd met plenty of clients in my old life who were more than happy to make up tales to ingratiate themselves, or to grab a headline or two. It could be that he was nothing more than a lonely storyteller who was grateful for an audience.

Flooding the sea with flammable fuel? To me that sounded like a rather crude and unreliable form of defence. I tried picturing the sea ablaze, a sheet of flaming oil, the dense clouds of choking black smoke billowing thousands of feet into the sky. Even if enough oil was fired onto the surface of the water, wouldn't it eventually burn out? And what was to stop the enemy from waiting for it to do just that? And did we even have the technology in 1940 to set the sea on fire?

But when I brought to mind my nightmare of the burning sea, I was bound to wonder if there was a connection here.

Hoped there wasn't. Because that would mean – what, exactly? That I heard things other people didn't? That I was psychic? Sensitive? Were those even the right words?

'Another urban myth?' I asked, testing Bill. There was strength in his assertions, the information boiling up inside him; a volcano of passion. Either it came from his imagination, or from decades of research.

'It happened!' he said grittily, and his face hardened. 'Or something *like* it happened. And I know, because I've scoured this shore for too many years, and I've found exactly what you'd expect to find – pieces of molten metal, jewellery, ammunition. German tunic buttons.'

I flinched at that, felt a brief pulse of anxiety, without entirely knowing why. Something he had said resonated with me, and for a single instant I was taken back to my youth. To Rendlesham Forest, with Nick. And the day things got weird in the woods.

I shook the memory off and asked what I really wanted to know: 'Was the Nazi invasion ever proven?'

He shook his head. 'The government denies all knowledge, but you won't be surprised to learn that there's a block on public access to the Shingle Street file at the Public Record Office.'

Bill was a believer, I realised now. An ardent believer. For whatever reason, he had a unique way of seeing things, almost as if he were tuned in to some wavelength that crackled with voices only he could hear. Overall, the effect was as unsettling as it was intriguing.

What convinced him? What was it about the shore that fascinated him, that rooted him here?

'It's to do with your shell line, isn't it?' I said.

The fire crackled, but Bill said nothing, only looked back at me with those inscrutable eyes.

'Bill, you said before that I wasn't the first to come here hoping to find myself. What did you mean?'

Finally, he drew a breath and said, 'As you may have sensed, I'm searching. You asked me about the shell line. Fact is, I lay those shells to honour the memory of my son.' He pointed to a framed picture of a sandy-haired teenager with bright blue eyes. 'Mark. Sixteen when he died. Drowned. Six years ago. Here, on Shingle Street.'

Of course, I remembered now; my father had told me about that when it happened. A tragedy. It had been in all the local newspapers. 'Bill, I'm so sorry.'

'Oh, no,' he said, grim-faced. 'I'm the one who should be sorry. You see, I saw it coming. And I failed him. In the worst possible way for a father to fail his son.'

What was this? What was he telling me?

'You were afraid Mark would harm himself?'

He stared at me, and I saw tears in his eyes. 'This was no ordinary tragedy, Lizzy – if such a thing exists.' His voice cracked. 'I did nothing. Even though the evidence of my senses told me all I needed to know . . .' He shook his head. 'I should have *acted*.'

'I'm sure you did all you could—'

'If I tell you, will you listen with an open mind?'

I nodded.

'Open heart surgery,' he said flatly, and patted the centre of his chest. 'Too many cigarettes, too many ignored doctors' warnings. When Mark went, I was flat on my back. Under the knife. Unconscious.' His eyes flashed. 'Until I wasn't.'

I looked questioningly at him. 'Sorry, I'm not sure I understand?'

'Maybe they didn't give me enough anaesthetic; or maybe they gave me too much; whatever caused it, I woke up just at the moment they cracked my chest open.'

'Oh my God, Bill—'

'Except I wasn't *on* the table any more. I was *outside* of my body, rising up and looking down at myself – on the damn operating table!'

I fell silent for a moment. This I hadn't expected, not even nearly, but that's not to say I wasn't fascinated – I was. Mostly because he struck me as a very stable, very serious man. With gentle incredulity, I asked if it was possible he had experienced some sort of hallucination.

He took a breath. 'Like you, I tried to rationalise it, even as I was floating up there on the ceiling, looking down on myself, I thought I must have stopped breathing, that I had died; but I could hear the surgeons talking calmly and the heart monitor beeping away.'

He raked a hand through his mop of grey curls. 'I realise how this must sound; crazy, right? But every word is true.'

'What did it feel like?' I asked.

'Honestly? For a moment, it was peaceful, utterly serene, as if time was standing still, and I felt as light as a feather. And then . . .' He swallowed. 'And then there was a lot of movement suddenly. The heart monitor was beeping faster and the surgeons were barking orders. Yeah, something was wrong all right, and the worse it got, the higher I seemed to float. I tried calling for help, of course I did, well wouldn't you? But speaking wasn't possible; the soul has no voice, Lizzy. No need of breathing too. At that moment, I was nothing but air and light.

'And suddenly, I was floating *through* the ceiling, until I was no longer in the operating theatre but outside, drifting under the stars and gliding over the countryside, towards this shore.'

His eyes widened with the memory.

'I saw it all, so vividly. The Martello tower, the fishermen's cottages; this very cottage. And for the first time in my life, I had an understanding of the universe beyond the everyday, comprehended its enormity. By now I was terrified, worried I wouldn't get back to my body, or even worse, that I had died during the surgery.

'Then I looked down and saw a figure ahead of me, just standing there, motionless on the shingle.'

An icy chill brushed my neck. 'Your son?'

He nodded. 'I didn't realise at first. He had his back to me. I began moving, *floating*, towards him, thinking whoever he was, he needed help. Call it a gut reaction. The closer I got . . . I saw he was distraught, bawling his eyes out.'

His voice cracked again and he shook his head as if in desperate denial. 'I realised that it was my boy. It was Mark, of that I have no doubt. Tears streaming down his face, just staring off into the black waves. Utterly oblivious to my presence. You see, we lived not far from here.

'A few weeks earlier, Mark and I had taken a walk here. He said he had something to tell me. He told me he was gay, or thought he might be. I wish I could say I reacted calmly and respectfully, but . . .' He tailed off, bowing his head. 'It was a shock, an adjustment for any parent. I'm sorry to say I didn't handle it well.'

'Oh, my goodness . . .'

'I should have connected with him, heart to heart. Told him I loved him no matter what. That night, out of my body, watching him on the beach, I saw to my horror what he intended to do.

The terrible inevitability of it. God bless his soul; like watching a car crash in slow motion.'

I swallowed, not sure I wanted to hear the rest, not sure telling this story was doing Bill any favours.

'Look, Bill, if this is too pain—'

'As my boy staggered towards the waves, I knew that he would drown himself. And I knew what had led him to do such an awful thing, I knew only too well. By then I was praying he would see me, *hear* me as I shouted silently for him to stop. Just *stop*! But he broke into a run, charging into the water, then wading in, deeper.' He shook his head, distressed. 'Oh, my boy. It must have been freezing. For a moment, a sort of understanding came onto his face. He looked stricken with fear and panic. In that moment I realised he had changed his mind, that he wanted to live – and he began to thrash about, shrieking for help as he went under.' He looked at me, grim with grief.

'Oh Bill,' I said, blinking back my own tears. It was a sad and shocking story.

'I wasn't just seeing all of this from outside of my body, but feeling it, too. The terror, the pull of the waves, the pain as his toenails were ripped off as he dug his feet into the stones in a hopeless attempt to anchor himself.' He took a shuddering breath. 'He had the shoreline in his view, but it was too late, the sea was claiming him. I could taste the salt; I could even feel the blows from those hard, heavy waves. The horror of it I can barely convey to you; the inevitability of my son's death. After a few seconds, one tremendous wave struck him head on. Pulled him under.'

He dipped his head and sat that way for a long time, trembling, gripping the side of his armchair. I wanted to get up and offer him some support, maybe a hand on his shoulder.

What stopped me were his eyes. Detached. Drifting. Outside, you could hear the waves crashing in. Bill's mental gaze, I knew, was fully focused on them now, and I had no desire to startle him out of his reverie.

I made us more coffee, then joined him next to the fire, sitting close to the flames to draw comfort from the heat. As I waited for Bill to go on, I pondered what he had told me. Several aspects of the extraordinary tale intrigued me: common themes like leaving the body, floating, looking down on himself on the operating table. Bill's account was remarkably detailed, but what did he think actually happened? Had his mind and body separated? Had Bill actually left his body and watched his son drown in real time?

I was open-minded, not completely convinced, but it was clear *he* believed it, and that was curious.

I waited in silence until he came back and raised his gaze to me.

'I awoke on the ward,' he said. 'My operation had been a success but I was agitated and distressed. The doctors promised me what I'd seen couldn't be real. An illusion induced by misfiring neurons in the brain, they said, probably brought on by the anaesthesia. Perhaps because I was so weak, or maybe because I couldn't stand the idea that what I had seen had been real, I accepted their theory. Put the whole experience out of my mind, convinced myself that of course Mark hadn't drowned himself. Which must sound reckless to you?'

I shook my head. *The lies we tell ourselves.*

'Well,' he said grimly, 'it sure as hell sounds reckless to me now, looking back on it. The guilt, Lizzy, goodness me, I hope you never have to feel guilt like that.'

He lowered his head. 'It was days before the doctors

considered me strong enough to hear the truth – Mark was missing. There's a saying that the sea always gives up its dead, and so it was. A few days later, his shoes were washed ashore. A week later, they found his remains.'

On his ruddy cheeks, fresh tears glistened. 'They said I howled when they told me. Well, I don't remember much about that, and that's probably for the best. What I do remember is the cold, raw numbness. My world, everything I cared about, went black. To lose a son . . .' His voice cracked with emotion and he clapped a hand to his mouth.

And now I went to rise from my chair to cross the room, but he held up a hand, clearly trying to gather himself, and so I sat back.

'I'm so sorry, Bill,' I said, knowing the words weren't enough. 'But you can't blame yourself, you mustn't.'

'For a long time, I didn't search for answers,' he went on. 'People say "you'll believe it if you see it", but I didn't want to believe. Easier to think I had hallucinated the whole damned thing, that my son's death that night was just a coincidence.'

'Well, maybe it was,' I said gently.

'But eventually, I took early retirement and came back here, rented this house. It was as if Mark was calling me. Do you understand?'

I did. 'You had an impulse?'

'Exactly! The instant I crossed the same bridge you did, I felt like I had landed behind some emotional iron curtain. Christmas Day. No one about. I wandered up and down the beach for what seemed like an eternity, gazing out to sea, listening to the surf. And thinking of Mark. Yearning to bring him back, if only for a minute. To say sorry, to say goodbye. Soon I found the spot where he did it and decided there was no point carrying on. What right did I have to live when I had watched my son die and done nothing?'

His voice was husky now. Little more than a whisper.

'I took my rucksack, loaded it with the heaviest stones I could find, then strapped the damned thing onto my back.'

I could see him now, a lone figure at the water's edge, the wind crying over the stones.

'I was about to wade in, but I saw something that struck me as odd – a solitary white shell. Gleaming in the moonlight. Surreal. Like it wanted me to see it. All things considered, I'd have to say it was a sign. A very fortunate sign. Understand?'

I did. 'You lay the shell line to honour Mark's memory. It's your way of communicating with him.'

He nodded and gave me the saddest smile I think I've ever seen on a man's face. My soul ached for him.

'Picking up that shell, holding it, I knew Mark had meant for me to find it, you see? He was giving me a sign. I held that white shell next to my heart, feeling the weight of the stones in the rucksack on my back.'

I could hear the self-loathing in his voice, the self-reproach, and of course I empathised; it hadn't been so long since I'd contemplated taking my own life – I knew all too well what it meant to step up close to that line, and then to step back. To fear it.

'What did you do, Bill?'

'The only thing that I hoped could make a difference. Can you guess?'

I could. 'You said a prayer?'

'That's right; I got down on my knees and prayed to God to protect my son's blessed soul. I'll be honest, Lizzy, I'm not a religious man, never have been – but right then I meant every word, and I vowed that I would remain here, on this shore, until I found my boy again.'

It took me a moment to understand what he meant by that before the realisation hit me with a shiver: *He means found in the spiritual sense.*

Drying his eyes on the sleeve of his jumper, he said, 'Being here on Shingle Street gives me hope, do you see? And I'm telling you this because you deserve to know. In my research I have uncovered the most compelling evidence for the existence of life after death. Hard to believe, right? But there's a term for what happened to me,' he went on. 'An out-of-body experience. You know, during my surgery I saw things I couldn't possibly have seen – like the lead surgeon dropping a scalpel and reaching for a new one. Afterwards, they confirmed that was exactly what happened when I was flatlining – when I was technically dead! So, how could I have known? How?'

I shrugged. It was a good question.

'Science tells us that consciousness is created by the brain. But I'd gone into cardiac arrest. So when I was floating up on the ceiling, my brain wasn't even functioning. And if my brain wasn't functioning when I perceived true information, does that not suggest that consciousness and body can separate?

'I was compelled to answer that question, Lizzy. Because it seemed to me that my experience was extra-dimensional – it had to be. I drifted through a ceiling! Moved through time and space. Clear evidence for the existence of a soul that can leave a living body or even – just imagine – live on *after death*. Do you understand what I'm saying?'

I thought I did. 'You're still looking for your boy?'

He nodded firmly. 'I never got to say goodbye, and I'd do anything to see him again. I need proof. I need to understand

and I need him to know that I accept and love him no matter what. Nothing else matters to me, Lizzy, and if I'm here long enough, I believe I may see him again.'

I considered him, this educated, well-spoken man. Clearly, he was caught in the throes of grieving a loss. I remembered well, after Mum died, how that could derail you.

'I don't know, Bill,' I said. 'I believe things aren't right here, not even nearly, but it's hard to process.'

He nodded. 'I get that. But I'm not crazy, Lizzy. If I saw Mark from outside of my body, then why shouldn't he see me from outside of his? *After* death?' Bill leaned forward. 'And why couldn't others, too? The evidence for life after death is right here on this shore. The others – they're all around us. Sometimes, I hear the voices of the men who died here, I hear their screams. They want us to know what happened. Whatever injustices occurred out here need to be told. The dead insist upon it. I believe it's them you've heard, echoes of tragedies right here on this beach.'

'How is it possible that we could hear these sounds and others can't?' I asked.

'Not everyone can hear the dead,' he said quietly. 'But some have a gift, that's what I think. A mind like a radio that tunes in to frequencies inaccessible to most people. Stress, anxiety, trauma – they can make you more attuned. More sensitive. What about your helper?' Bill asked. 'Hazel? Has she heard what you've heard?'

'Not as far as I know,' I said. 'She thinks Dad is hallucinating. Delusional. One night I heard these strange sounds, explosions, and she dismissed them as by-products of seismic shifts . . . from the earthquake.'

Bill snorted in disdain. 'Know what I think? I think things get weird before earthquakes. It's as if the ground holds a secret it needs to get out, and some of us tune in to that. We sense it. Like an awful darkness, rising.'

I caught my breath at that. But then something made my mouth dry: I was remembering the books under Hazel's bed, the old military photographs.

'Perhaps she does know something,' I said. 'Perhaps she's here for the same reason you are – digging up the past?'

'Well, it deserves to be dug up,' Bill said. 'Some people believe that supernatural entities feed off fear. I don't know about that, but if it's possible, then it stands to reason that the occurrences on this shore may, over decades, have become self-perpetuating. How many, like yourself, like my own boy, poor Mark, have been drawn here by the sadness that has gone before? How many have felt the pull of that sadness and met their demise because of it?'

He looked at me earnestly, eyebrows raised, then nodded his head. 'I *must* know the sum of what has happened here.'

I got up out of the chair and Bill rose to stand with me. 'Listen, Lizzy, spirits of the dead haunt this shore – they exist. Can I show you something?'

'Sure.'

Two seconds later, he was scouring his bookcase. Except it wasn't a book he plucked from the shelf, but an old VCR tape.

'Makes me feel old,' I quipped, and I wasn't lying. 'You know we've gone digital?'

'Watch this.'

I was too curious not to. Because now the tape cassette was in the VCR machine, and it was whirling and clunking, and a grainy picture was on the TV screen. I stared at it. Bill smiled.

'Yeah, not what you're used to, I know, but at least this sort of footage can't be played with so easily as on a phone. The film you're about to see was shot some years ago.'

His eyes were riveted on the screen as the shore came into focus. 'Look there.' He pointed.

I did. Got up close to the screen and looked hard. I wanted to see something. I genuinely did. For my sake partly, but more for his. The poor guy had lost his son; who could blame him for wanting so fervently to believe?

But if he thought there was some evidence of his son's lingering soul on this tape, or evidence of any supernatural phenomena, he was sorely mistaken. A flurry of flickering images. Some hissing static. That was all I saw. A grainy window on the past.

'Bill . . .'

He was still staring at the screen, studying it intently. The dark shingle, the murky waves rolling in.

I understood. His son's death had shattered his life. Now he needed a narrative that made sense to him. I had no desire to be disrespectful but neither did I want to encourage a delusion.

'Bill, I'm sorry, I don't see any—'

And suddenly, there it was. A figure, just in front of one of the tide-breakers. Dark and still, and staring right at the camera.

You could see right through it.

'Oh my God,' I said, drawing in my breath sharply.

'Now you see,' Bill said, nodding, 'why I stay here, wanting to believe – and waiting to be haunted. Life and death meet in union on this shore. Never doubt that, Lizzy. There are other worlds beyond our own. The happenings here stretch back decades, restless souls that must be understood. Something happened here, I'm sure of it. There's a secret that must be known.'

A thrill of supernatural possibility ran through me.

'Help me,' he said. 'However awful it may be, please help me discover the truth.'

The bell buoy was clanging its haunting note when Bill escorted me home. By then, it was close to ten o'clock. Freezing. Luckily, at Bill's suggestion I had taken some brandy in my coffee, and I was grateful for the warm glow it gave me as we crunched arm in arm through the low fog. We had bonded and I felt I understood this curious quest he was on.

'I know,' he said, when I was silent for a while. 'Life after death. Another realm permeating our own; it's a lot to take in.'

It was; a hell of a lot. What had I experienced the night of the phantom explosions and droning engines? My imagination? An earthquake? Or some gross violation of a natural law; the residue of past memories and events? Intangible, maybe, but no less real. And no less frightening. Something wanting, something *needing*, to be known, perhaps.

And to be heard? I wondered with a growing sense of dread. *To be seen*?

That mental question called up an image of the rusting watchtower on Orford Ness and I wondered: what was the significance of it? Why had I felt so compelled to climb the rickety steel stairs, and why was I consumed by such sadness when I reached the top? Why had the imprint of that hand in the thick dust affected me so? What was the mystery?

What was its meaning for me?

That was the question in my head as I told Bill to go back; I wanted to walk the rest of the way by myself. I wished him goodnight and waited until he was out of sight before continuing on to the Martello tower.

I went in, closed the door on the windswept darkness, and

was about to flick on the light when my mood abruptly changed. I didn't need to take another step into the entrance hall to know immediately that something was wrong. All around me, the air was thick with a pungent stink; like rotting cabbages.

Gas. Gas everywhere!

On impulse, I froze, covering my nose and mouth with my hand. My hand hovering, frozen, over the light switch. One flick of the switch, one deadly little spark, that's all it would take.

Then I shouted out to Hazel for help. No response; just the deadly hissing of gas. That sound was only in my head of course; but if I closed my eyes, I could picture the gas hob upstairs, unlit. Or the boiler cupboard next to the sink. Could envisage the gas slipping silently through the tower, filling the corridors, slipping through the cracks around Dad's bedroom door.

'Hazel?' I shouted again, then clamped my mouth shut; because in my mind, I could see Dad in his bed woken by my shout, his shaky hand reaching for the switch of his bedside lamp.

That would be it for us all.

Depending on how much gas there was; but who knew the answer to that? If the boiler or the kitchen hob were faulty, the leak could have been going on all evening; maybe all day. It was quite possible that Hazel was unconscious in her room.

I had to get to Dad.

But still I hesitated. What if he heard me coming? Snapped on his light?

As it dawned on me that I might be just seconds away from one almighty explosion, I drew a breath that was not at all steady.

What do you do?

Get some air in; open the front door!

I turned the handle and flung it open.

Now what? Run. Where? Downstairs or upstairs?

I decided to try to find the source of the leak and shut it off. One hell of a gamble, but I'd always been good at doing that, hadn't I? Now wasn't the time to lose my nerve. Now, if ever, was the time to roll the dice.

I looked directly ahead, at the shadowy staircase that looped up. Then I took a breath and ran for it.

In the kitchen, coat sleeve covering my nose and mouth, I raced to the gas hob. Sure enough, a ring had been knocked on. Not just one ring, I realised. Three! At once I turned them off. Then I worked my way around the room, throwing open every window.

I was at the sliding door to the balcony, taking in great gulps of the salty air, when I heard the slow scrunch of footsteps down below. Two figures approaching. They were coming up towards the front door. Hazel; and on her arm, walking steadier now, my father.

'Stay there!' I yelled. 'For God's sake, stay outside!'

I kept looking long enough to see her assist Dad to lean against the nearest wall, then she made for the tower entrance, stony-faced. A few moments later, I turned to see her hurrying up the stairs in her unflattering winter jacket that made me think of a sailor's waterproof coat. Her face was pinched red from the cold, her chest heaving with the exertion.

'Hazel,' I said, relieved. 'Are you okay? Is Dad okay?'

She came rushing towards me and seized my wrist in a vice-like grip. 'You are so careless!' she yelled. 'How am I supposed to care for Clifford when you go and do reckless things like this? HOW?'

Stunned by her hostility, I wrenched myself free and stepped back.

'Can you smell that? Jesus Christ, Lizzy – what's wrong with you? Thank God I'd taken Clifford outside for a late walk. The whole place could have gone up!'

I stared at her, confused. And then, too slowly – I should have realised faster – appalled. This wasn't an accidental leak. *She* had done this. To set me up. She was a gratuitously sly woman, clever, and I had to give her credit. Even to someone like Nick, this didn't look good for me: it wouldn't matter who you asked, a gambling addict with a memory problem wasn't someone to be trusted. Worse – sharing a home with a vulnerable adult, they were a liability.

I went to the window and looked down to check on Dad. He had his winter coat on but with his arms wrapped tightly around him, he didn't look warm. I would go and get him.

Before I could make for the stairs, Hazel said something that paralysed me with anger: 'If we're to make sure your father is safe in this godforsaken tower, you'd better start paying better attention to the way this household works. You're not drinking, are you?'

I whirled on her and yelled, 'Why are you doing this? Making me look absent-minded, unreliable; the way you've been treating Dad. Cruel. You won't stop, will you? Tell me what you *want*!'

'You already know what I want.' She smiled her awful, wintry smile. 'Only the best for *Dad*.'

'Property. Money. Dad's well-being – you want control of it all.'

'How much do you know,' she said, folding her arms, 'I mean really know about your father? This glorious architectural triumph of his? Sure, you've seen the awards, but do you have any comprehension of what he went through, what he did, to earn those glittering trophies?' She gave a contemptuous little laugh. 'I very much doubt it, Lizzy, and why? Because you're pathetically self-involved, aren't you? Too damned preoccupied with yourself! Why, look at tonight, for instance. I was walking on the beach with your father. He couldn't settle, wanted to take the night air. Where were *you*?'

She was trying to break my concentration, my scrutiny of her, but I had to focus. I made myself focus, and my memory skipped back again to the faded black-and-white pictures under her bed; the ones bound with that fragile purple ribbon. The tower before the renovation. The young military men. And the photograph tucked in a book: the teenager in the tight T-shirt and jeans at his birthday party with the beaming smile. Three separate moments from history. Somehow, Hazel's shadow loomed over it all.

'Secrets out, they always do,' I said, my voice thick with sulphuric fury. 'You *chose* us for a reason.'

She gave me a look of complete contempt. 'Why don't you keep telling yourself that, if it gives you any comfort?'

'You don't fool me,' I retaliated. 'You're hiding in plain sight, exploiting the very person you're supposed to be protecting – and I won't allow it!'

'Who are *you* to dictate orders to me?' she barked.

'What's with the blood spots, Hazel? On the floor in your room?'

She looked taken aback at that. Defensive.

'Nosebleeds?' I probed. 'Or do you also suffer with an addiction you need to share?'

Hazel, I realised, was holding her breath. It was the first time I had seen her clam up, but I was misguided, severely so, if I thought that silence was an admission of defeat.

'You'd better not push me,' she said with quiet menace. 'I'm at my wits' end, and it won't take much to tip me over the edge.'

Tip you over the edge? I thought. *No, Hazel, I think that happened long before now.*

She straightened her jacket, adjusted her spectacles. I wouldn't spend another moment in her presence. Dad was all that mattered, and it was him I had to see.

Downstairs, I led him in from the cold. 'It's all right,' I said, 'it's safe now. A foolish mistake with the gas, that's all it was.'

'Thank you, Lizzy.' In the entrance hall he hesitated, looking fearfully towards the stairs that looped down to the bedrooms. 'You know, I'm not quite ready for bed.'

'All right . . .'

'Upstairs,' he said, 'I'd like to sit a while up there, have a glass of wine maybe. To relax.'

'Dad . . . those stairs . . . I'm not sure—'

He let out a long exhale. 'It's all right, Lizzy. I don't want to take the lift, I hate using that thing. Makes me feel so feeble and useless! If I go slowly, and you help me, hold onto my arm, I'll get there.'

And he did. Not easily and not quickly (it took ten minutes or so). And when we finally emerged into the open-plan living area, although a little out of breath, he was smiling triumphantly. 'There,' he said, 'there's life in the old dog, yet, huh?'

Hazel, planted in the far corner of the room, was staring daggers at me. A moment stretched. I thought: *Why didn't you offer to help him climb the stairs?*

I didn't understand how she could possibly still believe her position was tenable here.

In my back pocket, my phone buzzed. I took it out and saw the blinking words: UNRECOGNISED NUMBER. Hoping it was Nick calling, I hit the green button and put the phone to my ear.

'Hello, Lizzy?'

Not Nick. Metcalf. And he sounded irritated.

'Won't you leave me alone?' I almost shouted. But I resisted the impulse to hang up. I could see him in his shiny office, working late. Maybe already looking through his contact book of thugs he used to deal with people like me.

'Elizabeth, I want you to listen to me.'

'I'm halfway through doing what you asked,' I said, turning away from my father. This was not a conversation I wanted him to hear. 'Just a little more time and—'

'We were expecting a second payment. When's it coming?'

The sly smile was on Hazel's face again. Her probing stare in my direction. Telling me this was her. She had spoken to Metcalf.

I quickly checked that Dad wasn't listening. To my relief, he was settling back into his favourite chair.

How often had she spoken to Metcalf? How much had she told him about me, my so-called 'paranoia'?

Screw her!

'You'll get your money,' I said into the phone and then gave the first lie that came to me. 'This property is under private surveillance now you bastard, so don't even think of trying to intimidate me or my father, or—'

The line clicked dead.

I couldn't look at Hazel. Couldn't bear to see that familiar triumphant, self-satisfied smile. *You need me*, that smile would say. *You need me and you won't forget it – because I won't let you.*

Sleep. I needed rest.

Needed to be anywhere she wasn't.

But I couldn't leave my father up here, alone with a mad woman. When she was out of sight, I would speak with him. About our family. About our past. About our future. Didn't he say he had money in his pensions? Perhaps, somehow, I could take him away from this place. Away from her. That thought was unformed, but it gave me a tiny spark of hope.

Alas, as I turned to him, I saw that there would be no conversation tonight. Already he was asleep. His flickering eyelids and mutterings suggested not peacefully.

– 11 –

DARKNESS FALLS

During the night, a half-formed plan came to me. I had remained awake, thinking and wondering. My plan wasn't perfect, because it meant leaving the tower for a few hours the next day, and how could I possibly leave Dad alone with a mad woman? At the same time, I had to get a grip on this situation, because I knew otherwise it would only get worse.

If beating my addiction had taught me anything it was this. There's always hope. Always a solution. Right now, I thought that solution involved Nick, and I didn't feel good about that. He was away with his ex, in Wales. Still, what are friends for? It was the only option I could see, so I took out my phone and hit the call button.

'Lizzy . . .' His voice was muted, clotted with sleep. 'What's up? It's three in the morning.'

'I need you back here, tomorrow. Please.'

'What? Lizzy, you know I'm—'

'I'm sorry,' I whispered, looking at my father asleep in his favourite chair. He looked a little stronger, I thought. Healthier. 'Truly, Nick, you know I wouldn't ask this of you if it wasn't absolutely necessary.'

That got through. 'What's happening?' he asked.

I explained about the way Hazel had been treating Dad, about the gas leak and her veiled threats towards me.

'Lizzy, are you sure—'

'She's plotting against us, I know it. Trying to make me look unstable. Why, I'm not sure, but I've got to do something.'

'Jesus . . . Give me a minute.' I heard him slip out of bed and pad into another room. Then, when he was alone, he stopped whispering. 'These are serious allegations, Lizzy.'

'Which is why I need proof. Tomorrow. I have a plan. But I need you to be here to watch Dad for me, please.'

'That's almost a six-hour drive . . . Can't Colin—'

'He's not in a good place right now. Nick, you can say you're calling by to check up on Dad. I know it's a lot to ask, but honestly, there's no one else now.'

There was a long sigh on the other end of the line. 'All right, Lizzy. If I leave early I could be with you by late afternoon.'

'I owe you for this,' I said, and draped a blanket over my sleeping father. 'Oh, and Nick, I need a small loan, too – a few hundred quid, maybe? You'll get every penny back, I promise.'

There was a brief pause, and then he said, 'Of course. No problem. Now . . . about this plan?'

It was just shy of four p.m. the next day when Nick called back.

'Lizzy, I'm sorry . . . the traffic.'

I'd been with Dad all day. I'd taken him for a short walk on the beach, and then sat with him in his room. Now I was pacing the top floor of the tower, tense, looking down onto the beach where Hazel was walking along the shore. 'Where are you?'

'Held up on the M4. Hell of a jam. There's a bad road accident up ahead but I'm hurrying.'

No time. The shops would be closing soon. What I needed

I could not order online for delivery; these days Hazel was all over the post.

'Can't it wait?' he asked. 'Until tomorrow?'

I thought of the gas leak. Hazel's determination to blame me. 'No, it can't wait. This can't continue another day. Stay in touch, Nick. Keep me updated.'

As I hung up, I knew what I had to do. While Hazel was still outside and out of earshot, I went down to Dad's room. He was reading in the chair next to his bed.

'I have to drive to Ipswich,' I told him. 'I won't be long, but I'd feel better if you locked your door until I got back, okay?'

He looked alarmed. 'Lizzy, what on earth for?'

'Because,' I said in a low voice, 'I don't trust her, and I don't think you do, either. The way she speaks to you – how do you even tolerate it? And why?'

He swallowed and allowed his gaze to slip away from mine; and that only made me more convinced there was something about their relationship he had kept from me.

'Dad?'

'Oh, Lizzy,' he sighed heavily, 'our family history is a little more complex than I would wish. Some of it . . . is a blur to me; and Hazel takes . . . an unhealthy interest.' He looked solemnly at me. 'She knows some things, personal information about the time we moved here; information about my relationship with your mother. Things I'm not proud of – you know it wasn't always perfect, don't you?'

I nodded.

'Some of the details, well . . . they're a little sordid. Things I would rather you never knew; and I worry every day if she would ever share those things with you. It's the hold she has over me.'

'It's a hold we have to end,' I said strongly. I reached into my back pocket and produced the key to his room. 'I'm not going to lock you in; I couldn't do that. You decide. But please, Dad. Please. Do this for me. Lock the door. It won't be for long. Nick's on his way here to check on you.'

'Nick?' Dad looked slightly uncomfortable. 'I'm not sure I'm up to seeing people.'

'He'll be here soon.' I crossed the room and crouched down at his side. 'Just do as I ask. I need to go and get something, all right? I won't be long.'

Cautiously, looking worried, he took the key. I told him I loved him.

'Stay here. And don't open that door for anyone but Nick.'

Woodbridge was much closer than Ipswich and would have been far easier. But I'd already checked online and the shops there didn't have what I needed. So it had to be Ipswich.

On the journey I tried calling Bill. At least he could keep watch on the tower for me from a distance. But there was no answer. He was probably out walking.

I glanced at the dashboard clock. 16:20 now. The shops were shutting any minute. I drove faster, trying not to think about what would happen if Hazel were to discover what I intended to buy.

By the time I got to the grimy electronics shop in Ipswich they were near to closing, but a young Asian man agreed to help. Eagerly, he recommended a home surveillance camera that, he claimed, was almost guaranteed to avoid detection.

'Oh yeah, it comes with night vision,' he said. 'That's pretty standard now. And it supports remote mobile viewing. It's all done through the broadband.'

He took a good half hour to show me how it worked.

'You clear about how to use it? Great. You can take it away today.'

I did.

On the drive back, my gaze dropped to the photo frame that wasn't a photo frame in its box beside me. I wondered briefly what Colin would think if he knew what I was planning to do: *'Crazy, Lizzy, Hazel was right, you're losing it!'*

And what about Hazel, what would she say?

She's not going to notice, I thought, *because it'll fit with the other photo frames in Dad's room.*

The closer I got to Shingle Street, the heavier I felt. If only I had the money I could return to London, take Dad with me. The colour had melted from the sky and the shadows were creeping longer. I couldn't say why, but it no longer felt comfortable out here, or even familiar. What it felt was threatening.

As my car rattled over the small bridge, I slowed to a crawl. Ahead, in the gravel car park, was Nick's car. *Thank God, he's here*.

But then I saw another car, and that one dropped a stone of unease in my stomach.

It was a police car.

'What's wrong?' I asked, getting out of the car.

A uniformed officer was already approaching. He held up a hand in a stop gesture. 'This area's restricted access.'

'Sorry, what?'

The roar of the waves was almost deafening.

'Do you live here, ma'am?'

'At the Martello tower. Why?'

His face was grim.

'Please come with me.'

He escorted me over the shingle, to the tower. With every

step, the world around me was slowing, the slamming of the waves now barely registering. What the hell was going on? Was this connected with the police's arson investigation? Or maybe Hazel had called them, reporting an intruder?

Before the police officer could tell me anything, I saw Nick. He was waiting for me at the bottom of the steps that led up to the main door, his eyes solemn, and that's when the gravity of this situation really hit home.

'Where's Dad?' I said.

'Oh Lizzy, I came as soon as I could.' His tone was flat. He took my hand and I noticed he looked pale, and he was staring at me with a sort of stunned expression that was far from reassuring.

'What is it, what's wrong?'

'There's no easy way to say this,' he said. 'Your father . . .'

I held my breath.

'Hazel thinks he was suffering one of his episodes.'

'What are you saying?' I asked, but as soon as the words were out of my mouth, I was dreading his answer. I looked steadily at him and saw the awful confirmation of my fears in his averted gaze. A sickness of horror rose within me.

'Somehow he got outside and—'

I recoiled, pulling my hand from his.

'I've been gone two hours. I told him to *stay in his room!*'

'This was before I arrived, Lizzy. Seems he made it upstairs. To the front door . . .'

Not like this, please, not like this. My whole body began shaking.

Nick let out a long sigh, looking at me with such tenderness and concern. 'I really fear the worst, Lizzy. We found his clothes in a small pile, at the edge of the sea . . .'

He looked past me, and I turned instinctively. Saw the police officer who'd escorted me walking down to the shoreline,

where his colleague was already standing, looking out to sea.
Searching.

For my father.

'No,' I said. 'No. This makes no sense!'

I told Dad to stay in his room. And he couldn't get up the stairs
without assistance. How the hell did he get upstairs without—

With a stab of horrified alarm, I had a vision of Hazel
quietly letting herself into his room; gently waking him; coax-
ing him out of his chair, out of the room, and up the stairs
to the open front door. Beyond it, the boom of the tide in the
early-evening gloom.

'Where's Hazel?' I demanded.

'Lizzy, listen—'

'WHERE IS SHE?'

Nick led me inside and down the stairs. In Hazel's room we
were hit at once by the powerful aroma of rosemary. She was
sitting on the side of her bed, her eyes large and frightened,
her skin clammy and the colour of milk.

'What the hell happened?' I demanded.

For a few moments, no reaction. She was immobile. Shell-
shocked, I guessed. Or guilty in her silence?

'He was working himself into a frenzy,' she said at last, still
not looking at me, and I registered the quaver in her voice. 'He
was raging against me, lashing out. Uncontrollably violent. I
was alone with him, Lizzy—'

Which meant that Dad had not locked himself in, as I had
advised. Why not? Either he had thought me over-cautious and
decided not to, or . . .

He forgot.

I pressed my fingers against my temples. I should have
insisted!

'What did you do, Hazel?'

'I locked him in his room.'

She did what? I stared, perplexed. 'Then how did he get out?'

Her head snapped up. 'He must have had a spare key!'

A thud of the most horrific understanding. He had let himself out of the room with the key I had left for him. I didn't even know there were two keys.

Oh God, Oh Jesus.

My fault.

And hers.

Back in the hallway, Nick made me sit on a chair as I wobbled and shuddered – and then spewed out my fury at Hazel that she had left Dad alone, vulnerable.

As had I.

'Lizzy,' Nick said, 'you're in shock. Wanting to blame someone is perfectly natural. But it won't bring him back.'

'I'm just . . . I don't . . .'

He gave me a look that told me he understood, that he cared. And that was all it took to break me.

I clung to Nick, his arms around me, as I wept. I needed that hug like I needed oxygen.

'I should have been there for him,' I said.

'You did your best, Lizzy,' he replied gently. 'You can't see it clearly now. But you will. Grief takes time.'

'Yes,' I heard myself reply, but my own voice seemed to be far away now. I could almost have forgotten about my plan, about the secret camera I had bought.

We drew apart.

'Will you stay here?' he asked. His voice was calm and soothing.

'Would you like me to?'

He smiled. 'You know I would, but this isn't about me. Sometimes, at times like this, a change of scene can do you good.'

Leave? No. That would feel like an abandonment. And what about Colin? We would need to be here for one another, to look for Dad. Or wait until a body was discovered.

Just processing that thought ripped me apart. My father had been home and safe. He was supposed to be getting better. And I was supposed to be looking out for him. I had let him down.

'Dad did know I was here for him, didn't he?' I whispered, looking for reassurance in Nick's eyes.

'Oh Lizzy – yes, of course he knew,' he said, squeezing my hand. 'He was your father.'

Then we were interrupted. The police officer who had met me in the car park had some questions.

At the top of the stairs, I turned and looked down at the bedroom level. Still, it needled at me: how could Dad have climbed up without assistance? And who else could have assisted him but Hazel?

'Why aren't you questioning her?' I asked the police officer. 'She was alone here with him. Hazel, who manages his financial affairs, who regularly took him on walks, and who was supposed to be responsible for his personal care. Why don't you ask her how my father climbed those stairs without assistance?'

'I already did,' the police officer said flatly, and I tracked his gaze to the top of the stairs. My breathing stilled.

The stairlift. I had forgotten about it. But there it was, in position at the top of the stairs.

Which meant it had been used. Recently.

I swallowed, realising my assumption of Hazel's involvement

here had been over-hasty. Had made me look paranoid. Even Nick's sad expression suggested he thought that, too.

The police officer asked, 'How's your father been recently? Anything distressing him?'

'He had a stroke. He was suffering from night terrors.'

'I see. Was he depressed?'

'Yes, but I didn't think he would go and do something like this!'

The policeman stared at me.

'He was stronger than that,' I said, even as I remembered Hazel's earlier warnings and Colin's concerns.

'Had he previously spoken about his intention to enter the sea and take his own life?'

I opened my mouth to say no; but a memory – like a shard of glass sliding into my head – made that answer die on my lips.

At the hospital. Visiting hours.

To my horror, I realised Dad might have told me *exactly* what he intended to do.

A black day. And the remainder of it passed in a blur. What I remember most was the beat of the search-and-rescue heli-copter overhead until late into the evening. All my hope was focused on that helicopter, it had to be. There was no way to make what the police said had happened to Dad acceptable, or to live with the knowledge that his body was out there, decom-posing in the lonely sea, while I went on living in the home he had cherished, without him.

And it wasn't just hope that prevented me from accepting his death. Unbearable to think that he was so unhappy as to have taken his life; equally unbearable that the tragedy might have been prevented if only I had stayed at home.

That made me wonder what Colin would say. What Sandra would say.

They'll blame, you, Lizzy; whether Dad is found dead or alive, they'll still blame you. And maybe that's right. Maybe that's what you deserve.

Later that evening, when the police had suspended their search and Nick had gone, and I had been alone in the tower but for Hazel, shut away in her room, I called Colin. He sounded drunk, and this time, I didn't blame him.

'I thought you could come home?' I said. 'We should be together now; it's what Dad would want.'

'You should have been watching him,' he said bitterly.

Yes. I should have. But I was only trying to do what was right. When I left him alone I was sure he was going to do as I asked and stay in his room.

'Listen, Colin,' I said. 'Something isn't right here. Something was disturbing him.'

'Do you hear yourself?' he shot back. 'Don't you think you should've been around more these last few days? Instead of sodding off for hours to God-knows-where?'

'You've been talking to Hazel?'

'Yes, because I trust her. Because things only started going haywire when *you* turned up. Have you thought about that, Lizzy?'

I opened my mouth to reply; closed it. Now Colin was saying something else. I tried to listen but my attention had wandered to a mental image of Dad's body bobbing face-down on the waves.

'Are you even listening?' Colin roared, jolting me from the awful vision. 'I'm not ready to see you, Lizzy. Leave me alone. I mean it.'

He hung up on me, and I stood there, numb. I went down

to my bedroom. Shut the door, locked it, and undressed. Then I crawled into bed, hugged myself under the covers, and lay there shivering, listening to the relentless rolling waves, trying to process it all.

If my father was dead and it wasn't a stroke that had got him, it was suicide. Isolation. Depression. Disappointment in me? Perhaps in the end it had all got too much for him. Like Bill's son, perhaps he'd chosen to end it in the loneliest place possible – a watery grave, here at Shingle Street.

Desperate to forget, just for a while, I took two sleeping pills that night, pilfered from Dad's supply in his medicine cabinet. Whether it was the pills or the exhaustion I don't know, but I remembered nothing between getting into bed and waking to the scream of seagulls the next morning.

There followed several days when I roamed the beach, raking it with my gaze, desperate for any sign of my father. Sometimes people who were swept out to sea turned up again, alive. Not often, but it did happen, and knowing that imbued me with enough hope to keep searching for the duration of the week.

Hoping he would be at home, one evening I decided to call on Bill at Dumb Boy Cottage. Wouldn't he have seen the police on the beach? I kept thinking about our last conversation about all the suffering that had occurred on this shore, how he had asked me to help him discover the truth about its dark past. Bill would have a view on this, he would help.

I hurried across the shingle to his door. I knocked and stood there for a few minutes, shivering. No answer. I wanted so badly to hear his voice, but now, in the roaring darkness, all I could hear was my own breathing and my heartbeat pounding in my ears.

Not home . . .

I felt tiny. Inconsequential. Deserted.

Eventually, that smallest spark of hope within me diminished, giving way to a grim acceptance. And the grief came upon me in waves.

Sometimes I would lie in bed, listening to the seawater slipping over the shingle, thinking of Dad's empty room across the hallway, and imagining him being in here. Safe and warm in his bed. Sometimes I would get up and go into his room, wishing him back. Sometimes I would go up to the top floor of the tower and stand at the glass, and stare out into the darkness. Wondering: was there anything about our home he had concealed from me?

When I was feeling up to it, late one morning, I went up to the kitchen to make a coffee. Hazel was already in there, boiling the kettle. She kept her back to me as she spoke.

'I can't begin to imagine how you're feeling,' she said. 'Such a terrible blow. Your dad was a special man, in his own way.'

Something about her voice didn't sound right to me. It was more purposeful than sympathetic. Without offering me one, she made herself a coffee, then turned to look at me.

'We shouldn't wait too long before seeing to the administration side of things,' she said.

'Sorry,' I blinked hard at her. 'You've lost me?'

Her head turned slyly. 'I mean Clifford's estate.'

'Hazel, I—'

'I know it's normal to turn away from such matters. Having someone close to you just disappear without a trace is bound to be confusing and difficult. Still,' she took a breath, 'it's right now that we get his affairs in order, don't you think?'

'What are you talking about?' A flush of anger heated my cheeks. There was no body. 'His estate remains his, until or unless—'

'You can't keep running from what's happened, Lizzy. He's missing, yes – but missing presumed *dead*. The sooner you face that, the sooner you can move on. Without a body, we will have to make a claim for a declaration of presumed death. So much to sort out, complicated papers to sign; it's a real muddle, but we'll get on top of it. Together.'

'Your help won't be necessary, thank you.'

Her eyes narrowed. 'But Colin already asked me to help.'

'He what?'

She came towards me slowly. 'It's a maze of complex legal procedures; I can do all that for you – if it's easier?' A pause. 'Then there's the pensions, the life insurance policy and, of course, this place to consider; what happens to the tower?'

Astonished by her tactlessness, I snapped, 'My God, Hazel, it's too soon. I can't . . . think straight. I need time . . . to process this.'

Her smile widened into a contemptible smirk. 'These matters must be dealt with, Lizzy. And swiftly.'

And she went out of the room without saying another word.

To distract myself from all the feelings threatening to overwhelm me, I got busy. Cleaning. Vacuuming. Tidying up in a frenzy.

I was mostly keeping it together until I laid out a pile of old books I'd brought from London on my bed. A photograph was poking out of one; I must have used it once as a bookmark. The book was a play, one of Dad's favourites: *Death of a Salesman*. But it was the photograph that did it, a cracked Polaroid, all the colour seeping out of it.

As I held the photo, unimaginable grief broke over me in a wave. I remembered the day this picture was taken – Mum, tense, telling me to smile, smile, as Colin snapped the shot. I'd promised myself I would have this photograph restored. Now, it looked beyond restoration. Dad's face wasn't just a blur, it had vanished completely; even the flannel shirt and baseball cap were hard to make out. The only thing that remained clear, imposing, looming over us, was the Martello tower.

I remembered Mum telling Dad the project wasn't viable, we didn't have the money, and my legs gave out on me. How had he afforded it? How?

I collapsed on the bed and buried my head in the pillow and wept. Tears for a family I had never known, not fully. And now, it seemed, never would.

– 12 –

A RECKONING

Over the next few days, I wandered around the tower, achingly sad and as lonely as one of Bill's ghosts. *The sea always gives up its dead*, he'd said. If only it would, I thought. That would have made the loss easier to accept. To have a funeral, lay my father to rest.

At the top of the tower, I stared down to the beach where he had taken his last walk.

'Was he depressed?'

I saw now why the policeman had asked that, but I still didn't want to believe Dad had killed himself.

Hazel was alone with him. She was always alone with him.

There's no evidence of wrongdoing – is what the police would tell me. *No evidence except your paranoid suspicions.* As if all this was in my head, like Colin and Hazel had implied since the beginning. They wouldn't believe me.

I went downstairs. Looked around Dad's room. Something about it was troubling and sad. It was cold, smelled of old sweat and emptiness. I stood there, scanning the room very slowly. What had brought me in here, I knew, was a question.

Was anything missing? His medication? What about the confidential papers in the drawers next to his bed, the bank statements and deeds to the tower?

I searched; there were many boxes here, some of them decades old, and dusty enough to make me sneeze. Some of them were marked with dates that would mean they were from his school days. Old work books perhaps? Temptation got the better of me and within minutes I was crouching in front of an open box, rifling through pictures of Dad in his school uniform; pictures of him in his rugby kit, beaming an ambitious smile. It was not a smile I ever remembered him showing in adulthood, not even long before Mum got sick, when life was good.

Who stole that smile? I wondered sadly. *What made you such an insular figure? The same thing that happened to me; the weight of a secret addiction, pressing down on you?*

He would have been fifteen or sixteen years old here; I was curious to see more, because it occurred to me now that I'd never seen many pictures of him in his late teens or even in his early twenties. In fact, now I thought about it, I didn't think I'd seen any.

I looked at his bed. The sheets were a mess, scrunched up and wrinkled. The sight unleashed a fresh wave of sadness and helplessness. The idea that he wasn't coming back was intolerable. So I stood and walked to the bed and began making it neatly, smoothing down every crease.

And as I plumped up the pillow and laid it down, I saw it, scratched into the wooden cabinet on the side that faced the bed.

Two words that drove ice into my heart.

HELP ME.

I stared at the etching, remembering Dad's broken fingernails, the scratching, gnawing sound I had heard coming from his room. For one nightmarish moment, all I could hear was my heartbeat.

Had he been trying to tell me something?

Was this desperate message a sign of his mental distress at the onset of dementia, and the things he believed were haunting him? Or did it confirm his fear of Hazel?

I thought of how she had humiliated him, the callous cruelty, the gas leak. I thought of the power of attorney, how she had taken control, reviewed the named beneficiaries on his pension funds. Whose names did she list? Had he consented willingly?

And the most disturbing question of all: what else had she done that I didn't know about?

Wait.

Hadn't she mentioned a life insurance policy? Did policies like that cover suicide?

That thought was a challenge. I searched and searched. When was that policy taken out? Who were the chosen nominees?

Eventually, I found the policy documents at the bottom of a cardboard box under a heap of other papers and letters. A quick perusal of the forms confirmed what I wanted to know. Suicide was indeed covered by the policy. It had been taken out twelve months ago, when Hazel arrived. And the people who would benefit in case of Dad's death were me and Colin.

Except here was another letter, with a recent date. It was addressed to my father:

Dear Mr Valentine,
We have received your request to change the nominees on your life
insurance policy held with us. Please be advised that the necessary
forms will be forwarded to you by post forthwith.

At that, I fell onto my knees as a conviction rose in me like bile. *Hazel had done it. She had murdered him.*

Why? was all I could think. *Why?*

She wanted the life insurance money; she wanted power of attorney; she wanted the tower. Everything. I felt sure of all of this; so what was I going to do about it?

What can you do? There's no proof. If Colin won't believe you, why should the police?

Right then, kneeling beside Dad's bed, I remembered how keen Hazel had been to stay, how utterly content she was spooning food into Dad's mouth.

Except there was more to it than that, wasn't there? That malevolent little smile.

Did it make her feel important, to be needed, knowing Dad relied on her so? Did it make her feel powerful to humiliate him in front of me, talking about Mum the way she had? How twisted was that?

I felt hatred blooming within me. Hazel had done it. Somehow. And she had to be held accountable.

I sat on the end of the bed, heart hammering, hands shaking with adrenaline, and asked myself: *What will happen if I don't act? How many more will suffer at her hands if I do nothing?*

Hazel would not win. That plea for help scratched into the side of Dad's bedside cabinet was a reminder of her abuse. It was also a warning not to let anyone else suffer at this woman's hands. Hazel would not triumph.

I would not allow it.

The next few days may have been the worst of my life. I went nowhere, spoke to no one, was afraid even to call Nick, just in case I was tempted to reveal the awful thing I was contemplating. The weather turned and the battering winds and hail storms made walks on the shore all but impossible. I remember thinking if there was a hell, I wouldn't mind so much ending up there as it would have been preferable to this.

Hazel stayed in, too. Just the two of us. Horribly cosy in our mutual solitude. I heard her plodding footsteps on the stairs, the buzz of her alarm clock and the click of her bedroom door, and I hated her. She had infested the tower, infected it, and I seethed at the mere thought of her. The way she had sat for hours at my father's bedside while, I imagined, quietly dripping poison, whispering secret tortures that kept him from sleep, or traumatised him when he did.

You confront her, face to face.

Confronting Hazel was hardly without its risks. Even if she did agree to sit and talk, when I challenged her, laid bare the truth, there was every chance she would run. Or worse, become violent.

For a while, my ideas were murky, unformed. Then I remembered Dad's sleeping pills, how drowsy they made him, how they'd helped me wipe out the night he died, and wondered if those pills could be the key to Hazel's undoing. And one afternoon, while she was napping up on the top floor, I went down to Dad's room and to the medication cabinet there, grabbed a few bottles of pills – and gave myself permission to do the unthinkable.

It was never my intention to kill her. That's the truth. But with a coldness that would once have been alien to me, I *did* want to scare her, to intimidate her into giving me the answers I needed, and this seemed to be the only way.

The sleeping pills would do their job, eventually, but how to deliver the payload? It wasn't as if Hazel would swallow them voluntarily. To engineer a situation like that, I would have to slip the pills into a drink, and Hazel kept her wine bottles in her bedroom, and kept her bedroom locked. Hazel was also very observant; whenever I was near, her eyes turned hawkish. So I knew that she would be suspicious of any attempt to cosy up to her. And the thought of doing that was, undeniably, repulsive.

The hurdle seemed insurmountable. Then there were the obvious risks. I'd checked online. Mixing the sleeping pills with red wine would send her out like a light, but even one drink mixed with the pills could be dangerous. Many more could cause memory loss, sleepwalking. Or death. Which wouldn't have worked. Because I had to know – I had to hear her say it as she looked me in the eye: her reason for tormenting us.

That's what Dad deserves, I told myself. *I have to do this. For him.*

And just knowing that was good. A relief. Similar to the relief that had washed over me in Mitch's office when I had finally admitted my addiction.

Maybe it's true, I thought, maybe the truth really does set you free.

The next morning, I showered, dressed, and made scrambled eggs, beating them into a frenzy. My hands weren't trembling, and the frayed wires I had expected to feel sparking in my stomach just weren't there; in fact, my stomach felt as calm as the sea looked that morning.

My mind however was a different matter. My mind was a fury. I downed a double espresso, then another, and then my hands *did* begin to tremble, ever so slightly.

I heard her come up the stairs, her stony gaze boring into my back. Turning, I cautiously suggested she join me for dinner so that we could talk. Given how badly she wanted to discuss Dad's estate, it seemed a reasonable assumption that she'd accept.

Her gaze narrowed slightly.

'I'll cook, if that's what you would like?' I offered.

She sat down, kept her gaze on me. 'Cook what?'

Just . . . you . . . wait.

I reached for the pile of recipe books stacked under the coffee table; handed her one.

'Why don't you choose?' *Involve her all the way, or she'll never trust you.* 'Lasagne?' I suggested.

'All right,' she said, putting down the book.

'I'll buy the tomatoes, from the market.'

She frowned. 'What's wrong with tinned tomatoes?'

'Fresh are better. This recipe was one of Dad's favourites. We'll need fresh basil, too. Lots of it.'

And although that kept her frowning, she managed a prim nod. 'Fine. Seven-thirty?'

'Seven-thirty,' I agreed, 'and we'll toast Dad's memory, together. He'd like that, wouldn't he?'

Again she nodded, and then she smiled. 'And after we've eaten,' she said with a light in her eyes, 'we can discuss business matters.'

'Yes,' I said, knowing that here was the moment to seize my chance, 'that's exactly what we'll do.'

When I got back from the market, I checked in the drawer next to my bed, half fearing the sleeping pills I'd hidden there would be gone, magicked away by the sheer force of Hazel's domineering will.

I was relieved, and a little afraid, to see that the pills were still right where I had left them.

So you don't have an easy excuse to back out now, Lizzy.

Part of me wanted to, of course. He had been so unhelpful, so cynical, but I wished that my brother would step up. I fantasised that he would appear at the front door at any moment with profuse apologies, admit he'd got it all wrong, send Hazel packing. But I knew that wouldn't happen, so preparations had to be made.

Eight pills ought to do it. Nine to be sure.

What would Bill say? If only I could ask him, but there was still no sign of life over at Dumb Boy Cottage. Probably he would say that one bad decision leads to another. Probably, but that wasn't enough to overcome my rage, my need to know the truth.

Certainly I found it difficult grinding up the sleeping pills into a fine dust and sprinkling it into the sauce, and a part of me wondered, as I put the dish into the oven, if I might just be losing my mind after all.

'The problem with your father,' she said, greedily aiming another forkful of pasta into her mouth, 'was his stubbornness. Never listened. Always thought he knew best. Stubborn as a mule was Clifford!'

I sat across the dining table from Hazel. The orange candlelight flickered devilishly on her face. The kitchen area was a nest of shifting shadows. It had gone eight, according to the clock over the stove, and I could hear the sea kicking the shore outside.

My breath was short and light, my eyes on the pasta she was forking into her mouth. My own fork was cold between my fingers and felt unnaturally heavy, a potentially deadly weight. A misjudged dose was all it would take and she'd be dead.

To settle my nerves, I tasted my wine, then set it back on the table. Took a small mouthful of food. Wouldn't want to arouse her suspicions; not eating would have been a hell of a red flag! And I didn't have to worry about the possibility of drugging myself. The ground-up sleeping pills had only gone into one side of the lasagne.

She droned on, with an endless stream of bile, and I, playing my part, pretended to listen. But the longer I watched her sitting there opposite me, stuffing her heavy face, glugging Dad's wine, the more I thought of what she'd done to him; and the more furious I became; and the more I began to fantasise about seeing her suffer.

I saw it happening, a mental rehearsal: her eyes widening with panic as a piece of that lasagne went down the wrong way and lodged in her windpipe. Her face would turn a deep shade of scarlet, and I would be glad to see it. It was wicked of me, but for one wild and darkly magnificent moment, I could even see myself sitting back, contented, watching as her arms flailed desperately; her bulging, watery eyes pleading with me to jump out of my chair and whack her on the back. The more I thought about it, the more I actually *wanted* to see her choke, right there and then. Admittedly, that would be tantamount to murder, but an elegant solution – she'd be out of my life for good.

Except that's not quite true, my inner voice warned. *What about the body?*

An appalling practical difficulty: I mean how, exactly, does one dispose of a body?

Until this moment, I'm not sure this question had ever occurred to me, and if it had, then only in a hazy, dream-like way. But seriously? No. And now that it did, the very idea of having to handle a corpse made me feel ashamed and physically sick.

I put down my fork, turned my head and caught sight of myself in the mirror above the coffee table. My hair was tangled, my face was pale and grave, with dark circles under my eyes.

How did you become this person?

Suddenly I remembered something Bill had said about his son: *'If only he'd known what I thought of him.'* That startled me, made me question what my dad would say if he could see me now.

He'd be ashamed, I thought, *ashamed and appalled. He would never have wanted you to kill. Not in his name. And besides, what use would Hazel be to you dead? If she was dead, you'd never understand why she's done all this.*

That brought me back to the plan I had so meticulously strategised and was now, at this very moment, putting into action. Would she notice something was off with the lasagne? She hadn't yet, and I didn't think she would. The extra herbs and spices in the sauce would mask any foreign taste, assuming the sleeping pills had any.

She swallowed another mouthful; was already on her second glass of wine. Surely it wouldn't be long before she began slurring?

'Dead now; I don't like to say I told you so, but—'

'Hazel—'

She adopted a preaching tone. 'I *did* warn you. If you'd listened to me, you'd have paid greater attention to his needs. You knew about the previous suicide attempts; you knew full well that your father wanted to harm himself, and yet you turned a blind eye.'

'Something is wrong with this place,' I said. 'You may not believe that, but Dad certainly did; and he was right. The strange sounds he heard – the explosions and screams? I've heard them, too.'

'Do you think that means anything to me?' she said with a roll of her eyes. 'The only thing haunting your father was guilt.'

'What's that supposed to mean?'

She spread her hands on the table. 'And you should feel guilty, too, because when Clifford needed you most, you weren't there for him, were you, Lizzy? He told me that he was ashamed of you for staying away for so long. That you'd let him down. He just never mustered the guts to tell you how he really felt.'

I didn't believe her. I didn't believe a damn word she said any more.

I thought of the documents I'd found, the things she'd done, the feeling I couldn't shake. There was really little point in containing what I suspected – what I knew – any longer.

It was time to confront Hazel.

'Why were you so cruel to him?' I demanded. 'Tell me, what did he ever do to you?'

She took another large gulp of wine.

'Tell me about his life insurance policy, Hazel?'

'No idea what you're talking about.'

'Oh, I think you do,' I said, feeling oddly calm. Or perhaps it wasn't so odd; for in my hatred of her, I had made peace with what needed to be done. 'That policy was taken out just after you arrived here. Interestingly, it's one of the more expensive policies; even covers suicides. You advised him on taking out that policy, didn't you?'

She shrugged it off, forked more lasagne into her mouth.

'We both know you had your own reasons for getting him to take out that policy.'

'You're listed as a nominee, Lizzy, you may not believe that, but it's true.'

'Which is strange,' I replied, 'because on the day you and I met, you feigned ignorance; said he had never mentioned me. His *disappointing* daughter.'

Her face darkened. I'd caught her out and she knew it.

'Did I encourage him to take out a life insurance policy? Yes, of course, because I could see the pressure your brother was under, and your father was not a well man. It was *necessary*. I even had Colin review the policy, he was involved at every stage. Which is why, Lizzy, both of your names appear in the documentation.'

Her gaze kept drifting to the flickering candle flame, and when she spoke again I detected a slur in her voice. 'You avoided your father for years, left your brother and me to get on with it. And yet you sit here, pious and self-satisfied, in judgement over me?'

'I'm just amazed you thought I'd never find out. Or maybe you *did* worry about that. Is that why you offered me money? To make me complicit? Because you *knew* I had financial trouble? You exploited me.'

'Your imagination is almost as lively as your father's.'

'No, Hazel, it's *your* imagination I've been wondering about.' I stared accusingly at her. 'I know you've arranged to change the nominees on his life insurance. Did you tell him you were doing that? Hoping for a windfall, are you?'

Now she looked at me, and what I saw in her eyes was genuinely frightening. A look of naked cold detachment. Here was her deceit laid bare – yet she didn't seem to care one bit. If anything, her eyes were smiling with the satisfaction of one who has triumphed. But I thought they also looked drowsy now.

'When you arrived on this shore,' I said, 'my father all but disappeared. You never took him anywhere. Turned him into a living ghost.'

'What's that supposed to mean?'

'Locked him in his room, did you? Taunt him?'

Still chewing her food, she held my gaze. Swallowed.

'You made him cry? Out of cruelty? For pleasure? Because it amused you? Why?'

She put down her fork.

'I *want* an answer.'

'You're hardly one to dictate orders,' she said. The grogginess was more obvious now, and that was good. It gave me the confidence to say what I said next.

'You invaded my life. And now I want it back.'

'That's a little theatrical, Lizzy, even for you.' Thick, furry words. She blinked, shook her head, then went on. 'I've noticed that drama seems to follow you around, doesn't it? Any impartial observer would say the same. Your brother, your friend Nick – you should know they both have grave concerns about your mental health. Even your dear father.' Her dark eyes glimmered. 'My, what a disappointment you've been to everyone.'

An expression of satisfaction fluttered across her face, and I detested her for it.

'You're crazy,' I said, 'you know that, right?'

'That's what *you* say,' she said, in a slow, thick voice. 'But how am I to know? The problem with crazy people, Lizzy, is that they never see it in themselves. And you?' she sneered. 'I think you're a walking testament to that. Former employers hounding you for money? Accusing me of insincerity? Whatever next?'

'You'll find out,' I said, allowing some menace to creep into my voice – and why not? Whatever happened now, there was no going back. I would see this through.

'You're in my debt, Lizzy – or have you forgotten that?'

'I don't forget much; my memory's pretty good, on the whole. Even though you've tried your hardest to convince me otherwise. But I do remember useful things. Things that matter.' *Like where Dad kept his medication.*

She took another mouthful of lasagne. I watched the fork travel slowly to her mouth. There was a tremble in her hand and the glazed, drifting look was back in her eyes again.

'You okay, Hazel?'

'Tired,' she mumbled, fuzzily.

'Wine gone to your head?'

With a foggy look in her eyes, her face crumpled with confusion and she shook her head as if trying to clear it. 'What is . . . wrong with me?'

I held her cloudy stare; tense.

'Lizzy?' She looked bewildered. 'What is this?'

'Just a little surprise,' I said, smiling. 'You do like surprises, right?'

She looked at the lasagne at the end of her fork. Understanding slithered across her features, and she threw it violently down onto her plate.

'What did you put in this?' she said, or tried to say; the words were so thickly slurred they came out in an ugly tangle.

And yes, I could have answered her question then, but there would have been very little point.

Because a few seconds later, after stumbling to her feet, Hazel went out like a light.

'I must have . . . dozed off.' Slurring.

I had planted her in a chair in the centre of the living room area, well away from the window, where the moonlight was streaming in. Two a.m. Standing at the sink, staring right at her, I felt my heart beating too fast from adrenaline. But I wasn't in the least bit afraid. A little masking tape, it turns out, does wonders for your sense of protection.

She looked vaguely around the room, head lolling, until her gaze found me. 'Lizzy—' She tried to move. Strained against the tape that bound her arms and legs to the chair.

'If I were you,' I said, 'I'd save my strength. Don't know yet how long you'll need it.'

For a moment her face was blank, uncomprehending. Then an ugly red fury exploded in her. '*What's going on? What have you done to me?*'

Silently, I stared at her.

'*LET ME OUT OF THIS CHAIR!*' she shrieked.

'Maybe. When you tell me what I want to know.'

Her eyes were wide and filled with murderous intent. Then she began struggling, thrashing like a wild animal, until the chair toppled over. If it hadn't been for the pillows I'd scattered around her she might have knocked herself unconscious. She lay on her side, looking up at me, her hands balling into fists.

'What the hell are you playing at?' she demanded.

'My father had a life. *We* had a life. And you cheated us out of it. I have no doubt that you murdered him. What did you do, take him out for a walk? Push him? Or did you encourage him to do it? Make him feel worthless and urge him into the water?'

She stared at me, defiant, eyes burning with hatred.

'Why did you do it, Hazel? To inherit this place? Change his will, did you? And the money in the bank, you got at that, too, am I right? What did you spend it on?'

'You're delusional,' she spat at me. 'Crazy.'

'Ha! That's rich, coming from you.' I walked over and leaned over her. 'They're going to lock you up, Hazel. Pick your charge: elder abuse; obtaining money by deception. Murder. Be very sure, you're going to jail.'

'Just who the hell do you think you are?' she seethed.

'I'm the person who's going to put you there,' I said curtly. And I walked out of the room.

On shaky legs, I went down to Dad's old room, sat on his bed, and the hard reality of what I had done hit my conscience.

You drugged another person and bound them to a chair.

Now the unimaginable was done and the adrenaline rush had subsided, my limbs were jittery and it was hard to make sense of my surroundings, let alone my conscious thoughts.

With a shaky hand, I picked up the glass next to the bed and swigged a large gulp of water. It almost made me throw up; then with an upsurge of shame, my former confidence crumbled to self-doubt.

What the hell have you gone and done, Lizzy? Mum, Dad, Colin, they'd be ashamed. You know that, right?

I did know it. Which was why, involuntarily, my hands covered my face. I had one fleeting thought as I closed my eyes: *Now she'll have to tell you, now you'll get the answers you need. She has no choice but to tell you.*

I told myself that, but it did little to calm me. Like a child shuddering uncontrollably from self-reproach, I wept. I left it an hour to gather my thoughts before going back up.

To face her.

– 13 –

THE VANISHING
AT SHINGLE STREET

She was secure and there was little prospect of us being disturbed, and perhaps you think knowing that made it easier for me, as I ascended the stairs?

It didn't. Every footstep was an effort. This had to end somehow. What worried me most was the possibility of a stalemate. *What if she refuses to confess? What then?*

As I neared the top of the stairs, a smell made me pause, familiar and distinctly unpleasant. Hesitantly, I climbed the last few steps. 'Hazel?'

Pitch black. I stepped forward, reaching for the light switch, and my foot slid, as if I'd stepped on a pool of oil. By the time I clicked on the light I was bracing myself for something nasty, but nothing could have prepared me for the scene that confronted me.

What? What?

I recoiled in horror. So much blood.

Everywhere. Blood up the walls. Blood soaking the floor.

I didn't see the colour red; the floor seemed to have turned *black*. And in the centre of the room was something that shouldn't have been; something that filled me with disbelief: Hazel's chair, toppled on its side. And empty.

It was impossible, but at the same time, horribly true.

Hazel was gone.

How long did I stand there doubled over, clenching my fists, telling myself this wasn't happening, *couldn't* be happening? Impossible to say for sure, but eventually I summoned the courage to look again.

Blinking away black floaters and spiderwebs, I locked my gaze on her toppled chair. I had been wrong about something: it wasn't in the centre of the room, it was nearer the kitchen. Which was wrong. Next to the chair was the masking tape I had used to bind her arms, now torn and in tatters.

I advanced slowly into the room, taking care to step around the pools of blood. And here was something new. On the floor behind the chair, glinting in the light, was a kitchen knife. Barely able to control my shaking hands, I picked it up. The blade was horribly bloodstained.

I remember thinking, *She's escaped, Dear God, somehow she's escaped.*

But how . . .

Looking down at the knife again, I began forming a gruesome picture of what had happened. Somehow, she had loosened the tape enough to get some movement in the chair; gone for the knife in desperation.

No, that can't be right. The chair toppled over and she was lying on her side, remember?

So how did she reach the counter?

I had no answer for that, yet; but I saw her bringing the serrated blade through the tape, across her wrist, splitting the skin, accidentally – then the blood pulsing out.

Was that possible? The arteries in the wrist were deep;

you had to really cut to get to them. But still . . . accidents happen.

Where the hell is she? With this much blood loss, she can't have got far.

I turned to the flapping curtains, which concealed the glass doors leading out onto the balcony: the doors were open a little.

After a moment's hesitation, I went out onto the balcony into the gusting wind. 'Hazel?'

No sign of her out here.

'Jesus Christ, she must have fallen,' I said, and in a split second I was barrelling down the stairs and across the darkened entrance chamber to the front door. Outside, on the shifting stones, I scanned for any sign of a body, calling her name, over and over. 'Hazel! HAZEL!'

But my cries were answered only by the wind and the pounding waves.

No. This couldn't be happening.

She *had* to be here! Somewhere.

I'd be lying if I said I felt safe out there on the exposed beach at that moment, especially on *this* beach.

'The files are missing. Something happened out there.'

With the tide coming in, I hastily retreated inside, scoured the whole tower, beginning in her room. Finally I returned with dread to the top floor.

So much blood . . .

What was I to do, report it? If I didn't and the body was found, the police would ask why I hadn't wondered about her whereabouts. I started for the telephone on the wall and had plucked it from its cradle before a thought stopped me: what about the money she had lent me? What if the police checked her bank accounts?

And now a new thought broke in, and it terrified me.

'Oh Christ . . . oh, no.'

I looked down at the darkening spread of blood and reminded myself that this was probably an accident, that she had cut too fast and too deep, and bled out.

That's right, Elizabeth, LIZZY, I bled out, because you left me in here, with no food and no water and no help until all I could do was reach for the knife. That's what I get. That's my reward for taking care of your blessed father. And you, what do you get?

From an objective perspective, this didn't look anything like an accident or even a suicide. What it looked like was a crime scene.

This room screamed murder.

And me? Elizabeth Valentine, who owed Hazel Sanders forty grand? I looked like the prime suspect. I'd had the motive, I'd had the means, and with Dad no longer here, I'd certainly had the opportunity.

I thought: *I wish I had killed you now. At least that way I could have controlled things.*

But this? My eyes surveyed the room. This could not be easily controlled.

She just had to be dead. No one could have survived so much blood loss.

In my mind's eye I saw the police leading me away from the tower in handcuffs. I knew what I had to do. Now, under the mantle of darkness, with the wind seething outside.

'I have to clean it up,' I said to myself, hearing my voice as if from far away. I had to try, because otherwise everything about this situation pointed damningly at me.

I made my way carefully towards the corner kitchen cupboard, opened it and reached for the mop with a sense of such need I might have been reaching for Excalibur. At the sink, I blasted the tap on, filling the bucket, all the time thinking, *Where the hell did she go? Where's the body?*

Back and forth went the mop, streaking blood, probing every corner, swabbing every square inch. Then plunging into the bucket with a mucky wet slop.

I don't know how long it took to remove the visible blood, hours I think. But when it was done, I emptied the bucket into the sink for a final time and watched the red-hued water disappear down the plughole. Next, I went down to the bathroom for towels. Dried the surfaces. My shoes and my jeans were bloodstained, so I took them off, lit the wood-burning stove and watched them turn to ashes.

Only then did I sit, trembling, and think.

Hazel had escaped, somehow. Injured herself. Lost so much blood, she *must* be dead now. Her body, I thought, would soon be discovered along the beach, or close by.

And then what?

They're going to work out you were responsible, a voice in my head said. *The gambling, the corporate fraud, the money she lent you, it's all going to come out. And they'll want to know all about the suspicious restraint marks on her wrists.*

Listening to the wind howl around the tower, I told myself not to panic. The dawn, I had to pray, would bring clarity. Answers.

None came. The dawn was creeping and grey and lowering to the spirits. In the days that followed, storms battered the shore, but the tower remained overwhelmingly quiet. Horribly, unnaturally quiet. I was alone, trapped in purgatory, frantically worrying about Hazel and the mystery of her vanishing. It was a relief when Bill called. He had heard about my father's disappearance from the Grayling family, his landlords in Woodbridge.

'Oh, God, Lizzy – I'm so sorry I can't be there with you. Still no body?' he asked.

'Sadly not. It would be a relief though, some sort of closure.'

'Lizzy, if it's any consolation, I know what you're going through.'

He did, I had no doubt; but that didn't make the blow any easier.

'Anything I can do?' he offered.

'No, thank you; but that's kind.' Just hearing his voice was a comfort.

I wished he were nearby. But his sister needed company so he had gone to see her in London.

'But I'll come see you as soon as I'm back.'

As far as I was concerned, that time could not come soon enough.

As the days passed, wave after wave of terror washed over me. I knew I had locked the front door, and yet I could sense Hazel's taunting presence. If I closed my eyes I could almost smell her. And hadn't it always been that way? The relentless scent of the sour, mendacious charlatan? Since the very first day we met.

I grew hopelessly depressed, and began to suffer from headaches and weakness, so much so that for hours each afternoon I would lie down – but instead of resting, I would go over and over the horror of that blood-soaked kitchen.

Every night before bed, I hugged myself, wandering from window to window, peering out for some sign of monsters. In a haze of grief and guilt and perpetual confusion, time in the tower stood still for me.

Sleep, when it did come, was fitful and plagued by horrible phantasms, vague memories, hideous dreams that filled me with indescribable terror.

In these new, darker dreams of Shingle Street, the focus wasn't Hazel, and it wasn't my younger father gazing off towards Orford Ness. In these nightmares I was venturing into the forest b*ehind* the shore. Where . . .

. . . *A darkness is rising* . . .

. . . where strange and indefinable forces were creeping nearer. The definite sense of a presence, felt.

A presence that wanted . . .

. . . *something, from me?*

Nick was beside me and I could *feel* the heat from a crackling campfire. Everything felt good, until *something* made me glance over my shoulder.

Something that said: *Help me. Find me.*

Each of those dreams left me nauseous. Partly because, deep down, I knew they were trying to show me something; mostly because, whatever that something was, I didn't want to see it. It was exhausting, draining, to continually wake and look for intruders who never materialised.

Then things began to happen. Unnatural things. On one occasion, as it was growing dark, I was walking through the hall, past the bottom of the spiral staircase, when I was startled to see a woman coming down the stairs. As I stepped nearer, she disappeared, and in her place I saw a reflection of myself in the mirror. I wondered how the lights and mirror could have tricked me.

This happened twice, and yet I was left wondering if it had even happened at all.

*

The loneliness was consuming, a physical ache in my chest, and although Bill Durrant, who lived so close, would have helped if he were here, the person I thought about constantly was Nick. Who had returned to Wales. To be with his partner. I missed him, missed our friendship. I would write him a letter, I decided; even if I didn't send it, the act would be a comfort in the gloom.

Dear Nick,

As we settle into a chilly winter, I wanted to drop you a line to wish you well and thank you for coming when I asked, at such short notice.

I thought long and hard before writing you this letter because I want to say something meaningful. It's also why I'm writing by hand, which might be a mistake, because my penmanship, as you can tell, is a little rusty.

While looking ahead during the last couple of weeks, I also looked back, and I reflected on something that you said to me when we had lunch in Woodbridge. You said I'd been your best friend, remember?

Those words stayed with me. This may sound overly sentimental, but I believe we came into one another's lives for a reason. I remember times that were difficult – because of my indecisiveness and need to get away. But I also remember so many good times, like when we would cook meals together or take a long walk into Rendlesham Forest.

As we step into a new year, I'd like to apologise from the bottom of my heart for the hurt and humiliation I caused you. We were friends for so many years, and we shared a lot together – laughter and pain. I miss that. I miss us.

I realise that I have lost the right ever to ask you for anything

*more than friendship. But thank you for being there for me. Can
I see you soon, please?*

   Yours truly,

   Lizzy x

I put down my pen and sat quietly at the hall desk, looking
out over the waves rolling ashore. In the distance, veils of rain
were sweeping across Orford Ness.

Two things happened then.

An icy shiver ran down my spine and I suddenly felt, though
I could not explain why, as though another pair of eyes was in
the room and fixed probingly upon me.

The second thing was worse, because it seemed impossible.

Thud, clump, thud.

From above, on the top floor. The sounds were startling and
inexpressibly terrible. Unmistakable dragging sounds. The
scraping of a chair across the floor.

My heart gave a small leap, then seemed to stand still. I held
my breath, gripped the corner of the desk, and it came again,
louder this time. Heavier.

Thud!

That might have been a chair toppling over. A chair with a
heavy woman bound to it, perhaps.

Uneasiness swirled into terror; I felt the blood drain from my
face and glanced towards the stairs that looped up, my mouth
trembling. What the hell was this?

Thud, clump, thud.

Above me, the same as before, repeating.

Thud!

Was there someone up there? An intruder? How could there
be? Wasn't it more likely that this was yet another grief- and

guilt-induced hallucination? Some sort of complicated bereavement disorder?

Bill wouldn't have said that. I could imagine what he'd say:

'It's Hazel, you know it's her. Didn't I say, Lizzy, that there's a stranger world than the one we walk through every day? Didn't I say that the longer you stayed here, the more you might learn that? Well, you're learning it now. But it can't harm you; take solace in that. These are just echoes of a past trauma, that's all.'

But that wasn't all, was it? Because, whether through reckless impulse or noble vengeance, it was *me* who had triggered that trauma – and now somehow, impossibly, Hazel intended me to know it. It would have been better for me, easier, to believe that she was still alive. But the sense of dread and foreboding that these inexplicable happenings stirred in me was as undeniable as her dark presence, which lingered.

Still.

If all of this sounds fanciful, superstitious, let me say that I'd never remembered the tower being so cold. Sometimes I saw my own breath as little puffs of frost, and when the sun went down, I had to wrap a blanket around me, even when the heating was on full.

Worse than the cold, though, was the smell. Cloying and thick. The smell of blood. Even after bleaching the kitchen, twice, three times, somehow I smelled the godawful odour everywhere.

One night, I thought I could smell it coming from Hazel's old room, next to mine. I hesitated outside her door, baffled by the light that was shining through the slit beneath it. Strange. If there was a lamp in there that she had left on, I should surely have noticed by now. Even stranger, when I opened the door and peered inside, I saw that the room was in full darkness.

Impossible!

That did it: with some misgivings, I called the only person I thought might understand.

I called Bill.

'Well, where is Hazel?' he asked. 'Lizzy, I didn't realise you were alone.'

'She left,' I said, 'vanished.' Although this wasn't the whole story, it wasn't a complete lie, either.

'You're sure you didn't leave the lamp on?'

'As sure as I can be.'

Silence down the line. I knew what he was going to suggest. Bill was a believer, but a judicious one.

'It's not my memory, it's not stress, and I'm not imagining things.'

'You know I keep a very open mind, Lizzy,' he said, 'but just hear me out a second, okay? What you saw *may* have been the moonlight. It's hellish bright some nights. It's fooled me more than once over the years. Now please, get some rest, and eat something.'

I told him I would try. The truth was, the idea of sleeping alone, after seeing that weird light, paralysed me with enough fear that I had no appetite.

Moonlight. Of course that's what it was. Moonlight.

I must have dozed off eventually, because my next memory is of snapping awake on my bed, still in my clothes.

Something had jolted me from sleep. I lay still and listened. The waves were pounding the shore, the wind whipping against the ancient walls of the tower. I saw through my arched window that Bill was right about one thing: the moon *was* bright, a silver disc riding high across the dark.

Soon I could smell it again. The air was heavy with the coppery smell of blood. A most repugnant scent. But not real, I told myself, only a memory.

Then, just as I was about to put my head down again, I heard something. From the floor above me, the unmistakable noise of the front door slamming.

The first thing I did was check it out, and I think you know I found the door just as I had left it, shut. Locked.

By now, it's fair to say that I was freaked out.

I thought about calling Bill, but my phone was downstairs, in the darkness, next door to Hazel's room, and going back down there didn't feel like a great idea.

Just then I heard a sound from up above me. A great muffled *thump*.

Slowly, I made my way up the looping stairwell. Breathing hard, I stopped at the top of the stairs. My eyes did a circuit of the room, from the giant oak dining table and benches, to the white dresser filled with blue and white china, to the sitting area and the wood-burning stove. Holding my breath, I listened. The whine of the refrigerator. The ticking of the clock. No one up here; only something I didn't want to see, right in the centre of the room.

The moonlight seemed to spotlight it.

A toppled chair.

The same chair to which I had bound Hazel.

I stood there, frozen, staring at that damned chair, but the sight of it left me thinking that she or something – some part of her – remained.

Behind me, suddenly, movement.

I swung around. For a moment I saw something, barely

a shadow, and then it was gone. But I *did* see it. A hulking, stooped figure. I suddenly wished I'd had the forethought to set up the home surveillance kit I'd purchased.

'What's the point in this? What are you doing? You had your time and you had your way. You took my father. What else is there? I never harmed you. Why do you want to traumatise me?'

Nothing. Not a sound. Only suffocating silence.

'What do you *want*?'

The silence thickened. The room seemed to pulsate. Coagulating with tension. My skin started to prickle.

I bolted. Almost tripped on the stairs. Didn't look back.

But it was worse downstairs, in the hallway. Here was a familiar smell. Hostile. Not the scent of blood, but of rosemary, all around me, suffocating.

As I pressed myself against the wall, I saw it again. A flicker of movement on the stairs.

'Get out. You're not welcome here; you never were. GET OUT!'

Silence then. The silence of freshly fallen snow. I couldn't hear the tide on the shingle, or the cry of the wind. Not even my own breathing.

It was the silence of nightmares.

When I awoke the next morning, it was to the sound of the hammering door knocker. I rolled over onto my side, doing my best to ignore it. But the knocking was urgent. And then I remembered the events of the night before and threw the covers off.

Shit! Police – it has to be. They've found her body, bloodless. They've tracked her to this address.

I put on my dressing gown and went anxiously up the stairs. Again, a loud bang on the front door.

'Lizzy?' A male voice, muffled through the door. 'I'm back. Thought you could do with some company. Hey, Lizzy?'

I squinted against the daylight as I opened the door. The crashing of the waves confronted me, the freezing air snapping at my face.

'What on earth has happened, Lizzy?'

Bill! Thank God. I felt like hugging him.

'You'd better come in,' I said, 'please.'

The tower's entrance chamber was large enough to accommodate a sofa, a coffee table, and an elaborately carved drinks cabinet topped with mugs and a kettle. Right now, wanting to avoid going upstairs, I was very glad about that. I nodded questioningly at it and Bill smiled, heading over to it and flicking the kettle on.

'What's going on? Tell me, Lizzy, because seriously, you sure as hell don't look yourself.'

He was right. In the hallway mirror, I saw a woman who was not just on the edge, but about to break. Hair dishevelled, dark circles ringing my eyes. Some would say I looked like a crazy person; hell, maybe I was crazy.

Hazel's words haunted me: *'Damned lonely. And that works on your mental health after a while.'*

'Please, Lizzy,' Bill implored, 'I know you're grieving, but something else is clearly wrong here, and I need you to tell me what's happening. Just level with me, okay? Where's Hazel?'

I thought about Dad suffering his slow decline and Hazel spending more and more time alone with him. I thought how she had humiliated him, the suspicious life insurance policy, and Dad's alleged suicide. But was I going to tell Bill about the awful thing I'd done? Sleeping pills in her food? Binding her to a chair? That Hazel had somehow cut herself free but injured herself in the process? That she had bled to death because of me? No. I was too ashamed to tell him about my outrageous plan. Instead, I took a deep, shuddering breath and said: 'I fear this tower is disturbed in some way. Spiritually, I mean.'

'Why would you think that?' he asked, keeping his eyes steadily on me.

'Because of everything that's happened since Dad left us.'

He looked surprised, but not entirely shocked. 'Tell me.'

I thought back to the unusual lingering smells, the cold spots, the distinct feeling of a presence, and despite my inner sceptic, I found the courage to elaborate.

'I just have this intuition – I guess that's what you'd call it – that there's someone here with me, walking on the stairs, or when I'm in bed, someone walking on the floor above.'

He nodded. Not judging me, which was good. Just listening. 'Anything else?' he asked.

I glanced up at the cavernous, circular brick ceiling and thought of the top floor, where she had vanished. I remembered the sickening pools of blood that had confronted me. An accident, I knew, that I would never scrub clean. Not from that room; not from my mind.

'Lizzy?'

'Hazel vanished,' I said, which was half the truth. I could damn her entirely by not mentioning the borrowed money; but that would be less than Bill deserved.

'Your life in London,' he said knowingly, 'what were you running from?'

I was reluctant to tell him about the fraud and my false expense claims; I think because it sounded grubby, and I was so desperately ashamed. But once I'd got through my sacking, my suicidal moment, and the debt, the rest came easily enough.

'I came here, and took a loan. From her. She blackmailed me.'

I waited for a judgemental reaction; none came.

'Hazel . . . she took advantage of us.'

'I'm sorry,' Bill said with warm compassion. 'How much are we talking here?'

I was seized with a jolting realisation: there would be no coming back from this. Once I said it, the truth about my terrible mistake was out. No more hiding.

'Lizzy?'

I swallowed. 'Forty grand. A little more than that.'

'This must have been one hell of a strain.'

I nodded. 'The only strain that ever broke me. The worst strain, I thought. Until these events started happening . . . this . . .' I couldn't quite get the word out.

'Haunting?' he ventured, and I nodded silently. 'Tell me more about the occurrences here.'

I was relieved to share details of the unexplained happenings in the tower as he made the coffee. And he let me talk without interrupting. No sceptical frowns.

He set down his mug.

'Any brandy to go in this?'

'If you like . . .'

'I think we could both use some,' he said. 'Agreed?'

'Agreed.'

'Know what I think?' Bill said quietly. 'There's something you've left out. Something you're reluctant to tell me.'

I remained silent.

'You think it's your father?'

Perhaps Dad was close to me still. On more than one occasion I had suspected he might be, and maybe that he was trying to communicate with me. But no, it wasn't Dad's presence that was haunting the tower. But how to explain in a way that made sense and didn't implicate me in Hazel's disappearance?

Suddenly, from directly overhead, came a heavy *thump*.

I saw Bill react with a jolt.

'You heard that?' I said. 'Please, for the love of God, Bill, *tell* me you heard that!'

He nodded and said, 'What was it? Shall we go and see?'

But before we could move, the noise came again, only harder this time. Louder.

Thump . . . thump!

Bill's eyes widened. 'Come on!' he said urgently. 'Quickly,' and together we bolted to investigate.

The thuds had come from the living-room area, of course. When we reached the top of the stairs, I motioned him forwards. We looked nervously around the room.

But the room was empty.

'No one in here but us,' Bill whispered. He now looked just the way I felt – distinctly unnerved.

I met his eye, but didn't say anything.

He was watching me with an almost paternal concern. 'Look, I don't think you should be alone here. There's a spare room at my place. Or, I could come stay here if you like?'

I did want that; but I couldn't take the risk that somehow these happenings would reveal to him what I had done. So I shook my head. Told him it helped just to share.

'You shouldn't be alone,' he said with a sigh. 'You remind me of myself, a long time ago, and I think you know when.'

I remembered how he had said grief had haunted him after his son's death, so perpetual it had tethered him to this shore,

laying that bright line of shells in remembrance. And so painful
that at first it had almost driven him to suicide.

We agreed to keep in regular contact. But if I had hoped that
confiding in Bill about the unusual occurrences would make
them cease, I couldn't have been more wrong.

Two nights later, I awoke suddenly, gasping for breath. Once
again the nightmare had found me; all the details were the
same. The forest. The campfire. Nick.

A memory hidden.

Still groggy from sleep, I groped for the glass of water next to
my bed and accidentally knocked it with my hand; it smashed
on the floor.

Dammit!

Out of bed, listening to the night, I wondered if it was the cry
of the wind that had woken me. But then I heard the rapping
of the knocker, resounding loudly through the tower. Not the
wind, then; someone was at the door.

A visitor, at this hour?

Nerves crackling, I went barefoot up the stairs. Who was it?
Bill, come to check on me?

God, I hoped so. But as I chanced a glance through the peep-
hole, I saw the security light had come on, but there was no
one out there.

How to make sense of this?

Suddenly, it came again: *Thud, thud, thud.*

I stood there, paralysed, staring in utter bewilderment and
disbelief. *No, please no. This is too much, way too much!*

The hallway suddenly felt too cold. Unnaturally cold.

Go back to bed, get under the covers, was the thought running through my mind. What kept me there was the certainty that I *had* heard knocking. Urgent knocking.

Which meant there had to be someone out there. Perhaps they needed help. Or maybe it was someone who meant me harm. So long as I remained indebted to Mitch, that had to be a serious possibility.

If you're going out there, you need protection, I told myself, and at once was blinded by a mental flash – a vision of Hazel on the day we met, looming over me with that awful claw hammer. Right now, not knowing who was outside, that hammer seemed as good a choice as any, so I found it in the toolbox in the cupboard under the stairs.

Shoes and coat on, I unlocked the door, opened it and held my breath as the security floodlight clicked on. 'Hello?' I whispered. 'Anyone there?'

I went out onto the illuminated porch and looked around, wishing I had set up the surveillance kit out here instead of in Hazel's old room. The churning of the sea made it hard to listen for any response to my question, but just then, against the wall of the tower, I glimpsed it – the flitting of a shadow.

'Hello? Who's there?'

But I detected no trace of a human presence; not even the ghost of a whisper.

Then my foot connected with something on the doormat. Slowly, I looked down.

This can't be, I thought, *this just can't be*.

But there it was, at my feet – a potted rosemary plant.

Spotted with blood.

I got back into bed knowing that sleep, if it ever did come, was certain to be filled with perturbing nightmares of Hazel.

In my head, Bill's words recurred to me: *'Life and death meet in union on this shore. Never doubt that, Lizzy. There are other worlds beyond our own.'* There was a time, not so long ago, when I would have dismissed sentiments like this as fanciful nonsense. Superstition. But now I believed it. Because not believing meant one of two things: either I was crazy, or I was living in denial. Neither were acceptable possibilities, not to me.

I couldn't see her, but I could *feel* her. Hazel. All around me. The scent of blood, the potted plant, these were demonstrations that even in death her hold over me was not yet relinquished.

– 14 –

THE OUTSIDER

The few days that followed are hazy in my memory – I remember crying, a lot, feeling a tornado of emotions, but mostly immense sadness. Part of that was grief for Dad, but a lot of it was the anxiety of not knowing what had happened to Hazel.

Either she was dead or she wasn't, and I'll admit it was curious to me that both she and my father had disappeared and neither of their bodies had yet been found.

But then there was the fact of the substantial blood loss; the strange happenings; and the scent of her rosemary plants and candles, which seemed to linger on in the tower. She remained present, even though she wasn't, and eventually that made me curious enough to get online and do some research.

I was interested, but not surprised, to discover a growing bank of scientific evidence suggesting that exposure to rosemary can boost memory.

That made me reflect on my father's mental condition. Sometimes lucid; other times – sometimes for days – flailing in waves of confusion.

The rosemary had aided his memory recovery, that seemed clear, but which of Dad's memories had she wanted to extract, and why?

And something else bothered me. Was rosemary the only herbal remedy she had been giving him? His mental state seemed to me bizarrely inconsistent, which might have been early-onset dementia. Then again, I had to wonder what other substances Hazel had administered. Was it possible that some of his apparent symptoms of mental disease were a direct result of her interference?

That question plagued me until Nick finally arrived.

'I'll do all I can to help,' he said, as we sat on the tower's top floor, drinking coffee. He reached over and gently wiped a tear from my cheek. 'I'm here for you, Lizzy. Now the police have concluded their search for Clifford, there will be all sorts of legal documents to deal with. I'm happy to help. But do you think you ought to stay? Here, I mean?' He cast his gaze around the enormous room. 'Alone? Why stay in isolation?'

Good question. Now the police had called off their search for my father, we knew that the death certificate would say, '*Missing presumed drowned.*' So what need was there for me to stay? Why not just pack my things, and leave?

I was sorely tempted (although God knows where I would have gone), but as much as I wanted freedom, the truth is I just wasn't strong enough to walk away from my brother. He would be hurting, too. I knew that. Since the news of Dad's disappearance, he had stayed away. I understood why, and the truth was, to be honest, I was a little relieved he had kept his distance, relieved Sandra had, too; because it meant I wouldn't have to explain what had happened to Hazel when I still didn't know myself.

I was convinced that sooner or later, my brother would return. However lost he was, whatever had happened to him in Scotland, I believed that when Colin felt ready to come home, he would want to find family waiting for him. His sister. He would want us to comfort one another in our old home, and to come to terms with our loss. Mum and Dad would have wanted that, too, I thought.

Ironically, if Hazel had been right about anything, she was right about this: in the end, siblings look out for one another.

Or should do.

When the outsider arrived on Shingle Street, I was taking a late-afternoon walk. By then, the day was drawing in, the weather damp and blustery, and the yellow fog was too thick to make a walk even remotely appealing. Nevertheless, I went out – to escape the intolerable atmosphere in the tower.

As I walked, I thought, inevitably, of that tainted rosemary plant left outside the front door, its needle-like leaves spotted with blood, and fear seeped through me like a black stain. It was a message, I knew that. Alive or dead, Hazel wanted me to know that she remained. Here. With me. However she had injured herself after I tied her up, it was my fault, and in vengeance she was determined to break me. I was cursed. The rosemary plant was her way of telling me that.

Something was missing that afternoon as I paced along the beach. I soon realised what it was: no gulls, squalling or shriek-ing. No sign of life whatsoever. It was hard to see further than my outstretched hand in the fog, which was disconcerting; and the noise of the collapsing waves bore down on my spirits.

Then, faintly, I heard approaching footsteps. Slow and purposeful.

Crunch . . . crunch . . . crunch . . .

Nearer and nearer, just a few yards in front of me, and there was menace in the sound.

Steeling myself, I whispered into the murk: 'Who the hell do you think you are – whatever you are?' In my fear, I assumed that I was addressing either the spirit of Hazel or some other non-corporeal entity that had languished here since the military tragedies that Bill had spoken of.

But now I saw something that gave me a jolt. There, just passing one of the long tide-breakers that stretched into the water, was a peculiar grey shape outlined against the yellow fog. It was at the limit of my vision, but it still made my flesh creep.

I'm not seeing this, I thought, *I just can't be.*

But this lonely figure was undeniable. I saw a long dark coat and a sagging hat that was pulled down low, obscuring most of the face. After a few more paces, the figure halted, raising its head; and now I realised the full extent of my misperception: this was no ghost, or anything so unnatural. Here stood a man in his mid-fifties, perhaps older, with a powerful face and piercing blue eyes.

I kept my gaze trained on him as he approached. What swept over me then wasn't so much fear as curiosity along with some trepidation. From the way he raised his eyes and studied me intensely, he clearly wanted to speak with me.

'Hell of a place this is,' he said, his breath pluming out. 'Feels like the land of the dead, not the living.'

'Tell me about it.'

His eyes, fixed on mine, were inquisitive. 'Now then, I'm really hoping I've not had a wasted trip. You're Elizabeth Valentine.'

It was more of a statement than a question, and he was staring at me so carefully that I had to wonder if we had met before.

'Can I help you?' I said.

'Oh, I very much hope so.'

'Sorry,' I said, annoyed by his cryptic manner, 'but have we met?'

'I'm Harvey,' he said, 'Harvey Proctor,' and he stuck out a hand that was quivering, only slightly, but enough to make me wonder if he might not be entirely well. Cautiously, I shook it. 'Look, can we go inside? I hope you don't mind me being so forward here, but really, it's vital we talk. Now, ideally – I mean, if you have the time? You see, I'm searching for someone.'

'Oh?' I crossed my arms, and Harvey removed his hat. His hand dipped into his right coat pocket and produced a tattered black-and-white photograph.

'Recognise this woman?'

Before studying the picture in any detail, my instinct was to delay. 'I'm sorry, but who did you say you were?'

His ice-blue eyes pinned me. The scrutiny of that gaze was intensely uncomfortable. *You know why I'm here*, it seemed to say, *we both know*. It had been a mistake, I realised, to assume that no one would come looking for Hazel.

'Take a look at the picture for me, would you?'

'Stop. Really. Who are you? Police?'

'Call me a fact-finder. How about that?'

So you're a private detective?

'Do you work for my old company; for Mitch?'

'Take a look at the picture for me.'

I made a show of scrutinising the photo. It was Hazel. She was younger, perhaps as much as twenty years younger, but there was no mistaking that flat round face or that mean, pouty little mouth.

'You know her?'

'Of course.' No sense in lying about that now, was there? Too many people had seen her here with me. 'She was supposed to care for my late father, but I'm going to assume you already knew that, right?'

'And where is she now?'

You really want to know, Harvey? Because somehow I don't think you'll like the answer. How do you feel about the supernatural? Stay here long enough, come into the tower she made my prison, and you just might find out.

'Vanished, two weeks ago; upped and left.'

'Just like that?'

I nodded, holding his gaze. 'Said she needed time to herself – last I heard from her.'

'You know her car is parked not far from here?'

I swallowed; said nothing.

'You didn't think to report her absence?'

'Report it to whom?' I asked. 'She wasn't from an agency. I just assumed that as there was no job for her any more, and—'

'It's not just you who's missed her, Elizabeth. As far as I can tell, for the last two weeks, Hazel hasn't been seen by *anyone.*'

'Really?' It was a strain then for me to feign surprise.

He raised an eyebrow. 'You weren't at all concerned for her well-being?' He held my gaze with unflinching determination; his close scrutiny of me was frightening and I suddenly wanted him to go.

'Let me be very honest,' I said, 'I won't pretend I liked the woman. She was bossy as hell, made me feel unwelcome here, and quite honestly she was abusive and negligent. If she'd done her job properly, my father would probably still be alive. So, was I glad to see the back of her? Yeah, you bet I was. But I'm sure she'll turn up; most "missing" people do, right?'

He studied me for a quiet moment, his brow furrowed. Could he see the secret on my face? 'Can we go inside?' he asked.

Our gazes locked. There was no chance of him leaving. I saw that.

'I won't keep you long. The light's fading, and it's date night with the missus.' He tipped me a wink that was just about charming.

I'm in the middle of something, is what I wanted to tell him, but saying that wasn't really an option, I knew. It would only raise his suspicions further. 'You have identification, I assume?'

'Nope,' he said, and his tone was disarmingly honest. 'What I *do* have is information about the woman you allowed into your home.'

My stomach rolled with anxiety as Harvey stepped up to me. 'I'm guessing your father needed care at home?'

I nodded, confused.

'She's not who she says she is,' he said weightily. 'She's done things I think you'll want to know about.'

I held his gaze for a long moment, the silence between us broken only by the collapsing waves.

Then I led him to the tower.

'Goodness me! Well, this is *something*!'

As Harvey's eyes strayed from the vaulted ceiling to the thick walls and the stairwell, I saw him taking in every detail, already compiling mental notes.

'Never been inside a converted Martello tower before,' he said admiringly. 'Can I have the full tour?'

You mean, can you look downstairs . . .

'Come with me,' I said, taking the stairs up. This was risky. He could be anyone, but whatever information he had on Hazel, I needed to hear it.

What did he mean, I was asking myself, *she's not who she says she is?*

'Peaceful here?' he asked, just as the wind moaned. 'Being so exposed, battered by the elements, I guess you hear all sorts of noises, right?'

Actually, that was true; just not the sort of noises he meant.

'You'd be astonished at the power of the wind,' I said. 'Coffee?'

'Thank you.'

He admired the room, as everybody did; then, as the kettle boiled, I bristled as he selected Dad's armchair, next to the fireplace. The mug was hot in my hands. He hesitated before taking his coffee.

'Something wrong?'

'Please don't think me rude,' he said, without embarrassment, 'but have you got anything stronger? Gin and tonic, perhaps? I'm feeling the cold like a knife out here.'

His hands were trembling again.

'No problem.'

I took the mug back to the counter, all the time keeping my eyes on Harvey, and suddenly it was like being back in London, in the office, sitting across from Mitch just before the inescapable confrontation. The fallout from that had been colossal. Where would the conversation with this stranger leave me?

I took out Dad's crystal decanter, which was chipped at the lip, and tipped a generous glug of gin into a glass and added tonic water; then crossed the room and handed it to Harvey.

'Thank you,' he said, 'most kind.' Then, after a sip, he cleared his throat. 'So, your father converted this place?'

The question was loaded with such authority he might just as well have shown me the character report he had no doubt already compiled.

'That's right, the tower was Dad's passion.'

'A peculiar one, if you ask me. Your mother died tragically young, correct?'

'You clearly already know—'

'Because I like to cross reference,' he stressed, tapping his leg. 'The facts are, your mother was a school teacher, your father an architect. They lived not far from here, right?'

I nodded.

His salt-and-pepper eyebrows knitted together and I could feel his sharp eyes scrutinising me. 'For a girl your age, barely a teenager, that must have been tough, moving out here, to the edge of nowhere. And then your mother died; you moved to London, but your father stayed. Entombed himself right here. Maybe he wanted to hide away, eh?'

He nodded to himself, as if to validate this.

'The point is, I suspected Hazel would come here, in the end. She doesn't realise this, but I've been observing her for a long time. Longer than I would like, and that's the truth. Who knows, maybe she suspects. Maybe that's why she's up here so many nights at the window, looking out, hiding. And maybe *that's* why she's disappeared. What do you think?'

'I really couldn't say.'

'Caught her scent almost a decade ago. I'm sick, if you can't tell, and I'm not sure I'm long for this world, Lizzy. But before I go, I want that bitch behind bars.'

'What did she do?' I asked, my voice low, as he straightened in his chair.

'I'll come to that.' He studied me. 'What you should understand, Lizzy, is this: anyone who associates with Hazel Sanders comes to my attention, eventually.'

'I didn't associate with her, not willingly.'

'Is that so?' His tone was cynical. 'At first, I wasn't sure; had to check the electoral register to determine that you did live here once, so you weren't necessarily her accomplice. And it was clear to me then that you were Clifford's daughter and maybe the situation was as clear-cut as that. But guess what? I've got a problem, Lizzy. I'm afflicted with an insatiable curiosity. So, I ran an online search and saw where you used to work, Red PR, and I thought, well, it couldn't hurt to give them a call.'

'You spoke to my former employer?'

He nodded. 'Had to be sure you were who you appeared to be, right? I mean, people steal identities all the time.' He took another sip of his gin. 'I pretended I was a potential client; asked specifically for you, your skills. They said you'd moved on. Mutual agreement, was it?'

I stared back at him flatly. 'Fifteen years. So what? It was time to leave.'

'Sure, I get that, but something bothered me. Guess there was something in their tone. But why am I telling you that? You know there was more to the story, don't you?'

My stomach was doing somersaults now. 'Listen, whatever you may think you know about me—'

'So I called them back, and this time I pretended I was a recruitment consultant, checking your references. Eventually I got through to some big shot – Mitch. Remember him? And he said he really didn't have the time for an old coot like me. To be fair, he did sound stressed and I sounded a bit shaky at the tail end of the afternoon, but he paid a lot more attention once I mentioned *your* name. In fact, I heard him get up and shut the office door before we went on with our little chat. Nice, I thought.' He tipped me a wink. 'Everyone deserves the courtesy of a closed door, right?'

I sat down. My knees were too weak to stand now.

'You stole a hell of a lot of money, and lied about it. Correct? Mitch skirted around the issue at first, but I got there eventually. When I mentioned some of your other employers had expressed reservations, he had an excuse to open the floodgates. Understand what I'm saying, Lizzy? He's bitter. Don't blame him, to be honest; he trusted you. Anyway, our conversation got me thinking: a woman who steals from her employer, who gambles with her corporate credit card – a woman like that would steal from just about anyone, right? Perhaps even from her own father.'

'You're wrong about that.'

'Am I? Then why are your hands shaking? Why's your face suddenly so white? You already paid back a substantial lump sum; where did that come from? The magic money tree?'

I thought of Hazel, bound to a chair in this very room. I couldn't explain to Harvey that the money had come from her.

He took a sip of his drink. 'Normally I'd be less candid than this,' he said, 'more discreet, so as not to compromise the investigation. But in this case I'm certain, and time is short for me. So I've levelled with you.'

'I'd like you to leave.'

Leaning back in his chair, he held my gaze steadily.

'Leave now,' I repeated, standing, 'or should I call—'

'The police?' He spoke over me. 'Why not? I reckon my old pals would be more than pleased to meet Hazel Sanders' accomplice.'

'I have no idea what you're talking about.'

'Let me tell you what I think,' said Harvey. 'I believe that Hazel was unduly influencing your father, and isolating him. Abusing him, and yes, I think she probably killed him. And I believe that *you've* been complicit in these crimes. If not actively assisting her. Which is it, please?'

I stared at him, horrified. 'You think I'd do that, to my own father?'

'Families hurt one another all the time; take my word for that. The horrible reality is that ninety per cent of elder abuse cases are perpetrated by family members. Which makes *you* a person of significant interest.'

'You talk like you're police.'

'Retired. But I've been observing this tower for months now. Day and night.'

I thought of Dad seeing a figure down on the beach approaching the tower. Hazel thought he'd imagined it – but it could well have been Harvey he had seen.

'And I was at the hospital,' Harvey went on, 'when your father was admitted.'

My pulse quickened as I realised what he was telling me: he was the figure I had seen at the end of the hospital corridor. Not a supernatural spectre. A man. Surreptitiously observing us.

'I wasn't entirely sure who you were then. You turned up out of nowhere . . . I had to know.'

'You wanted to intimidate me?'

'If you like.'

'Why?'

'Suggestibility, deception, these are effective techniques.'

I tried holding his gaze, but failed. My anger dissolved into bewilderment and my eyes drifted to the window. Bill's ghost stories came back to me.

'What about the weird sounds on the beach?' I asked. 'The rumble of engines, the muffled explosions?'

'No idea what you're talking about.'

'You mean you never heard anything like that, in all the time you've spent out here?'

'Never.'

We stared at one another. He was holding back on me. I had a distinct sense that he did know something about those unnatural sounds.

But what mattered now was Hazel. What she'd done. Why he could possibly imagine I had *helped* her. The suggestion was maddening.

'Please tell me,' I said, 'why did you trail Hazel? What did she do?'

What he said next shocked me to the core.

'By my reckoning, she's guilty of two murders. Three, if you include your father.'

The room seemed to tilt, as if the world was turning upside down.

'Hey, you with me?'

'Yeah,' I replied, my voice sounding odd to my ears. Distant.

'Sit down, will you. You look like you're going to pass out.'

I sat down heavily. 'This is . . . a lot to take in.'

'You're telling me you knew nothing about her past?'

'Only about the trouble at Rose Cross House. For administering her own herbal remedies without permission.'

He laughed, then started coughing. By the time he'd caught his breath, my dizziness had passed. But not the horror; I wasn't sure that would ever pass.

'By then, she had changed her name,' he said, 'started her new life. In her old life, she was Barbara Barnes. Home help, visiting elderly people in their homes, helping them with their lunch, that kind of thing. And that's when the trouble started. Wanna see?'

The sheaf of folded paper he was already drawing from his inner jacket pocket made it hard to say no.

He slipped a photocopied newspaper article onto the coffee table between us. 'The first victim – Peter Percival.'

I bent forwards to look. Drew a breath. The headline was almost too shocking to comprehend:

CARE ASSISTANT PLACED PLASTIC BAG
OVER PATIENT'S HEAD.

Beneath this:

Barbara Barnes denies ill-treating 72-year-old Peter Percival at his home in Woodbridge.

According to the article, she had been providing one-to-one care to Peter that day, when the postman, through the front-room window, saw Barbara holding a plastic bag over Peter's head. The postman, Walter Scott, said he had shouted at Barbara and banged on the window.

Asked by Joyce Hoskins, prosecuting, how Barbara had reacted, Walter said: 'She slowly removed the bag from off his head, she wasn't shocked or panicked, and then she came to the door and calmly claimed they were playing peekaboo.'

The headline of the next article Harvey showed me read:

CARE ASSISTANT CLEARED OF MISTREATING ELDERLY
PATIENT BY PLACING PLASTIC BAG OVER HIS HEAD.

*Barbara Barnes said she placed a plastic sheet in front
of the face of Peter Percival, 72, at his home as part of
a game of 'peek a boo'.*

'She got off on a technicality,' said Harvey. 'Lucky. Not for
poor Peter, though, whose body was found at home three
months later, after a concerned neighbour called the police to
report the smell of gas coming from his house.'

'Oh my God,' I said, thinking of our own gas 'leak' and
Hazel's reaction: *'How am I supposed to care for Clifford when you
go and do reckless things like this? HOW?'*

'As far as I can ascertain, the second victim was another
local man. But she was clever; she waited three years. She
needed time to settle into her new identity, and by then, she
was coming to the end of her employment at Rose Cross House.
During those years, from a distance, I kept an eye on her.'

My first reaction was confusion: the headline included the
word 'accident', but nowhere were the words 'suspicious' or
'murder'. My second reaction was shocked horror.

The article, from the *Suffolk Tribune*, reported on the death of
seventy-six-year-old Simon Firth, whose ribs had fractured while
he received emergency CPR. And this: *'Mr Firth also suffered injuries
from three "unwitnessed falls" during his time at Rose Cross House.'*

Harvey studied me. 'You all right; need a glass of water?'

I shook my head, thinking some of his gin would be preferable to water. I kept remembering how Hazel had sat in this
very room, not too long ago, tearful eyes fixed on me as she told
me about her father's agonising experience in a care home – *'his
eyes screwed up, his hands clenched into fists, crying out in agony . . .'*

How she remembered finding him in his bed, falling off his
bedpan, crying out for help. How his carers had 'unintentionally'

broken his ribs while administering CPR. It was an ugly thing to happen. What had she called it? That's right, 'a necessary evil'.

Evil indeed; for it was clear to me that some time between these horrible events and now, Hazel's memory had blurred with fiction, and the horrific reality of her own crimes. Negligence. Abuse. And . . .

'She's a monster,' I said slowly. 'I suspected, and now you've confirmed it. First Peter Percival; then Simon Firth; then Dad.'

Harvey scrutinised me. 'She's a killer; and a calculating, cruel liar. What sort of person targets the elderly and vulnerable, Lizzy?'

'You have to believe me, I had nothing to do with this. I want her found. I want her punished.'

'I want that, too. For a time, when she was on trial for abusing Peter, I thought I had her. The witness testimony was damning. There was no way she was getting let off . . .'

'What happened?' I asked, when Harvey didn't go on.

'Abuse of process. Physical evidence that should have been preserved was lost; a serious breach of duty on the part of the police. Meant her chance of a fair trial went out the window. She walked free but she wasn't content, not even then. Afterwards, she got nasty. Accused me of indecently assaulting her, in her cell.' He sighed, his frown returning, only deeper now. 'So they put me under internal investigation. It didn't help that they found some weed in my locker. That I admit to! Medicinal.' He tipped me a wink and a smile, but the smile soon faded.

'The CPS decided there was no evidence to support a prosecution. Small consolation. You think the stain ever left me? Did it hell. Always the knowing looks between my colleagues, always the suspicious glances. I was never left alone with a suspect again.'

'I'm sorry.'

'You should be,' he said drily, 'if you're covering for her.'

'I'm not. I want the same as you. I want her found.'

I was thinking: she might not be found, though. And this enigmatic stranger, Harvey, was probably thinking that, too. Hazel had vanished from the map, and the fact that I didn't know where she was had nothing to do with the stark truth that I was indirectly responsible. She'd disappeared when she and I were alone together, after a significant sum of money changed hands, after I had doubts about her innocence following Dad's death. However you cut it, this didn't look good for me.

'Just laying my cards on the table here, as honestly as I know how. Did you borrow money from Hazel?'

'It was a loan. A business agree—'

'No.' As he set down his mug, his smile turned cold. 'You took money from Hazel. And I'd wager she stole that money from your *father*. Oh,' his eyes flicked over me, 'don't try coming over so innocent. You knew. You were complicit.'

The conviction was back in his eyes, a look that told me he knew I was involved in this, and not in a good way.

'Well, if you should think of anything,' he said, standing and holding out a business card, 'please contact me on this number. You'll get straight through to me.'

I escorted him downstairs. He started across the shingle, then looked back. Punched a cigarette from its packet, and said, 'I'm not going to give up, Elizabeth. I want her found, I want her punished, and I want the truth about your involvement with her known. Understand?'

I watched him go, a part of me wishing that I could tell him everything, the rest of me haunted by the wretched secret I was keeping.

*

Back at the top of the tower, I took a long, disturbed look at Harvey's calling cards; the newspaper articles that bore the names and pictures of the pensioners whom Hazel had tortured and, it seemed, had very likely murdered in cold blood. Peter Percival, Simon Firth. Not names that were familiar to me, but they were permanently etched into my memory now.

'*Unwitnessed falls . . . fractured ribs . . . plastic bag over his head . . .*' Tears sprang to my eyes as I stared at those words, remembering Dad's broken fingernails, the scratching, gnawing sound I had heard coming from his room; and my heart folded in on itself. All I could think about were the days, months, Hazel had spent under this roof with Dad – with Colin's consent.

She signed a contract of employment, Colin had said.

Oh, but Colin. That contract ended everything.

How had we failed Dad so dismally? It was an appalling thought, but unwittingly we had let a monster in. And why had she wanted to infiltrate the tower in the first place – why had she targeted us?

I looked again at the newspaper picture of Simon Firth. If he had lived he would be Dad's age now. Maybe I was just desperate, clutching at straws, but it seemed to me that I had seen the old man before. Something about his features . . .

I paced the room, my mind registering the sibilant shifting of the shingle out on the beach as the waves crashed in, before finally I thought of the only other picture I had seen recently that had aroused my curiosity. The photo under Hazel's bed; the smiling birthday boy with tousled hair.

A minute later I was down in my room, slipping open the drawer and taking out the picture. Careless of me not to have replaced it before now; what if Hazel had missed it? Unframed, torn at the edges. There was the boy, on this beach, blowing out the candles on his birthday cake. Fifteen years old, or thereabouts. Again, it struck me that something about his smile wasn't convincing. The other boys weren't quite smiling – in fact, you could almost think they were sneering. I scanned their faces, recognised none, until . . .

There!

My eyes widened, I held my breath.

Oh my God . . .

In the foreground, looking on, was a face I *had* seen before, or rather a nose, because that's the feature that I most recognised. A prominent nose that bent ever so slightly to the left. Maybe that kid had a deviated septum; maybe he broke it playing football. What I knew for sure was that the nose belonged to Simon Firth, who, aged seventy-six, would collapse in a care home, and whose ribs would snap under the force of Hazel's cruelly vigorous chest compressions. Simon who, before his death, would endure many falls and abuse meted out by the hands of his carer.

Either Hazel had known the boys in the photograph, or they meant something to her. What seemed clear was that Simon, an elderly man whom Hazel had abused, had come here to the shore in his youth with a boy celebrating his birthday. But why did they come here? And how was this connected to my father?

Then I heard something, a slight creak of the floorboards above. I waited for it to come again, holding my breath, and was relieved when it didn't.

A question Hazel had asked came back to me: '*Did your father ever fear the shore?*'

I could almost feel her probing stare boring into me.

'Are you here, Hazel?' I asked the darkness.

I listened. Nothing, only the wind shrieking at the window, as if calling me. I moved towards it slowly and looked out onto the shore. The fog had cleared and, in the distance, I could just about make out Bill's shell line, gleaming under the bright winter moon. Yeah, she was near. Observing. Waiting for my sanity to break. But I wasn't yet ready to concede defeat, not even nearly.

'You knew more about this shore than you ever told me, right? Sly old Hazel; but not so clever, maybe? Because whatever you knew, I can know, too.'

Of course I could. My laptop was upstairs, which was where I went then, to get online and search 'Simon Firth . . . Woodbridge'.

As I clicked open the first result on the screen, my eyes widened. Simon's obituary was even more intriguing than I could have anticipated. I looked at the screen with my jaw hung.

'What the hell . . .'

'You're not the first,' I said to Bill when he answered my call ten minutes later.

'I don't follow, sorry?'

The line crackled as I stared at my laptop screen.

'I mean, you're not the first to come out here hunting what you called "the others ".'

'Okay? If you wanted my attention, you've got it, Lizzy.'

'A long time before you arrived, there was a teenager who attended a birthday party, right here on this shore. Now, decades later, he's dead. His death wasn't treated as suspicious, but it was. A vulnerable elderly man who needed care. Like Dad. And who do you think he had in common with my father?'

'I'm all ears.'

'Hazel. Or, as she used to be known, Barbara Barnes. She had a picture of this man, Simon, when he was a boy. Pictures of this Martello tower. Pictures of Orford Ness.'

'You think she targeted him in his old age?'

I did think that. What I didn't know was why; but one clue before me on the laptop screen suggested a connection that was more Bill's expertise. A link to the inexplicable happenings that my father had experienced here.

'Her last victim. Bill, I have his obituary here. His surname was Firth – Simon Firth. Does that ring a bell?'

There was a moment of silence, then an exhale of surprise on the other end.

'Jesus, Lizzy, Simon Firth was—'

'—an author and investigator,' I said, and I read out the obituary on my screen:

'Born 16 May 1939; died 6 February 2015 . . . Simon Firth, who has died aged 76, was the author of more than 30 books on the paranormal, including *Suffolk Hauntings* (1981) and *The Ghosts of Shingle Street* (1997), and was one of Britain's greatest authorities on hauntings.

'During the course of his life, Firth probably collected an unprecedented number of first-hand ghost stories. He was convinced about the reality of supernatural occurrences. In a debate held twelve years ago in Woodbridge, *The Meaning of Ghosts?*, he said:

'"We all have our own ghosts. Some are spirits of the dead, who may be capable of communicating with us. Other reports of ghostly happenings are impressions of events, recorded in our atmosphere. And there are ghostly happenings that occur only in the mind. For too many of us, and for me personally, ghosts are conscience."'

There was silence on the line as we both processed this.

Then Bill said, 'I think I should come over. You don't sound . . . yourself.'

I wasn't; because there was something very wrong here. Three men were dead, my own father among them, and what they all had in common was Hazel.

I needed to understand now how all of this connected.

'Come quickly, Bill,' I said. 'Please.'

I had to search through Dad's boxes of files for a couple of hours, crouched uncomfortably on the floor outside his wardrobe, but I was well rewarded for my efforts. Most of his records had gone up in flames with the boathouse, but judging from the dates of these files – early to mid-fifties – here were some pictures from secondary school. Just as Bill handed me a second coffee, I found what I was looking for: a class photo from when Dad was aged fifteen or so. The date scrawled in pencil on the back was 1954. The picture was black and white and faded, but there was no mistaking my father's younger, handsome features. I handed Bill the newspaper picture of Simon Firth and he studied it curiously.

'You think your father may have known this guy as a kid? Friends?'

Hazel. The tower. Too many coincidences. 'It's got to be possible, but we need proof.'

Now I spread four school photographs over the floor and put the picture of Simon in the centre of them all. We scrutinised the images in silence for a minute, perhaps longer.

'There!' Bill said, pointing over my shoulder. 'That's him, isn't it?'

It was hard to be sure; the boy in the picture, standing just a few paces away from Dad, was a teenager, not an old man, and he wore a school cap that cast a shadow over his forehead. But his nose was prominent, and it seemed a match. 'You may be right,' I said.

'I'm sure I'm right. And look!' Again he pointed. 'That kid off to the left, he looks remarkably like the other victim, no?'

I studied the picture, and indeed, the short, wiry boy at the end of my father's row did resemble a much younger Peter Percival. What gave it away was the prominent Y-shaped dimple in the centre of his chin.

'What does it mean?' Bill asked.

A moment's silence. 'It means that Hazel's attacks were definitely not random,' I said. 'She deliberately targeted my father, and two of his school friends.'

'But why them? What was her motive?'

My heart was hammering, my hands shaking.

I thought about the books under her bed and remembered how, before his stroke, Dad would often stare off towards the eerie and wild Orford Ness, as if into a blank and haunted void. I remembered Hazel at the window, gazing in the same direction, the rusting structures of military buildings a magnet to her eyes. Before, I'd thought little of their regard for Orford Ness. What if, I wondered, there was something meaningful about the old military test site for both Hazel and Dad? Something I didn't know about.

'Three teenagers,' I mused, 'sixty-five years ago, in one remote location. This shore. Where Dad completed this renovation. Hazel said he was convinced he was hearing voices. And one of his childhood friends grew up with a fascination in the supernatural.'

We locked eyes.

'That can't be coincidental, can it? What if Dad really could hear the voices? What if he and his friends were here and heard all about the local folklore? You said it yourself, Bill, this is a place of legends – those tales of the burning sea and the Nazi invasion. Bill, what if these kids were drawn to these stories? Came here on their own investigative adventure. And what if something happened to them? Something that stayed with them maybe, all the way to end of their lives?'

'I agree it's possible,' Bill said, after a moment. 'Speculative, but yeah, possible. You know what kids are like; into everything. However, why would any of that concern Hazel? When your father was a youngster she wasn't even born, surely?'

It was a good question, perhaps the only question, and I had an inkling that at the heart of it was the birthday boy in the photograph. Who was *he* and where was *he* now? I was just about to raise this question, when Bill said: 'Wait a moment, these pictures of your dad's . . . where are the rest?'

'What do you mean?'

'Well, all these photographs take your father up to at least aged fifteen; but then . . . nothing. It's like he vanished.'

'Could be in the albums that went up in flames with the boathouse,' I said.

'Yeah, but there are other pictures of him here, with you, presumably, as a baby. As a young man. But the in-between years, his early twenties, are all gone.'

That did seem a little strange, but at that moment I was only mildly interested. What interested me more was the mystery boy blowing out his birthday candles as the other boys looked on with sneering smirks. Who was *he*? Where were the other pictures of *him*? I put these questions to Bill.

'You can think about that when I'm gone.'

'What?' he said, alarmed. 'You're going somewhere?'

'The military watchtower. On Orford Ness.'

He stood up. 'No. Absolutely not. It's dark out there; it's not safe.'

'I have to, Bill. Because Hazel had an interest in that place, for sure; and it's where I felt most affected. Weird and wild. A place of mystery. Everything leads there.'

He was shaking his head, and I was shaking mine, remembering what it was like out there on that haunting strip of marshland where the instruments of death were developed and tested – the bitter wind, the enigmatic silhouettes of barracks and bunkers. Mostly what I remembered was the rusted watchtower: the compulsion to climb it, the profound sadness I felt at the top, the handprint on the wall. I knew that these memories, that place, were important. It had been as if the place was whispering to me.

Orford Ness could be the key to unlocking the entire mystery.

'In all my time here, that's where I felt the most sadness and the most fear,' I told Bill. 'Something dreadful is happening on this shore, you were right about that. And this isn't logical, but I have a feeling – like my mother used to have these feelings, an intuition if you like – that the Ness, that watchtower, is where some sort of trouble began. You asked me to help put the presences here to rest – so please let me try.'

'Then I'm coming with you,' Bill said.

'No. There are things I haven't told you,' I said, standing to meet his gaze. 'Things I've done that I'm not proud of.'

A shadow flitted at the edge of my vision and made me look around. A change had affected the bedroom; as though all the life had gone out of it, even though we were still here.

Bill looked inquisitively at me, a glint of excitement in those kindly eyes. It was the opposite of how I felt. There was a cold, sick feeling in the pit of my stomach.

'Hold still a moment,' I said. 'Can you feel it? All around us . . .'

'You mean a felt presence?' he asked. 'The sensation of being watched?'

I nodded and whispered, 'She's still here.'

'Hazel?'

'Yes.'

'Wait. You're saying she's *dead*?'

'Afraid she might be.'

His confusion was evident in his frown. What was the use in concealing it any longer? Time to level with him. So I did, and to his credit, Bill listened without any outward appearance of judgement. I was grateful for that, as I went over the horrid details. Listening to myself, it was as if I were describing the actions of another person, which, I guess, must have been wishful thinking. It disgusted me that I could have contemplated harming another human being. Even if she was vicious and vindictive.

'Bill,' I finished, 'there was so much blood. No way she could have survived. No way that *anyone* could have survived.'

'Yet you're convinced she's still here?'

I nodded.

His eyes remained fixed on me. Compassionate, I thought. And curious. Open-minded. They were the eyes of a scientist who had endured too many put-downs from climate change deniers and was now eager for some validation.

'Are you appalled at me for what I did? Disappointed?'

'I'm not here to judge,' he said. 'Let's say you're right. Somehow, Hazel injured herself trying to escape. Maybe she cut herself free and slashed her arm by accident. But then how did she leave without you noticing?'

'She must have made it down the stairs and out when I was asleep,' I said.

'But there was no blood on the stairs or in the hall?'

I shook my head, and he looked baffled.

'I always thought I'd be happier when she wasn't here any more,' I said pensively. 'Now I feel her closer than ever. Bill, you met Hazel, did you learn anything about her fixation with this place?'

'Can't be certain,' he said after a pause, 'but I believe she may have been looking for something.'

A great curiosity took hold of me.

'I told her I came here for closure. She told me she understood, that she hoped, one day, to find closure herself.'

'If she and my father shared any sort of secret, I must uncover it,' I said. 'Now. And at whatever cost. But I won't have you dragged into it. Okay? You're to stay behind. Bill, are you listening?'

'Oh yes,' he said, suddenly grave, 'I'm listening.'

Just then, we heard something out in the hallway tumbling down the stairs.

'Bill, wait! Please—'

But already he'd rushed out of Dad's bedroom to investigate. I moved to the doorway and saw him standing at the foot of the stairs, staring sadly at his left palm and the small white whelk shell it held. He exhaled, deflating; held the shell to his chest. Close to his heart.

'Bill?'

He came towards me then, a light of determination in his eyes, reached out and squeezed my hand.

'You're not going out there alone, Lizzy. If I'm not part of the solution, I'm part of the problem.' Nodding adamantly, he closed his fist around the shell. 'So,' he said, 'that's settled.'

I very nearly refused. What stopped me was something strange that happened in my father's room, directly behind me, at that moment. Something very small and precise yet totally intangible, like a change in the light.

'Okay Bill,' I said reluctantly, 'have it your way. We'll need to take some flasks. Let me find a rucksack.'

Darkness. The suck of the tide on the shingle. It was close to freezing outside. Side by side, we strode along the beach in our walking boots, bobbing torchlight leading us. The moon was a glowing white disc, bright enough for me to feel hopeful about locating Susan Winter's boat and making it safely across the river.

Soon we were walking past Bill's beloved shell line, which he laid in the hope that he might one day see his son again. His dead son. His drowned son. Taken by the waves.

He turned to me, his eyes gleaming, and drew a deep shuddering breath. 'Lizzy, I hope to God I haven't wasted my life chasing after things that don't exist. Do you think I have?'

I remembered the night of the muffled explosions; the dying men's screams carried on the wind. I shook my head.

As I looked into his eyes and saw in them a father's yearning, I felt a mixture of kindness and guilt. Kindness because I suddenly knew what was right for Bill: *He should stay here, near the shell line.* And guilt, that I would not take Bill with me to the Ness; I would go back on my word.

'We're going to need some more reserves,' I said. 'You got any more torches in the house? Maybe some blankets?'

He nodded. 'Should have more than a few.'

'Can you get them, please. Some warm jumpers, too. I'll wait here.'

He said he wouldn't be long.

The sensible thing would have been to explain what I was feeling. The charge of static electricity in my hair; the eerie sense that something unpleasant, perhaps even some danger, was folding around me. I felt it in my soul and in every muscle, a distance between two points in history closing in on one another. But I did not explain, probably because I knew he would try to talk me out of going alone. I wanted to protect him. I waited until he was in the cottage, and then, in a flash, I was running, and a few minutes later I was at the quay and the lonely small ferry boat moored there. Was I confident I could make it work? Of course not; but I did remember Susan operating the wheel and the throttle and thinking how easy it looked, and that gave me a little confidence.

Something else I remembered: the key for the engine, which she kept in a small waterproof container.

Get in, that boat seemed to say, *I'm going to take you somewhere you won't ever forget. Because something is coming. Like a storm on the wind. Something is coming.*

– 15 –

THE MAN I NEVER KNEW

The swish of water. The raised shingle bank of Orford Ness approaching.

I made it across in less than fifteen minutes, and although the estuary was calm for most of my crossing, from the moment I set foot on the wet jetty, the weather seemed to change abruptly. A blast of wind hit my face and sharp rain began to sweep down.

Welcome back, Orford Ness seemed to whisper, haunting and strange. *What kept you?*

With mounting trepidation, I looked around me. Shivered. Somewhere close by abandoned structures with DANGER, KEEP OUT signs were rattling under the force of the wind. Against the blackened sky I could just about discern the dark silhouettes of the old test labs and hangars.

I was alone, and yet, as I struck out over that desolate stretch of mud and pebbles and marsh, I couldn't shake the feeling that I was being watched. The sensation was so strong it felt like a finger pushing into the centre of my back. I felt vulnerable, reckless for doing this on my own; it would have been easier with Bill. Safer. I imagined him walking beside me.

'*Left me behind? Rather naughty of you.*'

'Sorry. I had to do this alone.'

'I hear you. So which way are we headed, Lizzy?'

'About half a mile from here is the military museum they're building. The guard tower I explored is right next to it. That's where I felt the sadness. The presence.'

'What do you expect to find?'

'Maybe nothing. Maybe something. Something that needs laying to rest, hey?'

The Bill in my imagination nodded. Then he said: *'Bet you wish I was really with you, huh?'*

I did. The sharp cold was in my bones and the air was thickening. A storm was coming. It would be wise to take shelter.

Briskly, I walked on, until the dark shapes of the hangars, the control tower, the half-cylindrical Nissen huts loomed into view. The harder I looked, the harder it was to imagine that this had ever been an operational establishment. Everywhere the shattered windows; relics of shattered lives.

'There!' I pointed towards the watchtower. A steel box on four stilts. It towered there, dark and silent in the gloom.

But something – I suppose you'd call it intuition – warned me not to go that way. Not yet. Instead, I felt compelled to pivot to my left, where the shape of a low hill loomed into view.

'Sure about this?' Bill said in my head.

I wasn't. But out here, alone, being sure about anything was a luxury I couldn't afford. What would Mum say? Now wasn't a time to be guided by logic or reason; if ever there was a moment to trust my gut, this was it.

I looked back at the low hill. Something odd about it. The front of the hill seemed to me a dull grey colour. Straining my eyes as I got nearer, I realised that it must be a bunker. How else to explain the pipes just visible, protruding from its rise?

And I wondered, as my gaze travelled over the rows and rows of similar small hills, if this was the weapons storage area Bill had mentioned. If so, any of these bunkers would offer me shelter from the rain – assuming they weren't all locked.

Instantly I felt a shock jump through me. A most extraordinary sensation that I was no longer alone. Someone was there; at my side, or just behind me. I can't emphasise enough how real it felt to me, this silent companion. Nothing was visible, nothing could be heard; but then an unseen hand pushed my shoulder. Gentle but firm; as if nudging me forward.

I cried out in surprise and my hand leaped protectively to my shoulder. For a moment all the curiosity that had fuelled my lonely expedition evaporated into fear for my safety.

And then something heightened my fear, a short burst of speech:

'*Help me. Find me.*'

It was the quiet, plaintive whisper I had heard before, and although it was impossible to be sure, I firmly suspected that this was the utterance of a supernatural agency.

A dead person.

But who? Why had they led me here? To guide or to haunt? To comfort or terrify?

My shock was so deep and so profound that for several seconds I couldn't move, and when I finally could, I opened my mouth to address the invisible intruder. What stopped me was a quick, almost fleeting movement of cold air that glided suddenly past me.

I was confused and shaken, but capable of collecting my wits, and that's what I did. Whatever it was, the presence had left me, for now.

A gust of wind slammed against me. I lowered my head,

steadied my footing and walked on. Straight ahead, a closed door confronted me. Here, a yellow and black sign read:

CAUTION, HAZARDOUS NOISE AREA.
HEARING PROTECTION REQUIRED.

The sound of movement on the other side of that door.

I had an abrupt irrational sensation that I was in danger. But I wasn't turning back. On my own, in the middle of nowhere, in darkness, in a place I knew was dangerous, I was going to push on this door, advance, and explore.

The door creaked as it opened. A startled bird flapped out of the blackness, causing me to leap back.

'Hello? Anyone here? HELLO?'

Just an echo bouncing back at me.

'*Stop,*' Bill said in my head, cautious. '*Just turn back now, Lizzy.*' But I didn't.

Feeling the dark pull of adventure, I stumbled cautiously through a clutter of debris, passing a rusting generator, ancient ammunition boxes. Another door confronted me. This one was heavy and rusted, and its padlock had come loose. Susan Winter obviously wasn't as diligent as she was supposed to be. I pushed on it and with a scrape it gave way. Stagnant air wafted out of the darkness beyond, but it did not deter me. Led by my torch, I took a few steps until I found the light switch, and with a heavy clunk the lights inside the bunker flickered on.

I found myself staring around a vast room. Freezing. No windows. Cracked concrete walls, a curving metal roof. And something I hadn't expected.

My heart lurched in my chest when I saw four figures standing at the far end of the space, and then with a surge of relief it registered that they were mannequins dressed in military uniforms. Was this the beginnings of the museum they were developing? Possibly. Although the workmen clearly had some way to go yet.

Broken glass littered the floor. There were rows and rows of filing cabinets. Shelves tightly packed with boxes full of papers and files. They smelled rank and damp. Neglected papers, possibly of historical importance, that should, surely, have been stored somewhere secure and not abandoned here, left to rot.

Sometimes I think certain locations speak to us, like our dreams do. We don't always know exactly what they're trying to tell us, but when those messages are imbued with meaning, we sense it acutely. That's how it was for me at that moment, as my gaze swept the desks and rows of filing cabinets. Documents. Highly classified. Secrets of a hidden history.

It was Susan's job to retrieve the documents from this site. I wondered whether she'd cleared this bunker yet. Or if she deliberately hadn't. What on earth was in these files?

Drawn to them, pulled like a magnet, I began to search, pulling out drawers in old desks and filing cabinets. They were all empty – until I reached a cabinet behind the mannequins. It was unlocked, which I took as an invitation to scan the file inside.

I remembered Bill telling me: '. . . *something happened out there . . . something the government worked very hard to bury.*' How eccentric and conspiratorial that had sounded. Well, if what I was reading was true, it didn't sound eccentric or conspiratorial now. What it sounded was downright sinister.

I ran my eyes over the text:

'*SECRET EYES ONLY . . . May 1940 . . . Imminent German invasion . . . Evacuation and minefields to be laid on the beach . . . soldiers burned alive with oil . . .*'

I know what you're thinking, and I was thinking it, too. Wasn't this just a little too convenient? That I should find this after such a cursory search in an unlocked bunker? And yet here they were, answers to the military questions Bill had been asking. Except what was written here wasn't what people thought. Not even nearly.

'Must be made to look accidental . . . petrol pumped onto the surface of the sea . . . Bodies washed up . . . Hundreds of causalities . . .'

'Oh my God,' I breathed, 'what did they do?'

Suddenly, behind me, a shuffling sound; and again, a powerful impression of a presence.

I whirled, seeing the line of military mannequins looming there. Had one of them moved?

No, of course not. And yet, I was almost certain one had.

Fear closed around me. Was there something in this bunker with me, some presence that inhabited this abandoned place and needed recognition? Or worse, revenge?

One of the bulbs began to flicker and fizz. Shadows danced. My stomach flipped, and a creeping horror began to take possession of me. I would not stay a moment longer.

The file went into my rucksack. For later, for Bill.

Only then did I notice that the mannequins' faces weren't intact. They were horribly burned. And now there seemed to be more of them . . .

Dead white eyes seemed to stare at me from out of the shadows. The blackened patches around those eyes accentuating the menace of those empty stares. What were they, crash test dummies, restored and dressed up? I felt my face crease in confusion – and then horror.

Crash dummies didn't have burns or mutilations; they didn't have scorched flesh . . . There was no mistake. No trick of the light. The figures before me, I realised, had once lived. These were spectres of military men who had perished here, and I was looking straight at the hideous injuries they had received in death.

This abandoned facility, I realised then, wasn't just haunted. It was *infected.*.

'No, this can't be . . .' I whispered into the darkness.

I never got to finish that thought. Because suddenly a strong arm wrapped around my waist, yanking me back, and I felt a sharp scratch on the side of my neck, and I was falling, fading, into darkness.

A campfire, crackling. Leaves and broken branches. The salty easterly breeze. Plastic champagne glasses.

I knew this place. A small clearing in Rendlesham Forest. With Nick.

Something caught my eye, something sticking out of the forest floor and glowing in the firelight.

'Leave it,' said Nick, but I reached for it. Prised it out of the earth. Regretted it at once.

It was metal, rough and chipped at the edges, tarnished to a mottled purple. The touch of it turned intrigue to fear. Just staring at that object made my stomach twist.

It's like me, I thought, it shouldn't be here.

A snapping branch. The oppressive sense of being observed. I twisted around, my heart thumping, and saw . . . something I could never understand or even admit to myself.

Someone was shouting at me.

'Come on, wake up now, that's it . . .'

In the velvety void, I swam towards that voice. But as my eyes fluttered open, I flinched away from the harsh white light.

'Try to focus. Lizzy? Hey, Lizzy!'

I was shaking. Someone was shaking me. Then a hand slapped my cheek hard. That brought me out of it.

I opened my eyes, but my vision was swimming. In the red glow of a paraffin lamp, I saw the blurry outline of a toppled chair; walls of corrugated metal sheets, rusting and tinted green with algae. Floorboards thick with dust and broken glass. And after a few unbearable seconds, I realised: this was the guard tower, the metal box on four rickety stilts. Freezing. And the atmosphere was pervaded by the same sense of grief and distress as before.

Whoever had been shaking me was out of sight, for the moment. Perhaps outside, on the viewing platform?

Suddenly, from my left, a pitiful sound, like an animal in pain. Turning my head, I saw a dark shape huddled against the wall. A person wearing a frayed blue hoody and a pair of equally frayed dark jeans. Their chin on their chest.

My first thought was that this dishevelled person was probably in a great deal of pain, and I was about to speak, to try to help, when the figure stirred and the head came up very slowly.

'Lizzy . . .'

His eyelids fluttered open, revealing milky eyes that were desperate. Devastated.

It can't be . . .

Frail fingers reached for mine.

'Oh, Lizzy,' he breathed through lips that were cracked and purple. 'You shouldn't have come, not for your stupid old dad.'

Disbelief held me motionless for a long second. Then, with exhausted determination, I dragged myself nearer to him. For a moment, I actually thought I was hallucinating. But then I felt Dad's papery skin as his hand slipped into mine, the gentle squeeze of those bony fingers, and the palpable fact that he was *alive* hit me, imbuing me with such amazement, relief and shock that I began to cry. Dad was alive and I had found him.

His eyes wandered the gloom, then fluttered back to rest on me, gleaming with tears.

'Oh, what have they done to you, my baby girl?'

His skin was the colour of clay; his face scratched and bleeding, his cheeks pitted and hollow. How long since he had last eaten?

'Where have you been all this time?' I asked, but then I saw the strewn blankets behind him, and knew the answer.

Here. He had been kept right here. With dawning horror, I realised that someone must have kidnapped him. Engineered his disappearance. Made it look as though he had drowned himself. Made every finger of suspicion target me.

'Tell me what happened?' I asked.

Dad suddenly leaned forward and gripped my wrist. His eyes, now, were shining with fearful clarity. 'Get out, Lizzy, hear me?' he said. 'Oh, my girl, get out *now*.'

'She's going nowhere,' said a voice behind me.

I jumped at the sound and turned instantly.

Not possible, I thought, *after losing so much blood, it's just not possible*. But there *she* was, aiming her torch at me, targeting me in it's beam. Hazel. Looking down on me with such disdain. Her mouth twisting into a smile.

'And so,' she said, with a note of satisfied finality, 'now, at last, you'll see his weakness, Lizzy. The horrible family truth.'

Outside, a gale was rising, rain drumming on the metal roof with tremendous ferocity. It was no calmer within that guard tower.

'What's happening?' I shouted. *'What have you done to him?'*

'Good to see you, Lizzy.'

For a woman who had apparently bled to death, she looked fine, sounded remarkably calm. Dad wasn't saying anything now, and I could hear him struggling to breathe.

'Don't be too concerned,' said Hazel, 'your dad's just a little sedated – but he's used to that by now, aren't you, Clifford?' She paused, then went on in a judicious tone. 'Of course, his memory's recovered a little, and that's good. You will be a witness, Lizzy. You have a right to know.'

'Stop this, please,' I said, 'whatever you're doing, please just stop. Let us go, can't you see Dad's sick?'

'Your father *is* sick – in the head.'

'As sick as you?' I challenged. 'As sick as someone who'd kidnap a vulnerable old man? Fake her own death? How are you even alive? How is that even possible?'

'It's possible because of me,' said a new voice. It came from the door that led onto the viewing platform. Someone was out there. A man.

Without speaking, Hazel gestured for him to come in. And after a moment, he stepped into the light.

What . . . what is this?

'Hi Lizzy.'

'Nick?' I said, bewildered. I went to stand up, but Dad gripped my hand.

'Please, Lizzy,' he mumbled, 'you've got to get out of—'

'Your father's right,' Nick cut him off, his tone mildly remonstrative. 'I'm sad you have to see this, Lizzy. Really. This isn't what I intended. I *thought* we had you fooled, and that was good. But this – you being here now – well, that changes things . . .'

His hair was stringy and damp, hanging in his eyes. He swept it back and looked bleakly at me. 'Sorry to disappoint.'

This I had not expected. I remembered then Harvey's idea that Hazel had an accomplice, and the realisation came through my body in a slow dreadful shudder.

'No, please, not you,' I said desperately. 'You're here to help, right? You followed me to help, *right*?'

Hazel suddenly gave a bark of derisory laughter. And I saw something that turned me cold. Clear and unapologetic loyalty as their eyes briefly locked. In that look, a secret knowledge passed between them.

'Nick?'

I had never seen him like this. That look of watchfulness. Calculating. Sly. What the hell was he doing here?

Then his hand twitched at his side, and as I looked at it I saw he was holding something. A syringe.

The scratch on my neck, I thought. *Jesus, he must have put me under . . .*

'You two. Working together. Why?'

'Tell her,' Hazel instructed. 'It's right that she knows.'

Nick fixed his eyes on me, and I felt none of the warm re-assurance I associated with my friend. What I felt was a prickle of fear.

'Nick, please, what the hell's going on?'

'Was kind of hoping dear old Dad might have explained by now,' he said.

I shook my head in confusion. Had I missed something?

'It's okay, Lizzy,' Nick went on. 'I don't want to see you like this – desperate, frightened. Please, just listen. Everything's going to be fine, everything can go back to normal. Once you understand.'

'What are you talking about?'

'Your father.' His mouth tightened. 'Everything you think
you know about Clifford is a lie.'

I looked at Dad, hunched miserably against the wall and deathly
pale. So vulnerable, so broken.

'You leave him alone!' I said, moving closer to shield him.
'This isn't right!'

'You won't be defending him once you know,' said Nick. 'He's
a *fraud*, Lizzy. You ever hear that song, "The Great Pretender"?
Well, that's him, your dad, right here. The greatest pretender
of them all.'

Nick's voice was low and solemn, entirely reasonable. 'Try
to remember,' he said, 'the good old days, before your mother
got sick; playing happy families at the tower. Were those times
ever truly happy?'

His words triggered a memory: the days when we had no
family car. I saw my Mum at the hall table tearing open a white
envelope. Reading the letter within. Collapsing to her knees
as Dad just stood there, saying nothing, staring despondently.

'Of course you remember. You know what? Clifford here was
steeped in debt, even then; never had control of his finances,
borrowing from anyone who'd lend. You told me about it at the
time, Lizzy, or did you forget that?'

The lies we tell ourselves . . .

I closed my eyes, and on the back of my eyelids now, another
memory: a man with a clipboard at the door, clicking his pen.

'Come on, Lizzy, you know this song, do I really need to sing
it for you?'

He didn't. The song was suddenly playing in my head, the
soundtrack to a flickering spool of memories: Dad telling Mum
it was his job to pay the bills, what business was it of hers? What

right did she have to ask questions about the family finances? Dad stuffing the mail under his jumper. Dad hanging his head when the bailiff left. And Mum at the door, trembling and crying, pleading: *'Clifford, talk to me! Clifford! What's going on?'*

'Told you he'd sort it, didn't he? Bet he sat you down in some family meeting and told you all how sensible he was with money, how he was going to put it right? When all he did was become more and more distant. And then your mother got sick and you all had an excuse to look away. Easier to believe his lies when you had your mother to think about. Or am I wrong?'

He wasn't. A silence stretched. How I wished, then, I could erase the past. Rewrite it.

'You know what surprises me, Lizzy? That you thought you could put it all behind you after the funeral. Move away, bury the past?' Nick shook his head. 'Memories like that never stay buried; darkness rises. Clifford here was the kind of guy who seemed to have it all sorted. Know what I mean? I'd wager you do. The apple never falls far from the tree.'

'Enough, please.'

'That all you can say? I mean, aren't you at least curious to know what happened?' He raised his chin. 'Yeah, I bet that deep beneath that cool exterior, you're just *burning* to know, aren't you?'

'I said that's ENOUGH!' I heard the coarse shock in my voice as it rebounded off the metal walls. Nick heard it too. And he smiled.

'Remember back when we were kids, Lizzy? We had a good time, right? Maybe the best of times.'

I closed my eyes and saw us, Nick and me, as teenagers, striking out across the shingle foreshore beneath the winter sun. Even on days when it was cold and wet and blowing a gale.

'Yeah, sure, life wasn't perfect. But we were happy. As far as we could be. We made the best of it, Lizzy. Until you *left*.'

'That's what this is about?'

'No.' His features hardened. His voice deepened with bitterness. 'What I'm trying to tell you is that we weren't alone. Our parents – Clifford here, my mum – they had a lot in common with us. *Way* too much in common.'

With dread, I said, 'What . . . are you saying?'

'My mum; your old man . . .' His fingers tightened around the syringe. His eyes on fire, fixed on Dad. 'Oh yeah, the other kids in school knew all about it. How could they not? What do you think they were sniggering about when they saw us together?'

At last I said, 'He made mistakes. But Dad's a good man.'

'No,' Nick said with contempt. 'He destroyed my family. Bet he didn't tell you that? Bet he didn't tell you he cheated me out of my inheritance?'

'Your *inheritance*? No. Nick, what are you talking about?'

'Never thought your dad had secrets? Never wondered why your mother was permanently unhappy?'

In a feeble voice, my father spoke up: 'Don't listen to him, Lizzy, please. It was so long ago and—'

Nick cut him off. 'They were going to be together. He was going to move her into the Martello tower, share it with her. Put the property in both their names once the renovation was done; that's right, isn't it, Clifford?'

I felt a horrible pang of fear as Dad looked pleadingly at me. *I'm sorry, Lizzy*, his eyes said, *I am so, so sorry.*

'And you can guess where he turned to for the money,' Nick went on. 'Yeah, my mother. By then, he'd gambled away most of his own, and he wasn't content to stop there. The tower, its entire renovation, that was a hellishly expensive operation,

Lizzy. I mean, didn't you ever wonder about that? Where the money came from?'

I glanced at Dad. His face was bone white, his mouth set. He was shaking his head despairingly, unable to meet my gaze.

'Yeah, the money's the clue, Lizzy. Hundreds of thousands. Clifford won't have told you this, I bet, but guess what? He got the money from *my mother*. That's love for you. Clifford asked and Mum provided. Except he didn't so much borrow the money as steal it. It's a question of the right signatures in the right place at the right time, isn't it Clifford?'

Doing the best I could to hold it together, I looked questioningly at Dad again. His eyes were shimmering with tears. Guilt?

'My mother mortgaged our house, just so Clifford here could fund his architectural grand design.' Nick's tone was thick with disgust and it showed on his face. 'She had to fake my father's signature to do that; but she did it. And that's why my parents broke up, Lizzy; that's why we lost our home. Because Clifford here took the money. Understand? He took the equity in our home, to pay for his.'

Suddenly my father started and his face creased with anguish.

I drew back. My throat clenched.

'So,' Nick said, 'still think this isn't right, Lizzy?'

I couldn't have spoken then, even if I'd wanted to. Dad's tearful reaction said it all. This was a truth that had festered for too long, mutating into a vengeful conspiracy. That need for revenge was real, all right, and it was visceral. Dangerous.

With scathing acrimony, Nick addressed my father. 'You allowed the years to tick by as you piled up the lies, higher and higher, until your kids didn't know you. Built a tower to protect yourself. Funded by *my family*. And now I'm entitled to an apology. A confession. Justice.'

Discharging Dad from hospital early. Certifying the power of attorney. The pools of blood so easily procured partly from her own arm, but mostly from the hospital blood bank.

A deception. All of it led to Nick.

Except it didn't stop with him, did it?

I turned my gaze to Hazel, who stood, solid and looming, in a corner, half concealed in a nest of shadows. She had a wolfish gleam in her eyes.

'Why did you do this?' I asked her. 'And what the hell ever brought you two together? You never knew one another, so—'

'Can you be sure of that?' Hazel spoke over me. 'How *can* you be sure, after being away for so long?'

To my chagrin I realised that she was right. Still, it seemed such an unlikely companionship that I was at least half convinced she was lying to me.

'We *came* to know one another,' Hazel clarified. 'Remember Clifford had an infection in his foot? That meant regular hospital appointments; and I went with him for every damn one. As you know, I'm good at noticing things, Lizzy, and what I noticed on those tedious visits was Nick here; always watching your father from the sidelines; but why?'

She turned to look at Nick, her head tilting to one side. 'I really had to wonder, because he wasn't treating your father, were you? Mostly, it was the silent seething bitterness on your face that told me you knew Clifford, that perhaps you two had history, and I spent a long time wondering about that, Nick. But in the end, I didn't have to ask, did I? You just came right up to me while Clifford here was with the nurse, remember? And you asked me: did I live at the Martello tower?

'You know what you were like then, Nick? A lost lamb

needing to be shown the way. All the anger was there, deep down, as it had been since your youth; you just needed a little encouragement to channel that anger, didn't you?'

She nodded to herself, smiling contentedly, then turned her gaze slyly on me. 'So you see, Lizzy, we found one another. Convenient partnership, wouldn't you say?'

I stared dumbfounded at the two of them, these betrayers, and felt suddenly very alone, very small, and very nauseous. 'What do you want?' I asked again, finally finding my voice, 'and what makes you think you'll get away with this?'

Hazel gave me a cunning sideways look. 'Because,' she said, 'to anyone who cares, Clifford is *already dead*.'

For a moment the words just hung there, but Nick looked oddly confused. As if she had just disclosed part of a plan that was hitherto unknown to him. Either way, I realised that she was right, and I felt a shiver of dread. Meticulous planning on her part.

'Hazel?' Nick spoke up, a half-formed question, but she swiftly silenced him with a gesture of her hand. She took a few slow steps nearer, eyes glittering, as the scale of her poisonous triumph fully dawned on me.

'In you, Lizzy, we found a rather ideal and unsuspecting accomplice.'

I wanted so badly for her to be wrong, but I could see the calculation in her eyes, the devious scheming.

'I saw such ambition in you, Lizzy. But your judgement . . .' She shook her head. 'No, pet, I'm afraid to say your judgement is a little . . . *off*. And I think that when the police eventually come asking questions, that's going to play to my advantage rather well, don't you?'

She came nearer still, dropped a hand on my shoulder and paused, carefully choosing her words. 'I'll tell you something,

Lizzy, and listen carefully now, because this is the story the outside world will hear. It's the story of a compulsive gambler, an out-of-control addict, a thief, who drains her own father's accounts. Accruing more and more debt. Only this time, you decide this isn't a debt you'll repay. Easier to remove me from the equation, right? Easier to make *me* disappear. And that's what I'll do, when our business here is concluded. I'll disappear for a while, let Nick here tidy up any loose ends, then I'll return and say you attacked me. You were unstable and I had to get away. People will understand that, I think.' She nodded primly to herself. 'People will think I deserve something in return for my loyalty to your father.'

Then a memory came back to me, something I remembered from our exchange in the tower: she had changed the named beneficiaries on Dad's pensions, or tried to.

I felt a shiver crawl over my flesh. Hazel was his care-giver. She was there for him, always. It was entirely believable that he would leave her money.

Now I was willing to bet that it was her name that appeared on those pension forms. It wouldn't be Nick's name – he was no one to my father, that would have looked suspicious. Besides, I was beginning to wonder from his paling expression just how much of her plan Hazel had omitted to tell him.

'And yes Lizzy, I know, you probably got a steam cleaner all over that kitchen already – if you didn't, then I'm disappointed, but' – she looked sharply at me, as if to ensure I was listening – 'when the police find my little note, explaining how afraid I was of you, how unbearable you made life at home until I agreed to lend you money, they'll scour the Martello tower for any trace of my DNA. Blood spots, for example. I'm sure you realise what that will mean for you.'

I did, and it meant that everything would point to me.

'You were never wealthy,' I said, knowing this was true but needing to hear her confirm it. 'The money you gave me. You siphoned it from Dad's accounts?'

She nodded, not in a smug or triumphant way, just matter-of-factly. 'The rest came from . . . other sources.'

I said nothing, but I could guess who those other sources were. Simon Firth, Peter Percival. Dad's childhood friends.

'Nick deserved this opportunity to scare your father, to confront him,' she said, giving him a solemn, satisfied look. 'An atonement for your father's sins.'

'Oh please, you don't care about Nick or settling his family's scores,' I said disbelievingly. 'Why would you? You two barely know each other. No. You did this for self-gain, for financial reward. That's it.'

She gave me a dark, withering look that said: *There you go, underestimating me again.*

'Want to know what brought me here? Why I did what I did?' She stepped forward, her eyes flashing with a fanatical gleam. 'All reason was for it. All justice. What I did was *fair*.'

Here it was – she wanted Dad's pensions, his property? Or maybe she was just one of the sadistic abusers you read so much about these days, who thrived on abusing and manipulating vulnerable elders, someone who thrilled to their repeated cries for help as their bedsores wept and their bodies dehydrated and they struggled with their bedpans.

Neglect. Abuse. Whatever her twisted justification, none would be good enough. Nothing would justify it.

'So let's hear it, Hazel. What *is* your problem?'

'How's this for a motive?' she hissed. 'Your father *murdered* my brother.'

Her words were a splash of freezing water to my face.

'What . . . what did you say?'

She was staring hard at me. With dread, my eyes locked on her lips as they formed an impossible sentence: 'Your father killed *my* Sammy, my older brother. The brother I never met. *Your father* killed him, right here, in 1954, on his fifteenth birthday.'

The rain was pelting the corrugated metal roof. A loud groaning of steel as the entire watchtower creaked under the blasting wind. The storm was almost upon us.

With my heart in my mouth, I turned to look at Dad. 'What's she talking about?' I whispered.

My father's eyes weren't vacant now. They were glittering and dark and yes, somewhat secretive.

'Dad, please, what the hell does she mean?'

Before he could attempt an answer, Hazel said to me: 'You already know what my Sammy looked like, don't you Lizzy? You found his picture in my bedroom, remember?'

How could she know that?

'Snooping, Lizzy,' she said, her voice chillingly calm. 'Good at that, aren't you? The way you went through your father's private papers. A real snooper. Did you really think I wouldn't want to keep an eye on you when I was away? When I was coming here, to make preparations? Had you on camera, that's right. With a live feed to this.'

She held up her phone. And there, glowing on the screen, was an image of me at her bedside, holding the photograph of the teenager blowing out birthday cake candles as the other boys looked on, smirking.

'Simon Firth and Peter Percival. They were here.'

Nick's head snapped up. It was surprising to see that gesture, because the look in his eyes suggested this was new information. I was sure of it: Hazel may have told him about Sammy's 'friends', but something in his expression told me he had not heard their *names*. And what struck me was the glimmer of recognition in his eyes. There was alarm there – the look of a man who realised he might be out of his depth.

Hazel didn't seem to notice that, though; she fixed on me. 'When they were growing up, Simon and Peter came here with my Sammy. And if it wasn't for your father, he'd still be alive.' Her face was flushed with hatred. 'You want to talk about abuse, Elizabeth? Isolation? Ask your father. I learned it all from him.'

She's lying. That's what I told myself as I watched my father groping for words, shaking his head wildly. And yet, there was a dreadful conviction in her tone that made me wonder.

'It's *not* true . . .' Dad spoke up, but his manner made me think of the day the bailiff had come to our door. The alarm on Dad's face when Mum asked him to explain the endless letters from the bank. The same denial I was seeing now? Or fear, perhaps? Panic?

Uneasy, I raked a hand through my hair.

'Oh Lizzy, you must have suspected,' Hazel said, her face grim and unforgiving. 'You worked in PR – you can smell bullshit like no one else. And in the short time you've been back, you've certainly rummaged through enough drawers and cupboards – haven't you?'

I looked at Nick, wanting to see reassurance on his face, but he offered none. Just stared flatly back at me. *You should not have come, Lizzy*, that look seemed to say. *Why did you? You weren't meant to hear any of this.*

'You were lucky to know your brother. Privileged,' Hazel said bitterly. 'But Lizzy, growing up an only child, in the shadow of parental grief? Can you imagine what that was like for me, the intense loneliness?'

She began to pace restlessly as what sounded like a lifetime's trauma came spooling out.

'I was born ten years after his death, but I never knew a normal mother or father. In Sammy, my parents had seen perfection. A good, gentle boy who did what he was told, never answered back. Sammy, who they hoped would grow into an ambitious successful man and continue my father's law practice. Then I came along. Unplanned. A surprise for them, but not, I feel, a good one. Was it inevitable that they'd look for the same perfection in me, and never find it? Who knows, but that's what happened.'

A crash of thunder. The storm sounded so much closer now.

'Forced to sleep in the living room, on a sofa, because the only bedroom that was free – Sammy's old room – had been a shrine for so long it was impossible for them to see it as anything else. They never got over the loss. When I reached the age he was when he died, my mother broke down in tears; told me she wished she had died, and not Sammy. And when I pointed out to her that if that had happened I would never have been born, she simply stared back at me, and nodded.'

Hazel shook her head as if in denial at that.

'Can you imagine how that felt? All I wanted was for them to *see* me, to *love* me, but nothing I did was good enough.

'Finally they told me what had happened to Sammy. Can you guess?'

I couldn't, and I didn't want to.

'After his birthday party, on the beach, Sammy came out here with Clifford, Simon and Peter – and I think you know why?' Hazel said, interrogative eyes fixed on me.

'They came to explore?' I ventured, remembering that one of the boys in the photograph had grown up to become an authority on supernatural matters. Joining the dots, the conclusion that they came here for the dark thrill of adventure made sense. The only question was: what did they find?

'Idiotic kids doing idiotic things. Not Sammy. Timid child, my parents told me. An introvert. Sammy had no interest in exploring somewhere like this, never wanted to come. But they made him. Your father and Simon and Peter – didn't you, Clifford. Suppose you found it amusing to scare him with the old legends?'

She flicked her eyes at my father; he caught the look, and something passed between them. A private exchange that was deeply unsettling to me.

'Your father, Lizzy, has lived with the shame of it ever since,' Hazel said. 'His night terrors? Those were born from guilt. And his precious Martello tower? He didn't renovate that out of a passion for the building. He did it to hide from his past. From his *shame*. Built himself his own prison, walled himself up, to look out on this wretched place. He could never escape it, could you, Clifford? Now you never will.'

Listening to this, an unbearable chill ran down my back. As I twisted around, Dad gripped my hand tightly. There was a look of utter desperation in his eyes now.

'Please, Lizzy,' he mumbled, 'you mustn't believe this.' He glanced up at Hazel, who was looming over him. 'It was an *accident*,' he stressed, 'you know that! I never . . .' He swallowed, choking back tears. 'I never meant for your brother – bless his soul – to come to harm. Sammy got into difficulty. What happened was a frightful accident. And we'd have taken it back, if we could. Even now, I wish I could take it back. I would do *anything* to—'

'WELL YOU CAN'T!' Hazel yelled, making Dad and me start violently. 'YOU CAN'T TAKE IT BACK!'

She began pacing back and forth, and the words flew from her mouth like daggers. 'Think about what happened, just think about how you treated my brother, the endless name calling.'

'*It wasn't my fault!*'

'Wasn't it?' She was closer now, fixing Dad with that righteous glare, and I saw the darkness behind her eyes that had festered, I suspected, for too many years. The insatiable need to right a wrong. *Siblings look out for one another*, she had said once. *Or should do*. In retrospect, that comment held a double meaning.

Dad shook his head. 'We all made a mistake!' he cried, this time holding up one hand as if swearing an oath. 'We never meant to—'

Hazel spat in his face.

'No!' Instinctively, I lurched forward, but Nick's hand clamped down on my shoulder. His other hand, I recalled, was holding a syringe.

'Listen to me,' Hazel said. 'Are you listening?'

Dad barely managed to mutter a reply.

'You're a murderer. Child killer. Say it.'

He shook his head.

'*Say* it!'

'I'm *not* a killer.'

'I need to hear you say it,' Hazel insisted. 'We all need to hear it. Tell us what you did! You remember – I *know* you do.'

I realised then why she had brought him here, of all places. Why she had filled his home with rosemary plants and candles to aid the reminiscence therapy. Why she had worked so hard to rekindle his memories. She was goading him. Forcing him to remember.

'Peter told me what happened in 1954, right where we're standing,'

'NO! Peter only told you what you wanted to hear!' Dad's lips trembled and his gaze drifted into the distance. He was remembering. 'Peter could never accept what happened . . .'

My God, Dad, what did you do?

Galvanised by rage, Hazel strode over to Nick. 'Give me that.' She snatched the syringe from him.

'Funny, isn't it,' she said, 'how the truth brings everyone to their knees, eventually?' She brought the syringe to the side of my neck and held it there, just inches away, ready to stab me with it.

'Let go of me!'

Dad stared in horror. 'No, no, please don't harm her.'

'Then tell me what I want to know,' she snarled. 'The Ness was off limits back then; why did you bring Sammy here against his will? To show off to your friends? To show you were *braver* than him, that you had the guts to explore when he didn't?'

'We were foolish, so foolish. Things got way out of hand, but—'

She grunted with disgust. 'You enjoyed seeing him afraid, didn't you? Oh, I bet you just *loved* that – bullies always do, right? You *feed* off fear.'

Dad was shaking his head vigorously, his gaze skittish.

'Sammy died because he fell from out there.' She nodded

to the lookout platform beyond the door. 'Because you *pushed* him.'

I said nothing. I couldn't speak. Never before had I been so stunned into silence.

'No, that's not what happened,' Dad said, grey-faced, and threw me a despairing glance. 'We weren't monsters! But yes, Sammy did fall and—'

'*Sixty feet!*' I heard the catch in Hazel's voice. 'Did you read the coroner's report, Clifford? Because my parents did. And I did – all ninety-eight pages. Know what I learned?'

Dad lowered his head as Hazel's flat round face contorted with emotion. I felt my heart break for her a little, in spite of all she had done to ruin our lives. Even if she was delusional, the trauma she was enduring was real enough. We could all see that. Standing next to her, Nick looked horrified.

She sucked in a breath. 'Sammy hit the ground on his front – on his *face*! His head cracked wide open, spilling his brains onto the concrete.'

Dad cringed, and I had to swallow down a surge of nausea. Unmoved, Hazel hurled yet another accusation.

'And before he fell, you and your mates beat him, mercilessly. Tortured him.'

'No, it wasn't . . . like that . . .' Dad stuttered, tears rolling down his flushed cheeks.

'The name calling had been going on for years, hadn't it? Because he was different. Sensitive. And out there that night, there was no one to stop you going further,' Hazel hissed. 'Then, when it was over, after you pushed him, what did you do? The three of you fled, like cowards – fled, thinking only of your-selves, and left poor Sammy . . . for the scavengers.'

She shook her head, and this time her voice didn't just catch, it broke and she sucked in a breath of grief.

'*Four days* until they found him – poor soul. Four long days, left to the crows and rats. My parents counted every one of those days, you can imagine. And by the time they found him, Clifford – did you know this? – they had to identify my brother by his *teeth*!'

None of us spoke.

'So, tell me what gave *you* the right to leave him out here, alone. Why didn't you at least make one anonymous phone call? Why did you just run?' She nodded, as if she already had the answer. 'Because you were guilty as sin. All that mattered was saving your own skins, when really you should have spent the rest of your lives behind bars!'

'We ran because we knew no one would believe us!' Dad said through his tears. 'And when we were put on trial for man-slaughter, no one did believe us.'

My breathing stopped. *Manslaughter?* Hearing that was like being punched in the gut. Who was this man beside me?

He looked at me, eyes leaking, his expression of hopelessness and remorse undeniable. 'Found us guilty,' he admitted, 'served eight years in a young offenders' institution. After that, a new identity. Not even your mother knew.'

'What's your name?' I asked, bewildered. 'Your real name?'

His mouth tightened. 'I'll never be that person, ever again. I'm Cliff. I'm your dad.' Then he turned back to Hazel. 'You want the truth? Here it is: the night Sammy died, all four of us experienced something none of us understood or knew how to deal with.'

I wrapped my arms around my body, bracing myself for what was coming, my heart thudding ever harder.

'What we heard up here,' he said, 'the impossible things we saw that night . . . it was the shock of those events that caused Sammy's fall.'

'What are you talking about?' Hazel demanded.

'You'll never understand, you can't, because *you weren't there!* But what we saw and heard changed our view of the world. Such strange, unearthly things . . .'

I took a moment to process this – as far as I could process anything with a syringe aimed at my neck – and then I thought of the papers in my rucksack.

'Something happened . . . Something the government worked very hard to bury . . .'

I thought of the ghostly figures in military uniform I'd witnessed in the bunker. Their burned and mutilated faces. I thought of the rumoured military disaster at Shingle Street. Is that what he meant?

When I'd heard ghostly sounds that night on the shore, I thought I'd heard the cries of dying men, aircraft lumbering through the sky . . . a deafening explosion that Hazel had dismissed as an earthquake. Had Dad and his friends heard something like that, too?

It had to be possible.

Outside, the wind gusted hard enough to shake the guard tower.

'Enough!' Hazel snapped. 'I heard these fantasies from Peter and I'll be dammed if I'll tolerate any more from the likes of you. Do you think you can miss someone you've never met? I do. I know it. You killed my Sammy. And you'll pay for that, by God you will. You'll pay for it *now*.'

– 16 –

THE HAUNTED SHORE

A gust of wind shrieked through the gaps in the steel walls. Nick moved swiftly towards my father, bent down so he was on his level, and took his arm.

What the hell are they going to do? I thought, terrified. Hazel was capable of anything, she had proven that. How far would she go to right the injustice that had blighted her life?

'Get up, Clifford!' she barked. A sigh of surrender shuddered through my father as he struggled to his feet. 'Take him outside,' she instructed.

Nick hauled Dad towards the viewing platform from where Sammy had fallen. I tried to move forward, then felt the point of the needle against my neck.

'Both of you, just stop and think,' I pleaded, 'it doesn't have to be this way!'

'Take him right to the edge,' said Hazel. 'Show him the drop that Sammy had to see!'

Nick obeyed without question, but as it dawned on me that I might be just seconds away from seeing my father placed in grave danger, I drew a breath that was not at all steady. Somehow, I had to break Nick's trust in Hazel. Surely he didn't know all of her background. He was a good man – angry, yes, and misguided right now, but still, I wanted to believe in him. Believe that he wouldn't be working with Hazel if he knew who she really was.

It was one hell of a gamble, but I'd always been good at doing that, hadn't I? Now wasn't the time to lose my nerve. Now, if ever, was the time to roll the dice.

'How many more people are you going to punish, Hazel? Weren't the others enough?'

She jolted, as if a live wire had touched her arm, and Nick hesitated, looking back at us. 'What does she mean?' he asked. 'What others?'

'It means she has form,' I said, eyeing that damned syringe and wondering if she was as crazy as I feared. Nick, who still had hold of my father's arm, was squinting in confusion.

'Oh, she hasn't told you this part?' I said quickly. 'What about her real name, has she told you that?'

'Her *real* name?'

'Barbara Barnes,' I said. 'It's not just Dad who constructed a false identity.'

Nick's eyes darted between me and Hazel; I guessed he was trying to discern if I was bluffing.

'Watch what you're saying!' Hazel said in a low voice. The syringe was even closer now. 'You're delusional.'

'Am I? Tell that to Simon Firth and Peter Percival.'

'Wait,' Nick said after a moment, sounding unsettled and surprised. 'That name . . . something in the local newspapers, seven or eight years ago?'

Dad's face, I saw, wore an expression of horrified understanding.

Nick pulled Dad back inside the tower, stopping just inside the doorway. 'Hazel,' he said, 'what the hell did you do?'

'She hunted them,' I said, glaring at Hazel. 'You had a duty of care, and you made two vulnerable men suffer.'

'Shut your mouth,' she hissed, shoving her face in mine. 'Just shut the hell up! Nick, take Clifford outside!'

But Nick no longer looked so certain, and his mouth was trembling. I was briefly hopeful that his resolve seemed to be weakening.

'Was it worth it, Hazel?' I asked. 'Did they tell you what you needed to know?'

'You're sick!' she spat. 'Sick and deluded, like your father.'

Only too aware of the syringe so close to my face, I leaned forward just a fraction and snarled, 'As sick as someone who'd murder two innocent men?'

She didn't like that, not at all. To have a light shone on your wrongs, to have them seen fully, is to know yourself. And for others to know you, also.

Holding her gaze, I drove the knife in deeper. 'Now Harvey's hunting you, Hazel. He told me everything. And you can bet he has a grudge against you for ruining his career – remember doing that?'

She looked stunned. So did Nick, whose mouth had formed a perfect O.

'Nick!' I shouted his name with enough accusation that he flinched. 'She got off on a technicality, but make no mistake: she's committed unforgiveable crimes. You understand what you've helped her do? Tell me you understand the gravity of what you've got yourself involved with here?'

He blinked, shook his head, but he never looked away.

'She targeted these men, tortured them, until they told her what she wanted to hear: how Sammy died. And then' – I turned to look directly at her – 'you murdered them.'

'No,' Hazel whispered, her face milk white. 'That's enough, that's—'

'Violence motivated by revenge. And to get at the truth.'

'She never believed the truth,' Dad broke in, frowning at Hazel, 'she never will.'

But – as we were all about to discover – that wasn't entirely true.

Suddenly, in the distance, we heard a rumble of thunder. In truth, it was so deep and resonating I had to wonder if it *was* thunder.

Dad's head snapped up. Uncertain, his eyes met mine and, for a moment, a heavy silence enclosed us. Even the wind and the pelting rain seemed muffled. I knew my senses could have been playing tricks on me, but the rumble from outside, from above, sounded like the drone of engines.

Hazel turned her head towards the noise, lowering the hand holding the syringe for only a split second, but that was long enough for me to take a chance. Now or never.

Many months of rage surged up, giving me all the strength I needed. With a *crack*, my right elbow impacted with her jaw, hard.

'That's for Dad!' I cried, already launching another punch, to the left side of the face. 'And this is for me!'

The shock of the blow sent her reeling back into the steel wall with a loud *clang*.

Stumbling to my feet, still groggy, I made it to my father's side and drew him close. He looked at me out of a gaunt, strained face, tears standing in his eyes.

'I'm sorry I lied to you, Lizzy,' he whispered, 'so sorry to you and Nick.'

I was relieved that Nick didn't intervene. Instead, my oldest friend lowered his head, and when he raised it and spoke again his voice caught and cracked, with a distinct tone of regret mixed with sorrow. 'Lizzy – this is *not* what we agreed. Honestly. I never signed up to murder anybody.'

'Oh, don't you play the innocent fool!' Hazel fired back at him as she hauled herself to her feet. 'You knew where this was headed all along.'

Nick recoiled as if she had struck him. 'No!'

'But he must die; surely you see that?'

'No, no, no! That's not what we agreed!' He was shaking his head vehemently, his eyes moving from her only to plead with me. 'Murder? Lizzy, *no*! Please, you know I'm not that person. She tricked me – said we would give Clifford a scare, make him confess to what he did. Make him apologise, but that was all, I swear!'

It was the stare he gave her that convinced me. A look of visceral bitterness.

'She was using you,' I said, placing my hand on his arm. 'You can't trust anything she—'

'Don't listen to her!' Hazel gasped, adjusting the glasses that had almost fallen off her face. There was a boiling anger in the eyes behind those glasses. Amazingly she was still holding the syringe.

And she thrust it out before her as she advanced on us.

I remember what happened then so vividly – mostly, I think, because shortly after I got back to Shingle Street I told Bill, and then wrote it all down. In fact, it was the first part of this account that I typed out – that's how afraid I was of forgetting any of the details.

Nick stepped forward, grabbed Hazel's arm, and twisted the

syringe out of her hand. 'Tell me what you did to those men,' he said viciously. 'Tell me, or so help me God, I'll—'

Suddenly a low vibration was rolling through the floor, the walls.

Hazel froze, we all did, as the vibration built, along with the ear-throbbing roar of an unseen plane and a new sound – a high-pitched whine.

Everyone held their breath.

THUD, THUD, THUD. Explosive sounds from afar, like detonating shells.

Startled, Hazel shrank away. 'What the hell?' she exclaimed, and her face took on the same look it had when she'd found herself tied her to the kitchen chair. It was the expression of a person who knew they had lost control of a situation and didn't quite understand how.

'This is what happened,' Dad's voice cracked with emotion, 'dear God, this is what we heard, in 1954, on the night Sammy died.'

I thought of that time alone on the beach, watching the ragged firelight out at sea, and remembered Bill's warning: '*Life and death meet in union on this shore.*'

Another *THUD* in the distance. Were these muffled detonations the incorporeal traces of some long-ago disastrous event? At that instant, yes, I thought that more than possible. And a mental tingling hinted at further strangeness to come. The air began to stir, the temperature plummeting.

A chill stole through me.

'What's happening?' said Nick. 'You feel that?'

The apprehension on our faces said it all: yes, we could all feel it – the air thickening with a weird static that crackled and made our hair frizz.

Suddenly, every source of light at our disposal began to flicker, a perceptual shift in the atmosphere, a new tension in the air. Dad's eyes locked on mine with dreaded expectation. We stayed that way, too tense for words, for perhaps a full minute, intently listening, eyes darting all about.

I suppose a psychologist might write off what happened next as a group hallucination. But it was as real for me as sitting here now writing these pages is real for me. Orford Ness, abandoned and in ruin, didn't feel like a dead place now – it felt as if it was coming alive all around us.

The wind gusted, rattling the walls of the guard tower cabin, bringing another sound to our ears.

Impossible. Hazel's mouth went slack. All four of us shook our heads in bewilderment. The new sound was faint and yet it seemed to be coming from just a few paces away. At first, just snatches of phrases, the odd word.

'Coward . . . piss yourself . . . Nobody thinks you're brave . . .'

I shook my head, half wondering, hoping, that some intrepid, mischievous youths were out here, below us maybe, acting up and playing tricks on us all. But then I heard another voice.

'Stop it, please . . . want . . . go home.'

It was coming from the watchtower ledge outside, a boy's voice. Weak and terribly frightened. I don't think I've ever heard such distress. The idea that someone could make a child feel that way was sickening to me.

'No.' Hazel shook her head, her eyes hardening behind her perfectly square spectacles. 'There's no such thing . . .'

'Mum will be worried . . . please, go home.'

'*Mummy's boy . . . pathetic . . . fat ass!*'

Ugly voices, caught on the winds of time.

I was powerless, then, to resist the dreadful images that rose in my mind, images of the kids spitting their verbal attacks at a terrified, sobbing boy. In my mind I could see them, their premature and horrific deaths still decades away: teenagers in their cuffed jeans and their crew cut short hair.

Peter Percival.

Simon Firth.

Dad.

I looked at him, horrified, but in his shame he was unable to meet my eyes. Why had he done it? Maybe because Sammy was overweight? Maybe because his haircut was wrong? Or maybe just . . . because? The answer probably had more to do with my father and his friends than Sammy. Poor Sammy, who had never wanted to be here. In the dark. In a desolate, nowhere place. Where he had wanted was to be was safe at home and warm in bed, remembering his birthday party.

'*Please, take me back,*' his small voice whimpered. '*Sorry, so sorry . . . please don't hurt . . .*'

Hazel was shaking her head, eyes flashing with confusion.

The insults cut the air like daggers.

'*They were all laughing at you as you ate your cake.*'

'*Too much cake, fatso.*'

'*Weirdo.*'

'*Queer.*'

And that was when Sammy began to howl.

With my heart in my mouth, I pictured the boy backing away out into the blustery darkness, onto the ledge. Behind him, a rusted metal railing. Unstable. Waiting to break.

*

An ear-splitting boom blasted the air, making the entire guard tower shake and rattle so violently that it felt as if at any moment it could collapse and kill us all. One thud, then another and another. The explosions were almost on top of us, as if the sky itself was falling.

'WHAT IS IT?' Hazel yelled, an expression of utter terror on her face. 'WHAT THE HELL IS HAPPENING?'

I looked wildly towards the exit, into the blackness. Lights in the sky, dark shapes – barely visible – of aircraft approaching us. And it was then I realised that it wasn't just us hearing this. The boys, in their own dimension of time, were hearing it too.

'SEE THAT? WHERE DID IT COME FROM?'

The sky cracked with another deafening explosion. We didn't just hear the boom, we felt it, like when a wave of sound at a concert trembles through your body.

Hazel's knees buckled in fear. She threw out a hand to support herself on the rusty wall, and the wind gusted again, strong enough this time to make the entire cabin creak. I looked around uneasily at those walls. Specifically at where Hazel's hand had landed.

Something about it . . .

Oh my God . . .

The handprint. Sammy's handprint?

Hazel had her hand on it.

An extreme coldness swept through the cabin, and at the same moment, the aircraft sounds outside grew even louder. *Deafening.* A rumble of explosions.

'Oh sweet Jesus,' Dad breathed. The strength had gone out of his legs. He was crouched down on the floor and gave a small shudder, turning his head towards the ledge outside. I tracked his gaze. We all did.

Any time I question my memory of what happened next, I remind myself of the tears that were rolling down my father's cheeks, and Hazel's cheeks too, at what they saw – what we all saw.

Out on the ledge, a teenager. He was visible in the shaky beam thrown by Hazel's torchlight, but the details of his clothes weren't easily seen, because the torch beam was shining right *through* him, onto the railing behind. His outline was blurry, his movements jagged and jerky, as if we were watching one of Bill's grainy VHS tapes.

'Sammy,' breathed Hazel. 'Oh God . . . Sammy.'

I don't know how long I stood there staring at what I had to assume was the shade of Hazel's long-dead brother. Long enough, certainly, for me to check Nick and Hazel's reactions. My oldest friend was silent, his face completely blank. As for her, she was a wreck, shaking and gasping and sobbing. Dad was crying too.

'We made a mistake!' he called out desperately, extending a frail hand to the young teenager. 'Sammy, we never meant you any—'

More booms, more vibrations.

Too near the edge, I thought, *he's just too near*.

'Please!' cried Dad.

'Sammy,' sobbed Hazel.

Oblivious to us all, untethered from our time, Sammy continued to back towards the rail.

From the darkness, suddenly, the loudest of explosions, sending a tremor through the tower.

The boy lurched backwards.

Hazel screamed. 'Sammy, for God's sake, please, don't!'

And the iron railing at his back snapped like a rotting branch.

'NO!'

Across more than half a century, Hazel's cry merged with her brother's as he dropped into the inky blackness.

Time snapped back; all four of us blinked into the present. A few paces away from me, Hazel was on her knees. She cradled her head in her hands, her shoulders shuddering as the shock and the emotion rolled through her.

'I told you,' Dad whispered. 'An accident – one that no one would ever have believed. Hazel?'

Words did not reach her.

Accident or not, Sammy had fallen more than sixty feet. In my mind's eye, I could see him, sprawled on the weed-infested concrete below us. His innocent face smashed in, his head cracked open and his brains spilling out.

Dad was hunched forward, gripping the wall for support. Looking up at me, tear-stained and shaking, he said, 'I wanted so badly to tell you what happened, about the person I was, the mistakes I made.'

I held my breath. I had many questions – not least of all: how could he have kept such a colossal secret from us, his family, for so long?

'Lizzy, please, can you understand how ashamed I was?'

I could. And yet knowing my father had victimised Sammy so cruelly, I could not in that moment look at him. And neither could Hazel.

She was crouched with her back to us, near the exit leading out onto the viewing platform. Sobbing uncontrollably. Defeated. How hard had it been for her? Not knowing why her parents were always so sad and distracted. Why they were always looking at photographs of Sammy instead of taking pictures of her. How many of her early years were spent at a graveside without knowing why?

No doubt she had thought of herself as an avenging angel. Probably the urge to take matters into her own hands and mete out justice had been overwhelming; how else to explain the appalling abuse she had inflicted on others?

But did that make her right? Justify her crimes?

I looked at my father, so frail and so devastated. Felt a pang of sympathy.

Manslaughter. Eight years locked away. Then a lifetime of self-imposed isolation in that dammed tower. Wasn't that punishment enough?

Let it be done, I thought. *It happened. Let it stay in the past.*

Nick broke the mood of frozen contemplation.

'We should leave,' he said, and he was right. Outside, the rain had ceased, the noise of the phantom aircraft had faded away. And yet, our platform, sixty feet up, was still creaking dangerously under violent gusts of wind. But Hazel was blocking the exit.

'Get out of the way,' Nick said.

She raised her head and I saw the raw agony in her eyes. I don't think I've ever seen anybody look as distressed as she did right then.

'I said move!' Nick snapped, and I shot him a look that said, *Leave this to me.*

Then I stepped nearer to her.

Careful, she's dangerous, my inner voice warned.

I watched her for a few more seconds. Then moved closer still.

'Please, Hazel . . .'

She flinched as my fingers brushed her right shoulder.

It was time to level with her, no matter how fantastic or incredulous it sounded. 'During the war, 1940 I think, something horrendous happened here.' I thought of the yellowed official papers in my rucksack, the ones marked 'SECRET EYES ONLY'. 'Something the military covered up.'

I told her what I believed: that what we'd heard and seen here were ghostly echoes of this event playing out around us, as they had played out around Sammy and Simon and Peter and my father all those years ago.

What – or who – was the cause of these disturbances? If I could uncover the truth about the great tragedy of this haunted shore, perhaps I could silence the echoes for ever.

'Whatever that secret is, it must be heard,' I said. 'It needs to be known. You can help me, but we need to leave. Now. Together.'

'Listen to Lizzy,' my father spoke up. 'Please, Hazel. From the bottom of my heart, I'm sorry for the way we treated Sammy. The bullying, the name calling—'

'Sammy's still here,' Hazel said over him. 'I'm staying.'

She sounded hollow-hearted with grief and anger. I could only guess at the turmoil in her mind, but in that moment I felt I understood her pain. Her need for an ending. And in good conscience I could not leave her alone.

'Hazel,' I said, 'if you let me help you, then—'

'I'M NOT COMING WITH YOU!' she roared, twisting to face us and lumbering to her feet. 'I'm not going back to the shore, I'm not leaving here, *I'm not going anywhere with YOU!*'

Quick as lightning, she lunged at me, swiping at my face, but I was already leaping back. Then Nick was stepping forward, the syringe in his hand raised high, aimed at her neck.

'Nick, NO!'

Instinctively I grabbed his arm and yanked him back, then stepped between him and Hazel.

He jerked the syringe into the air, furious. 'Are you crazy?'

I matched him with a cold stare. 'No more violence, it's done, it's over.'

For a moment, none of us moved. Behind me, I could hear Hazel's harsh breathing.

I twisted around and looked directly at her. Grief had eclipsed anger once more. She backed away, eyes streaming.

'Go,' she said weakly. 'Please go, please leave me.'

I thought then of Bill, his cherished shell line and his quest to be reunited with his dead son, how he had asked me if he had wasted his life searching for things that didn't exist. He hadn't. He was on his own path, and that was right. And now, for better or for ill, Hazel was choosing *her* path. This lonely guard tower was her beginning and her end.

She wiped her tears away with a slash of her sleeve and looked at me. *Please.* That's what her eyes said. I nodded my acceptance and, finally, I turned my back on her.

Deep down I knew that we would never see her again.

By the time we had helped Dad down the rickety metal staircase that ran around the guard tower, his breathing was laboured and he was unsteady on his legs. But the improvement from before was noticeable and his mind seemed clear enough. I had to wonder: was he always so physically impaired? How often, when it suited her, had Hazel sedated him?

And how much of his confusion had she purposefully induced?

A bright white moon was sailing through a bank of dark clouds, and that was good. It meant we would be able to find our way across the mudflats and through the wreck of the base to the jetty.

'I'm sorry,' Nick said as Dad rested on the bottom steps, and I saw the guilt in his eyes as he reflected on his part in aiding and abetting a woman who was not just an abuser, but a killer. A woman who had lied to him, too. 'I'm sorry for what I helped her do, sorry to you both. Listen, I'll put it right, okay? Somehow. I'll tell the police everything I know.'

'No,' I said at once, 'that's unnecessary.'

Nick nodded. 'Somehow I'll make it up to you.'

It was a relief to see something of the friend I remembered: sensitive and considerate Nick. But one unnerving question remained in my mind: what now? The police already thought Dad was dead. So how were we going to explain that he wasn't?

My father squeezed my hand and looked directly at me, long enough for me to understand what he wanted me to do. *I did wrong*, that look said, *Lizzy, I did wrong, and I need to put it right. Will you help me do that?*

I reached out for Nick's hand. Took it in mine.

'Nick,' I said, 'it's *us* who need to make amends to *you*. We're going to sell the tower. Pay back everything your family is owed.'

I glanced at Dad and he nodded his agreement. The two of us would find somewhere smaller, more manageable. A bungalow. I would find some freelance work. And whatever was left after we repaid our debts would be used to help Dad live well.

We flinched as another rumble came from the sky and we looked up, wondering what on earth was coming next.

'Come on,' Nick said, 'this place seriously freaks me out. Clifford, let me carry you.'

My father, exhausted and incapable, let Nick scoop him up. We set off through the mud, struggled through a torn chain-link fence and passed the deserted guardhouse. When we reached the broken-up concrete path that ran alongside the rows of small hills, the bunkers, I knew the jetty wasn't far – and yet instead of hope, I felt fear. It was the atmosphere of the place, the shattered buildings and dark pits once home to who-knew-what experiments. I could almost hear the men in their trucks who had lowered bombs into the underground testing labs. The base may have looked empty, but we weren't alone, I knew it. I wanted to get out of there, immediately. I wanted to get back to Shingle Street and examine the documents in my rucksack and unravel the truth; and I knew that Bill would want that, too.

Relief surged through me when I saw the small blue boat bobbing on the water beside the jetty. What I did not expect to see was another, similar boat. Empty.

Had Bill followed us? I shouted his name, but it was lost on the wind.

'Come on, Lizzy.' Nick gestured me on, and helped Dad into the boat as I got the engine started. My father sat beside me, shivering, and as we launched into the darkness, Nick looked back over his shoulder, towards the sprawling abandoned base.

Was I foolish to trust him? I supposed he might keep silent, but I worried that in the end his guilt would eat away at him and the nightmares would fester; especially once he had looked up the monstrous crimes Hazel had committed against Simon and Peter.

The cold snapped at our faces as the boat cut through the water, and the only sounds were the sloshing of water and the low rumble of the engine.

'Not far now,' I said to Dad, trying to reassure him. Fifty yards or so and we would be back on dry land.

Then, suddenly, Dad's head snapped up. He turned to us

both, his eyes wide with apprehension. I felt it, too. A palpable sense of danger, very near to us.

'There,' he said. 'Can you hear them?'

I could.

The noise of aircraft in the darkness, somewhere overhead, filled my ears. Rumbles and awful high-pitched whines.

Nick was looking around frantically, fear etched on his face. 'What—' he said. 'How—'

A dark, silent shape swept across the sky. An outline, no more.

Then the bombs hit.

All round us, catastrophic explosions.

Dad jumped in terror and slipped off the seat. I grabbed for him and ended up in the bottom of the boat too, my arms around him.

Nick shouted something I couldn't hear and then lunged for the engine and cut it off. He too sank down and huddled there with us.

We drifted in the darkness, the presence of the dead thickening around us, holding tightly to each other as if that would tether us to the land of the living. The noise was deafening. Engines. Shrieking bombs. Explosions.

And then a new sound. A man's desperate scream: '*HELP ME, HELP ME PLEASE!*'

We felt, then, an intense heat, radiating off the water.

It's on fire, I thought, *the sea is on fire.*

An oily burning smell in the air. Worse. The stench of burning flesh.

I saw it in my mind, these waters raging with flames. Columns of dark smoke billowing into a starry sky, a barge engulfed in flames; fiery fluid raining down. And in the water, uniformed men – so many of them – helplessly flailing, roasting alive, screaming in agony. Trapped in purgatory.

And then . . .

All was calm. The air was cool and clear. The only sound, apart from the wind, was the slide and drag of the nearby shingle.

Fear and confusion were roiling through me.

'Lizzy?'

I turned to look at my father. His eyes were wild with terror.

'It's okay,' I told him, 'it's okay now.' But as I held him close, I knew that was a lie. There was nothing okay about what we had just experienced.

We were being haunted, there was no other word for it. By restless, embittered souls. Why?

In my rucksack were the faded military papers stamped with the words '*Directorate of Military Intelligence*' and '*Secret Intelligence Service*' that I had stumbled upon – or been led to. The ghostly figures in the bunker, the ones I had thought were mannequins, maybe they had wanted me to find the documents. Maybe they held an answer.

'Help me, help me please!'

I felt a responsibility to do that. To understand. I determined right there and then that I would find out what had happened on this shore; I would reveal its secret.

One final wrong to right, one final secret to out. The biggest lie of all.

'What now?' Nick asked warily.

I started the engine. 'Now, we end this.'

EPILOGUE

THE BODIES
ON THE BEACH

Four months later.

Kindly blue eyes regarded me with open affection. 'I'm a little surprised you came back. But very, very glad you did. Good to see you, Lizzy.' Bill beamed me the smile I'd been waiting to see, but he broke off to peer curiously past me into the thicket of trees. From that direction faint men's voices could be heard.

'It's good to see you, too, Bill,' I said, and his attention shifted back to me. 'I expected you would still be here.'

Bill nodded firmly as if that could never be in any doubt. 'Someone needs to keep the shell line going. Keep the hope.'

'That's true.'

'You got everything ironed out with your brother?' he asked after a moment. 'All the proper help, I mean?'

'He's quit drinking. For now. Reckons he'll beat it this time. I hope he does.'

'And your own situation?' he asked delicately. 'How are you holding up?'

'Okay,' I said, and it was true. Finally, I could breathe again, free from the crushing weight of guilt and shame. After we

paid back every penny owed to Nick, there had been enough
money left from the sale of the Martello tower to take care of
Dad comfortably, and to clear my debts.

'We're renting a cottage in Woodbridge. Colin's with Dad
right now, and it's good they're spending the time together.
Dad's ...' I shook my head. 'Clearer in mind somehow.
Although. I don't think he remembers much of the Ness, or
what happened to us out there.'

'Perhaps that's a kindness?' Bill said.

'He's certainly calmer. It's odd, Bill, but I can't help wondering if he ever really had dementia, or if his confusion had
a different root cause. He's clearer with me now, day to day,
and yet he can't seem to recall everything that happened to us
over on Orford Ness.'

'You think his brain has shut out what happened?'

I nodded. 'I've read that trauma can bury memories, not
erase them completely, but hide them; our subconscious mind's
method for protecting us.'

'Well,' he said thoughtfully, 'I can relate to that; my son's
funeral is a blur to me.'

'Also,' I said, and this was a more sinister thought, but I
needed to get it out, 'I can't help wondering how much of Dad's
confusion – the way it came upon him so suddenly, his night
terrors – was caused by Hazel's "herbal remedies".' I shrugged.
'Maybe she was inducing altered states of consciousness in
order to—'

'Get at the suppressed memories she wanted him to face?'

'Exactly. Colin tells me that Dad's confusion worsened when
Hazel arrived. So, it's a disturbing possibility, right?'

Bill nodded. 'And one, I fear, that is likely.'

Both of us started then, as a hare darted out from the

underbrush. We laughed, making light of it, but our smiles soon died.

'Have you met the Martello tower's new owners?' I asked.

'Not to speak to, but they seem like good people. Young family. Three kids.'

He paused, adjusted his hat, and his eyes flicked to the trees behind me.

'I only hope they'll be happy here.'

I hoped the same. But how could anyone live peacefully on this shore until its blood-soaked secrets were known and its spirits finally laid to rest? With that question in my mind, I took my bag off my shoulder and drew out the file of yellowed papers I had been studying for many weeks.

Bill tensed. 'What've you got there?'

The first challenge had been to get the papers authenticated, and I was thankful to the Imperial War Museum for doing that. Bill's quest had cost him too much personally for me to risk any mistakes now.

'You had a theory,' I said. 'You believed something happened right here at Shingle Street in 1940. The burning sea. The Nazi bodies washed ashore.'

He nodded eagerly.

'Well, Bill – you were right. Partly.'

'What have you found?' he said.

I held his stare as I answered: 'The truth.'

The wind whispered through the trees, and I felt Bill's expectant gaze on me. It was hard to know how to start telling him what I knew.

Earlier that morning, when I had walked deep into

Rendlesham Forest, I had been retracing old steps. This was the way I'd come all those years back with Nick.

And as I'd waited for Bill and the other men I knew would be coming, the forest seemed as eerie to me as I remembered from that fateful night with Nick, when we had sat by the campfire toasting our future. When I had found that object glinting on the ground. When things got weird in the woods.

A memory suppressed.

Until now.

From somewhere not too far away came a mechanical sound. An exchange of voices. There was nothing untoward about these sounds, but they stirred my unease. How could they not? I knew only too well what was soon to come, the awful thing we had to face.

But first, I had to prepare Bill.

'You know,' I said, 'a long time ago, something bizarre happened to me when I was standing near this spot, something I never truly accepted. It never really left me. In a way, I think I've been running from it ever since.'

I looked down at the ground; caught my breath at the sharp stab of memory. The overbearing sense of melancholy. The metal object protruding from the earth, glowing in the firelight.

I reached for the memory, into the darkness, and heard Mum's voice: *We should never have moved here*. I thought of the secrets that had tormented my father and led to an adolescent's death. I thought of the roar of the aeroplane engines, the blanketing explosions and the splash of orange flames on the raging sea as it burned. I thought of all the sinful, shameful acts committed on this shore down the years, and felt in my soul that now, *now*, was the time to end them – to confront what my subconscious had blocked out. The answer had been there all along. The answer was in me.

'Lizzy, please.' Bill reached out for my hand. 'Tell me. What happened here?'

Rendlesham Forest. The year I graduated. A white flash of memory, and there it is: between my fingers: a button, rough and tarnished, fashioned from brass. It had an inexplicable quality about it, of mystery and danger. Also, it felt old to me.

Very old.

I was counting the beats of my heart as Nick told me to put it down, but my fingers held on fast.

A sudden snapping branch that made me twist around, just in time to see a lonely figure watching us from the nearest line of trees.

A man. Grotesque. Horrible beyond words.

I saw the burns on his face first, a horrible skein of ruined flesh. His hair was completely burned away. Then I noted his uniform – and the fact that I could see the trees *through* that uniform.

I stood there stiff and cold with my eyes riveted on the figure.

A soldier. Long dead, and yet standing. Not moving. Just staring. With horrible purpose.

'Nick, look! Can you see it? Nick—'

He gently shook my arm. 'What's wrong? What are you looking at?'

You can't see it? The green-grey tunic? The Nazi medals? The horribly burned face?

No, he couldn't see it . . . or wouldn't.

Hallucination? Perhaps, but it was inconceivably shocking. An icy, nauseating sensation rose in my chest and made me want to double over and vomit.

Now the spectre began to move, turning to a distant clearing, and I realised, with some horror and some curiosity, that it wanted to show me something, for it was raising its right arm. Pointing.

Reaching for Nick, desperate for him to see this, too, it registered that I was still holding the brass button and that it must be from this soldier's uniform. Reflexively, I dropped it.

And the ghost vanished. As quickly as a gambler's lucky streak.

I didn't want to believe that I had seen something supernatural that night, but I couldn't deny the very real and visceral fear it had provoked in me.

'You saw the ghost of a Nazi soldier?' Bill asked, but in his eyes I saw another question: *'Why did you never tell me?'*

I've had a long time to think about that, so I should have a good answer, but the best I could manage was along these lines:

Some experiences reach beyond any of us. They are the events beyond the limits of reason; the events we shut out and pretend didn't happen – because to admit they did upsets the natural order of things, invites uncomfortable questions about the sanctity of this world and our place within it. We neatly label them 'myths', 'fables', 'legends' – anything but face up to the possibility of something unknown, something foreign to our understanding of the world, lurking on the borderlands of normality.

But those things *do* exist. Waiting for us. I know that now. I know because I've seen them. Buried them.

And dug them up.

Bill nodded as if he understood; but he didn't yet, not even nearly.

'Can you hear that?' he asked suddenly.

I listened; from deep in the forest behind us came the mechanical sound again, and an exchange of voices.

'There are some people you ought to meet,' I said. 'They're going to help us expose the truth.'

'What truth?' Bill's gaze snapped back to meet mine. 'I'm ready,' he said, 'I need to know.'

'It's all in there,' I said, handing him the folder of documents. 'The dark story of a haunted battlefield that never was. Buried sufferings. The biggest of lies.'

'What do you mean?'

'A scandal reaching to the highest levels of power. The public could never know, not in wartime conditions. Not ever.' I gestured for him to follow me into the trees. 'Come with me. There's something you need to see.'

We walked towards the part of the forest where I had found the soldier's uniform button. And now we could hear a motor running. The chinking sound of pickaxes and shovels.

'What are they looking for?' Bill asked, taking in the workers in white hats and high-vis green jackets. Nearby were others: a small team of archaeologists and historians, some making notes, some taking photographs.

'It's not what they're looking for,' I said quietly, 'it's what they've *found*. What I helped them find, thanks to these documents.'

With a look of mounting dread, Bill started to walk towards the assembled group, but I reached out and gripped his arm. I needed to prepare him for this.

'It was May 1940. British intelligence started fanning the flames of a dramatic story – a flotilla of small vessels commandeered by the German army landing here at Shingle Street.'

He nodded sombrely. 'I told you, remember? British forces covertly laid a series of pipelines in the sea, just past the low tideline. When the time came, these pipelines were pumped full of a flammable liquid and the sea "set alight" to stop the Germans getting through.'

I shook my head. 'It was a lie, Bill.'

'Why do you say that? People living around here *saw* the sky light up with a red glow, heard the explosions. Went on until six in the morning! And that night church bells rang further down the shore – an invasion warning.'

'People saw and heard what they were supposed to see and hear,' I said.

'But there were so many reports of burned bodies scattered on the shoreline,' he insisted. '*German* soldiers. How do you explain that?'

'Black propaganda. As you know, this whole stretch of shore was an obvious target for the Germans. In 1940 we were on the edge of losing the war, and the government needed public morale here to remain as strong as humanly possible; they needed the locals ready to fight. More than that, they needed to convince the Americans they were up to the challenge of a war with Germany.'

'So?'

'You've heard of the Special Operations Executive?'

'The SOE?' He nodded. 'Churchill's secret army. Espionage. Sabotage.'

'Exactly. Their role was to create unrest and turbulence behind enemy lines.'

He blinked with a memory. 'And they developed weapons for irregular warfare.'

'Exactly.' I held his gaze. 'There was no Nazi invasion; only one our government fabricated. The failed invasion at Shingle Street was a lie.'

'But . . . you said yourself, you saw the ghost of a German sold—'

'A man *dressed* as a German soldier,' I cut in. 'Yes, the sea was set on fire; you were right about that. Petroleum warfare. And a great many bodies *did* wash ashore, terribly burned. But those men weren't Germans, Bill . . .'

His face began to pale. The truth dawning.

This time when he walked forward, I didn't hold him back. I walked with him.

'The site was discovered weeks ago,' I said, 'when the local MP persuaded the Ministry of Defence to conduct initial archaeological tests.'

We stopped at the edge of the enormous trench and Bill gasped in horror. Down in the mud, archaeologists were working on scores of skeletal human remains piled on top of one another.

A mass grave.

'Oh, my God . . . oh . . .'

'There's another pit just like it,' I told him, 'half a mile away in the forest. Bodies flung in without ceremony, and buried.'

He stared at me in utter shock, his eyes as wide as dinner plates.

'You were right about something,' I said. 'Many servicemen *were* killed in the exercise—'

'Exercise?'

'Patches of sea covered with flaming oil. Perhaps as many as a hundred men. Eighty at least. But there was no invasion.' I paused, reflecting on what I knew. 'Execution would be a better word. A bloodbath.'

He stared, as if lost for words.

'They were ours, Bill. *British men*. Dressed up as enemy troops. Burned alive.'

Bill gazed, appalled, into the burial pit. I found it hard not to look myself – to look and be overwhelmed by the horror.

I went on. 'The poor servicemen were buried in this mass grave, and the other one, in their uniforms and with their helmets. As you can see, not a lot of the uniform fabric has survived, just fabric around the buttons. Unacknowledged by our government,' I added sadly, 'unremembered. They deserved better.'

'So many young men,' Bill said. 'And they had a mother and father who missed them. Yet they have never been given peace.' He shook his head and turned his eyes on me. 'No, this can't be true. Why would our government do that to our own people?'

I gestured to the documents in his hands, the ones I'd found on Orford Ness.

'Desperation. This was 1940 – Hitler's troops seemed invincible. Don't forget, we had just suffered a terrible defeat in Europe. Bombs were raining on London. We needed to guarantee American cooperation, secure resources.'

'You mean we needed to show them we were capable of resisting the German army?' He sounded on the verge of tears.

'Exactly. The troops stationed over on Orford Ness were told they were on a training exercise. After the sea burned, set alight with incendiary bombs, these pits were dug, the bodies piled in, and the site was forgotten about – until now.'

As he stared at the litany of human remains, Bill's face was a study in strained composure.

'Now what?' he asked.

'We do what's right. Find as many bodies as possible, identify them and give them what they deserve. A respectful burial with full military honours. Peace.'

I watched him closely. Saw his back straighten, his chin come up. And I anticipated his next words:

'You've done enough. Let me take it from here.'

'Thank you, Bill. I was hoping you would say that.'

High above us in the trees, a bird cawed. The leaves rustled in the wind. An archaeologist's pick thunked in the dirt.

'The newspapers will be running the story tomorrow,' I told Bill. 'After decades of silence, the truth will out. Then, if we do it right, the troubles here will cease.'

'You really think so?'

I nodded. 'Hopefully, this will no longer be a haunted shore.'

Back on the beach at Shingle Street, we prepared to say goodbye. A look of pride came into Bill's eyes.

'What is it?' I asked.

He cocked his head to the side. 'The day we met here, you looked so lonely. A wanderer.' He smiled and nodded. 'But not all who wander are lost. I felt then that you were sent here for a reason, and I was right. So, what now for Lizzy Valentine?'

Dad needed me. For now, that was enough. I told Bill that as we walked up the beach and arrived at Dumb Boy Cottage.

'Would you like to come in?'

'Another time,' I said. 'It's a gorgeous day and I'd like to walk a while.'

He hugged me one more time and when we drew apart I

noticed a tear rolling down his cheek. 'Thank you,' he said, 'thank you so much. I feel my boy around me still.' He looked out to the sea, at the rolling waves, and he took a deep breath of salty air and smiled peacefully. Then he said, 'Oh! Just one thing. Wait here for me.'

He went inside the house and returned a minute later. 'I have something for you,' he said, his face lit with a smile. He held out a small, slim envelope. 'Take it, Lizzy, please. Open it.'

I did. And now it was my turn to cry.

'Oh . . . Bill . . . oh, my goodness.' My voice cracked with emotion. In my hand was the Polaroid photograph from my youth. Shot by Colin. Showing me, Mum and Dad, with the Martello tower looming behind us. The image was crisp and clear. Recoloured. Restored. Dad's face was no longer faded. Now at last, I saw it clearly.

'There's always hope,' Bill said, and gently wiped a tear from my cheek. 'I hope you don't mind that I took the liberty of having this photo restored for you.'

I didn't mind; it was the sweetest thing that anyone had ever done for me.

'Thank you, thank you, Bill.'

I hugged him with all the strength I had.

'Well, you take care, Lizzy. And good luck.'

As he went back into Dumb Boy Cottage, I saw him cast one more hopeful glance at his cherished shell line, which was glowing white in the morning sun. I wondered if Bill would ever move on from Shingle Street, or whether knowing what he knew now would only make him more determined to remain here and wait, in the faith that he and his son would one day be reunited.

And I believed, now, after all I had experienced, that they

would find each other again. Death was not the end. Souls lived on. Which meant – and the thought made me clutch the photograph in my hand and smile – that somewhere out there, *she* existed still.

My mother.

'Someday,' I breathed into the wind.

A shrieking seagull drew my attention, and my smile faded as I gazed out over the water. A fisherman's boat was bobbing in the pale blue distance. With the water sparkling like diamonds it was a few seconds before I could focus on the spit of land across the river that was the source of so much suffering. Orford Ness shimmered for a moment on the horizon, as ethereal as a mirage, before crystallising, the enigmatic silhouettes of its beacons, bunkers and blast chambers darker than ever.

Though it was too far off, I fancied I could see the watch-tower. Where Sammy had met his end – and Hazel too. They'd reported the discovery of her body by a National Trust employee in the papers later that week. Perhaps she just fell, but the look in her eyes when we left her that night – I'm not so sure she didn't jump. Or . . .

But that was ridiculous, wasn't it? The second boat at the jetty wasn't Harvey Proctor's. The former policeman who'd been hunting Hazel wasn't out there on the Ness. He wasn't the stranger Bill had spotted watching from the Shingle Street car park when the police brought her body across the water – watching with grim satisfaction. And if he was . . . well, Harvey had good reason to be glad she was gone. That didn't mean he had ended her life.

Still, when I looked over to the Ness, a shiver ran through me.

I began walking, across the shifting shingle, parallel to the restless water. Soon enough, the newspapers would write about the atrocity committed here, the nation's greatest secret. I wondered then if at last the shore would rest, its infernal truth finally known. I wondered what the implications would be, the massive public outrage, and if me writing down what I knew, telling my story, might be a good idea.

And I wondered about Hazel, whether she was at peace. Finally.

Something told me she was. From here, the Martello tower was out of sight, and as far as I could see, the sky curving above me was clear and blue, not a cloud in sight.

ACKNOWLEDGEMENTS

My deepest thanks to:

The whole team at Quercus, especially my editor Stefanie Bierwerth.

My literary agent Cathryn M. Summerhayes, and Luke Speed my film and television agent.

And thank you to Celine Kelly for her attentive, perceptive edit, and to Guy Black, Charlotte Webb and Charlie Wilson, for their most valuable suggestions.

I'd also like to thank my mum, Pamela Spring, for all her love, friendship and encouragement.

Most of all, thanks is due to Shingle Street itself, and its many dark and fascinating legends which helped inspire this book. This rare vegetated shingle beach possesses a profoundly mysterious atmosphere that I knew I wanted to capture from the very instant I visited, and its history is even more intriguing. Rumours that a small German invasion had landed at Shingle Street and that Germans had been burned alive with petrol being pumped onto the surface of the sea persist to this day and have even led to questions in the House of Commons.

Although many of the locations featured in the book are real, I have taken extensive artistic liberty in changing their geographical locations as well as historical dates of significance. Orford Ness, for example, was not abandoned in the fifties but in the early nineteen seventies. The area is now open to the public, though access is strictly controlled.

Neil Spring
June 2020